Beloved Counterfeit

KATHLEEN Y'BARBO

Fairweather
Key
BOOK 3

BARBOUR
PUBLISHING

OTHER BOOKS BY KATHLEEN Y'BARBO

Fairweather Key Series

Beloved Castaway
Beloved Captive

© 2009 by Kathleen Y'Barbo

ISBN 978-1-60260-342-4

All scripture quotations are taken from the King James Version of the Bible.

This book is a work of fiction. Names, characters, places, and incidents are either products of the author's imagination or used fictitiously. Any similarity to actual people, organizations, and/or events is purely coincidental.

For more information about Kathleen Y'Barbo, please access the author's Web site at the following Internet address: www.kathleenybarbo.com

Cover design by Müllerhaus Publishing Group

Published by Barbour Publishing, Inc., P.O. Box 719, Uhrichsville, Ohio 44683

Our mission is to publish and distribute inspirational products offering exceptional value and biblical encouragement to the masses.

 Member of the
Evangelical Christian
Publishers Association

Printed in the United States of America.

CHAPTER 1

July 1819, O'Connor Plantation, Jamaica

You were supposed to be watching."

"I have been. Not a ship's approached." Claire O'Connor turned at the sound of her sister's voice and held up the most special shell in her basket of prizes. "I found some sand dollars. Come and look. This one's the biggest yet."

"No, I don't want to see them." Opal hurdled over the small dune and bounded toward Claire. "You weren't watching, either. He's back."

Looking toward the horizon, Claire spied nothing but low-hanging clouds and a sun hot enough to shrivel all that it touched. With no slaver in sight, the only reason for the announcement was obvious. "Papa?"

"Yes, Papa. Who else?"

"He couldn't be." Claire set her basket down carefully, making sure not to spill the shells she'd spent the morning collecting. "If Mama had expected Papa to return, she'd certainly have sent away her gentleman friend."

That's what Mama made her and Opal call them, but none of the fellows who climbed the stairs of the big house while Papa was away ever looked like gentlemen to Claire. And they certainly weren't friendly.

Most of them weren't, anyway.

"Now come on over here and help me look," Claire said. "I don't think I've seen this many sand dollars on the beach since the big storm blew over last fall."

No explanation of their destination was required as nine-year-old Opal raced across the sand to catch Claire's wrist and give it a jerk. "I think Papa killed this one."

"Don't be silly," Claire said even as her heart thudded against her ribs.

Though Claire was almost a full year older, her sister's legs were already longer, so keeping up took some effort. By the time she reached their secret hiding place beneath the front steps, Opal had already lifted the loose board and scrambled inside.

Their father's voice rose and fell like heat waves and blew past toward the dry expanse of land that tumbled downhill toward the beach. By contrast, their mother's birdlike responses chirped across the storm with all the effect of a whisper in a gale. Words like *slave* and *bankrupt* and oaths against the monarchy and Parliament bounced past, all just a part of what they'd heard from Papa since he'd heard the news that any slavers would be arrested should they dare bring their cargo into Caribbean waters.

Thus far, nothing had been said about what went on while Papa was at sea. Perhaps things weren't as bad as Opal claimed.

Claire pressed her finger over her lips to hush her sister, then crept toward the parlor window. She might have risen up to look inside had something not whizzed past her head and landed in the yard, sending Claire racing back to the steps. A glance over her shoulder told her the object was the sparkling necklace Mama had put on for the first time this morning.

"Hurry up," Opal called in an urgent whisper. "You can't let him see you."

"I'm not afraid of him," she blustered as her trembling fingers refused to take instruction. Claire let out a long breath. "He can't get you here. He can't get either of us."

Finally, the board slipped back into place, and Opal hauled Claire back. They cowered against the rocky foundation in a spot the pair had claimed as their own so long ago neither remembered who found it first.

" 'Sides, he's mad at King George again, not Mama," Claire added. A reminder to herself and her sister that no matter who took the blame, someone or something other than them generally started the ruckus.

"Tommy says the slaves are gonna kill us in our sleep," Opal whispered. "He said he hears things when he's on the ship with his papa." She paused. "Evil things."

"I told you to stay away from that boy," Claire hissed.

"He's nice, Claire, and I'll not hear another word about him."

"You will so." Claire held her tongue a moment. " 'Cause if I find out you've been talking to him, I'll tell Mama." Another pause to appreciate Opal's gasp. "No," she said slowly, "I'll tell Papa."

Opal put on her stubborn look and let loose of Claire's arm.

She'd hit on a sore subject, sure enough, but she'd not be the one to make things right again. As the older sister, Claire was responsible for keeping Opal from things that would hurt her.

And keeping company with a boy whose papa supplied half the Caribbean with slaves could lead to nothing but trouble. The fact that he was some years older and had already begun to sprout whiskers didn't seem to matter to Opal, but to Claire it meant he'd soon be just like Papa and the others who called themselves grown men.

Claire rubbed the spot on her leg that still plagued her when she stepped on it wrong. Every bruise she got was another reminder of what grown men were capable of.

"Tommy said his papa would take us far away from here."

For just a moment, the idea tempted. Far Away. It was a place where her dreams took her, though she never expected her feet would land on the spot.

"I don't like him, Opal," Claire whispered. "Bad things happen on his papa's ship, so we can never sail upon it. And he calls me Ruby Red, though he knows I hate that."

Heavy footsteps thundered overhead, signaling that the brawl had moved from a respectable inside spat to a potentially public one. Claire's heart sunk. Those were always the worst, and it was either Opal or she, and not Mama, who would likely bear the scars of the day's battle.

"Don't leave me, Claire," Opal whispered as she scooted closer.

"Never, ever," Claire said.

"Vow it," her sister said so softly Claire almost missed the words.

Claire held up her pinkie and Opal did the same. Linking trembling fingers took some work, but they managed. "I vow it," they whispered in unison, their father's shouts nearly covering up the statements.

A determination welled up in Claire as Papa's footsteps faded. Despite the fact that their combined age didn't add up to twenty, she'd leave this place soon enough and take Opal with her. And as the big sister, she'd surely see that nothing happened to Opal ever again.

Right then and there she promised it—swore it before the Lord whom the Methodists down in Port Royal called on every Sunday—even as the footsteps turned and headed back in their direction.

November 1828, Galveston, Texas

Nine years later, and Claire could still remember the day Papa hauled her and Opal from under the stairs. Likely she always would, for every time she lifted her dress, the scars reminded her. Most of the time, however, the gentlemen didn't notice. She, in turn, tried not to notice they weren't gentlemen at all.

It was an agreement between them, this mutual ignorance of plain fact. A bargain struck in coin and flesh that promised should they pass on the street neither would acknowledge the other.

Yet here in this rented room with the window shut against the sea breeze and the curtains closed to the prying eyes of anyone who might be strolling by, names were whispered and secrets shared. Sometimes she played the old piano jammed against the far wall, but most of the time it remained silent once the lamps were turned low.

As much as she hated what transpired here, Claire nonetheless entertained banker and businessman, politician and policeman, and others whose names and employment she never knew. During the day, the same rented room hosted children whose mamas insisted they learn to sing a fine tune or play the piano.

To these children, she was Miss Claire. To their mothers, she was Miss O'Connor. More than one of their fathers, however, called her endearments that would scorch the ears of any who listened.

All of it she endured rather than experienced. It was how she managed. Perhaps it always had been.

Claire sighed as she waited for the door to close and the heavy footsteps to fade into silence. When the clock struck the hour, another would arrive, so she hurried to set herself and the room to rights.

She was troubled that she'd found no other way to supplement the pittance she made teaching, but time would be kind to her and Opal, of this she was sure. She just had to get through the next hour. Then the next day and week, and eventually time would pass—and so would their situation.

In the meantime, Opal and all the respectable wives and daughters of Galveston would know Claire O'Connor as a woman who taught piano lessons in a rented room above the Cotton Exchange and kept to herself in the little house three blocks from the ocean.

Sitting at the piano to play helped Claire pass the time and gave anyone within hearing distance the idea she had another lesson. She played louder, faster, and with more abandon than she'd played in ages.

Tonight felt different. As if something was about to happen. Something big. Something that would change things.

Then came the familiar knock, and she knew nothing had changed at all.

Later, she shut her door against the fellows who might show without warning and donned her winter coat. Though November's chill touched Galveston with a gentle brush, it nonetheless painted the streets with ice on this rare occasion.

Of late, Opal had taken to spending her evenings away, so Claire smiled when she saw that the lamps burned bright in the front parlor. At eighteen, her sister could hardly be called a girl anymore, but to Claire, she would always be more child than woman. Too young, indeed, for the potential suitors who gathered on the porch or called to her from the street.

The price of finding refuge on a slaver all those years ago had been Tommy's knowledge of their whereabouts. Two girls left on the Galveston docks might have found nothing but a bad end, but Tommy's papa saw to placing them in a home with an elderly relative

KATHLEEN Y'BARBO

of his who was in need of cooking and cleaning.

Claire had hoped both father and son would forget them, but Tommy never did. To her great chagrin and Opal's delight, the slaver's son had arrived unannounced some months ago. Thankfully, his visit had been brief and not repeated, for the years had not been kind to the man.

Oh, his looks were unaffected, for he was quite a handsome fellow. But something else about Tommy Hawkins, something she couldn't quite put her finger on, bothered Claire. Maybe it was the way he watched her, or it might have been the easy and familiar way he treated them.

Whatever it was, the man's presence set her on edge.

"I'm late," she said as she pressed open the door. "I hope you've not waited dinner on me."

She stepped inside and found the parlor empty. A fire burned low in the hearth though the lamps still glowed bright. "Opal?" Claire called as she shed her coat. "Are you here?"

The kitchen echoed as she passed through, and she noted the cold pots on the stove. Claire doubled back to the eastern-facing bedroom, where she found Opal's bed still neatly made.

Moonlight slid across the wide boards and bade Claire to enter. She did and found the note. Opal was gone. Ran off with the slaver's son.

Thoughts scattered then came into focus as Claire stalked through the house to the kitchen, then back to the bedchamber. She threw what little mattered to her in a bag, along with the note.

She would catch up to Opal and put a stop to this foolishness. Surely her sister didn't intend to break the vow they'd made all those years ago under the steps.

"That's it," Claire whispered. "That Hawkins fellow's got her brain addled. We'll just see how sweet his words are when I find them."

Closing the door to the little cottage, Claire walked out into the evening's chill without bothering to extinguish the lamp or bank the fire. Surely Opal hadn't gone far. Indeed, they'd both be back in time for a warm meal and a long chat about the bonds of family and the importance of keeping a vow once made.

But Opal didn't come back. When Claire reached the docks, she

found a familiar vessel about to weigh anchor. On the deck stood her sister.

"You've come," Opal called. "I hoped but didn't dare ask."

Claire glanced behind her at the bustling port city she'd come to call home. How many years ago had she stood on this same platform and stared back at a Hawkins vessel in the hopes that she'd found a new life?

It seemed like yesterday, yet she and Opal had lived a lifetime since then.

"That you, Ruby Red?"

Claire suppressed a groan. He hadn't called her that since their childhood days.

Tommy tossed a rope to a crewman and came to stand by Opal, placing his hand on her shoulder. "Isn't that something? I didn't expect I'd get two lovely ladies for the price of one."

Ladies. Price.

Claire sighed. An unfortunate choice of words, though she knew he likely did not make the same reference as she.

"You know what your problem is?" Tommy released Opal to lean over the rail. "You're far too serious."

"Am I now?" This from a man who hadn't said two words to her in six months.

"Yes," he said as he offered a courtly bow. "What if I promised to help you bury the serious Claire O'Connor at sea? Next time your feet touch dry land, you'll be Ruby Red, sailor of the seven seas."

His laughter was contagious, though she'd not let him know. "I never liked it when you called me Ruby Red," she called back.

Tommy pretended to think. "How do you feel about plain old Ruby? Not that you're either," he said.

"Look here, Tommy." Opal came to the rail and gave Tommy a playful nudge. "She's my sister, but I'm your wife, so you'd better be careful."

"Your wife?" Claire swallowed hard. "Since when?"

"I married her weeks ago," Tommy said, "but she was afraid to tell you."

Opal looked apologetic. "I know you wanted big things for me,

Claire, but I love him. We'd planned a fancy ceremony. You would have liked doing that for me, I know." She linked arms with Tommy. "We didn't count on being blessed with a little one so quickly."

By degrees, the picture became clear.

"Come aboard," Opal called. "I'll play, and you can keep watch. When the baby comes, you can be her auntie Claire."

"His," Tommy corrected.

"Or perhaps one of each." Her giggle sounded almost like the Opal of her youth. "Claire, please. We'll have this adventure together."

Together. In a moment, Claire made her decision; for a lifetime, she would regret it.

CHAPTER 2

March 1837, Fairweather Key

Ruby O'Shea stood at the surf's edge and forced herself not to stare at the horizon. It had become a bad habit, this watching for a ship she prayed would never arrive, and today she resolved to break it.

Seven Sundays ago, she'd started thinking about allowing the Lord to bury the name of Claire O'Connor and all the ugliness that went with her. Yesterday she'd gone and done it. Now she was well and truly Ruby O'Shea.

At least that was how she figured things worked. After all, the Bible said Jacob wrestled his way into a new name and a clean slate. If he could earn the name of Israel and get the promise of a nation rising from him, maybe she, too, could claim a fresh start and a name change.

Her conscience prickled, a sure sign according to the preacher that she still had some business to attend to with God. "I'm new at this, Lord," she said as she lifted her skirts and stepped over the skittering surf. "Maybe You could give me a nudge and tell me what I've forgotten to confess."

She lifted her eyes to the cloudless sky and waited. Nothing. Maybe it was the change of name, though she'd found no other way to leave the past behind and keep the future safe. The last name he'd expect her to have would be Ruby. The name she hated.

"Lord?" An east wind lifted her braid and slung it over her shoulder, and a lone gull screeched overhead. Still, God did not answer.

"Maybe I didn't ask right," she said as she turned her back to the water and dug her toes into the wet sand. "At least when I get it wrong, You don't whack me like—"

No. She'd been promised her past was just that—past—and her scarlet sins were white as snow. That meant all of them. Even the ones so shameful she couldn't tell a soul except the Creator, who'd promised He would toss them down to the bottom of the ocean.

"Now that's something I know a bit about," she said as she picked up a tiny shell with her toes and kicked it into the air. It landed a few yards away and rolled down into the water.

"Just about everything I ever cared about except the girls is down there at the bottom of the ocean. My sins might as well be there, too. Sort of evens things out."

It didn't, but Ruby figured if she said it enough, she'd believe it. The idea wasn't any more far-fetched than the thought that anyone could forget who and what she'd been.

It was all too much to figure out, so she decided not to try.

The island of Fairweather Key was so small she could walk the whole of it in an afternoon. She knew because she'd done it before, though that dark day was another she'd cast into the depths.

Today her walk was with a purpose and must be completed before the hungry souls back at the boardinghouse came looking for their lunches. The fact that she'd been taken under the roof of the most respectable establishment outside of the church still astounded Ruby, for Mrs. Campbell, the owner, was not only the wife of the former judge but also the only live soul to whom Ruby had told the whole truth.

When she had confided in Mrs. Campbell, Ruby had fully expected to be turned out on her ear, along with the girls. Instead, Ruby had been clothed, fed, and given the keys to the front door. Where she came from, people didn't treat scarlet women that way.

The whole thing made her regret she'd chosen the name Ruby. In her mind, the name had been a joke based on the condition of her character, and one she'd only carried forward once she found herself hauled soaking wet and shivering onto the shores of Fairweather Key by rescuers.

Only the Lord could have planned a trip that ended in a ship-wrecking and then began all over again with a new life. Ruby certainly hadn't figured things to go that way. Now the joke was on her.

"Keep moving," Ruby said as she stepped over a tiny skittering crab, being careful to keep her skirts above the wet sand.

She was a lady now, and ladies did not tromp through town with wet, sandy skirts. This much she remembered from her childhood, though she'd been hard-pressed to remember it even then.

Months of living like someone else on Fairweather Key had taught her well enough that the urge to throw off her frock and dance in the waves was a desire best left in her old life. Yet the yearning plagued her even now.

So did the craving for the one thing that would take away the memories.

"There," she said as she spied what she had come for.

The pale circle disappeared as the surf rose, the grainy sand playing havoc with the neat reminder of where it had been. Ruby waited to grasp the sand dollar when the water slid away.

"Ahoy there," a familiar voice called, and Ruby turned to see Micah Tate strolling her way.

Handsome as the day was long, and twice as nice as any other man who'd come within smiling distance of her, the wrecker-turned-preacher never failed to set her jaded heart fluttering. It surely wasn't his charm; from what Ruby had observed, the fellow hadn't learned a thing about courting the ladies. Nor was it persistence of any kind, for Micah Tate seemed determined to ignore her every time she stepped into the room.

Oh, he'd compliment her cooking and thank her for the seconds or thirds he always ate, but he rarely spared her more than a passing glance. What she'd really wanted was to ask him about the notes he seemed to be forever making in that big Bible of his.

The only possible reason he would be calling to her now was either mistaken identity or empty belly. She was, after all, in charge of the kitchen at the only boardinghouse in town. And though he lived up near the ridge in a place that reportedly offered a view of the key that none other had, by prior arrangement with Mrs. Campbell, Mr. Tate took all of his lunches and some of his suppers at the boardinghouse.

"Ahoy," Ruby called in return, though the greeting felt silly.

Spying the sand dollar, she made a grab for it just as a wave surprised her. The impact knocked Ruby sideways, and she skittered like a crab to keep her footing.

"Hey there," Mr. Tate said as he closed the distance between them in long strides. "I hope whatever you fetched was worth the soaking."

And soaked she was, from the hem of her skirt to the sleeves she'd starched just this morning. So much for acting the lady.

He seemed to be studying her with some measure of amusement. Or was it disdain? From where she stood, it was hard to tell.

Ruby spared no further time trying to decide. Long ago, she'd decided there were only two things a man wanted from a woman. Given his lack of friendliness, likely this one just wanted his belly full. They always did, even when that wasn't the ultimate goal.

Mr. Tate continued to stare, though he seemed to be a bit short on words. She dropped the sand dollar into the pocket of her apron and counted to five lest her temper get the better of her. "I assure you I can cook even in wet clothing."

Her statement startled him, or so it seemed from his expression. "I didn't worry—that is. . .well. . .I'm sure you can cook just fine even with your skirts clinging to your legs like that."

So that was it. His belly had taken second place. Well, there had once been a day when that sort of line might have landed a fellow behind a locked door, his wallet significantly lighter, but no longer.

"What are you looking at?" Even as her temper flared, Ruby felt a certain satisfaction that Micah Tate was finally paying her some measure of attention.

The man lifted his cap to run his hand through hair just a shade darker than her own rusty red. Likely he was teased about it as mercilessly as she.

Not that she'd dare let down her guard to feel sorry for him.

Yet in all the times she'd watched him sidle up to her table and partake of whatever meal she set before him like a man half starved, Ruby had never really *looked* at him beyond taking notice of his better-than-average features. Only when he turned and walked away did she realize Mr. Tate had not responded to her question.

Guilt, her constant companion, plagued her just enough to cause her to call after him. "Didn't mean to speak so rudely," she said, one hand shielding her eyes from the ever-present sun.

He turned and regarded her no less harshly. "Yes, you did."

The truth, and she knew it. Ruby met his steady gaze and almost smiled. "Yes," she admitted, "I did."

The Tate fellow shrugged. "I figure whatever's got you mad's something I'm not asking about, so don't bother to tell me." He had the audacity to grin.

"There's no danger in that," she said.

"I didn't figure so."

He shrugged and seemed in no hurry to move as Ruby shook out her soggy skirts and reached for her shoes. Maybe he was like her in that a walk on the beach with only the gulls for company kept the rest of the day on a smooth path toward a good night's sleep. Maybe when it rained, he, too, paced the confines of whatever room he was stuck in and wondered what sails were heading over the horizon undetected.

Perhaps that was why he'd chosen to build his home on the highest ground in Fairweather Key—so he could keep watch. *What a stupid thought.* But then, her head was full of stupid thoughts.

At least that's what Tommy had told her. And Papa before him.

Ruby pretended to fret with her apron strings as she cast a furtive glance at the fellow now standing with pants wet halfway to the knees from the surf. So she had the worrisome habit of forever keeping watch. Life had taught her that things happened when she looked away. Bad things.

If only she'd kept watch that night when Tommy thought to choose her bed over Opal's. For once, he had been the one who would bear the scars—not her.

She threw another glance toward the horizon; then, as if she were more interested in the weather, she turned her attention to the sky. Puffs of white cotton waltzed across a sky as blue as the girls' eyes.

The girls.

Her heart caught in her chest as it did whenever she thought of them. Right now, twins Carol and Maggie would be learning their

17

letters and numbers from Miss Emilie—Judge Spencer's new wife—at the schoolhouse. Smart as whips, those two, and quick to fit in with their adopted home.

Ruby smiled to think of Tess at the parsonage, helping the reverend's wife entertain her grandbaby. How much help a four-year-old could be was questionable, but Mary Carter seemed to thrive on having the little girl underfoot. Tess, too, had blossomed under the Florida sun.

"Well, what do you know?" Micah Tate drawled. "I've witnessed a miracle."

She looked his way but didn't respond.

"Yes, indeed," he said as he fitted his cap back in place. "I saw a genuine miracle just now." He laughed, deep peals of humor that rumbled as they rose. "Indeed," he said a moment later, "had you been standing where I am, you'd say the same thing."

"I'll not play your game, Mr. Tate," she said.

He grew somber. "No, I should've known you wouldn't."

A nod of good-bye would have to be sufficient, she decided as she felt her apron pocket for the sand dollar. As she made her way past him, Ruby had already redirected her thoughts to the noonday meal and what she'd be serving with the stew.

The diversion served her well. By the time she'd decided on warming last night's bread and slathering it with fresh jam to go along with the stew, Ruby had all but forgotten her worries.

Not forgotten, exactly, but she'd certainly shoved them to that dimly lit part of her memory where only the occasional shaft of light and remembrance pierced the darkness.

"Miss O'Shea?" Mr. Tate loped up to join her, his pant legs rolled to the knees and his boots in hand. "Aren't you curious as to the miracle I saw?"

She picked up her pace and counted off the ingredients for the pie she'd bake this afternoon. Soon the larder would need to be refilled. Thankfully, Mrs. Campbell had trusted Ruby with the household account while she was away visiting her daughter on the mainland. Without the ability to purchase what she needed, the boarders would soon be doing without almost everything except the fruit that grew readily on the trees in the side yard and the scrawny chickens that ran about like they owned the place. Humility rolled over Ruby in waves as she thought again of the dear woman who knew the ugly truth of her past and trusted her anyway.

"Really, Miss O'Shea. I don't recall meeting another woman with less natural curiosity."

Ruby sighed. Truly the man was too much. "I fear it's a natural state for me. It was beat out of me as a child."

Realizing she had said the words out loud, Ruby froze. By degrees, blinding anger replaced abject humiliation.

Anger for speaking aloud what should have been kept private.

Anger at the Lord for blinking when He promised not to.

Her feet began to move, and Ruby could only follow. A slow walk became a trot and then an all-out race to find her way back to the boardinghouse and safety.

CHAPTER 3

Micah stopped to fully appreciate the beauty of the woman who wouldn't give him the time of day. Blue skirts the color of a noonday sky fought the sea breeze but did not slow Miss O'Shea's progress as she vaulted over the sand with the agility of one seemingly used to such activities.

She did not falter once, even when an oversized wave jumped the shoreline to pelt her with a saltwater shower. What sort of citified lady was so sure of foot on shifting sand? He shrugged. For all he knew, the best cook in all of Fairweather Key spent her spare moments perfecting the ability to run barefoot on all sorts of turf for just this kind of situation.

She'd certainly perfected the ability to dodge the slightest attention he'd tossed her way over the past few months. How a woman could put lunch in front of him every day since the first week of August and never once look directly at him was beyond understanding.

He continued to observe her, unwilling to look away as her braid swayed from side to side. Something small and pale flew from her hand, but she barely gave it notice.

When she reached the cut where the sea grass gave way to the path toward town, Micah watched her pause, and for a second, he thought she might look back to see if he'd followed. When she did not, he set off in her direction.

A wave danced over his feet and chased a sand crab up into the remains of someone's campfire. As had become his habit when coming across these kinds of things, Micah checked for signs of a Seminole raiding party—not that he was entirely sure he'd know such clues if he saw them.

Still, it seemed that bad news traveled twice as fast as good and lasted three times as long. For the better part of two years, stories arrived through travelers and transients that the Seminoles were intent on adding to the land they were fighting to keep. Forays into Indian Key and other places up north near the mainland looking for who-knew-what had folks in those parts running scared.

What the Seminoles wanted, Key West got, with refugees bypassing Fairweather Key to go as far south as possible without moving to Havana. The last time he'd traveled to Key West, the city had seemed to have quadrupled in size with enough militia and guns to outfit its own war if need be.

And to think he'd given serious thought to pulling up stakes and heading there. With his wrecking boat gone and the woman he thought he loved now promised to another, Micah could surely throw what little he owned into a bag and disappear with the next tide.

The trouble was, the Lord wouldn't let him. Every time he tried, something waylaid him. Now he wondered if maybe Ruby O'Shea was the reason.

He couldn't blame the woman for being skittish, what with her having arrived on the island courtesy of the local wrecking fleet after being plucked off a sinking ship. What she was doing aboard that particular vessel, Micah refused to contemplate.

"Hawkins was holding her and those girls captive," he said to the wind and the lone gull that slid past just overhead. For good measure, Micah repeated the statement. If he did that enough, he'd start believing it.

Not that he'd ever seen a woman and three little girls leave a ship of that sort looking fit and fine as these four had. It was almost as if. . .

"No, they were *captives*, and that's all there is to it."

Yet in his heart, he knew any man with a pulse would take notice of a woman like Ruby O'Shea, even if she was the mama of three.

Micah liked to think his interest in her was different, his purpose in getting to know her based on proximity and good cooking.

Then there was the issue of his future plans. With Rev. Carter mentioning retirement and Micah as his replacement at nearly every opportunity, there was little doubt he'd eventually turn to preaching full-time.

Any woman he took an interest in would have to agree to serve alongside him. Micah chuckled. "My thoughts are running away faster than Ruby O'Shea."

Still, many questions needed to be answered before he could consider a courtship with the winsome Miss O'Shea. "Winsome?" Another chuckle. "I'm sounding more like the reverend every day."

He fitted his stride to the footprints she left and found, even with his height, he had to stretch to do it. It appeared the tiny woman was almost flying over the rocky beach.

At the cut, he paused to see if he might find the object she'd either thrown or dropped. It only took a minute to spy the round sand dollar among the spikes of sea grass.

Micah snatched up the shell and dusted off the grit before slipping it into his pocket. Miss O'Shea might ignore him again at the lunch table, but surely she'd pay attention to what he'd be bringing her today.

He'd walked halfway back to town before remembering what had brought him to the beach. Rev. Carter's offer, made in the form of a less-than-convincing offhand comment, bore hard on him. Warring with the strong temptation to take the pulpit from the soon-to-be-retired pastor was the reminder of a past he'd literally swum away from.

He hadn't thought of that day in years—not until this morning when the words from 1 Samuel 12 flew off the page of his Bible and struck him in the heart.

Micah walked three more steps then settled onto the fallen tree trunk that had acted as a bench since its arrival after the last storm. He scrubbed at his forehead, and sand raked his face. *"Only fear the Lord, and serve him in truth with all your heart: for consider how great things he hath done for you."*

As much trouble as he had memorizing scripture, how ironic that this verse had returned to his mind several times since daybreak. While the Lord had certainly kept His end of the bargain and done many great things for him, Micah squirmed at the thought of how he himself had been elusive with the truth. Even his closest friends knew him only as a good man who worked hard and loved the Lord. Josiah Carter, the reverend's son, was privy to the fact that Micah had come to Fairweather Key as a widower who'd lost not only a wife but also a child. Others no doubt wondered why he named his wrecking boat the *Caroline*, but none had inquired. And he'd not offered an explanation.

Now that the *Caroline* lay in pieces on the reef, he'd been thinking long and hard—and praying in equal measure—about what he'd do next. Hezekiah Carter wanted him for a preacher, but Micah still felt the pull of the sea and wrecking. For that, Josiah Carter would gladly take him on as partner. It seemed as though Josiah never tired of pestering him about the subject, and Micah had begun to give the proposition more than a passing thought.

Doing both seemed possible, but was dividing his time between the two what God had deposited him on the key to do?

Somehow Micah had figured to return to the place where thinking came best to him and sort it out. Instead, along came Ruby O'Shea to complicate things further.

If he was going to court her—which just might happen if he could catch her attention—or if he was going to go back to owning his own wrecking boat or even think of acting as pastor to the citizens of Fairweather Key, there was only one thing to do.

Micah rose and walked toward the parsonage. With each step his purpose got stronger—until the minute he reached the gate to the churchyard. There the questions he'd ignored caught up with him, as did the doubts.

Before he could put his hand on the gate, Josiah Carter called to him from across the street. Micah turned to acknowledge his friend even as he gave quick thanks for a postponement of his decision.

Josiah dodged across the busy street to give Micah a hearty slap on the back. "Just the fellow I've been looking for." He pointed east toward the docks. "Come with me. I've got something to show you."

Micah knew where this was heading, yet he chose to take the path of least resistance and play dumb. Let his overanxious friend try his best; he'd certainly done that more than a dozen times since the sinking of the *Caroline*.

Given the direction of his thoughts, investing in another wrecking boat was the last thing Micah planned to consider today. Then he saw the craft.

She was a beauty. Long and sleek with a mainmast that jutted toward the sky in a fine straight line. Micah picked up his pace, only realizing when he arrived at the dock that Josiah had been speaking to him.

"And the best thing about her," Josiah continued, "is that she can be had for a song."

Micah stopped short, his purpose renewed. "I don't sing."

Josiah laughed. "You will when you hear how much the judge wants for her."

He tore his attention from a hull that sliced upward from the choppy water with what would surely be an almost flawless curve. "The judge?"

"Come on," Josiah said. "Caleb's expecting us."

Micah stalled right there on the dock. "Hold on a second. What do you mean Caleb's expecting us?"

The wrecker pulled a watch from his pocket and checked the time. "We're a little late, but I'm sure he'll understand when I tell him how difficult it was to find you this morning." Josiah set off again and yanked Micah into step beside him. "Where were you, anyway?"

"Went for a walk," was all Micah would admit. "So you just up and decided that boat was for me?"

"No." Josiah turned to take the courthouse steps two at a time.

"No?" Micah beat his friend to the door and stood between him and the knob. "Look, Josiah, I told you the last time you mentioned it that I'd let you know when I was ready to go back to wrecking."

"That's what I said, Micah, but your friend doesn't seem to listen." Micah turned toward the new voice and found Naval Lieutenant Caleb Spencer, presiding judge of Fairweather Key, standing in the

open doorway. Caleb grinned and shook Micah's outstretched hand. "You do speak the truth, but there appears to be no cure for it. You see, Josiah doesn't heed my words, either."

"Yet he jumps to do his wife's bidding."

Caleb grinned. "Perhaps there's the secret. Neither of us can fill out a bonnet quite like Isabelle Carter."

"Nor shall I try," Micah said with a chuckle.

Josiah ignored the good-natured ribbing to lead the group inside. "So, Caleb," he said when they reached the judge's chambers, "tell Micah what you told me this morning."

The judge settled behind his desk. "This information cannot go any farther than this room." He steepled his fingers. "Considering he and I are family, I've come to rely on Josiah in certain matters of great importance."

Indeed, with Caleb's recent marriage to Emilie Gayarre, Caleb Spencer and Josiah Carter were now brothers-in-law. Caleb gestured to the two chairs opposite him. While Josiah made himself comfortable, Micah opted to stand.

"Suit yourself, Tate," Caleb said, "but I think you'll want to hear this." He paused. "It's not often a man's offered one of the finest examples of a wrecking craft at so little cost."

Micah shook his head. "I don't mean to be rude, Caleb, but I don't need to hear the story. The last thing on my mind today is buying a new wrecking boat. I'd hoped to have a conversation with you about something else altogether." He nodded toward Josiah. "You, too."

Caleb held up his hand. "Then I propose a deal. First you listen, and then you speak." He looked from Josiah back to Micah.

"Fair enough." Micah sank into the empty chair. "Go ahead."

"Again, I must remind you this is highly classified information."

"You know I'm not a man who carries tales, Caleb," Micah said.

"That's why you're here." He leaned back, and the fancy chair, one Micah recalled hauling off a vessel some months ago, protested with a groan. "It's no secret our government won't back down from its position in regard to the Seminole. It appears there are few men in Washington who care that innocents are dying as well."

Understanding dawned. "No, thank you," he said as he rose. "I'll not be buying a boat belonging to a dead man, no matter what the price."

"Sit down, Micah," Josiah said. "That's not it at all. The Seminole are too busy up north to come hunting for blood down here."

"Josiah's right." Caleb turned his attention to the window that looked out on the docks and the ocean beyond. "And so far they've been more inclined to strike where there are fewer who can fight them." He glanced back at Micah. "At least for now."

Micah shook his head, impatient for his turn to speak. Already the idea of confessing didn't settle well in his gut.

"You'll like this, Micah," Josiah said. "So keep quiet until you've heard it all."

"It's simple, really." Caleb reached for the handle of the topmost desk drawer and slid it open. "I've got a commission here that I'm prepared to offer you. Captain of the Fairweather Key Militia. Doesn't pay much, but a boat and plenty of free time to preach or farm or do whatever you please comes with the salary." He shrugged. "Unless the Seminole decide to pay us a visit. Then you'd be plenty busy."

"Fairweather Key Militia?" Micah took the paper from Caleb but did not bother to read it before letting the correspondence fall to the desktop. Whether this opportunity was from God or the devil, he couldn't be sure.

"You've got the wrong man."

Caleb rose. "I'm rarely one hundred percent certain of anything, Micah, but this time I've got no doubt I have exactly the right man. You're a natural leader. I've seen it for myself out on the reef and in my warehouses. You've had chance after chance to do the wrong thing and profit from it, yet I've never seen you do anything but make honorable choices."

Honorable choices. Any other man would've busted his buttons at such a compliment. For Micah, it only deepened his shame.

"He's right," Josiah added. "We didn't exactly start off on the right foot. Remember when I took the *Caroline* to go back to my sinking ship and find Isabelle when the others refused to? You ended up the only man who would stand up to Judge Campbell and fight to free me from jail, and you were the one I stole the boat from."

Micah shrugged and decided to lighten the mood with humor. "Some days I have to wonder if that was such an honorable thing."

Josiah gave him a good-natured jab. "And my wife would likely agree."

"In all seriousness," Caleb said, "I'm being pressured to provide the name of a man who will take on the organization and training of men to protect the island in case of Seminole attack. Emilie's got her heart set on a trip to Santa Lucida, so this issue must be settled today."

"Then pick Josiah. He's a better man for the job than me."

"I'll not argue the point of which is the fittest for duty." Caleb nodded toward Josiah. "But I also doubt there would be much happiness in the Carter household should I name Josiah to that role and keep him from accompanying his wife to Santa Lucida."

"She's been looking forward to meeting the woman who has become Emilie's substitute mother," Josiah said.

"Yes," Micah said carefully, "I see the dilemma."

"Then we're agreed." Caleb returned to his seat. "All that remains is for me to send word to Washington that I've found my man."

Micah swiped at the beads of sweat gathering on his brow despite the November chill. How easy it would be to take on that role, to accept the vessel that would take him out of his job at the warehouse and back onto the open ocean.

He'd carried on the ruse of being an upright citizen for all these years. What were the chances he'd ever be found out?

Yet God knew.

He had always known.

And loved Micah anyway.

"I've done as you asked and listened to your proposal," he said to Caleb. "Now I'd like the same in return."

Caleb's nod gave him the go-ahead to speak, yet Micah found his voice would not come. Twice he cleared his throat, but the words refused to dislodge. He was left studying the toe of his boot and praying the Lord would allow him the confession that was long overdue.

The judge seemed to sense his trouble. "Is there something in your past that might prevent you from accepting this position?"

Micah nodded, unable to lift his gaze.

"Did you kill anyone?"

He jerked his head to meet Caleb's even stare. "No."

"Are you a thief?"

Again Micah replied in the negative.

"In that case, I'm satisfied in offering you this position." Caleb shrugged. "Whatever you've done, it can't possibly disqualify you from the work the position requires. Unless you can't shoot a gun. That's not the case, is it?"

"No," Micah said, "I'm a decent shot."

"Then it's settled." Caleb paused to run his hands across the edge of the desk. "Look, you don't have to tell me anything, Micah, because I'm certainly not asking. I'm living proof a man can have a past and still have a future."

Micah considered the statement. Certainly the Washington lawyer turned Fairweather Key judge had overcome the fact that his mother's Benning family tree held more pirates than lawyers. He'd even managed to snatch up Emilie Gayarre from right under Micah's nose.

"I don't need to know, either," Josiah said. "You're a good man. I've watched you, and I know it to be true."

The temptation to shake hands on the deal weighed heavily on Micah. How easily he could see himself at the helm of that vessel. What he couldn't see was standing up on Sunday morning to preach with this lie hanging over his head.

Micah swallowed hard. The Lord was fair even when what He asked was hard.

"Only fear the Lord, and serve him in truth with all your heart: for consider how great things he hath done for you."

Serve Him in truth. Indeed, it was time, even if he served the Lord from a jail cell instead of the pulpit.

"I'm a deserter, Judge Spencer," he said before cowardice could take hold again, "and I'm thinking you might want to throw me in that jail of yours rather than promote me and give me a gun and a boat to patrol with."

CHAPTER 4

"Viola, darling, you know I love you." Dr. Daniel Hill rose from the blanket so quickly he nearly stumbled over his own feet.

"Yes," she said. "Of course I do."

"Then I want you to understand that no matter what may happen, anything I do is out of love for you."

"All right." She gave him a sideways glance as she folded the blanket and set it aside. "Is something wrong, Daniel?"

"Wrong?" He shook his head then reached to give her a quick kiss on the cheek. "Of course not. It's just that, well, one never knows what the future holds."

Yet one might hope it held a wedding.

As Viola Dumont made short order of packing the remains of the picnic lunch back into the basket, she watched Dan without caring whether he noticed. He did not, of course, for the shock of mentioning a wedding had sent him into fits of panic once again.

An exaggeration, but only slightly.

She did know he loved her—or at least she knew he called it that. After all this time measured now in years rather than weeks or months, it was something, this thing between them. But she'd begun to wonder if the course of love had run dry—at least on Dan Hill's part.

Yet today he'd suggested a picnic at their favorite spot on the bluff, the place where the mangroves grew so thick that the tiny crabs skittering about under their limbs were the only sign of life. He'd taken her boating beneath the canopy of green once before. The crabs had terrified her only slightly less than the feelings that threatened to overwhelm her when Dan Hill kissed her for the first time. Odd how their kisses would always bring her back to the creepy tunnel of crab-infested mangroves.

Dan jerked at his collar and grimaced as the salt-tinged breeze lifted a strand of dark hair and brushed it against his jaw. She noticed the bead of perspiration tracing a path down his freshly shaved cheek only to be swept away by the back of his hand.

Only an idiot would think he perspired because of the weather.

No, it was Viola's uncanny ability to send Fairweather Key's only physician into either total silence or inane proclamations with one word: *wedding.* "Not ours, Dan," she quickly added as she stuffed the folded blanket into the basket, though the words tasted sour against her tongue.

He tore his attention from the horizon and offered a far too quick smile. "Of course not."

Of course not?

Her hopes plummeted, though she plowed on. "You see, I was down at the McGregor home this morning. Ella, her eldest, the one who sells eggs at the market, said she had heard a wedding was afoot for—"

"And the baby?" Dan ducked his head to swipe at his lapel.

"Baby?" Viola paused to try to understand the question. "What baby?"

"You're a midwife, dear. I assume yours was not a social call given the advanced state of Mrs. McGregor's confinement." His tone held nothing but reproach, sending the last of Viola's dreams of an imminent proposal skittering to the dark place where she hid them.

"Yes, of course," she managed, clutching the handle of the basket so tightly it would surely break at any moment. Perhaps if she remained silent, the topic of weddings could once again be broached.

Green eyes wandered to the horizon where the sun danced behind the sails of a vessel heading for port. "I trust the delivery went without complication," he offered.

Leave it to a doctor to try to turn a conversation about weddings into a discussion on medical issues. "It did," she said as she paused to contemplate once again how to best recover their lost topic.

Dan stopped short and took the picnic basket from her, setting it at his feet. "Vivi?"

He rarely called her by this name, the one he'd somehow convinced her to admit had been her childhood nickname. Like the gulls overhead, Viola's battered hopes once again soared.

"Yes?"

Reaching across the distance between them, Dan took her hands in his. Viola's heart leaped as she hoped. . .prayed. . .this would be the moment she'd waited for.

"You're quite a woman."

She waited. And waited. Nothing. Instead, he stared at a spot just above her head, not quite making eye contact, yet not ignoring her altogether.

"Thank you," she finally offered. "And you're quite a man."

It was her turn to cringe. She sounded like an idiot, yet most times in Dan's presence she felt like one.

The only thing she did better than he was the one thing that kept them apart. Perhaps he'd found the ability to finally move past that impediment.

"This is not easy," he said, and she felt his fingers tighten around hers. "I've waited until the last minute to tell you lest I show myself to be the coward I'd prefer you not see."

"Coward?" She shook her head even as she struggled to remain still. "You're frightening me, Dan."

He released her hands to cup her face. A fleeting memory of another man doing the same thing on the cathedral steps sent an involuntary shiver through her.

"You're chilled." Dan stepped back to remove his jacket and place it around her shoulders. "Now that's better. Come close so I can hold you until you're warm again."

She went into his arms without argument, and she might have stayed there until far past the point at which it might be considered proper. Ever the gentleman, Dan released her before reputations could be harmed.

Not that anyone cared what a woman of her age did. After all, she was no Emilie or Isabelle Gayarre.

"Yes, thank you," she said as she blinked hard. "I'm much better now."

A lie, but she kept her mouth shut against retracting it.

Dan gave a curt nod before lifting the basket with one hand and sliding his arm around her waist with the other. "Perhaps this is a topic better broached another day."

"What?" she said as she kept her attention fixed on the path ahead. "The baby or the wedding?"

He stopped short, nearly sending her toppling forward. "Neither, actually. You see, I was about to tell you that I must—"

"Kiss me."

"Must I?" His expression softened as he set the basket aside and pretended to consider the situation.

"Indeed, you must. At once." She smiled. "I insist."

A daring move, yet it worked. Whatever bad news Dan Hill was about to deliver would now be postponed—if not indefinitely, at least momentarily.

The kiss ended, Dan once again took up the picnic basket. Without a word, he forged ahead. Tempted as she was to remain in place until the doctor realized he walked alone, Viola was smart enough to realize that might not happen until he arrived on her doorstep and found her missing. With a sigh, she shouldered her pride and followed Dan Hill yet again down a road that led away from the question of matrimony.

"Micah Tate a deserter?"

The expression on Caleb Spencer's face said much more than the words he'd just spoken. Having known Josiah much longer than Caleb, Micah couldn't bring himself to chance a look in his direction.

The hope of finding relief in telling the truth of his past shriveled under the two men's stares. Now that he'd opened his mouth, there was no turning back. Rather than pace, Micah sank back into the chair and then, in defiance of his shame, straightened his backbone.

"Yeah," he said as he tried not to match his tone to the way he felt.

"It all started back in January of '28. We'd come to Texas with Austin in '21 and were doing pretty well for ourselves on a piece of land that ran right up to the Brazos. Caroline and the baby were puny, but I figured it to be the cold weather, you know? Weren't more than a few sneezes and a sniffle. Seems like I would've known if it'd been worse." He paused until the memory dimmed, then swung his gaze to Caleb. "Maybe you heard about the Fredonia Rebellion."

Caleb nodded. Josiah, however, looked puzzled.

"The alcaldes in Nacogdoches declared independence from Mexico," Micah explained. "Something about disputes over land grants, if I remember correctly. Austin sided with the Mexicans and mustered up our militia to head up there and help them put down the rebellion. Didn't take long. Those who didn't run ended up in trouble with the Cherokee for involving them in the spat. I was standing guard outside the Stone Fort when I got the letter."

He rose, unable to sit any longer.

"You don't have to go any further with this," Caleb said. "I believe I understand."

"No. You can't possibly. I walked—no, I pretty much ran when I couldn't hitch a ride in some farmer's wagon—all the way home, only to find two fresh-dug graves and a whole bunch of people looking at me like I was responsible."

"So you left." This from Josiah, who now stood and placed a hand on Micah's shoulder.

Micah shrugged away from his friend. "Yeah, I left. Seems I was good at that. I left Caroline when she needed me. Left the militia without asking for leave." He paused only to draw in enough breath to continue. "Figured it was just as well I kept on walking until I found a vessel leaving out of Galveston with need of a deckhand."

"And you ended up here." Caleb shrugged. "I can find nothing to hold against you, Tate," he said. "The way I see it, you did what was asked of you then returned home with good cause. Unless I'm mistaken and you left the battlefield."

"No, the fighting was done," Micah said with the last of the air from his lungs.

"And your homestead?"

Again he was back on the banks of the Brazos; again he pushed away the memory. "Closed the door and walked out with the clothes on my back and the money we were going to use for spring supplies. Far as I know, it's all still there gathering dust."

The judge leaned back in his chair and seemed to be thinking. Finally, he reached for pen and ink then opened his drawer to find paper.

"What're you doing, Caleb?" Josiah asked, his voice rising. "You're not turning him in, are you? Micah Tate is a good man, and you know it. Why, just last night over supper my father declared him to be the only candidate to replace him in the pulpit."

"He's likely to change his mind when he hears my story," Micah said.

Josiah stepped into Micah's line of sight. "If you believe that, you don't know Hezekiah Carter very well. He'd likely just tell you that to whom much is forgiven, much is expected."

The truth, and Micah knew it. Trouble was, he hadn't quite decided what it was like to be forgiven.

Caleb continued to write. When he finished, he set the pen aside. "I've written a letter of inquiry regarding one Micah Tate—that *is* your proper name, is it not?"

"It is."

Nodding, Caleb continued. "I've written to ask of any charges against you, Micah, and to inquire as to whether I should send you back to the Austin Colony to face them. As for me and my jurisdiction, I've got no reason to hold you lest you've committed more crimes to which you'd like to confess."

Micah's attention went to the page where the ink had all but dried on his future—and his past. "That's fair, Caleb. More than fair, actually. And no, other than coveting Miss Ruby's cooking, I've done a decent job of behaving myself since I landed here."

"This militia," Caleb continued. "Did you join up formally, or did Mr. Austin take volunteers?"

Micah swiped at his brow with the back of his sleeve. "We were volunteers, all of us who lived in the colony. Those who could fell in with Mr. Austin and the Mexicans when called. Those who couldn't were free to stay behind."

"Free to stay behind?" Caleb looked as if he might be thinking hard on the topic; then he shook his head. "If only those went who could, then what of those who found their situations had changed? Would they not, then, be free to go and attend to whatever called them back?"

A slight glimmer of something close to hope began to dawn on him. Micah looked over at Josiah then back at Caleb. "I suppose."

"What makes you so bent on punishing yourself for desertion when you just told me what you did, if it were done by anyone else, would be permissible?"

"I, well. . ." His gut tightened even as something in his heart loosened. "I guess I didn't think of it that way."

Again the judge seemed to be contemplating something. "Then here's what I figure," he said. "A man takes a commission—then he's obligated. If he's volunteering and it's not wartime, that's another matter altogether."

Slowly Micah managed a nod. "But the militia. I was obligated and I left."

"Let it go, Tate." The judge shook his head. "You were called home by bereavement. That's a different matter altogether."

Josiah clasped his hand onto Micah's shoulder and gave him a firm shake. "You did what any of us would have done, Micah. You went home. There's nothing dishonorable in that."

"You did not walk away from the battle," Caleb added. "Though I warrant you must have felt you walked into one."

Micah recalled opening the door to his—their—home and feeling as if he'd been hit in the gut by grapeshot. Caleb Spencer spoke the truth. He lowered his gaze.

As soon as he could manage it, Micah would find his escape. He had plenty to think about.

"I appreciate your candor, Tate," Caleb said. "Now if there's nothing further you'd like to discuss, I would prefer to talk about that boat out at the dock and the job you'll be doing for me."

Micah lifted his head and found Caleb staring, his expression almost daring him to disagree.

Caleb reached over to offer his hand while Josiah tightened his grip on Micah's shoulder. "You're a good man, Micah Tate, and the only one I want watching my island while I'm away. What say you? Will you accept my offer?"

It took only a moment to manage a nod, but in that moment, Micah wondered whether he would ever see himself as Caleb and Josiah did.

As God did.

"Can I pray about it?"

"I wouldn't have it any other way," Caleb said.

"Just don't let my father talk you out of it," Josiah added. "I figure you can patrol weekdays and preach Sundays."

Micah almost laughed as the glimmer of hope brightened. "Hey, now," he said. "Keep in mind I've agreed to neither."

Yet as he said his good-byes and stumbled into the afternoon sun, Micah felt as wrung out as a morning's wash. He also realized he'd like nothing better than a heaping plate of the redhead's lunchtime fare.

That is, unless he was too late for that, too.

CHAPTER 5

Viola watched the doctor's straight back as he marched down the steps and made his way to the gate. While the distraction of the kiss had done its job and postponed whatever news Dan intended to deliver, he'd nonetheless left her with the feeling the delay was only temporary.

But then, what sort of permanence had he ever offered her? Viola frowned at the thought. His admissions of love came more frequently now, yet somehow the doctor seemed to feel these required no further commitment from him.

Wandering through the empty rooms of her little home, Viola halted at the wardrobe, its carved surface glowing in a slender shaft of sunlight. The door opened on silent hinges, revealing a half-dozen dresses suitable for a woman of modest means and one fit for a princess.

Her fingers trembled as she reached for the gown she'd not touched in more than a year. A moment later, it was in her arms, soft silk against her cheek.

Only the scent of soap remained, the acrid odor of dried blood and too many days of traveling aboard ship long banished. "Oh, Andre."

She let the dress crumple to the floor. Something in the gesture felt wrong, so Viola snagged it by the sleeve and draped it over the end of the narrow cot that served as her bed.

Her hand lingered over silk brought to New Orleans all the way from the Far East. The pearls she'd worn at her neck had long since been lost, having scattered across the steps of the cathedral back in New Orleans, but those that decorated the bodice and sleeves remained.

So many fittings, standing for what seemed to be hours on end in front of Mama's gilt-edged mirror until the very shape of the dress seemed to stay long after Viola had stepped out of it. She didn't dare complain or, for that matter, even consider uttering such words.

And the cost. . . What she wouldn't give to have half the price of this dress in her account over at the grocer's or the mercantile.

She allowed her mind to tiptoe backward to the cathedral steps but refused to let her thoughts remain there. Remembering how she came to the island served only to offer up the opportunity to forget all the things God had done with her and through her since her unexpected arrival. Had she remained behind in New Orleans, she'd likely be wed and in need of a midwife rather than having become one.

No, she decided, she'd be dead. "Andre would have seen to it."

Yet even now, some two years after her fiancé's death, Andre Gayarre reached from the grave to control her life and stand between her and the man with whom she'd fallen in love. By default, so did her father.

From her window, she saw Emilie Gayarre approach. Viola put on her best smile. Was it not for Emilie, she'd never have found Fairweather Key. Neither would she have managed to become what she was: a midwife who often worked alongside the doctor she loved.

Somehow the fact that she helped to bring new lives into the world seemed to atone in some measure for the life that had been lost at her hands.

Again the scene unfolded in her mind. The angry man she'd left waiting at the altar on their wedding day stood before her.

A gun in the hand that more than once had bruised her body. Words from the mouth that more often bruised her soul.

A shot. Andre Gayarre lay dead.

Viola shrugged off the image and reached to grasp the blue gown, her only possession when she boarded Josiah Carter's ship for freedom. Placing it back in the wardrobe, she swiped at the tears she hated and turned toward the door.

Before Emilie could knock, Viola opened the door with a smile firmly in place. As pleasantries were exchanged, she invited her old friend in.

"I've come bearing news." Emilie grinned. "And a letter."

She glanced at the handwriting and found it vaguely familiar. "How did you get this?" Turning it over, Viola could find no evidence that the document had been mailed.

"It was handed to me," Emilie explained, "by a mutual friend who arrived on my doorstep some moments ago."

"Have you time for tea and conversation before I return to school for the afternoon?" Viola gestured toward the parlor, good manners trumping her curiosity at who might resort to this kind of silliness. Then an idea formed.

Dan.

Of course.

Likely Micah Tate had talked some sense into the hopeless bachelor.

Micah let the courthouse door close behind him then took a deep breath of salt air. He felt ten years younger, his shoulders a measure lighter now that the weight they'd carried no longer rested upon them.

The door opened, and Josiah stepped outside. "Want some company?"

He looked back at his friend, weariness suddenly threatening. "Not if you're going to ask me why I didn't tell you this before now."

Josiah shrugged. "No."

"Well, good." Micah set out walking, unsure as to his destination. The stretch of his legs and the pace of his stride served to quickly restore his mood. As he contemplated the conversation with Caleb Spencer, his thoughts turned to prayers.

"This is where I leave you."

Micah jerked his attention toward the friend he'd forgotten walked beside him. "What? Oh yes, of course."

Somehow they'd arrived at the cottage Josiah shared with Isabelle and little Joey. The lad must have been watching, for he burst through the door calling for his papa, Isabelle on his heels. Micah thought of Caroline and the babe she surely chased around heaven, and for a moment, all Micah could do was stare.

"Come back here, young man," Isabelle called. When she caught sight of Josiah and Micah, she stopped and offered a grin. "So this is why he's ignoring me. Go ahead," she said to the boy, who'd now turned to regard his mama with an innocent stare. "Go to your papa."

"*Your papa.*" Another stab to his heart, and Micah turned away. With a wave, he left the happy couple and their son and resumed his walk toward the boardinghouse and the meal he hoped would still be available.

"Hello there, Micah Tate."

Doc Hill. Not an unpleasant man, but certainly not anyone he'd be willing to pass the time of day with in this condition. Micah ducked his head and pressed forward, ignoring the call, unwilling to let go of the grief that seized him.

Unfortunately, the doctor caught him at the corner while Micah waited for the funeral director's horse and wagon to pass. Rather than offer his true opinion of the man's company, Micah met his gaze and nodded, then followed the gesture with the required pleasantries.

"Have a moment?" the doc asked as his gaze followed the wagon until it disappeared around the corner. "I could use some help. Some wisdom, actually."

Micah's chuckle held no humor. "If it's wisdom you seek, I'd head toward the church."

Daniel Hill seemed no less enthusiastic. "No, I doubt the reverend would understand. Now if you'd spare me just a few minutes, I'd be grateful." He gestured toward the clinic. "I figure you're heading in that direction anyway, so allow me this, please."

His tone carried a desperation Micah not only recognized but had felt more than once. Still, he'd already had one companion on a walk he'd intended to be one of solitary prayer. He thought to explain that Hezekiah Carter would likely be much more helpful than himself at anything.

But the doctor appeared to have his mind set on talking to Micah and not waiting for the better man to assist him.

"All right," Micah said, "but I'm in a hurry, so you might have a bit of trouble keeping up."

"I'll risk it." With a nod, they set off across the street. The doctor waited until they'd cleared the corner before he looked ready to speak. "I've a problem. Of the female variety."

Despite his irritation, Micah grinned. "Might the problem be named Viola Dumont?"

"It is." Doc paused. "Rather, she is. No," he corrected. "I must admit I'm the real problem."

"Why tell me?" Micah said. "Go tell Miss Dumont."

"I tried." He tugged at his collar. "I thought maybe you could help me with that."

"Talk to her for you? Oh no." Micah stopped short then shook his head and took off walking again. "Look," he said when Doc Hill caught up to him, "I'm not a man who gets himself involved in this kind of foolishness."

"It's not foolishness, Micah."

He slid the doctor a sideways look. "When there's a woman involved, it's almost always foolishness."

"She wants me to marry her."

Micah had to laugh. "Is this news to you? Anyone with decent eyesight would know that. What none of us can understand—likely her as well—is what's taking you so long. Seems to me a man with the opportunity to land a fine catch like Miss Dumont ought to go ahead and do it."

A pair of ladies from the choir emerged from the mercantile to greet them, and the doctor tipped his hat, as did Micah. "I can't," Daniel said when the women were out of earshot. "I'd only be a disappointment to her."

"Is that all?" Micah shrugged. "I reckon if a man's not being a disappointment in some way to a woman, then he's likely about to be. It's the nature of the arrangement, I'm afraid, though women don't seem to mind it so much."

"Be serious, Micah." The doc paused and seemed to be considering his next statement carefully. "The truth is, I did intend to marry her.

I knew it from the minute I saw her. Then when Andre Gayarre walked into my clinic with a gun in his hand, everything changed."

"I see."

This conversation had gone far past comfortable and was reaching the point of needing to be over. The growl in Micah's gut reminded him that every minute he tarried was a minute he was not eating Ruby O'Shea's fine cooking.

Dr. Hill seemed to be waiting for more. Irritation and impatience converged to remove any intention on Micah's part to offer up understanding or even humor. Doc needed to handle his business like a man: in private and without consulting anyone or taking a poll to figure out what to do.

"That was two years ago, Doc. You can't use past history as an excuse." Micah paused. "You wanted my advice, so I'm giving it to you. Marry the woman and be done with it, or leave her be."

"That's it?"

Micah nodded. "Yes, that's it. Now if you'll excuse me, I've got some eating and some praying to do, and I am long overdue on both."

The doctor reached out to stop Micah. "Thank you," he said with what seemed to be great relief in his voice. "I knew that's what should happen, but I resisted it." He paused. "For all the obvious reasons."

Micah studied him for a moment but found nothing to understand in the man's sudden change of attitude. "Yes, well, glad to be of service," he said as he resumed his walk. "Give her my best if you think of it."

"Micah?"

Biting back a sharp retort, Micah let his shoulders sag and his pace slow. "What is it?"

"Thank you."

"I didn't do anything," he said, though when he turned to see what sort of response his statement might have garnered, Dr. Hill was gone. "Odd fellow," Micah muttered as he stretched out the arm the man had patched back together after last year's accident on the reef. "But a good doctor. That much I'll give him."

CHAPTER 6

"Tea, no," Emilie said. "I have a few visits to make. Though it would take little to see me staying long enough for you to read that letter."

Viola shook her head as she broke the seal. "I fail to understand how. . ." She read the first line twice before she fully realized whose hand had composed the words. "Remy?"

"Yes." Emilie moved into her line of sight. "He was a bit concerned about surprising you, so he came to me first and asked that I pave the way for a reunion."

Viola found the nearest chair and sank onto it, unable to remain upright. "That's impossible. My father would never allow it." She took a deep breath. "I'm sorry. I don't doubt you. Tell me where I can find Remy, and please understand I still find it a bit difficult to believe it's true."

"I think that story is best told by him. Shall we go, then?"

"Yes, I'm anxious to see him." Viola shook her head as she rose to find her bonnet and wrap. "When I left it seems he was barely out of knee pants." She felt the tears sting her eyes but blinked them back. Some things that she'd left behind when she stepped aboard the ship with Isabelle and Emilie had caused her more pain than others, her relationship with her younger brother chief among them.

"An exaggeration, to be sure," Emilie said, "and yet when I posted my answer to his letter, he responded quickly and with great enthusiasm. It seems as though the law was not his forte, and neither was the prospect of joining Henri."

"Wait." Viola stopped short and looked at Emilie. "He sent a letter to you? When? And why not to me?"

"Some months ago," she said, "and he asked that I not mention his desire to see you." Emilie paused. "He has a particular purpose in coming here, but I will let him tell you that."

Viola thought of Remy, the gentle younger brother who called her Vivi because it irritated her. The scholar who, from a young age, was more likely to be found with his nose in a book than not.

The lad whose interest in books was bested only by his interest in the fairer sex.

"I wonder what he's like. Is he handsome?"

Emilie's grin was her answer.

"Of course he is. And what of his studies? I suppose he's done with them now and is likely practicing the law, though perhaps he joined the family business. Does he have a wife with him?"

Viola closed the door and joined Emilie. Together they turned toward the eastern side of Fairweather Key, where Emilie and Caleb's cottage sat at the end of a narrow lane.

"No," Viola answered herself, "he'd likely be chasing away any potential wives and be miserable toiling away under Henri's command. Henri is still in charge of the company, I assume. Do hurry, Emilie."

Emilie shrugged as she hurried to keep up. At the corner, they met several children on their way to the parsonage for some of Mary Carter's afternoon treats.

"Don't be late, children," Emilie called as Viola dragged her away. "We've a busy afternoon ahead."

"Henri always did fancy himself at the helm of Dumont Shipping," Viola continued when she had Emilie's attention again. "Even as a boy. I can remember while Remy and I were playing school, Henri would be ordering about the cats or the chickens or whatever else he could find. Later it became the servants and, I suppose, his wife and children. Surely by now he has children. And Papa? Likely he still lives."

"Likely."

That she did not know gave Viola pause. Another regret of leaving

New Orleans without saying good-bye. "Yet he did not come himself nor seek any further contact with me after news returned of Andre's death."

"I cannot explain it," Emilie said, "though I do suppose that he and my father may bear much grief and burden over Andre's death."

"Grief and burden? They merely sent him. It is because of me that Andre is dead."

Emilie linked arms with her, likely as much to slow Viola's pace as to offer comfort. She smiled at the baker's wife, who waved from the building across the street, then turned her attention to Viola. "Might you have lived had you not?"

"Perhaps. Or perhaps not." Viola met the gaze of the woman who might have become her sister by marriage. "I have tried on many occasions to offer this up as an excuse, and the words fall flat when compared to the result."

"My brother had a horrible temper, Vi," Emilie said. "Andre did not go to the doctor's home that day with good intentions."

Viola stopped to lean against the fence rail, her eyes falling shut. "I tried to love him. I wanted so to please Papa and make this a good match."

Emilie let her cry until the tears were spent.

"I've made such a mess of things, Em," Viola said.

"And now you are making Remy wait." Her friend's tone was gentle, her purpose obviously to distract.

She decided to allow the ruse to work. "Indeed," Viola said. "A moment longer, and I'll be ready to meet Remy. Do I look awful?"

"No, Vivi. You look every bit as beautiful as I remember."

Viola whirled around to find that her little brother was not so little anymore. He towered a head taller and wore his mop of dark curls in a much more adult manner than had the young man she left behind.

"Remy!" She made to hug him and felt her feet leave the ground. The horizon swung about, and when the ground rose to meet her, Viola nearly stumbled.

"Easy there," her brother said as he gathered her close. "Didn't mean to knock you off your feet."

"If you two will excuse me." Emilie pointed to the end of the lane. "I see two of my students I've been meaning to speak with. Carol and Maggie, would you come here, please?"

Viola looked past Emilie to see the O'Shea twins scampering toward the beach. As Emilie chased them down and turned them toward town, Viola stepped out of her brother's embrace to hold him at arm's length.

"Remy Dumont," she said as she blinked back tears yet again, "what in the world are you doing on Fairweather Key? Shouldn't you be reading for the law or choosing a wife by now?"

He winked. "I should, but I'd rather be here with you."

"Surely you're not planning to stay here."

"No, but I plan to take you with me when I leave."

CHAPTER 7

R uby stirred the stew then tapped the edge of the pot with her spoon. Behind her, she heard little Tess do the same. "What are you cooking, Miss Tess?" she called over her shoulder as she counted up the plates and utensils for the noon meal.

"I need a spoon to make my stewp," the four-year-old said, peering up with eyes that made Ruby's heart lurch. So like her father, those eyes, and yet nothing like him at all. Well, perhaps in her bursts of temper, but beyond that, Tess bore him no resemblance.

"Stew," Ruby gently corrected before hefting the tray onto her shoulder to deliver it to the barge-sized dining table.

A tug at her apron string caused Ruby to turn. "No," Tess said. "You made stew. I made stewp. I'm gonna feed Red."

Another day, she might have bent to gather up the girl or join her in her nonsensical talk. She might even have allowed her to put some of her imaginary creation out to feed Red, the rooster that snapped at the heels of everyone except Tess.

Today, however, Ruby had yet to shake the morning's trip to the beach or the reason for it. Then there was the troublesome reminder that she'd likely soon see Micah Tate.

Would that the man might actually miss a meal. Dared she pray it?

She turned her thoughts to Tess, who now sat on the kitchen floor with her favorite wooden spoon and a scowl. "So you made soup?"

"No," came the sullen response.

Ruby picked up the empty tray and retraced her steps back into the kitchen. She'd handle Tess later. Likely the girl would emerge from her mood as quickly as she'd settled into it. She generally did. For now, however, the noon meal must hold Ruby's attention.

Besides, with all but one room in the boardinghouse claimed, there'd likely be at least ten around the table. A glance at the clock warned her they'd all be coming through the door soon. Wrapping the fresh bread in a tea towel, Ruby reached up to retrieve a basket then placed the barely cooled loaf inside.

Ruby pressed past Tess with the bread in one hand and a stack of linens in the other.

The place might have been only a modest boardinghouse in faraway Fairweather Key, but Mrs. Campbell insisted on proper manners, proper meals, and good linens. She'd boasted that her entire collection of napkins and tablecloths—reportedly once used by royalty—had been purchased for next to nothing at a wrecker's auction. To back up her claim, each item bore the crest of Britain's ruler in the corner.

Though Mrs. Campbell had left Ruby to do as she pleased both in the kitchen and with the rules of the boardinghouse, Ruby had kept all in order as if the former judge's wife still ruled the roost. Should she return tomorrow, Mrs. Campbell would indeed find everything quite unchanged. Except the recipes. Those Ruby had adjusted a bit.

Another tug at her apron strings caused Ruby to nearly tumble backward. The bread basket, however, was not so fortunate. While the basket clattered to the floor and slid toward the kitchen, the bread parted ways to skid to a stop near the window. In her rush to help, Tess stumbled and stomped on the cloth-covered loaf.

Or perhaps the act was intentional.

Surveying the damage, Ruby decided the bread was ruined, though she might salvage enough of it to make a bread pudding for tomorrow night. She turned to walk back to the kitchen, and with each step, she prayed she might tamp down her anger lest she—

The crumbled mess that had formerly been a stellar example of her bread-making skills went flying past Ruby's head and slammed against the far wall. "Stewp! Say it. Stewp. Stew and soup!"

"Maria Teresa—" Ruby covered her mouth even as her heart sank. One name more and, well, she'd not contemplate it.

Tess looked stunned. "You said never to—"

"I know what I said." Ruby's fingers shook, rendering her unable to retrieve what remained of the bread. "It was a mistake, Tess."

The door opened then shut, indicating the first of the hungry boarders had arrived. "What are you making, little one?" a familiar female voice called.

"Stewp, Miss Emilie!" Tess said with more than a little quaver in her voice. "For Red."

"Soup and stew?" Ruby turned to see Emilie Gayarre standing in the doorway. "And look at this." The schoolteacher stooped to reach for the mangled loaf. "You've made mush to go along with it." Her gaze met Ruby's, and Ruby thought she detected more than a note of sympathy there. "Busy morning?"

Ruby mustered a smile before taking the remains of the bread and depositing them into the slop bucket. "I've had better."

Before Emilie could respond, Carol and Maggie burst through the back door and clattered to a halt when they spied their teacher. Looking like the cat that ate the canary happened too often with this pair, but today the expression was especially pronounced.

Ruby glanced over at Emilie then back at the girls. So often since the twins were born, Ruby had wondered if there might be some sort of unspoken communication between them, some language of signals and expressions that only the two of them were privy to.

As if hearing her thoughts, Carol stared at Maggie, who slowly and solemnly nodded.

"There's nothing a bit of practicing won't cure," Emilie said. "Isn't that right, girls?"

Both nodded, though Ruby noticed there was little enthusiasm in either response.

"And what, pray tell, are you practicing, girls?"

"Our names," Carol said.

"We spelled the wrong ones," Maggie added.

"The wrong. . ." Ruby felt her stomach clench. Little troubles like this would surely add up to one big problem should she be foolish enough to remain in Fairweather Key for long. Poor children. She'd asked much of them.

Possibly too much.

Yet what else could she do? Almost every evening since August 2, she and the girls had spent their last few minutes before bedtime going over the story of who they were and how they came to be on Fairweather Key. Not the whole truth, but a reasonable version of it with the proper protection included for the innocents.

More than once since she'd decided to heed the preacher's warning, Ruby had wondered if she ought to come clean with the townspeople like she'd come clean with Jesus. She'd decided, at least for now, that while the Lord would love her and the girls no matter what, the church folk likely would not. The hardest part of this realization was trying to explain it to the girls.

What she'd ended up with was something Rev. Carter said two Sundays ago. "When you can't tell anyone else, you can always tell Jesus." The who and the where of their past were matters, Ruby told the girls, that were just for Jesus to know.

Ruby turned around to give the stew a vigorous stir it didn't really need. "You'll stay for lunch, won't you?" she inquired of Emilie.

Emilie touched her shoulder. "I thought we might speak in private, Ruby."

"I know what that means," Tess said. "It means you're in trouble."

"Hey now," Ruby said, pointing the spoon at Tess then cringing when she realized she'd dripped gravy down her skirt. "You've got troubles of your own. Unless you'd prefer we discuss your behavior right now."

Tess stuck out her lower lip as she reached to grasp Maggie's hand. Maggie, in turn, linked fingers with Carol.

"It's stewp," Ruby heard Tess mutter just before she yanked her sisters outside.

"No, Tess O'Shea," Ruby called, using both names carefully but deliberately as her temper flared, "it's bread that you've ruined, and a mess you've left all over the kitchen floor just when I'm expecting the boarders back for lunch. Rest assured, you'll be sorry later."

Ruby clamped her lips shut and reached for the towel to swipe at her skirt, the second she'd ruined since dawn. Except for her Sunday dress, she was without a clean spare.

What was wrong with her?

"Ruby?"

She'd all but forgotten about Emilie. "I'm sorry you had to hear that," Ruby said without sparing her a glance. "Sometimes Tess is a little, well, hard to handle."

The front door opened, and the sound of several deep voices sent Ruby scurrying into the dining room with the pot of stew. Over the next few minutes, the boarders streamed in to take their places at the table.

Micah Tate was missing.

Ruby shook off any thoughts of what his absence might mean as she returned to the kitchen for the coffeepot. There she found the schoolteacher hard at work, scrubbing the last of the bread crumbs off the floor.

"When do you and the girls manage to eat?" Emilie asked without looking up.

"I generally chase off the chickens and set a table for the girls back on the porch." The truth was, the table was really a rain barrel with a board set across it, but it gave the girls a place of their own to take their meals without upsetting or interrupting the boarders. "I'll fix their bowls soon as I get dessert on the table."

"Let me," Emilie said.

Ruby gave the teacher, who'd recently become the wife of the town judge, a look. "You don't have to do that."

Emilie smiled as she dusted bread crumbs off her skirt. "I want to."

The sound of a boarder calling her name didn't give Ruby much time to think. "I suppose there's no harm in it. Just don't let Carol convince you she's allowed more than one serving of dessert. She's got quite the sweet tooth, that one. And watch out for Red."

"Red?" Emilie asked.

"The rooster. He thinks he rules the yard." Someone in the dining room called her name again, and Ruby responded then turned her attention back to Emilie. "Just wave him away and he'll run."

Another call, and Ruby left Emilie standing in the kitchen. The group of boarders was still missing Micah Tate. Ruby was too tired to worry about why the persistent wrecker had missed lunch for the first time since she'd come to work in Mrs. Campbell's kitchen.

Perhaps this God she'd only just come to know really did love her. He'd certainly smiled on her by not causing her to face Micah Tate twice in one morning.

Ruby shrugged off the unwelcome reminder and cleared the table, then piled the dishes together for washing. A moment later, she went back for the soiled linens and tablecloth. Only then did she pause to sigh. An afternoon of laundering and more cooking awaited her, as did the nighttime routine of preparing for the morning meal, yet Ruby gave thanks for the work.

At least it was an honest living that kept a roof over their heads.

A giggle drew her attention to the window overlooking the back porch. There Ruby spied the very proper schoolteacher sitting on the back steps, watching what appeared to be wild heathens turning and spinning like tops and scattering Red and three hens to the far corners. Just as one girl would fall, another would jump up and take her place.

If they continued, none would be able to hold down her lunch. Yet it seemed a shame to stop the very thing that made them shriek with happiness. After all those three had endured the past year, happiness was certainly due them.

Had Emilie not spied her, Ruby might have let the dancing and spinning go on indefinitely. Instead, she offered Emilie a smile then hurriedly divided the remains of the stew into five bowls, being careful to fill the other four before spooning what remained into her own.

At Emilie's command, the girls ran to the rain bucket and doused their hands and faces. While Maggie used the corner of her skirt to dry Tess's hands, Emilie shooed away Red and replaced the board atop the bucket.

Ruby placed spoons into all five bowls then situated them on a fancy ebony and silver tray that likely came from one of the wrecker's auctions. Backing out the door to keep it from slamming on her, she stepped onto the porch.

"Oh no," Emilie said as she rose, "I didn't intend to interrupt your lunch. We can talk another time."

"Girls," Ruby called, "how would you like to have a picnic over in the churchyard again?" All three squealed with delight, a sure sign the answer was yes. "Maggie, go and get the tablecloth from the laundry pile. Carol, you see to Tess's bowl."

In a flash, the girls were headed across the yard, scattering chickens as they slipped through the gate. When the last blond head disappeared from sight, Ruby collected her bowl and settled on the top step. Exhaustion began its familiar trek from the tips of her toes past knees that had bent one time too many, finally settling at the small of her back, where she refused to acknowledge it.

"What is it about that churchyard that makes the children love to picnic there?" Emilie asked. "Not a day goes by that I don't see at least one group of boys or girls there during their lunchtime break."

Ruby grinned while she waited for her arms to comply with her wish to lift the spoon. "Mary Carter's the reason. She's forever baking sweet treats and offering them up for the children if they can show her they've cleaned their plates."

"Well, that does explain it, though knowing my sister's mother-in-law, I shouldn't be surprised. Maybe I'll start taking my lunch over at the churchyard, too." Emilie dug into the stew with a gusto that told Ruby she'd forgotten her reluctance to intrude on lunch. "This is delicious, by the way," she said when she'd swallowed a bit.

"Thank you." Her stomach's protest overpowered Ruby's need to rest, giving her the strength to spoon up a portion of the gravy along with a tiny bite of meat. She looked down at the watery dregs in her bowl, the remainder after all other hungry mouths had been fed. "Stew and soup." Ruby chuckled. "Stewp."

The schoolteacher looked up from her meal. "I'm sorry?"

Ruby's chuckle became a giggle that, by degrees, dissolved into tears she was nearly too tired to cry. "Stewp," she said as the events of the day, the week, and the years came rolling down her cheeks. "I'm eating stewp."

CHAPTER 8

Home?" Viola shook her head. "Why would I want to go back home, Remy? I have a wonderful life right here, but—please understand I mean no offense—it doesn't include being bullied by Papa and Henri."

Her brother seemed to study her for a moment. "Tell me about your wonderful life, Vivi."

"I'd be happy to," she said, "though might we leave Emilie's gate? I've a lovely little home in town that I'd like to show you."

"Would you, now?" He held up his forefinger then bounded up the walk to the porch. There he hefted a small trunk to his shoulder and retraced his steps. "Show me this lovely little home, then."

"Is that trunk heavy?" she asked after they'd gone a few steps. "I can send someone back for it."

Her brother laughed, and the sound sent her mind reeling back to childhood days. "I'm not a child anymore," he said. "I'll manage."

"No, you're not a child," she said. "Tell me what I've missed."

"It's more what I've missed, actually, and that's you." He glanced down at her. "Though I must admit I'm not at all displeased that you didn't marry Emilie's brother."

"You never said so," she countered.

They walked in silence through the heart of town, and more than once, Viola waved to a familiar face. As they passed the courthouse, she saw Micah Tate and Josiah Carter deep in conversation. When neither looked her way, she went back to talking. "It's just ahead," she said when they reached her block.

"You didn't ask."

Viola paused at her gate and shook her head. "What?"

"About Andre. You never asked my opinion. To offer it unasked would have been disloyal."

She thought a moment as she struggled with the latch. When it finally gave and the gate swung inward, she shrugged. "Yes, I suppose that's true. And you were always loyal to me. I thank you for that."

"Brothers are loyal," he said, "or at least they should be."

"I'm thankful all the same." Viola stepped ahead of Remy to open the door. "Here we are," she said. "This is my home."

"Why is there a bell on your porch? Has your cow gone missing?"

"Very funny. I am a midwife, and that bell is for emergencies. While I might miss a knock in the dead of night, I've not yet slept through a ringing of that bell."

"Nor, I wager, have the neighbors." He reached for the bell and gave it a jangle. "Indeed, a handy alarm. Perhaps I should keep it at my bedside in case I have need of coffee or breakfast in the morning."

She gave him a playful but gentle elbow to the ribs. "Put that down. Your height might proclaim you to be an adult, but I've just seen evidence that the little brother I left still exists."

"Long may he live." Remy shifted the trunk into his arms and then set it on the floor. Stretching his arms over his head, he grinned. "So—a midwife? This is very much the home of a woman, Vivi. Is there no husband? No man in your life?"

How to answer?

"I see this is a question I've obviously no business asking."

She dropped her things on the nearest chair. "Oh, you can ask. Doesn't mean I have to respond." Viola paused. "Yes," she said with a sigh, "there is a man, though I've grown weary in trying to figure out whether he's actually in my life or merely just in the neighborhood."

"Meaning?"

"Meaning he's spent much time courting and little time considering what comes next." Viola leaned against the doorframe and watched her brother heave the heavy trunk about as if it weighed nothing.

"What of you? You've certainly grown up. Is there some woman pining away back in New Orleans while you're away?"

Remy raised a dark brown eyebrow in response as he walked to the other side of the room. He picked up the worn copy of *Paul Clifford*, the book she'd left on the table when Mrs. Vincent's husband had fetched her to deliver little Arabella in the wee hours, and opened it to the first page.

"It was a dark and stormy night; the rain fell in torrents—except at occasional intervals, when it was checked by a violent gust of wind." He looked up. "Brilliant novel, though it always intrigued me how this fellow Mr. Clifford could live a dual life as a criminal and a gentleman."

Viola strolled over to take the book from his hands. "Surely a dual life isn't all that difficult, though I'd not recommend it. Now what of your lunch? Are you hungry? As I recall—"

A ring of the bell stopped her, and a moment later she opened the door to find the eldest of the Vincent girls on the porch. "Is it time?" When the girl nodded, Viola sent her off to let her mother know help was on the way. "It appears you will be left to fend for yourself for a while," she said to Remy as she reached for the bag she kept nearby.

"How long do these things take?" he called from the door.

"Things? Oh, babies?" She shook her head. "There's no predicting. Would you like to come along?"

Remy's stunned expression made her chuckle even as she turned her attention to the task ahead. The last time she'd delivered a baby at the Vincent home, things had not gone well.

"Vivi?"

She turned to see Remy standing in the doorway. "Miss me already?" A poor joke, she realized as soon as the words tumbled out.

Ruby let her spoon fall into the bowl and swiped at her eyes. Had she not a full day's work still ahead, she might have leaned her head against the porch post and claimed a quick nap. Out of the corner of her eye, she spied Emilie Gayarre watching her and resumed eating.

It seemed the only way to avoid conversation, at least for the moment. The stew—stewp—was good but might have been better had she a slice of bread to go with it.

She took another bite. Maybe later she'd find time to start another loaf. Yes, with her dinner plans all but done, she could surely do that. Another bite and then one more, and the bowl began to empty.

A pie, perhaps. Yes, she'd serve the pie instead.

"I don't know how you do it all."

"Oh," she said with a start as she set the bowl aside and scrambled to her feet. "I'm terribly sorry. I'd all but forgotten you were here." She smoothed her apron and offered a shrug. "My mind tends to wander sometimes, though I never let it go any farther than the kitchen."

"There's no need for an apology." Emilie shrugged as she rose and reached for the bowl. "Actually, I rather enjoyed the quiet. It's lovely here."

Before Ruby could protest, Emilie had deposited the dishes inside and returned to stand in the open door. "I wonder if perhaps I've chosen the wrong time to discuss the girls with you, Ruby. I can surely wait until you're not so. . ." She paused, and Ruby figured her to be weighing her word choice against her upbringing. "So tired," Emilie finally said.

"Best we talk now," she said, even though dread snaked up her spine.

The schoolteacher had been the first to take them in, offering shelter on that rainy night in August. She'd offered clean clothes and soft beds and never once inquired of the how or why of their arrival. Along with her sister, Isabelle, Emilie had made them feel welcome and offered a measure of dignity to a woman who'd had none for a very long time.

Ruby took a deep breath and said a quick prayer the best way she knew how. "I'll answer whatever questions you've got." She paused. "At least I'll try."

Emilie seemed to consider the statement a moment. "All right, then." She came to sit next to Ruby. "The twins," she said tentatively. "I've noticed, well. . ." The schoolteacher turned her attention away from Ruby to study something off on the horizon. "I think perhaps there's more to your story," she finally said. "To their story."

Here was her moment to tell the truth. To take God at His word and offer up only that which was accurate.

Ruby opened her mouth, fully intent on telling the woman who would soon become the judge's wife everything. Or at least most of it.

Then she heard herself say, "I don't know what you're talking about."

CHAPTER 9

An opportunity missed, Ruby knew. Yet when Emilie rose and offered a smile, all she could think was how very much she wanted to be anywhere but in this place at this time having this sort of talk with Emilie Gayarre.

There would be time again for the truth; this she knew. For the look on the schoolteacher's face told her the subject would be broached again.

Ruby's stomach began to churn, and she knew it was not from the stew.

"Of course," Emilie said as she rose and sent the chickens scattering. "Where has the time gone? I'm certain the children will be wondering where their teacher is."

Ruby forced a smile, but she could not bring herself to meet the woman's gaze. "I reckon so," she said. "I'll go and fetch the girls and see they get themselves back to the schoolhouse."

"No need," Emilie said. "I can do that." She reached to touch Ruby's sleeve. Only then did Ruby look into Emilie's eyes.

"Leave Tess to Mary Carter this afternoon," she said. "Isabelle will be there with Joey, and you're in dire need of some time to yourself."

Time to herself? She'd gone without so long that she didn't know if she remembered what that was. Even in her sleep, she shared a cot with Tess, and depending on whether one of the notorious Florida storms rolled in, sometimes with all three.

"I couldn't impose," she said, imagining what she might accomplish with even one undivided hour.

"Then it's settled." The schoolteacher smiled. "You see, my nephew may not yet be two, but he adores Tess. She's quite a help to Isabelle in keeping him busy."

Tess did love to amuse the little fellow.

"Will you tell the ladies how much I appreciate the help?"

Emilie looked as if she was about to say something, but after a moment, she nodded and headed for the gate. "I'll be baking pies for the both of them," Ruby called, "and I'll have no argument about it."

Emilie paused at the gate and rested both palms on the whitewashed wood. "Someday perhaps you'll tell me where you learned to cook so well, Ruby."

The schoolteacher's expression seemed innocent enough, but Ruby couldn't help but feel they were no longer talking about pies. A sudden urge to gather up the girls and run for the nearest oceangoing vessel bore down on her, but Ruby forced a smile.

"Yes," she said as she took an unsteady step toward the back door. "Perhaps I will."

And then Emilie was gone, leaving Ruby to sort out her aching bones from her painful conscience. Neither could be done in the kitchen, where bread crumbs still dotted the floor and the lunch dishes awaited cleaning.

A trip out back to the room she shared with the girls would likely allow for private reflection, but no doubt being alone would only invite tears. "And the last thing I need to do is cry over something that's easily fixed."

Indeed, Ruby could remedy the problem with a quick trip to the docks and a discreet inquiry to the captain of whatever ship might be sailing soon. This decided, Ruby bypassed the kitchen altogether and walked to the front of the boardinghouse, where the wide parlor windows offered the best view of the street.

She lifted the corner of the heavy drape and pulled it back. From her vantage point, Ruby watched Emilie stop at the church gates and wave at someone inside. A moment later Isabelle Carter appeared at the gate to embrace her sister.

Seeing the two conversing put Ruby in mind of her own sister and all the times since the accident when she had wished for Opal. "I will not cry," she said even as tears stung her eyes.

Releasing her grip on the fabric, she watched the drape fall back into place. Her fingers traced the heavy brocade, its golden threads burnished to a dull copper along the edges. Mama had had pretty curtains like this. They were green. No. Blue. Yes, a lovely shade that Papa said reminded him of the Cornwall sky.

She'd had no idea where Cornwall was, but she imagined it was a lovely place where the sun shone most days and danced across a sky painted in Mama's favorite color. The image had been ruined when Tommy Hawkins told them that Cornwall was a bleak and cold place known more for smugglers than anything else.

Just one more in a long line of disappointments associated with either Papa or Tommy.

Or both.

Why do I do this to myself? "You think too much, Claire. You always did."

She jumped away from the window, stunned at how easily the name had slipped from her lips. At how very much she sounded like her sister.

Indeed, the pronouncement held much truth. From her earliest days, if she wasn't thinking about the past, she was fretting about some distant part of the future. Neither seemed to do much good.

Ruby straightened her aching back and felt her bones slide against one another in protest. A corresponding twinge in her neck caused her to massage the ache.

"I could do that for you."

She froze, unable to breathe. Just as she'd conjured up Opal's voice, surely this one, too, was from her imagination. Then she heard the floorboards creak and knew he'd come to stand behind her. To find her vulnerable.

Again.

"What do you want, Jean Luc?" A whisper rather than anything like actual words, but to speak them any louder would be to cast doubt on what she hoped was her calm demeanor.

"Sweet Claire."

Ruby refused to flinch even when Thomas Hawkins's second in command placed his hands on each side of her neck. Fully expecting the Frenchman to strangle her, she gasped when he used the strength in his fingers to massage her aching muscles.

In the past, she'd have melted under the tender massage. Today she found his touch repulsive, a reminder of who—of what—she was.

"I suppose Ben and Jamie are with you." She paused and said a prayer against it even as she added, "And Tommy."

The fingers stopped their movement. Jean Luc Rabelais moved closer. "I've come alone, Mrs. O'Shea," he added in a mock Irish brogue.

His meaning was unmistakable. It was also familiar, owing to the times she had perpetrated the fraud of acting as silent wife to his Scottish husband during certain business transactions. At the time, the ruse had seemed harmless, mere window dressing to the actual crime of offering up such contraband as fine silks and baubles to those who could afford them. A genial couple who'd just happened to stumble upon a few trunks of contraband goods made for much better sales. Somehow contemplating a purchase from ruthless smugglers set the well-to-do on edge.

Ruby had received nothing for this ongoing playacting except continued passage aboard Hawkins's vessels and the knowledge that she would live to see the girls grow to womanhood under her protection. Harmless then. The opposite now.

"I see," she managed, angling away from the window and toward the kitchen door. Likely Jean Luc was merely doing the bidding of the man who would be more than happy to see her dead. "You're here upon whose orders?"

"Claire, Claire." The voice deceptively sweet and tender; the man anything but. "He'd have my hide, and you know it."

She braved the slightest glance and found that Jean Luc had changed little in the months since she'd last seen him near the docks. Features that set him apart from others of his ilk were better suited to some silk-covered drawing room. He'd certainly used his charm to find more than one comfortable bed for a night or a week of nights.

Rumor held that Jean Luc had a wife comfortably ensconced in a chateau near Gouvieux, where she believed her oft-absent husband to be traveling the world mapping uncharted lands and garnering large sums of money. Wherever the truth might lie, Jean Luc Rabelais had never seemed much concerned with the bonds of matrimony.

"Might I ask the reason for this visit?"

"You've got something I want." He moved closer. "And something Hawk wants." Jean Luc practically fitted himself against her. "I've considered this dilemma at some length and have come to a conclusion."

His right hand snaked around her neck and cupped her jaw. A braver woman might have bitten him and run or at least thrown open the curtains and screamed for help.

Their shared past, however, gave Ruby a third option.

With care, Ruby ducked out of Jean Luc's vile embrace and, backbone stiff, walked toward the kitchen as if she hadn't just been confronted with evidence of her past. While her hands shook, Ruby held her head high. With luck, she just might be able to bluff her way out of this.

Then she'd somehow fetch the girls and leave Fairweather Key behind for good. How this would happen, she'd figure out as she went.

Jean Luc was upon her before she'd taken three steps. He whirled her around to face him, and Ruby lost her balance. As she tilted, the floor rose to meet her with a thud that sent stars dancing before her eyes. Jean Luc lunged to grasp her hand but missed. Lurching forward with skirts tangled about her legs, Ruby crawled toward the kitchen.

This morning's careful braid had loosened and covered her face, rendering her unable to see. He'd turned her around, this much she could tell, and they'd left the kitchen, though she was far too disoriented to know in what direction.

Boot heels stomped a noisy symphony as she swiped at her face and scooped a handful of hair from her eyes. A door slammed, and darkness fell. The parlor. It was the only room that could be put in near darkness though the sun shone brightly outside. Slowly, tiny shafts of light from the edges of the drapes brought the room into focus, and Ruby's mind worked frantically to find a solution.

Long ago, the window frame had been painted shut, a state of affairs she'd vowed to remedy the next time she found a handyman to help. Now her lapse was Jean Luc's gain. A key turned in the lock, and without warning, he released her.

Much as she hated it, Ruby held tight to his hand until she could guarantee her ability to remain upright. As her eyes began to adjust to the dim light, so did her mind adjust to the situation.

"Jean Luc," she said in what she hoped was a firm and disinterested tone, "might we discuss this? I'm a woman of considerable means." A lie, of course. "Perhaps we could discuss terms of whatever it is you believe I owe you."

CHAPTER 10

The smuggler moved toward Ruby; this she felt more than saw. When Jean Luc reached to touch her, he did so gently. "I'd marry you tonight," he whispered as his lips found her ear.

Ruby pressed her palms against his chest, and for a moment, he allowed it. "Last I checked, a man only gets one wife," she said as she gave him a shove. "I'm sure yours has no idea what you do when her back is turned. Perhaps someone should tell her."

He was on her in half a heartbeat, leaving no trace of the civil man she'd known. "I could murder you in your sleep, Claire," he said. "And those girls, too."

The girls.

Her breath caught. Of course he would figure she had them. Or did he just assume? She began to back away from him as her mind reeled with things to say.

"Jean Luc," she finally said as she felt the familiar settee bump the backs of her legs. At least she knew where she was again. "Come and sit beside me. Here, I'll guide you with my voice."

Carefully she sat, perching on the end nearest the door. Something crashed and shattered, and the sound of glass crunching told her the smuggler had walked over whatever delicate treasure Mrs. Campbell had placed in the room.

He cursed as he kicked another object out of his way. She rose to guide him to the settee.

"Light a lamp," he demanded as the sofa groaned under his weight.

"I prefer not," she said as sweetly as she could manage. Giving away her advantage would never happen, especially in light of the fact that he knew the girls were with her. "Now lean back and make yourself comfortable," she said, struggling to figure out what to do next.

"Sweet Claire?"

She eased up from the settee, her movements so slow they caused her already-tired bones to ache. Finally, she was standing, the door only steps away. "Yes?"

"Were I able, I'd have long ago made you my wife. You know this, don't you?"

Perhaps she did, though she'd found it easier to ascribe only bad intent to any man who forced his attention upon her. To consider he might be telling the truth was to change the past, and nothing could do that.

Still, there had to be some reason why the smuggler Rabelais would risk his neck to stand between her and Tommy Hawkins.

Ruby sighed. How had things become so complicated?

He shifted positions toward her, and Ruby panicked. "You did know this, did you not?" In the dim light, she could see him watching, waiting. Did he figure her to be readying her escape?

"I suppose," she allowed evenly, reaching up to set her hair to rights. It would never do to have a boarder return and find her looking like she'd, well. . .it just wouldn't do.

"Then you must know nothing has changed."

But something had.

No longer was she Claire O'Connor. And no longer was Ruby O'Shea dependent on her own means. While she was still working out the details, Rev. Carter had assured her that walking with the Lord meant she had a rock to cling to even while the storm raged.

If being trapped in a parlor with Jean Luc Rabelais wasn't a storm, then she didn't know what was.

A chuckle, though there was no humor in it. "Claire?"

"No one calls me that here."

A door opened somewhere outside the parlor, and Ruby jumped.

Heavy footsteps thundered past the door then disappeared even as she heard her name.

Micah Tate.

So he'd come for his lunch after all.

"Oh, I see how it is, Claire." Jean Luc busied himself with adjusting his cuffs. "Well, there's nothing for it." He strode by without so much as a sideways glance.

Panic rose as she realized her past was about to intrude into her present in what promised to be an ugly way. "Where are you going?"

Jean Luc paused before throwing open the parlor door. "To meet this man who calls your name," he said in a perfect imitation of the Irish accent that sent terror through her once again. "Surely he's the reason you're reluctant to renew our acquaintance."

"Wait." Her voice surely gave away her fear, but it worked. For a second.

Then Micah Tate called her name again, and the smuggler swore under his breath. "None were better than you. Together we made quite the team, my dear Mrs. O'Shea," he said in an all-too-familiar Scottish brogue as he disappeared into the hall, leaving Ruby to chase the humiliation and shame he left in his wake.

Micah wandered through to the kitchen and found the pots empty and nothing but bread crumbs to show that a meal had been prepared. He swiped at the mess then decided to leave it until after he found something to fill his belly.

Beginning with the nearest cupboard, he began his search. Jars and tins hid some things he recognized and others he didn't, but none could be called a decent meal.

Sounds from somewhere on the other side of the house caused him to stop his pilfering. He hadn't been a bachelor so long as to forget how territorial a woman could become in regard to her kitchen. Still, the jar of jerky he kept at his nearly empty house was nowhere near an even substitute for whatever scraps he might find here.

"Didn't intend to bother you, Miss Ruby," he called when footsteps headed his way.

KATHLEEN Y'BARBO

Micah straightened his mess as best he could then turned to wait for the mistress of the house to arrive. He even put on a grin just in case.

Instead of Ruby, a stranger appeared. "I'm sure she'll not mind you helping yourself to anything she has. Who is. . .Ruby?"

Micah stared down at the man, a fellow who looked to spend as much time in front of the mirror as he did polishing the pistol that hung at his side. His accent gave him away as French, his expression as trouble.

Miss O'Shea came flying around the corner as if her skirts had been set afire. Skidding to a stop on what was surely a freshly cleaned floor, she worked a strand of hair back into a braid that looked as if she'd fashioned it in the dark. Splotches of color just a shade lighter than her mussed-up hair stained her cheeks.

It didn't take a genius to figure out he'd arrived either at the wrong time or, he hoped, just in time. "Miss Ruby?"

She averted her gaze and seemed to study her shaking hands. "Mr. Tate, I'm afraid you've missed lunch altogether."

"Nonsense." The stranger laughed and gathered her to his side in a way that made Micah's temper bristle. Something about the man and his treatment of Ruby O'Shea didn't set right. "Surely you can use your considerable talents to please Mr. . . ." He snapped his fingers. "Forgive me. I didn't get your name."

"Tate," Micah said as he watched Miss O'Shea shrink from the man's grasp. "Micah Tate." He returned his attention to the Frenchman, who seemed a bit less sure of himself now that he'd felt the handshake of a wrecker. What the fellow didn't realize was that his hand was still weakened from last year's injury. "I trust I've not missed anything important other than lunch."

"Tate?" When Micah nodded, the fellow grinned then winked at Miss O'Shea. "Sadly, you've missed nothing at all, though not for lack of trying on my part."

That was when Micah hit him.

68

CHAPTER 11

Two things Micah hadn't bargained for: that the Frenchman would fall so easily, and that Ruby O'Shea would land beside the man as if she, too, had been struck. She hadn't, of course, though anyone who stumbled upon the scene might think otherwise.

He watched her tug at the man's arm then pat his forehead as if her efforts might undo the damage Micah's fist had done. All the while she made little whimpering sounds.

"Get up," Micah demanded, wondering what in the world had caused him to react so strongly. When she refused to comply, he hauled her to her feet. When she wobbled a bit too much for his liking, Micah set her on a three-legged stool and told her to stay put.

"You don't understand." Miss O'Shea looked as if she might bolt, so Micah made a point of standing between her and the door.

"What's there to understand?" he asked as he watched the man for signs of movement. "He was practically begging to be hit."

Not completely the truth, but the best Micah could come up with while Ruby O'Shea was staring at him like that. The pink had disappeared from her cheeks, replaced now with skin gone ashy white.

"You really have no idea what you've just done, do you?"

"I've defended your honor, and I'll not apologize for it." He straightened his backbone, warming to the topic. "I reckon you've not had anyone take up for you, Miss Ruby."

Her silence spoke volumes.

"Then it's high time you know that a man doesn't talk to a lady that way, nor does he stand for listening to anyone else who does." A fat tear slid down her cheek, taking some of the starch from Micah's sails. "And another thing," he said. "I fail to see how you can be worried about him when he went down faster than an anchor in a rainstorm."

For emphasis, he nudged the Frenchman with the toe of his boot. The man groaned in response but made no move to open his eyes.

Miss O'Shea, however, seemed to come to life right before his eyes. While he watched, she jumped to her feet and stormed over to stand toe to toe with him. He was two heads taller at least, but she seemed not to care. She looked ready to do to him what Micah had just done to the Frenchman.

"Before you go and hit me, Miss Ruby, I think you ought to know the judge has asked me to be his second in command here on the key."

"You go ahead and make jokes, Micah Tate, but you've just gone and ruined everything."

She looked serious, but even as she poked at his chest with her forefinger, Micah found it hard to imagine things were that dire. One Frenchman with a headache surely wasn't the end of the world.

"What have I ruined other than this man's day?" Again he nudged the man with his boot. "And if anyone deserved what he got, it's. . .what's his name, Miss Ruby? I don't think he gave it."

"No." She stepped back and looked toward the window. "I don't recall that he did."

"Yet you're acquainted with him." He paused. "That much I can see."

"You can't see a thing, Mr. Tate." She turned to slip past him, and for a moment, Micah thought she might be heading for the back door. Instead, she found the basin and dipped the corner of her apron into it, then returned to kneel beside the rogue.

"What are you doing?" he asked as he watched Ruby bathe the man's swelling cheek. "Do you not appreciate the fact that this man showed you no respect?"

"What I appreciate," she said as she repeated the process of soothing the now-rousing Frenchman's face, "is that Jean Luc will be fine." She offered the man a smile. "Won't you, Jean Luc?"

Jean Luc. He'd have to remember that name, especially if he took on the responsibilities the judge offered. Likely he'd see this one again, and it wouldn't do to forget who he was.

"What happened?" the man asked as he struggled to rise up on his elbows.

"You fell," Ruby said as she continued treating the man as if he were long-lost royalty.

It didn't take but a few seconds of watching her to fuel Micah's temper past the boiling point—again. He stepped past Ruby to stand in front of Jean Luc.

A lesser man would have waited for the fool to try to stand, then knocked him down and seen that he stayed there. Micah decided to ignore the urge to do just that.

Reaching down to grasp the Frenchman's wrist, he gave the man a yank, and the stranger stumbled to his feet. Holding his grip a little tighter than before, Micah made sure to look the man in the eyes when he shook him loose and finally spoke.

"Apologize to the lady." He pointed to Ruby, who now looked as if she might throttle them both at any minute. "And take care that I don't find double meaning in your words."

A grin began to form on the intruder's soon-to-be misshapen face. It disappeared when Micah's eyes narrowed. He shifted his attention to Ruby.

"Mr. Tate, this is really enough." Her voice was high, thin, and her face still pale though her eyes sparkled with what looked to be unshed tears. She clenched and unclenched her fists, and when she caught him staring, she stuffed her hands into the pockets of her apron.

"I didn't ask your opinion, Ruby."

The Frenchman had the audacity to look amused. "So you're Ruby to him, too, are you?"

The question seemed to startle Ruby as much as it confused Micah. "Who else would she be?" he demanded.

"She's crafty, that one. She can be anyone she wants."

Ruby O'Shea might tolerate his behavior, but Micah surely would not. "Leave," Micah said through clenched jaw, "while you can still walk out on your own."

The man seemed ready to argue. *Good.* Micah's fingers itched to silence any complaints the stranger might have. Instead, the man smoothed his lapels then appeared to study the toes of his boots. "He is right." Jean Luc shrugged. "I've treated you poorly," he said, "and for that I beg your forgiveness."

"Accepted." Ruby stepped between them. "Now I'd prefer if you left, Mr. Tate," she said.

"Me leave?" He chuckled. "Not until I know you're safe."

Her look of desperation almost convinced him to do as she asked. Then he spied the Frenchman and knew he'd not be the first man to depart the boardinghouse. Not while there was a woman with more cooking skills than good sense to be protected.

From the expression on the Frenchman's face, Micah figured he held a similar sentiment. Time to end this game.

Micah reached for Ruby and gathered her to his side. "I know I'm late, but I'd much appreciate you fetching me something to eat." He paused. "Dear," he added with what he hoped was a convincing smile. "And while you're doing that, I'll see our visitor to the door."

He released her, trying not to smile at the stunned look on her face. Clamping his hand on the Frenchman's shoulder, he half guided and half pushed him to the front door. When they reached the front porch, he stopped short.

To be sure there was no mistaking his intention, Micah held tight to the man's shoulder. "I don't know who you are or what your business is with Ruby O'Shea, but if I ever see you on Fairweather Key again, it'll be you who's sorry, not me."

The fellow didn't seem in much of a hurry, though he did shrug out of Micah's grasp. Only because Micah let him.

He seemed to be sizing Micah up. "If I am to believe you, Mr. Tate, I would know your relation to. . ."

"Ruby?" Micah supplied.

"Yes, of course," Jean Luc said with a nod. "*Ruby.*"

Out of the corner of his eye, Micah noticed the curtains part.

Surely Ruby had decided to spy on them rather than rustle up some lunch. Fine enough, he supposed, for once he disposed of this fellow, he'd likely find his own meal of jerky back at his place up on the bluff.

The Frenchman backed up three steps, seemingly unwilling to turn his back on Micah. It did not escape Micah that the man with the gun seemed to be the one who was afraid.

Nor did it escape Ruby that the Frenchman had retreated without putting up much of a fight. By the time Jean Luc whoever-he-was had disappeared around the corner, the redhead was storming across the porch boards to continue the discussion they'd started before the Frenchman found his feet.

At least the look on her face told him it was going to be that kind of talk.

In his limited experience with women, Micah had never seen one pace like Ruby O'Shea. If he let her, she'd likely wear out the boards around the edges of the big front porch.

"Slow down there," he finally said, reaching out to grasp her wrist.

She hauled back and nearly swatted him, so he let her go. "I am stunned," she fairly sputtered, "at the complete lack of respect you've exhibited today, Mr. Tate."

"What?" Only after he stamped his foot did Micah realize how silly the gesture was. "I just chased off a man who obviously meant you harm, and all you can do is tell me I've shown a lack of respect? What about the things he said?"

"I don't recall what you're talking about," she said, though her statement didn't seem to be delivered with much enthusiasm.

He stood his ground. Nothing the redhead could say would turn him from his task. "Where I come from, a woman is treated with dignity and respect."

"And where I come from, a woman is. . ."

She didn't say it; she didn't have to. The lone tear that slid down her cheek spoke for her.

A southerly breeze lifted a strand of her hair and teased her neck. The same fingers that itched to obliterate the Frenchman now reached to press the curl behind her ear.

While he hadn't intended for the gesture to be intimate, Micah nonetheless felt he'd somehow stepped beyond the bounds of propriety. He was about to apologize when she turned her back on him to look toward the sea.

"You've killed us all," he thought he heard her whisper.

"Ruby?" He moved to her side, unable to say anything more than her name.

Her sideways glance revealed a woman who, in the afternoon sun, looked to be more vulnerable child than hardened woman. The moment passed, and the old Ruby returned even as she swiped at her cheeks with her sleeves.

"I'll see what I can do about finding you some lunch," she said as she brushed past him and disappeared inside. "Likely the chickens have left an egg or two, but don't expect anything fancy."

Micah followed her into the kitchen and waited in the doorway while she bustled around doing whatever a woman does when she wants to let a man know she's displeased. He let her storm just long enough for her to blow off some steam, and then he caught her.

"Mr. Tate," she said as she looked up at him with wide eyes. "You'll release me this instant—else your lunch will burn."

A fussy one, this gal, though whatever scared her about the Frenchman had her more high-strung than usual. "Let it burn, Ruby," he said. "I've a mind to say something, and I'd appreciate doing it while you're standing still."

"Surely you're joking." A change from irritation to fear crossed her features. "Unhand me, or I'll scream."

"No, you won't." Emboldened by her lack of commitment to the claim, he leaned forward. "And soon as you listen to what I'm about to promise you, I'll not only let you go, but I'll leave you be and not bother you for any more free lunches. How's that?"

Her only response was to blink.

"All right, I'll have to take that as a yes." He let out a long breath and made himself look into her eyes. "You're something special, Ruby O'Shea, and until today, I didn't realize just how much you don't know that. That man, that. . .Frenchman. . .you let him speak about you in a way that. . ."

Anger got the best of him, and for a minute, all Micah could do was try to breathe. "What I'm trying to say is you should never let anyone treat you like that."

She opened her mouth to protest, and he shook his head to silence her. "Don't argue, Ruby. Now I don't know who this Jean Luc fellow is to you, nor do I care. What I do know is if I had a woman like you, I'd never let anyone treat her poorly nor speak ill of her."

If I had a woman like you. . .

The words hung in the sea-scented air between them.

For the first time, it occurred to him that he might have a woman like her. That he might have her. He'd entertained the thought in passing, for sure, but until now, he'd not actually given it serious thought.

Here he stood, still in the boardinghouse kitchen, yet he felt as if he'd been hit by a bolt out of the blue. Micah looked away, suddenly realizing that Ruby had slid from his grasp to hurry back to her cooking.

If I had a woman like you. . .

He watched her move, noted the sway of her braid as it teased the center of her back, the set of her jaw as she took to her work. Something inside him went a notch off balance, and he had to find the stool and land on it quick.

If I had a woman like you. . .

"Ruby?" he called, working to bring some sort of normal sound to his voice.

She paused to regard him. "What is it?"

"That promise I said I'd make?"

Ruby turned back to her work. "What of it?"

"I intend to make it before God and everyone."

She looked at him like the crazy man he was. Micah thought she might say something, likely comment on his fool talk. Instead, she shrugged and went back to the business of cooking.

In a moment, she reached for a plate and slid the contents of the skillet onto it. "It's the best I could do," she said as she passed him without looking and set the plate on the farthest corner of the dining room table. "Best eat it before it gets cold."

"I'll see he doesn't bother you, Ruby," he said when she returned. "You'll be safe here."

That did it. She froze then slowly turned to face him. This time it was she who caught him by the arm.

"Nothing makes me madder than a man who boasts about something when he has no idea what he's talking about." She lifted his hand and shook it in his face. "These fists of yours won't stop a bullet, Micah Tate, and they certainly won't keep me and the girls safe when Jean Luc and his men come back and slit our throats in our beds."

He wrapped his free hand over hers. "It will if I'm in the bed with you, Ruby."

She slapped him. Hard.

Before he realized what happened, Ruby O'Shea was out the door and halfway down the street.

"No," he called after her. "I didn't mean it like that. I want to marry you."

CHAPTER 12

Well, that did it. Ruby whirled around and the madman nearly slammed into her. "Leave me alone, Mr. Tate. I've had enough trouble for one day without enduring more."

"I'm trying to remedy that, Miss Ruby."

The wrecker almost looked sincere. For a second, she considered what it might be like to wed a man like Micah Tate. Yet even as she thought on what might be a life of respectability, she remembered what others thought of Papa.

"I've no need of your remedy." She turned her back and marched toward town, knowing her pride had gotten the better of her. Where she'd go, Ruby had no idea, for where she needed to be was back at the boardinghouse, awaiting the girls' return and preparing for the evening meal.

While the beach beckoned, she figured Micah Tate would only follow. The last thing she needed was a repeat of this morning's humiliating scene. No, she'd walk all the way around the island before she'd make that mistake again.

"Please wait," Micah called, but the plea only caused her to walk faster.

Up ahead, she spied Viola Dumont. The always-friendly midwife appeared to be rushing off somewhere, for she responded to Ruby's call with only a quick wave.

Ruby caught up easily. "Might I walk with you?"

"I'm afraid I can't visit today," she said. "Mrs. Vincent's in need of me."

"Might I accompany you?" Ruby cast a glance over her shoulder to find that the wrecker continued to follow, though at a distance.

Viola glanced at her as they turned the corner and headed for the docks. "Why the sudden interest?"

"Well," Ruby said as she searched for an answer, "I figured there might be times when you would need some help with doctoring the ladies."

"We have a doctor," she said.

"Oh yes, well, of course." Micah turned the corner, and Ruby suppressed a frown. "I've done some doctoring," she blurted out.

And she had, though likely not the same sort Viola or the doctor practiced. While they cared for civilized folk, Ruby had often been pressed into service to remove pieces of grapeshot or to sew up a knife wound. She'd not been particularly good at either, but with no one else willing, the role was cast upon her.

None of this would she tell Viola Dumont, however, at least not in detail.

Word was, Miss Dumont came from quality. Her papa was some sort of New Orleans rich man. Why she landed here on the key was a story shrouded in mystery, but the reason she'd stayed wasn't: Viola Dumont was crazy in love with the town doctor. Unfortunately, the fool man seemed to be the only one who couldn't see it.

"Might I ask a question?" Ruby said.

Viola shifted her bag to the other arm then shrugged. "I suppose."

Wonderful. Now she had to think of something to ask. "How does one become a midwife?"

Another glance. "Why? Are you thinking of taking my job?"

Ruby giggled. "Oh, my, no. Of course not. It's just that I was—"

"Trying to avoid talking to Micah Tate?" Viola's wink gave her humor away.

"I might be," she said.

"As it happens, I may have need of an extra set of hands. Unless I miss my guess, there may be two babies this time instead of just one."

Ruby smiled. "Now twins are something I know more than a little about."

By the time they turned into the front yard of the Vincent home, Micah looked to have given up on following her. Ruby remained with Viola, however, long enough to rock Mrs. Vincent's newborn daughter while Viola examined the infant son and then handed him over as well.

"The babies are small but healthy," Viola said. "I'll just go and see to their mama now." She looked down at Ruby's armful of babies then leaned forward. "Are you sure you don't mind?" she asked softly. "The Vincent girls are a bit small to help, and their papa is hopeless."

She stole a glance at the rest of the Vincent family, four girls of stairstepped ages and their ashen-faced father, now gathered at the long dining table eating in silence. The irony was that Mr. Vincent seemed to have built the furniture with the idea of filling the two benches on each side with a multitude of little Vincents. From what Ruby observed, he did not look to have the ability to last through even one more birth, much less the half dozen it would take to complete the group.

"It's my pleasure," Ruby said. Holding the infants put Ruby in mind of Carol and Maggie. How long ago had she held them like this? Ruby noted the babies' dark hair and thought of how fair the girls' hair had been in contrast. "Soft as down," she whispered as she allowed the memories to flood her mind.

"I'm afraid you'll have to give them back now," Viola called from the bedchamber door.

Ruby rose and reluctantly handed the children back to the midwife, then bade Mr. Vincent and his brood good day.

A moment later, Viola appeared on the porch. "Precious little ones," the midwife said. "And thankfully healthy. A blessing, as multiples often don't fare as well."

For lack of a suitable answer, Ruby nodded. Indeed, she knew this to be true.

As she walked with Viola toward town, Ruby cast the occasional glance about to search for signs of Micah Tate. Thankfully, she found none.

Just beyond the mercantile, she made to turn toward the church, where Tess was likely overstaying her welcome. "Wait," Viola called.

KATHLEEN Y'BARBO

"Don't go so quickly." When Ruby turned around, Viola smiled. "You did a great job with the Vincent twins."

"Thank you," Ruby said. "I do love babies."

"Well, you should," Viola replied with a grin. "You had three of them."

"Yes." Ruby nodded, though she felt sick inside. "I suppose so." She took a few steps toward home before Viola called to her again.

"I was just wondering," Viola said when Ruby glanced back at her. "About Micah Tate."

"You're not the only one," she muttered.

The midwife shook her head. "I'm sorry. I didn't hear you."

Ruby looked around before closing the distance between them. "Can I trust you with a question?" Somehow she knew she could even before Viola nodded. "I wonder if you know what it's like to turn things over to God. What I mean is, have you ever—"

"Given my life to Him?" Viola nodded. "Yes, though I'm still learning how that works."

"How long has it been since. . ." Ruby paused to consider her words. "That is, did it take a while for the Lord to start speaking to you?"

Viola leaned against the gate and seemed to consider the question. "I suppose He spoke to me all along. It did take me a while before I figured out how to be quiet enough to hear Him. Why?"

Ruby shrugged. "No particular reason," she said.

"I see." Viola nodded. "Now it's my turn. What does all of this have to do with Micah Tate?"

Ruby sighed. "That's what I'm trying to figure out."

"He's a good man, Ruby," Viola said. "If it weren't for him, well. . .I'd likely not be here, and neither would Emilie and Isabelle. He and the wreckers saved us off the reef."

"Seems like a lot of people come to the key that way." Ruby thought of her own arrival on Fairweather Key then shrugged away the memory. "I just wonder," she said, choosing her words carefully, "if a man like Micah Tate's any match for the criminal element. You know, the smugglers and such."

"The smugglers and such?" Viola echoed. "Well, I'd have to say

I've not seen our island plagued by anyone of that ilk." She leaned conspiratorially toward Ruby. "Why? Do you know something I don't?"

"I, well, that is, I just wonder about a man's, well. . .his penchant for violence, especially if he's used his fists in front of you."

Viola's eyes went wide, and she clutched Ruby to her side. "Come inside now."

The midwife propelled Ruby through the door and into a world that smelled of cleanliness, of flowers, and of the ever-present sea air. While Viola dropped her things on a lovely tapestry-covered chair, Ruby could only stand still and wait.

"Come in here and have a cup of tea," she said. "We've got some things to discuss, I'm certain."

"Things to discuss? No, really, I can't leave the boardinghouse for more than a few minutes." Yet she'd done just that—and then some.

If Viola saw through the flimsy excuse, she had the kindness not to say so. "All right," she said. "Then perhaps you'd allow me to ask something personal. You have my word anything said will never leave this room."

"Perhaps," was the best Ruby could do.

She nodded and walked to the window to push back the lace curtains and peer outside. In profile, Viola Dumont looked like some sort of royalty, so straight was her posture and so fine her features. None save those who knew her would think the woman had come from examining a new mother rather than dancing at some fancy ball.

When she turned to face Ruby, however, her expression had gone grim. "You're afraid of Micah, aren't you?"

"Afraid?" She had to think only a moment. "A little."

Viola's eyes searched Ruby's face. "With reason?"

That took a bit more concentration. She had reason to fear all men, not just Micah Tate in particular. Yet something about the wrecker sent a different fear coursing through her.

The fear that, should she allow it, he might take the one thing she'd so carefully protected: her heart.

"Ruby?"

"I'm sorry." She shrugged. "I suppose my reason's not what you're thinking. I just don't believe a man can be that good for that long. In my experience, none have managed it."

"So this is based on past experience?"

There was a sadness in Viola's voice that almost sounded like she, too, knew of this kind of thinking. "It might be." Ruby straightened her spine and let out a long breath. "Yes, past experience."

Viola lifted her hand to the windowpane then slowly reached to touch her face. For a moment, it seemed as if the midwife were far away. Then abruptly she seemed to return, a lingering sadness on her face.

"I had a fiancé once," she said softly. "I don't suppose you knew that." When Ruby shook her head, Viola responded with a nod. "His name was Andre, and he was Emilie Gayarre's brother."

This was news. No wonder the two women were so close. They'd come near to being family.

"He's dead now," Viola said, her hand still resting against her cheek.

"I'm sorry."

"Don't be." She turned to face Ruby, releasing her grip on the curtains then watching them fall together as if that were the most interesting thing she'd seen all day. "Suffice it to say I know what a man's capable of when provoked. I also know sometimes what provokes a man is a woman who loves him unconditionally."

"Your man hit you." The words tumbled out, and even as she heard herself say them, Ruby longed to gather them back up.

"As did yours," Viola said softly, her expression unchanged.

CHAPTER 13

How to tell a lady of quality that ducking a man's fists started well before Ruby was of age to have a man of her own?

"No need to answer, Ruby. I've found that the past fits much better where it belongs—behind us." Viola moved from the window and slipped past to open the door. "No sense in dredging it up and wearing it for all the world to see. That's what I say, anyway."

"Vivi, is that you?" A dark-haired man eased around the corner, wearing a sleepy expression and a wrinkled shirt half tucked into trousers in a similar state. "Oh, I'm sorry. I didn't realize you weren't alone." Dark eyes locked with Ruby's as one corner of his mouth turned up in a crooked grin. "Remy," he said as he lifted a dark brow and moved toward her. "Remy Dumont. And you are. . . ?"

Viola stepped between them. "Ruby O'Shea, meet my brother."

Her smile was as much for Viola as for the man who stood behind her. "Pleased to meet you."

"He's only just arrived." Viola turned to give Remy a look then a swift peck on the cheek. "So forgive his unkempt appearance. I'm sure he was just off to repair himself."

Remy pushed his hair from his face then smoothed the front of his wrinkled shirt. "Indeed," he said as he winked at Viola, "I was off to do just that." His gaze swung to Ruby. "If you'll excuse me. I'm certain we'll meet again before Vivi and I return to New Orleans."

"You're leaving?" Ruby turned her attention to the midwife. "I had no idea."

"Neither did I," Viola said with some measure of what appeared to be exasperation. "And for the record, my brother has not consulted me on this decision of his. Shall we?"

Ruby followed Viola outside, unsure whether she'd just made a friend or lost one. She paused when Viola did, watching while the midwife snapped the head off a perfectly beautiful flower of some sort.

"Micah Tate," she said as she studied the flower. "Where does he fit in all this?"

"I don't know," Ruby said. "I thought maybe the Lord would tell me, but it seems He's left me to figure it out."

Viola gestured toward the docks. "Better think fast, because here he comes." With that, she threw open the latch and opened the gate for Ruby. "Know this," she said as she paused to close the gate once Ruby had passed through. "Micah Tate has never shown me to be anything but a good man. I understand Rev. Carter's decided he'll pastor the church someday."

From the corner of her eye, Ruby watched the wrecker approach. "Yes, I've heard as much."

"I know him to be a man of his word, Ruby," Viola said. "So if he's made you any promise, you can stand on the fact he'll see it through until he shows you otherwise."

Ruby groaned as she waved to Viola and walked away. "That's what I'm afraid of."

By picking up her pace, Ruby reached the parsonage before Micah could catch her. There she found Tess playing tag with a tolerant William Carter. The younger son of the Reverend and Mary Carter had allowed Tess to charm him into tying a handkerchief around his eyes, rendering him nearly helpless as she danced just out of his reach.

"Mind the child, William," Mary Carter called from somewhere inside the parsonage. "I'll not have you stomping her with those feet of yours."

Tess screeched with glee when she spied Ruby. At the sound,

William removed his blindfold and caught the child before she escaped. "Wait for your mama," he told her patiently. "It's not safe to chase about in the street."

Tess seemed to consider arguing but instead climbed aboard the boy's shoulders and allowed him to carry her across the road to where Ruby waited. "Look, I'm riding a horse," she called. "A big horse named William."

"You're quite the tolerant young man," Ruby told him when William made a circle around her.

"I don't mind," William said. "Between Tess and Joey I'm never bored."

"Joey had to take a nap on account of he's a baby," Tess said. "And William is his uncle."

"Yes, I know," Ruby said. "Joey belongs to Miss Isabelle and Mr. Josiah. That's William's big brother."

The girl peered down at Ruby with blue eyes the color of the afternoon sky. "Someday when my sisters have babies, I'm going to be an uncle, too."

No point in correcting her, Ruby decided, though she did wink at William. "Indeed, you may," the young man said as he lifted her easily over shoulders nearly as broad as his brother's.

Tess skittered to the ground and headed for Ruby, grasping handfuls of her skirts as she launched herself forward. Ruby caught her—barely—then knelt to offer a hug. Impish Tess rarely tolerated such hugs lately, for she spent much of her waking hours in motion, unavailable for this sort of loving.

"Where have you been?" Tess demanded.

"Well, let's see." Ruby pretended to consider the question carefully as she refused to allow anything but a smile. "I cleaned up after lunch, and then I went and helped Miss Viola. I got to hold the new Vincent babies while their mama got her examination."

"Not fair," Tess said. "I didn't get to hold a baby today, and you did. I tried to hold Joey, but he's too big."

"Yes, I suppose he is," she said.

"I want a baby at our house," Tess demanded.

"Honey, I hardly think this is a discussion we should be having.

85

You're my baby, and that's enough for me."

Tess wriggled out of Ruby's grip. "I want a baby at our house," she repeated.

"That's quite enough, Tess," Ruby said. "I've told you it's not as simple as all that. You can't just decide you'd like a baby and then have one arrive."

"Why not?"

When Tess looked to William for the answer, his cheeks went pink. "I think I hear my mother calling," he muttered as he hastily made his way back to the parsonage.

"Why?" Tess demanded, her fists still full of Ruby's skirts. "Tell me why we can't have a baby at our house like Miss Isabelle has at hers."

Ruby sighed. Her patience, what was left of it, had worn thin. Worse, Micah Tate had not only caught up to her, but now stood close enough to hear the entire conversation. "Dear," she said carefully, "I'd love to discuss this with you. I just can't talk about it right now."

"No." Tess's favorite word in years past was resurrected and spoken at great volume and with much gusto. "Tell. Me. Why."

Ruby grasped the child by her wrist and headed toward the boardinghouse without giving the wrecker a glance. At first Tess complied; then she decided to dig in her heels and protest. That was when Ruby stopped and prepared to pick her up.

Instead, Micah scooped the child into his arms. "Do you mind some help?" he asked.

Any help would be welcome, Ruby decided, except his. Yet the way Tess climbed onto Micah's shoulders as she had with William did make the walk home faster and quieter. Though she chattered away with Micah, at least she was talking and not screaming in protest.

They arrived at the picket fence, and Micah settled the girl back on the ground. "Mind your mother and go inside," he said. "She's worked hard today and is likely going to need your help with dinner."

With Tess trotting happily toward the door, Ruby relaxed a notch. "Thank you," she said to Micah then slipped inside and closed the gate. "She adores you," Ruby added when the man remained where he stood.

"And I her." Micah lingered a moment longer then turned away with a wave of his hand.

Just as Ruby had begun to relax, Tess fairly flew past to reach the gate. Rather than escape through it, she climbed atop the lowest rung and leaned over to address Micah. "Mr. Micah," Tess called. "Come back."

Micah stopped but thankfully did not make a move to return.

"I want a baby at my house and Mama won't tell me how to get one. Can you bring me a baby tomorrow when you come to eat lunch here?"

The wrecker had the decency to turn several shades of red before shaking his head. "I can't do that, Tess," he said, though his attention was squarely on Ruby. "Not tomorrow, anyway."

"When, then?"

"Ask your mother," he said as he turned to head back toward town.

Of all the nerve. Ruby offered the wrecker her back and stormed to the front porch. "Not funny, Micah Tate."

"It wasn't intended to be, Ruby O'Shea," he called just before she hustled Tess inside and slammed the door.

CHAPTER 14

The first thing Micah did after the door slammed was to go home and fetch the last of the jerky he kept on hand for emergencies. The second thing was to find Caleb Spencer.

"So you've come to your senses and accepted my offer so soon?" Caleb met him halfway across his office to shake hands.

Micah suppressed a smile. "What makes you think that's why I'm here?"

The judge shrugged. "I had no doubt you would. I only thought it might take a day or two."

Micah took a step back to look out the window at the docks and the broad expanse of ocean beyond. "What you're asking is a tall order, Judge."

"It is. Which is why you're the man for it, Tate." Caleb strolled back to his desk and motioned for Micah to follow. "I was so confident you'd take the job that I've already had the papers drawn up." He glanced up at Micah. "There's a salary to go along with the position."

Micah read the paper without comment, though his eyebrows shot up when he saw the amount he'd be paid. "I can't take all of that, Caleb," he said. "It's too much."

"It's enough to support a man and his family." He paused. "Figured I'd allow for any future plans you might have."

"But this is—"

"Enough for a widow to live on should something happen to the militia captain?" Caleb supplied.

"And then some."

"Wrecking's been good to this island," he said. "You know from working in the warehouse while you were recuperating that there's a wealth of goods going through the auction house each month. Suffice it to say our coffers are quite full even after the building of the new school."

Again Micah made to protest, but Caleb silenced him. "Understand, I'm buying not only your services but your loyalty. You receive a salary and a seaworthy vessel along with the ability to raise up a militia and train them. For that, I am willing to pay full value." Another pause. "Do not sell your abilities short nor assume your loyalty should come cheap."

With nothing left to say, Micah went back to reading until he'd scanned every line of the document twice. When he looked up, he found Caleb watching him carefully.

"The nature of this job is that it exists only as it is needed and will cease to exist when the need for it has passed. That's the only drawback. Any questions?"

"Makes sense." Micah shrugged. "I'm sure I'll have plenty of questions along the way, but right now, no."

"All right, then." Caleb settled behind the desk and reached for his pen, then dipped it in ink and handed it to Micah. "Sign the papers," he said, "but not for the salary. Do it only if you feel you can conduct the duties the citizens of Fairweather Key require of you. I warn you they are hefty, yet I have no doubt of your ability to surpass any expectations."

Micah scratched his name across the bottom of the page and committed his life to defending the safety of the key. Considering how poorly he'd done the last time, the promise struck more than a little fear in him.

Yet he'd do it, and he'd do it well.

Caleb continued to make much fuss over Micah's taking on the job, but Micah shook it off. The way he saw it, the Lord had given him the opportunity to make up for the last time he'd been part of a militia. This time he'd carry out his duties without any thought of leaving his post, no matter what.

If only the Lord would provide a remedy for his other regret. Micah had thought the feisty boardinghouse cook was sent to give him that opportunity, but so far, Ruby O'Shea was having none of it. No matter. With all the resources of the Fairweather Key Militia at his disposal, he'd keep her safe whether she appreciated the effort or not.

The way he figured it, since he'd missed lunch, he'd show up for dinner and see if she shooed him off. This he decided as he walked down the steps of the courthouse and turned toward the docks.

It was Monday, and the mail boat stood at anchor when he passed. Beyond it was the vessel he'd been given, and a beauty she was. He'd yet to decide what to call her, though a few ideas had already come to mind.

After spending a good while examining every inch of the boat, Micah set sail and found her to be every bit as agile a vessel as he'd hoped. It felt good to be back at the helm, so good that he circled the island twice before turning her for home.

Josiah Carter met him on the docks with a grin. "Caleb told me the news."

Micah returned the smile. "I'll not disappoint him." *Nor Ruby.*

"I know you won't," Josiah said. "Though I wonder about how quickly you made your decision."

All he could offer in response was a shrug.

"So tell me." Josiah grinned. "How was your first sail on her?"

"Everything you'd think and more." He gestured Josiah aboard. "Let me show you."

A tour of the boat followed. Josiah convinced Micah to take her for another sail, and by the time they returned, the sun hung low on the horizon and the wind had begun to kick up.

"Isabelle will be wondering where I've gone off to," Josiah said.

"I suppose so," was all he could offer in response. As he watched his friend hurry home to his wife and son, Micah felt yet another stab of jealousy.

It didn't take him long to wash the day's work off and put on his Sunday clothes. With the lamps now lit up at the boardinghouse on

Beloved
Counterfeit

the hill, Micah followed them to the gate, intent on seeing just what
Ruby O'Shea might think of his uninvited return.

Then he spied her through the front window, and all he could do
was stand and watch as she went about the business of setting the table
for dinner. A few boarders had already seated themselves, and at least
two more stood within view.

He opened the gate then closed it carefully so as not to alert anyone
to his arrival. Still, the door opened before he managed to knock.

"Hello, Tess," Micah said, fully prepared to discuss babies, yet not
prepared at all.

"You're to find a seat before Mama changes her mind about serving
lunch guests at dinner." Tess's innocent face told him the child had no
idea of the meaning behind her words. Her sisters, however, snickered
as they entered the dining room with napkins and silverware and
began placing them around the table.

"Is that so?" Micah slid into a spot at the end of the table and
ignored the looks of the others assembled there. "Well, please tell her
that once she marries me I intend to be at her table for both."

"That's enough joking, Mr. Tate," Ruby called from somewhere
back in the kitchen. She appeared in the doorway, tray in hand. "Your
humor has lost its luster, I'm afraid."

"Yet my promise remains."

Ruby ignored him to serve the best roast chicken he'd tasted in all
his years. Even as he reached for seconds and then thirds, Micah kept
his attention equally divided between the food and the cook.

"I understand there's big changes afoot on the island," the diner
to Micah's right said.

Micah glanced at the man and pegged him for the indoor type,
though he did wear a sheen of red under his fringe of blond hair that
showed he'd spent a little time in the sun lately. Likely some fellow on
his way to and from without caring what went on here.

"I overheard a bit of celebration down at the courthouse this
afternoon. The judge is most happy that he's found a man to take on
the job of heading up the Fairweather Key Militia." The man stabbed
a slice of meat then warmed to his topic. "He said there'd be a big
announcement made once the man gave his official acceptance." He

91

paused to finish chewing. "Wonder who it is."

An inelegant snort was Micah's only response. If this fellow wanted news, he'd have to read the newspaper.

Ruby, however, had warmed to the topic and was grilling the guest with a half-dozen questions. Interesting that she'd be so keen on wanting to know who was protecting the island when the man in charge had first offered this service to her alone.

"Who do you suppose it is?" he heard her ask.

Her inquiry launched a discussion that called a number of familiar names to the fore. Micah remained silent, using the time to enjoy the last bites of his meal.

Then a thought occurred, and Micah turned to face the stranger. "What I wonder," he said with what he hoped would be a casual tone, "is how you came to overhear something the judge obviously didn't want overheard."

"Yes, well, I. . ." He sputtered a bit more before releasing a long, loud sigh. "All right. The truth of it is, I was at the warehouse hoping to get a look inside. Yes, I know no one's allowed inside except on auction days, but I had to know if a certain piece of treasure with value only to me might be among the artifacts pulled from a recent wreck. Unfortunately, I failed in that matter."

"Is that so?" Micah made a mental note to speak to Caleb about the man first thing tomorrow. He also decided to check the logs to see just which vessels might have been of interest to the stranger—that is, if he didn't manage to pry the information from him before then.

The man nodded. "I'm not proud of what I did, if that's what you're thinking." He glanced around the table; then his gaze landed—and stuck—on Micah. "But the fact remains that I heard what I heard. We're to have a second in command to the judge."

"We?" Ruby shook her head. "I don't believe I know you. Are you new to the key?"

The fellow turned two shades of purple. "I, well, what I meant was while I'm not a citizen *per se*, I am interested in possibly relocating." He waved away further questions with a sweep of his hand.

Micah set down his knife and fork and turned to face the talkative stranger, noting the square jaw, above-average height, and crescent-shaped scar just below his left cheekbone. "I don't believe I caught your name."

"I'm Drummond," the man said as he offered his hand to shake Micah's. "Clay Drummond."

Micah stared at Clay Drummond's outstretched hand a few seconds past proper before clasping it to show the city fellow just how strong a wrecker's grip could be. To his surprise, the stranger gave as good as he got.

"And what's your line of work, Mr. Drummond?" Micah asked. "Because given that you're here looking for something that doesn't belong to you, the only thing I can figure you for is either a smuggler or a thief."

Drummond nearly swallowed his teeth, such seemed to be his surprise. "Oh, I see how it is," he finally said. "You're a prankster."

The room fell into silence. Ruby stepped into Micah's line of sight to give him an angry stare. "Ignore him, Mr. Drummond," she said. "He does tend to say things that aren't appropriate."

"I do?" Micah feigned surprise as he released his grip. "I'm sure Mr. Drummond here understands I meant no harm." He punctuated the statement with a look intended to tell the stranger just the opposite.

Drummond met his gaze in such a way that Micah had no doubt the message had been received. He appeared about to say something when Ruby barged into the conversation. "So, Mr. Drummond, tell us more."

"Yes, like when you're leaving," Micah said.

The question went unanswered as the conversation soon turned to other things, leaving Micah to enjoy his meal in peace. If anyone was to hear the announcement of his appointment early, it would be Ruby O'Shea.

He waited around to do just that, remaining in his place even after the others had excused themselves. To find a reason for staying, Micah chewed slowly and refilled his plate until nothing remained on the table.

When little Tess climbed up onto the chair beside him, Micah set down his fork and gave her his full attention. Or at least he did the best he could, considering his too-full belly.

"Mama says she can go fry up another chicken if you're still hungry."

"Does she now?" He looked past the child to the pantry and the kitchen beyond. "You tell her I'm much obliged, but I'd rather speak to her than eat any more of her fine cooking."

Tess climbed down, nearly upsetting the chair in the process. Micah grabbed the chair and righted it as he watched the girl head back in the direction she'd just come, her bare feet padding away seemingly as fast as they could go.

His statement was obviously duly repeated. A second later, as pots and pans began to clang behind her, Tess peered around the corner. "She says she's busy and you should go home."

Above the noise of the kitchen symphony, Micah gestured for Tess to approach. "Did she say anything else?"

The girl nodded. " 'Cept I'm not supposed to tell you."

"I see." Micah pretended to think a moment. "I don't suppose she's happy with me."

"Tess, where are you?" This from one of the twins—not that he could ever tell them apart. "Come and help us finish our chores, or we'll tell."

Tess leaned close. "You should probably do what I do when she's mad."

"What's that?" he whispered.

"Hide," she said as she once again bounded from the chair. This time she left in the direction of the front hall, her footsteps disappearing up the stairs rather than heading in the direction of her sister's persistent call.

Both older girls came running through a moment later. "Where is she?" one of them asked.

He pointed to the stairs. "Something about hiding."

The girls looked at one another. "If she's hiding. . . ," one began.

"Then we are, too," the other finished as the pair raced off to join their sister somewhere on the upper floor of the boardinghouse.

Micah sat a moment longer then quietly pushed away from the table. He'd sat there so long that his feet took a moment to listen to his head, but eventually he got as far as the doorway. From there he

94

could see Ruby working over a basin of water. She appeared to be scrubbing something.

So intent was she on whatever she was doing that she obviously never heard him until Micah stood right behind her. It was all he could do not to reach out and massage arms that were surely sore and in want of care.

She paused in her endeavors to swipe at her forehead then continued with her work. Again Micah itched to relieve her of some measure of the duties she'd likely performed every day since coming to the boardinghouse.

For a tiny woman, she certainly bore much on her shoulders. Shoulders that practically begged for his fingertips. He reached out slowly, intending only to imagine for just a second what she might do should he make good on his thought.

Then he saw those shoulders heave, watched the hands go still in the basin. A sniff confirmed what he suspected.

Ruby was crying.

All the glee in telling her about his appointment fled. He reached into his pocket to offer a handkerchief, and his fingers touched the sand dollar.

"Ruby, I've brought you something," he said softly as he reached toward her back, extending the delicate shell.

She whirled around, took one look at what was in his hand, and ran. This time, however, he didn't let her get away. His long strides easily matched hers until he caught her just the other side of the fence.

"Let me go," Ruby said, and he did, though he made sure to stand between her and the path to town.

The last rays of the sun burned streaks of gold across her hair and cast her face in shadow. Micah longed to turn her toward the light so he might see her better.

"I only wanted you to have what was already yours," he said as he tried again to give her the shell. "You dropped it this morning at the beach."

Her gaze landed on the object in his hand and lingered. "Was that only this morning?"

Micah lifted her palm and placed the sand dollar in it. With care he closed her fingers over the shell then lifted her hand to his lips.

"I'll not forget my promise, Ruby," he said, "nor will I withdraw my offer."

She shook her head as she turned to face the ocean. "I don't understand. This morning we were practically strangers and the sun hasn't set on the day, yet you're offering to marry me."

Micah came to stand beside her, following her gaze toward the water. "Why does it matter?"

"It matters." Ruby paused but did not spare him a glance. "You know nothing about me, Micah Tate," she said, "and I warrant once you've heard my story, you'll change your mind."

"Interesting statement." Micah thought of Caroline, of how this time things would be different. "For I was about to say the same thing to you. Likely you'll not appreciate my reasons, either." He stepped between Ruby and the ocean. "So don't tell me your story and, unless you're wanting to hear it, I'll not tell you mine."

She shook her head. "That will never work."

"Why not?" He warmed to the topic. "Many a marriage has started out with the couple knowing too much about each other. I'm offering to protect you from whoever and whatever frightens you."

"And in return?"

"In return, I get a warm bed and a good meal." When she turned her back and started walking toward the boardinghouse, Micah knew his jest had fallen flat. "Look," he said when he'd caught up to her, "you really want to know what I get?"

Ruby nodded.

"I get someone who needs me. I get a place I can call home that doesn't echo when I step inside. True enough, I get food in my belly and a soft place to lay my head." He paused then decided to just come out with the rest of it. "And you'll get a man who will stand by you, Ruby O'Shea. The way I see it, you're long overdue for a man who will take up for you. Am I wrong?"

Her glance told him he wasn't.

"Now I guarantee there's nothing you can tell me that will change any of what I've just said." It was his turn to pause. "That's not true."

Ruby's sharp intake of breath was enough to let him know she heard. "I'm a man, Ruby, and a man—a husband—has certain needs of his wife."

"Is that all?" She asked the question as if she weren't surprised at his statement.

"No," he said. "There's just one more thing. That baby Tess wants. . ."

The redhead gave him a look. "Don't get ahead of yourself, Mr. Tate. I haven't agreed to take you on yet."

"No, but you will," he said with a bravado that tarnished a bit when she had the audacity to laugh.

CHAPTER 15

I want to meet this man, Vivi. As your brother, I insist on making the acquaintance of the man who has designs on my sister."

Viola set her needlepoint aside and turned her attention to her brother, who had only just stopped pacing the room. His questions peppered their evenings together, but rarely did he bring up anything related to Dan Hill.

"Must we discuss this now? I was so enjoying myself." Viola maintained her smile, barely. *Lord, lead me, please.*

"It is as I suspected. This man is a cad bound on taking your affections and offering nothing in return." Remy began his trek around the parlor, his fists clenched. She'd seen his temper and knew his way with anger would either cause him to do something stupid or send him into a brooding silence that might last for hours or even days.

But he spoke at least a bit of truth. She had neither seen nor heard from Dan Hill in days. She'd not yet lowered herself to make a visit to his clinic, though more than once she'd considered it.

"You'll find a changed man in Father, I warrant," Remy continued. "Your absence has mellowed him greatly."

"My absence?" She stifled a humorless chuckle. "I doubt anything I may have done, past or present, has made any impact on that old man."

Remy paused at the window and lifted the edge of the curtain to peer outside. "Tell me about Ruby O'Shea," he said.

The abrupt change of topic took a moment to settle. "Why?" she finally managed.

He let the curtain drop. "No reason," he said, though she knew there must be.

"Well, let me see." Viola shifted positions and dropped her needlepoint into the basket beside her chair. "She's a hard worker and decently good at acting as the midwife's assistant." When he turned to lift a dark brow, Viola explained, "She accompanied me to assist in a difficult birth recently and did a splendid job. I understand she has some doctoring skills."

When Viola paused, Remy shook his head. "Go on."

"She's got three adorable daughters and somehow manages to raise them and run the boardinghouse in Mrs. Campbell's absence. Mrs. Campbell is the wife of the former judge. She's away seeing to her daughter's—"

"Back to Mrs. O'Shea. What of Mr. O'Shea?"

Viola grinned. "Remy Dumont. Are you interested in our Ruby?"

"Nonsense." He took up his pacing once again.

"You are." Viola rose and caught him by the arm. "You are."

"I find her interesting," he said, wrestling out of her grip. "And as she is obviously a friend, I wish to know more about her."

"Liar." She giggled. "Though I will oblige you. I've not asked outright, but the understanding is Ruby is a widow. A pity considering the children."

"Yes," he said slowly, "you mentioned the children." He paused. "Repeatedly. And, I assume, with purpose."

"With no more purpose than you've colored our previous conversations."

"I have no idea to what you refer," he said with a wink, "though I'll admit I've made no secret of the fact I intend to leave here with you, and sooner rather than later."

Indeed, he had not. What Remy didn't know was that he had already begun to wear on Viola's resolve. Were she to listen much longer, she might find herself packed aboard a New Orleans-bound vessel without settling the issue of her feelings for the doctor who held her heart.

"Vivi, you cannot continue to skirt the issue of why I'm here," Remy insisted.

"And you cannot continue to ignore the fact that while I am very pleased to see you, I am quite uncomfortable with this topic." She averted her gaze. "So tell me more of what you've been doing since we parted."

"What I've been doing?" Remy exhaled, a familiar sign of frustration. "I've been reading." He shook his head. "Actually, I've been driving myself to distraction trying to figure how you got all the way to the steps of the cathedral before you decided Andre Gayarre was not the husband for you."

"The truth?" When he nodded, she drew a deep breath and continued. "I never thought there was a choice to be had, Remy. Our fathers were bound and determined to merge families." She paused. "I rather enjoyed Andre's company. He could be quite charming, and he did court me as if ours were not a marriage arranged in a boardroom."

"Which it was."

"Yes." The admission hurt, even now. Somehow she'd managed to convince herself Andre Gayarre had fallen in love with the woman he would have married regardless of emotions. It helped to believe that much.

Her brother shook his head and gave her a look that said he would suffer no further nonsense. "Andre Gayarre came to Fairweather Key to bring you back or kill you, but instead he lost his own life." Her gasp seemed to cause him to pause. "You didn't think I knew of this?" Remy shook his head. "The benefit of being the studious youngest child is that my elders take for granted that I am neither listening nor competent to decipher their hidden meaning."

Opening her mouth to respond, Viola found no words. She settled for closing her eyes. Indeed, Remy was one not to be underestimated.

"So about the guilt you've been carrying," he said.

Unable to remain still, Viola rose. Her feet traced a path to the hallway and her bedchamber beyond. "I'll not have any further mention of Andre in my home," she tossed over her shoulder for good measure.

An attempt she knew would give nothing but fuel to the fire that was this discussion.

"No need to speak of him," her brother called. "I've my answer, Vivi."

Viola turned to retrace her steps. She found that Remy had returned to the comfortable chair near the window. "What answer?"

"I had to come here and see for myself," he said. "I needed to know whether it was true."

"You're talking in circles." Viola shook her head. "I've had a long day. I'm sure you'll find another way to amuse yourself in my absence."

"Indeed," he said. "I thought I might clean the pistol I gave you. Where might I find it?"

"Pistol?" Viola grasped the doorframe for balance and took a deep breath, letting it out slowly.

"Don't be coy," he said. "I merely wanted to offer up my help. I've nothing to do, so cleaning the weapon seems to appeal." He rose and took a few steps toward her before halting. "Where is it, Vivi?" Abruptly he turned on his heels and headed back to the chair. "No need to explain," he said. "I'm sure the doctor is taking good care of it."

She froze. "It's been two years since I thought of the location of that pistol, Remy. What are you insinuating?"

"Me?" Again Remy shook his head. "Nothing. Though the next time you're tempted to evade my questions, I would remind you that I'm the one who taught you to shoot." He sank onto the chair and stared. "I recall you rarely missed whatever you aimed at."

"The nerve."

Ruby yanked another set of bed linens from the never-ending pile and threw them into the basin. That this man, practically a stranger, would assume she would fall into his arms and be grateful for his proposal of marriage.

"The very nerve."

In truth, she did feel the slightest bit of appreciation for Micah Tate's valor and, in retrospect, for his honesty. Still, even the men who'd pushed actual dollars into her hand rather than a sand dollar hadn't asked her for a child.

"And before I even agree to give him the time of day."

She rubbed the soap cake until her arms hurt, then paused and started all over again. By the time she finished every piece of bedding in the boardinghouse, Ruby was no closer to taming her aggravation.

The real trouble, beyond any issues of pride or preference, was the fact that Micah Tate had stirred up a hornet's nest by treating the smuggler Rabelais as he had. With Jean Luc no longer feeling charitable toward her, he'd likely go straight to Thomas Hawkins with the news of where she now lived and with whom.

It was the *with whom* that bothered her most.

While she alone was responsible for her circumstances, the girls were innocent of anything save their birth to a mother ill equipped to raise them and a father who would never see them again.

"At least as long as I'm alive, he won't."

Ruby tipped the basin and sent a stream of sudsy water flying. She thought of the sand dollar upstairs in the attic room she shared with the girls, of the promise made by the man who had pressed it into her palm.

She didn't love him. All Ruby knew of love was that people who had no idea what it meant bandied about the word as if bestowing it was some sort of reward. Or withholding it a punishment.

Yet Micah Tate offered something no other man had: protection. He of all the men who'd sought her attention had offered nothing but safe harbor. Even Jean Luc Rabelais had not offered this—not without asking for something in return.

Then again, the wrecker's already discussing babies. "And there's only one way to accomplish that."

The thought took her back to the indignation that fueled her irritation. Was she destined to always be worth only one thing to men?

Gathering up the linens, she hauled them toward the rope where the sun would dry them in a few hours' time. Hefting the heavy fabric over and over made her arms ache, but the labor gave her the release that screaming could not.

She sighed. Nothing would come of this fretting except possibly blisters and wrinkles—blisters from scrubbing away her aggravation and wrinkles from worrying about when this sham of a marriage would turn ugly.

It doesn't have to be a sham.

Ruby froze, her fingers releasing the soggy linens to puddle on the damp ground. A real marriage was something she'd never considered.

Dare she hope this God she'd only recently begun to trust might have something like that for her? Surely a woman with the past she carried around wouldn't be fit for any man who might worship the Lord.

Yet she'd been promised she was a new creation. Claire was gone, and Ruby had taken her place.

She reached for the topmost bed linen and shook it clean, then draped it over the rope. As she worked out the worst of the wrinkles, Ruby considered the dilemma before her. To stay and face either fear or marriage, or to go and pray that her past and those associated with it did not follow.

The wind whipped her hair about, obscuring her vision until she returned the errant strands to her braid and moved to turn her face to the wind. Wet fingers went back to their work as she glanced out toward an ocean so green it hurt to look at it. No unfamiliar sails pierced the horizon, nor did any stranger stand at the gate.

Yet she kept watch, waiting for the inevitable even as she considered her options.

Leaving Fairweather Key was a possibility. It always had been. The trouble with that was twofold: She had nowhere to go and no way to get there.

If she was being truly honest, Ruby had to admit she'd never felt more at home than in this place. And the girls were happy here. In the months since they'd landed on the reef, she'd seen the twins blossom into normal children who had friends and enjoyed their schoolwork. And Tess, well, she never met a stranger no matter where she went.

That Tess had found surrogate grandparents in Mary and Hezekiah Carter and a host of pretend aunts and uncles in the extended family they'd collected in Fairweather Key made Ruby thank the Lord for their unexpected arrival here.

The only fly in the ointment was the specter of Thomas Hawkins. Logic told her by now Jean Luc was halfway back to wherever

Hawkins's band of ruffians was holed up to puff up his wounded pride by telling Tommy where he could find her.

Ruby finished hanging the last of the linens then reached for the basin. Maybe the next time Micah Tate asked her to marry him, she'd think a little harder about saying yes.

Trouble was, he'd have to hurry, or leaving would be the only answer.

CHAPTER 16

Given that his first try at proposing to Ruby O'Shea didn't turn out as he hoped, Micah decided to change his strategy. In his experience, the more a body missed something–or someone–the more dear it grew.

Since he'd been a fixture at Ruby's table every day, he decided a little absence might make her heart grow fonder. So for the next three days, Micah took his lunch down at the harbor with the others who made their living on the sea.

He'd almost forgotten how very much he enjoyed the company of the wreckers and fishermen who called the vessels in the harbor their homes. Spending time with them also gave Micah an idea of who might be included in the band of men who would be charged with seeing to the island's safety.

To be sure, he kept a close eye on the comings and goings of the boardinghouse on the hill, visible as it was from the sleek vessel that came with his new position as captain of the Fairweather Key Militia. He'd even begun entertaining the idea of selling the house on the bluff that never quite felt like home to him.

A boat was no place for a family, however, and should Ruby O'Shea ever take him up on his offer, he'd need a decent home for the trio who came along with her. To go from a family of one to a family of five would stretch the confines of the vessel for sure, so keeping the house would be the wiser choice.

The thought of what he'd said—what he'd promised—weighed heavily on Micah. He spent a decent amount of time pacing the deck, wondering if he'd made a promise to Ruby he couldn't keep.

Yet the Frenchman's possible return didn't frighten him one whit; he welcomed it. Another opportunity to show Ruby O'Shea he could take care of those whom the Lord had assigned him.

With each day that passed, he was more certain Ruby was his second chance at doing things right. This he knew he wouldn't mention as he headed to the courthouse to meet with Caleb Spencer. On his list were the names of those men he deemed fit for duty should the island need to muster up a militia.

He'd heard that Viola Dumont's brother had arrived on the island and made a note to contact him to see how long he planned to stay. To his mind, any man fit and worthy would serve.

As he turned to climb the courthouse stairs, Micah glanced up at the boardinghouse. About now, Ruby was likely helping the girls with their schoolwork or perhaps starting the preparations for the boarders' dinner. More important than this was the knowledge that she did these things while under his distant but watchful care. For where he could not be, his militia could.

Micah opened the door of the courthouse and stepped inside, then greeted Caleb. "I've got the list if you're of a mind to look at it."

"Bring it over," he called as he shifted aside piles of documents to make room for the paper. "And while I'm at it, we should discuss your duties while I'm away."

Micah settled in across from Caleb. "How soon?"

"A few weeks at most." He leaned back in his chair. "Emilie is still sorting through applicants to replace her. I never anticipated it would be so difficult to find a teacher."

"The place is somewhat remote," Micah offered.

Caleb shrugged then gestured to his desktop, filled with several neat stacks of papers situated among a landslide of others. "Anyway, I'll expect you to handle all this and present me with a clean desk upon my return."

Micah swallowed hard. What had he gotten himself into?

As serious as the judge appeared, his jaw began to twitch. A

moment later he chuckled. "That's wishful thinking on my part, Tate. You're familiar with the paperwork required when we have an auction."

Something he'd done a dozen times or more since injuries from the sinking of his wrecking boat forced him to take a job as the judge's warehouseman. "I am," he said as he flexed the arm that still plagued him on occasion.

"I pray you won't have to use that knowledge, but I am comforted that you won't be caught by surprise if you need to act on it." Caleb paused. "The next auction should clear the warehouse by the middle of next week."

Another detail Micah was glad not to have to handle. "What about that fellow I told you about? The one who opened his mouth at the boardinghouse table?"

Another shrug. "He and I had an interesting conversation yesterday morning. After being presented with the option of spending some time in jail or producing identification, he admitted and proved he was an insurance man. Peterson Life and Trust out of New York City."

Micah shook his head. "Why not come out and say so? He claimed to be here looking for an object of sentimental value."

Caleb's grin surprised Micah. "I'm sure that was partly true, only the object he was looking for was money. Seems as though he figured he might uncover something to take back to the boys in New York City."

"Like what? You run a tight ship here."

"And that's all the man's got to take back to his superiors." He sighed. "Turns out he's been going up and down the coast, checking up on things for quite some time. Said mine was one of the few islands where there wasn't some question as to where the profits went."

"Well, at least he turned out to be legitimate. I fear not all who appear harmless are."

The judge gave him a stern look. "You know more than you're saying, Micah. What is it?"

"Nothing I'm free to say just yet," he said, "though between you and me, I'm of a mind to marry up with Ruby O'Shea."

There. He'd said it. Out loud. Micah leaned back to watch the play of emotions cross Caleb Spencer's face. "Surprised?" he finally asked.

"A little." He braced his elbows on the desk. "Have you declared your intentions to her?"

"In a matter of speaking, yes."

"And she's accepted your proposal."

It was Micah's turn to sigh. "She will."

He knows. Viola thought for a moment she might blurt out the obvious. Might say the words long awaiting release.

With deliberate slowness, Viola turned to face her brother. The expression she'd seen so often applied to schoolyard bullies or used in moments of irritation was now squarely fixed on her.

"The truth," she said as she felt the life drain out of her, "is that I do not remember. Indeed, had I the chance, I know I would have done it, but I truly remember only fragments of the day."

"Fragments?" he echoed. "Come and sit. You look to be ready to topple."

Remy led her back to the settee and situated her there. As patient as he was persistent, her brother merely stood in silence while she worried the lace on her sleeve. Then a loose button caught her attention and held it.

Each inane thought pushed away a more dangerous one. Even so, snippets of a complete memory surfaced. Andre's shouts. Fear she might be hauled back to New Orleans to face the marriage she'd fled.

And then two guns. Andre held one, and the other. . .

Or was Andre unarmed while she and the doctor both carried pistols?

Viola sighed. Like pearls on a broken strand, the memory fell away and disappeared. Retrieving the final clasp that would complete the strand proved once again impossible, though she walked in her mind through each moment of the horrific event as if she were actually there.

She might have remained so occupied had Remy not plopped down beside her. "Careful," she said. "This is not a particularly sturdy piece."

"Then I'll buy you a new one." Remy rested his hand on her shoulder, his jesting mood obviously gone. "I feared I would find you rotting away in some jail cell."

"A fate perhaps better than not knowing," she said.

"This doctor." Remy shifted positions and faced her. "What does he say of it?"

Viola sighed. *That this shooting will forever stand between us.* "That a woman of my delicate upbringing could not possibly shoot with such deadly accuracy."

The look that passed between them caused Viola to shiver. At once, she knew. The string of pearls met and closed.

"Come home, Vivi," Remy said. "Think on it no more, and come home."

How easy it would be to do as he asked and put the world that was Fairweather Key behind her. To be sure, the specter of Andre Gayarre would never leave her no matter where she went, but perhaps it would rise up less frequently once she was no longer forced almost daily to walk past the place where he died.

"I want to meet him." Remy rose and hauled her off the settee with a yank of her hand. "Where might I find this doctor who has you so enthralled?" When Viola did not answer quickly enough to suit him, Remy grabbed his hat and marched out the door.

Viola trailed just far enough behind to watch where he went without being close enough to be coaxed into following. She held her breath until he turned right at the corner, a direction that would take him decidedly away from the person he sought.

Then she spied Ruby O'Shea hurrying past and stepped onto the porch. After calling to her, Viola went to the gate. "Might I trouble you to do me a favor?" she asked. "If you've the time, that is."

CHAPTER 17

R uby suppressed a grin. She saw how it was: an overprotective brother intent on giving a slow groom a push toward the altar. What might that feel like? Still, she'd come this way in hopes she'd find someone altogether different: Micah Tate.

The basket on her arm held an offering of sorts. A few slices of bread, some of last night's fried chicken, and the first slice of what promised to be a particularly tasty pie.

"Thank you, Ruby," Viola said. "I'm much beholden to you."

"Oh no," she said as she turned her attention to the situation at hand, "though I wonder why it wouldn't be a proper good idea to let your brother and the doctor have a conversation."

Viola's grin went south. "I, well, you see. . ."

Adjusting the basket, Ruby shook her head. "No need to explain. I'll do what I can, though I can't promise I'll even find him."

She needn't have worried. Quickly reaching the clinic, she found Remy Dumont seemingly waiting for her. Something in the way he smiled made her wonder, though she quickly removed all traces of a grin in response.

"He's not in," Viola's brother said as she reached for the latch on the gate. "There's a note if you'd like the details. I didn't bother."

"He?" Ruby glanced toward the doctor's office and noticed that a slip of paper had been tacked on the doorframe. "Oh yes, of course, Dr. Hill. Well, I will have to come back another time, won't I?"

"Don't know. Something I can help you with?" His gaze swept over her in that manner some men have of making a woman feel indecent when she wasn't. Or in her case, when she wasn't anymore. "You don't look as if you're in need of medical attention."

"I'm not. I just. . .well. . .it can wait." *Mission accomplished.*

Turning on her heels, Ruby headed back in the direction she'd come. He was an impertinent man, that Remy Dumont, and though she'd come to respect his sister, Ruby couldn't be sure how she felt about him. Perhaps it was his youth, though at most he likely bore a year or two more than she.

No, she decided as she reached the corner. There was something to Remy Dumont that reminded her of herself. Something that threatened to be unleashed should good manners or restraint give way.

She breathed a sigh of relief that she'd not been forced to entertain some sort of lengthy conversation with the man. What could they have possibly discussed beyond the weather and perhaps a shared story or two about Viola?

The handsome newcomer suddenly fell into step beside her, and Ruby found nothing to say at all. Not that she needed worry, for Remy Dumont quickly filled the silence with a barrage of questions about Fairweather Key and its inhabitants.

She answered each one as best she could, considering she'd only been a resident for a short while herself. Finally, silence reigned, and she felt obligated to ask a question of her own.

"So what do you do back in New Orleans?" was the best she could come up with.

Long fingers that looked as if they belonged dancing over the keys of a grand piano in some elegant salon swept a dark curl from his face. "How did you know I'm from New Orleans? Have you more interest in me than you let on?" Before she could respond, he laughed. "My, but aren't you easy to flummox?"

"Flummox?" She shook her head. "I've no idea what that means, but I don't think I like it."

"I assure you, confusion renders you no less lovely."

She shifted her basket, putting it squarely between them. While Remy Dumont might present an attractive distraction, Micah Tate was the only man who'd offered protection. Pretty wouldn't protect the girls should Tommy and his men come calling.

"Miss O'Shea, are you lost in thought or merely lost?" When she reluctantly gave him her attention, Remy shrugged. "Forgive me if I'm wrong, but it appears you've no particular destination in mind."

"To the contrary," she said, "I'm visiting."

"Tell me the truth, Miss O'Shea." Remy leaned close and gripped the edge of the basket, blocking her plans to leave. "You appear to be a woman of some passion. And a widow. Might I arrange to see more of you?" Closer still. "My sister regards you highly, but I don't feel she sees you as I do."

The nerve. Anger rode high in her mind and in the heat flooding her face. Were she a man, she might have called him out. A woman, however, had two choices: Endure the ribald comment and walk away, or consider the attention a compliment.

In the old days, there would have been a third option. But these were not the old days, and she was a new creation in Christ. Once lost but now found and made clean.

Her vision tunneled, and Remy Dumont alone filled her field of view. Back came the long-absent gnawing urge, an old familiar want that could be so easily remedied in the arms of Remy Dumont. She closed her eyes. Prayer was so close, yet the choice to do so evaded her.

Temptation.

The word rose ugly before her. Remy Dumont, young and handsome, sweet with words. He bade her return to a life she swore she'd abandoned.

Tempted her to forsake the real for the temporary.

What harm would come of a stolen afternoon? It's not like I'll become what I was. The curve of his mouth told her he'd be a man of practiced abilities. A man who could kiss a woman and make her forget her cares.

And there were many cares. Fears. Worries.

"Yes, that's it, Ruby. You're thinking about it, aren't you?" Now he held her forearm, and though the basket hid them, his fingers were not still. "Steal away with me," he whispered as he leaned close enough for her to feel his breath on her cheek. His free hand tangled in the

ribbon holding her hair in place. "I long to loose this braid of yours. Such a lovely shade, this scarlet hair of yours."

Scarlet.

"Though your sins be as scarlet, they shall be as white as snow."

Shock poured over her like cold bathwater. *Sins of scarlet.* So easily she'd nearly fallen. Her heart sank as a mixture of humiliation and sorrow filled her down to the bone.

When she looked at Remy Dumont again, all she felt was the need to run. To flee before good sense and seven weeks of newfound faith were tossed aside once more.

"Excuse me, but I must. . ." Without bothering to finish her good-byes, Ruby turned on her heels and fled, nearly slamming into Mr. Russell's prize mare. "Excuse me," she said to the animal as it stood tethered before the mercantile.

The mercantile.

A slow glance up at the windows showed her that their exchange had been witnessed by a half dozen of Fairweather Key's citizens.

She ducked around the tail end of the horse so as to avoid the condemning stares and found herself ankle deep in the muck that was Main Street after a decent rain. Her head held high, she plodded across the street and paused to shake what mud she could off the hem of her dress.

"I'm hopeless," she said as she reached the boardwalk then nearly slid to her doom from the mud on her shoes. "Truly hopeless," she added when she righted herself.

Thankfully, Remy Dumont seemed content to remain on the other side of the street, though he shadowed her as she continued to walk. Her fingers shook, but she formed a fist with her free hand and forced her attention forward.

To turn around would be to meet Remy at the point where Main turned upward toward the boardinghouse. Better to keep walking until he tired of the ruse and let her be.

If he tired of it.

She cast a sideways glance and found him watching her. Ruby wished for the distraction of a familiar face who might want to stop and chat. None appeared.

Just keep walking. Don't stop. So she did, and by the time she realized where she'd gone, she was standing within a stone's throw of the docks.

And so was Remy.

And so was Micah Tate.

CHAPTER 18

So the Dumont fellow had designs on Ruby O'Shea. That much Micah could easily discern from their walk down the hill and the conversation they'd obviously had in front of the mercantile. He shifted his attention to Ruby, who wore a flushed expression.

For a moment he allowed himself to believe she hadn't been walking with the fellow. Then, by degrees, the reality of it sunk into his tired bones.

Dumont was young, as was she, and obviously interested in the lovely redhead. But then, what man with a pulse and no wedding ring wouldn't be?

Micah reached to shake Dumont's hand, making sure to squeeze extra hard as he said, "Tate, Micah Tate."

To his credit, the young man didn't so much as flinch. Rather, he gave as he had received. "Yes," he said, "I've heard about you. Good things," he added with a glance down at Ruby, "from my sister."

To answer would have been the proper thing, but watching Remy Dumont wither under his stare was more amusing.

"His sister is Viola Dumont." Ruby must have realized she'd jumped into a conversation in which she did not belong, for a lovely shade of pink dusted her cheeks. "Of course, you know her."

Again he might have answered, but where was the humor in that? And with all the grief he'd endured at the hands of Ruby O'Shea, a bit of fun was certainly due him.

KATHLEEN Y'BARBO

Then came the all-too-familiar twinge of conscience that caused him to soften his expression and take up the lost thread of conversation. "I'm responsible for mustering up a militia of able-bodied citizens of Fairweather Key." Micah gave Dumont another long look and pretended not to notice Ruby's discomfort. "Planning on being here long?"

"I wasn't, actually," he said in a tone that let Micah know what he thought of their backwater town. "I've only come to fetch my sister home and perhaps see a bit of the island's lovely attractions as well."

Ruby's sharp intake of breath drew Micah's attention and stopped the Dumont fellow cold. "I had no idea she was. . ." She shook her head. "That is, Viola never told me she planned to leave."

"Vivi was not expecting me," Dumont said. "I must confess I have come to appreciate some of the beauty she told me I would find here."

Remy Dumont's smile might have been called charming, and had he not been aiming it at the woman Micah intended to marry, it might also have been appreciated. Instead, he felt something welling up inside that was completely foreign.

It had started when Micah had seen the pair walking toward the docks. Viola's brother had the audacity to reach over and touch Ruby's shoulder. Perhaps he merely swiped at the bloodthirsty mosquitoes that infested the cove upon occasion. Or maybe he'd only seemed to touch her.

Then he did it again, and this time Ruby stopped short and turned to face him. Her bonnet hid her face, but Micah could see the midwife's brother clearly. Their conversation went on for no more than a minute, but the damage was done.

Right there in broad daylight with half of the fishermen and wreckers in Fairweather Key and all of the customers in the mercantile within watching distance, the two had practically tested the bounds of propriety. Or at least Micah imagined they might have.

He had been struck by jealousy.

His plan to stay away from the boardinghouse wasn't working out as he expected. Or was it? While Dumont watched Ruby, she most definitely had turned her attention elsewhere.

To him.

"Beauty?" Micah smiled under her gaze. "Indeed, beauty abounds

116

here." He added a wink then grinned when Ruby made a face at him. "But back to the militia. Every able-bodied man on the island is expected to do his part. Long as you're here, I'll expect you to join us."

Dumont met his stare and, for a second, seemed to be intending to respond with some measure of enthusiasm. Finally, he nodded and turned his attention to Ruby. "Might I walk you back to the boardinghouse?"

"Are you staying there, sir?" His tone was sharp, and Micah knew it, but the image of Ruby and this man abiding under the same roof warranted nothing less.

"He's not," Ruby hastened to say even as she slipped past his glance.

"I am burdening my sister with my presence," Dumont said with what was surely youthful sarcasm, "though I count on a short stay."

"So you mentioned," Micah said. "Perhaps I might inquire as to when the next vessel sails." He paused, as much to let his words soak in as to tame his grin. "It would certainly be no trouble."

"Yes, well, you're a good man, Mr. Tate, but I warrant when the time comes, I'll manage to find my own way."

"A pity," Micah said under his breath.

"So, Miss O'Shea," the midwife's brother said. "Might we continue our walk? You mentioned something about going visiting, and I'm keen on meeting more of the nice people of Fairweather Key." Dumont linked arms with her then looked over Ruby's head to glare at Micah. "If you'll excuse us, then."

She appeared to consider the question just a bit longer than Micah liked. "Thank you, but I've a bit of business to discuss with Mr. Tate," she said as she shrugged from his grasp.

"As you wish," he said before taking his leave.

"The militia, Dumont. I expect you on the courthouse steps three days hence at dawn." When the fellow continued walking without any response, Micah gave in to his temper. "Ignoring the call to duty will not keep you from serving, Mr. Dumont."

Again he ignored the statement. Micah's blood boiled. How dare the fool show such insolence?

"Excuse me," he said, "but I'm of a mind to teach that man the manners he's sorely lacking."

"Leave him alone," Ruby said. "I'm sure when the time comes he'll do what he should."

Micah's mistake was looking away from Dumont and focusing his attention on Ruby. One look, and all irritation evaporated.

"I'm not sure I agree with you," he said, "though I hope you're right. Just so you understand, he could be thrown in jail for refusing to serve."

Something in her expression surprised him. "Really?" was all she said, but Micah got the impression that the idea of Remy Dumont behind bars did not distress her as much as he expected it would.

"So," he said as he searched for another topic. "What's in there?"

"This?" She let out a soft, "Oh," and then thrust the basket in his direction. "It's for you. That is, I made it special." Ruby shook her head as a charming red color climbed into her cheeks. "It's lunch. Unless you've eaten, and in that case, I suppose it's dinner."

Micah lifted the cloth to see a feast hidden beneath. "Is that pie?"

"It is," she said. "I hope you like it." Ruby paused, seemingly uncertain as to what she should do next.

"Will you join me?"

"No, I couldn't really." She cast a glance over her shoulder and appeared to be trying to determine in what direction the Dumont fellow had gone.

Micah spied the man taking his time as he strolled back up Main Street. Likely he would keep watch to see just when Ruby would follow his path.

It would never do to allow her to leave now. Yet she appeared poised to do just that.

Before she could run away, Micah pointed to the as-yet-unnamed vessel. "Come on aboard and sit with me while I eat." Lest she argue the point, he gestured to the basket. "I'll make short work of this, and then you can bring it back to the boardinghouse."

Was it his imagination, or did she seem disappointed?

Ruby tried to hide the glance she made toward town, but as she turned back to look at Micah, she knew she'd failed. For lack of anything else

Beloved Counterfeit

to say, Ruby shrugged. "I suppose I am a bit hungry."

She wasn't in the least, but staying with Micah was the much better alternative to walking home and risking another encounter with Remy Dumont. To be sure he had no idea of the turmoil of her thoughts, Ruby offered a smile.

Micah gestured to a smart-looking vessel then began walking toward it, leaving Ruby to figure he intended her to follow. She did and in short order found herself facing a plate of the same food she'd dished up to the boarders what seemed like no time ago. While Micah said grace over the meal, Ruby sneaked a covert glance at the wrecker.

Her impression on the beach had changed some, though her thoughts on his appearance had not. Unlike Remy Dumont, whose rakish charm made for most of his attractiveness, Micah Tate was solidly handsome and solidly nice.

It was a combination she rarely saw in the men with whom she came in contact. Men who might, at any moment, show themselves on the horizon. She checked to be sure none were approaching then ducked her head once more.

Like the preacher he was rumored to become, Micah Tate made full use of the moment to pray about everything from the food to the sunshine and beyond. At least it seemed so.

Though she tried to listen to his words, she was more taken with the way the breeze blew across the back of her neck and chased a pair of gulls past the mainmast. While Micah offered a blessing for the hands that made the food, Ruby let out a long breath, only then realizing she'd not once been aboard a vessel and felt such a sense of peace.

Even when she and Opal had finally fled the madness that was Papa's world, there had been nothing like this.

"Amen," Micah said, "and next time it'd help if you kept your eyes closed and your mind on the praying."

"I have no idea what you're talking about," she said as she sat back and watched him tackle the food with the gusto of a man who'd not eaten in days.

"Admit it," he finally said between bites of chicken. "You're considering my proposal."

He caught her off guard, yet she couldn't have formed a response she'd be willing to say even if she'd had time to think on it. She decided to change the subject. "Why haven't you been taking your meals at the boardinghouse?"

Micah chewed maddeningly slowly, and then, as he swallowed, his grin bloomed. "So you've noticed."

"Of course I've noticed," she said. "The food goes twice as far." When he gave her a look that seemed to ask if she was jesting, Ruby felt obliged to continue. "And of course Tess misses you terribly."

Again he merely stared.

Ruby shifted positions and tried not to flinch under his stare. "So I wondered if you were perhaps planning another trip up the hill tomorrow or if I should stop setting a place for you."

"Who is the Dumont fellow to you?"

The sudden change of topic took her by surprise. "I hardly know the man," she said with a truth that belied the conflicting emotions she'd felt on Main Street. "Now about tomorrow's meal, will you be with us?"

"I'll come back when you ask me to, Ruby," he said as he rose and dumped the chicken bones into the water.

Of all the infuriating nerve. "I just did." She took a deep breath and attempted a tone with less of a bite to it. "Well, of course you're welcome to come back. Mrs. Campbell made provisions for you, and I'll not go against her wishes." She shook her head. "I can't imagine why you'd think you weren't welcome."

Micah seemed to consider her statement, though he gave no indication he might respond. Finally, he lifted the basket. "Why did you bring me this?"

Caught. What could she say?

"Have you come to accept my proposal?"

"What?" She exhaled. "I, that is. . ."

"I see." He set the basket at her feet and stepped inside the cabin. "I thought you'd have come to your good senses by now," he said.

"It's not about good sense." From where she sat, Ruby could see Micah moving about but could not tell what he was doing. "For I've enough of that for the both of us."

"Is that so?" he called from the depths of the vessel. "I warrant not, for you're in quite a situation, Ruby O'Shea."

"I've handled situations before, Micah Tate, and though I will grant you that you're partly to blame for it, likely I'd have been found out eventually. So," she said as lightly as she could, "I absolve you of your obligation to marry me."

"You absolve me?" His laughter rolled toward her. "It's not your absolution I seek. Though perhaps I should be concerned that you see me only as your protector and not as someone who might bring you the occasional smile."

That was an odd statement coming from the serious wrecker. What sort of man cared whether he brought a smile to the face of his wife? Surely none whom Ruby had met, except perhaps for the Carters—father and son. They, she'd decided early on in her stay on the key, were the exception and not the rule.

The mail clipper slid past on the tide, a bell calling out its arrival. She glanced across at the deck and returned the wave of whoever stood at the helm. The vessel's wake jostled the boat, causing her to grip the wood to keep from falling. Still, Micah remained inside.

"I should go," she called.

No response. She crept closer. All activity inside had ceased. Perhaps there was some sort of exit that took him below. Leaning forward, she saw only a dim interior with a shaft of light where the sunshine spilled through the door.

"Micah, I—"

Someone grabbed her from behind and whirled her around. Micah. Were she able, she might have swatted him.

"You frightened me, Micah Tate," she managed to say, though her heart still pounded in her throat.

Immediately he released her. "I'm sorry, I. . ." He stepped away. "I thought to surprise you, make you smile actually, by going around the other side and. . . Dumb of me."

"You thought to surprise me?" At the thought of the serious Micah Tate planning any kind of surprise, Ruby began to giggle. The more she thought of it, the funnier the idea became, until her giggle became full-blown laughter.

Poor Micah obviously didn't have any idea what to think. "It's my turn to apologize," she said. "I just didn't think of you as someone who would do anything silly."

"I told you I would." His grin fell. "I see."

"Oh no, I didn't mean it like that." She searched for the words to bring back his grin. "What I meant was, you're the solid kind. The kind a woman can depend on to take care of her." She paused, noting his frown lines were no longer so deep. "You said so yourself, so I just assumed you'd find silliness something you'd prefer not to engage in. Me, however, I think it's just fine. Why, when the girls are—"

"Ruby?"

She took a breath. "What?"

"I asked you a question you never answered." His gaze swept her face as he crossed both arms over his chest. "Why did you bring the food?"

"I told you. I thought maybe—"

His eyes seemed to plead with her. "The real reason."

"When are you coming back to the boardinghouse?" Not the answer wanted, but a question in need of a response all the same.

He leaned closer, and for a moment, Ruby thought he might kiss her. "Do you miss me?"

"I don't know."

"Then I'm going to have to answer your question in the same way. I don't know."

Her temper flared. Was there a man on this planet who didn't have the ability to irritate her? It seemed not.

Surely no such man was aboard this vessel. "Micah," she said slowly, "I have just been kind enough to bring you food, though you've questioned my motives. Now you have the audacity to ask me if I miss you?"

Micah's grin returned. "Thank you, Miss O'Shea. You've just answered my question."

Irritation rose a notch as she reached for the basket. "I've not done any such thing."

"Yes, you did," he said as he leaned back against the cabin wall and crossed his arms over his chest. "And I must say I'm very glad to know you miss me enough to be sensitive to the topic, though I must insist you cease your carrying on with Remy Dumont. Perhaps you didn't realize this, but it appeared you two were much too close for decent folks."

"I, well, oh!" Ruby turned on her heels and stormed across the deck. Only her years of experience aboard ship kept her on her feet.

"One more question," he called, even though she seemed to ignore him. "I'll be seeing Rev. Carter tomorrow. Shall I go ahead and book the church, or would you prefer to go with me and help choose the date?"

Ruby stalled and forced herself not to turn and look at him. "You wouldn't dare," she said through clenched jaw.

Surely he wouldn't. But as she turned toward town, his laughter followed.

And she wasn't sure.

CHAPTER 19

On the fourth day of Micah's self-imposed exile from Ruby's table, Hezekiah Carter came to visit. Like Micah, the pastor had obviously spent time in the sun recently, as evidenced by the red color on his face.

Micah swiped at his forehead and stepped onto the dock to shake hands with the pastor. "What brings you here, Rev. Carter?"

"Working on a garden for the parsonage," he said. "Something I'd planned to do in my old age." A chuckle. "It seems to have arrived, and quite before I expected it, I might add."

"Old age?" Micah shook his head. "Hardly."

"Be that as it may," he said, "I've a favor to ask. It's a bit of short notice, but I wonder if you might be willing to conduct the Sunday service this week."

"Sunday service?" He gave the pastor a looking over. No sign of ill health. "Why?"

Rev. Carter shrugged. "It's time."

"I suppose."

"Excellent." He clasped his hand on Micah's shoulder then excused himself to walk away. A few steps down the docks, he turned. "Oh, Micah, one caveat. You'd do me a great honor if you speak on one of the Lord's promises."

"Which one?"

He grinned. "Oh, that's easy. I'd like you to talk about His promise to wash us clean and put our past behind us."

"Of course," he said, but as he watched the old man stroll away, Micah couldn't help but wonder why the pastor had chosen that topic. And this Sunday to preach it.

Never before had he come to Micah on such short notice, though he'd offered up the pulpit on several occasions over the past few months. And never had he given any instructions on what message to give.

With only good intentions and a well-worn Bible, Micah sat beneath the shade of a coconut palm and tackled the job. In short order, he had quite a list of verses applicable to his topic but no sermon.

Again he opened his Bible, and this time Micah wrote a few notes. A very few notes.

It seemed as though his mind refused to wrap around the task of making something out of the words. When his stomach growled, Micah set his scribbling aside.

He wondered what sort of meal Ruby might be serving up at the boardinghouse today. Not that it mattered, for he had no immediate plans to return. At least, not until he was certain Ruby missed him.

Micah gathered his sermon notes for Sunday and rolled them into a bundle that he carried under his arm. He'd found much to talk about but had little success putting it into some semblance of order. Then there was the uncomfortable feeling he had while reading a few of the more pertinent verses.

He decided to set to walking in the hopes he'd find inspiration along the way. To his dismay, his traitorous feet took him to the front gate of the boardinghouse. He looked to the side yard in the hopes of finding Ruby or one of the girls but saw nothing but laundry hanging on the line.

Micah ticked through his options. The last, which was staying right where he'd landed, appealed the most—and the least.

Of course, Micah knew he had every right to walk up the front steps and seat himself at the table in his usual spot. Pride wouldn't feed a man for long, and neither would he get a thing written on the sermon lest he sit in his favorite chair and think.

Besides, according to his empty belly, it was near to suppertime.

Micah saw only one way to swallow his pride, and that was in one big gulp. He took the steps two at a time and opened the door as if he'd not missed a day or a meal. When he stepped into the dining room, Micah gave a brief nod to the other boarders then winked at Tess when she brought him fresh cream for his coffee.

"Where's your mama?" he whispered.

Tess pointed to the kitchen then leaned toward him, a conspiratorial look on her face. "I think she's mad at you."

"Is that so?" He stooped to get at eye level with her. "Did she tell you that?"

"Tess, come in here please," Ruby called.

The child placed her finger over her lips.

Micah chuckled as he watched her skip from the room and, for a moment, envied her easy way of transitioning from one situation to the next. If only the world were as simple a place now as it had been when he was Tess's age.

When Ruby brought out the food, she placed it in the center of the table then made her exit without sparing him a glance. He thought he noticed, however, that she paid him special interest when she returned with the bowl of conch chowder.

What was *he* doing here? Ruby peered around the corner and watched Micah Tate turn the pages of his Bible, obviously intent on remaining seated at the far corner of the table indefinitely.

"Should I tell him to go home?" This from Carol, who had little tolerance for anyone lately.

"Shh," Ruby said as she stepped away from the door. "We'll not be treating the guests that way."

"But he's not a guest," she whispered. "I think he's just here to court you."

"Court me?" Ruby lowered her voice. "Court me?" she repeated. "Why would you think that?"

"We know what he asked you," Maggie said as she stepped inside with a bucket of fresh water. "Tess told us."

126

"Tess told you?"

"Why do you keep repeating us?" Carol asked.

Ruby took the water bucket from Maggie and set it on the floor, then led the twins out onto the back porch. "I'm not repeating. . ." She sighed as she closed the door. "All right, maybe I am. And maybe Mr. Tate *did* declare his intentions."

The twins exchanged an I-told-you-so glance.

"But I have neither accepted him nor taken him seriously."

"And that's where she's gone wrong."

She whirled around to see Micah Tate standing at the door.

"I'm sorry," he said. "Was I not invited to this party?"

The girls giggled. "It's not a party," Carol said.

"We're just talking." This from Maggie.

"About you," they said in unison before scampering away across the backyard. "And whether you were here to court our mama."

Ruby felt the heat flood her cheeks, partly from embarrassment and partly from irritation. "That's quite enough, girls," she called, though her words might as well have been puffs of smoke for how quickly they disappeared in the salt air.

Their giggles followed them as the twins disappeared around the corner of the boardinghouse. "Traitors," Ruby muttered as she tried to ignore Micah.

Busying herself with work came easy to Ruby, yet as she cast about for something to do, she found all her chores were waiting inside. With Micah standing between her and the door, she could only talk her way back inside or stay and remain silent. Neither appealed.

"If you'll excuse me, I need to go inside now," she finally said. "I've work to do."

He looked as if he might argue but stepped aside. She reached for the bucket but found he had snagged it first. "Please put it in the basin," she said, and he did as she asked.

Micah stood looking quite out of place among the dishes and pots lining the countertop. "Thank you," she finally said in hopes he'd get the idea and leave.

"You know I was just teasing about going to the church to reserve a date."

"No," she said as she turned her back on him. "I didn't."

"Well, now you do." He paused. "And Viola's brother—"

"Nothing to it," she said. "Not that I owe you this, but I've not seen the man since that day on Main Street."

It was the truth, though she decided not to let on how ambivalent she felt about the Lord answering her prayer to rid Remy from her life should he be a bad influence. Praying that prayer had been the best thing she'd done, yet she couldn't help but feel disappointed that the rogue hadn't at least come calling to apologize for his familiar behavior on Main Street.

"Yes, I know," Micah said.

"You know?" Ruby tried to absorb the meaning. "How could you know?" She paused. "Unless you've been watching me."

His gaze collided with hers. "I made a promise."

Realization dawned. "You *have* been watching me."

Micah looked away. "If you don't need anything further, I'd be much obliged if you'd allow me a corner of the table to work on my Sunday sermon."

"Go ahead." Ruby went back to clearing the aftermath of supper, though her mind wandered to the ways Micah might have found to keep her in his sight while she remained unaware. That she had not known frightened her, yet finding he was capable of such covert behavior gave Ruby an unexpected feeling of satisfaction.

As she worked, however, she found herself sneaking peeks at the man inhabiting her dining room. At first he seemed distracted and then intent on whatever he was writing. A few times when she passed the doorway, he seemed to be talking to himself.

The sun sank lower, and the room fell into shadows, so Ruby decided the neighborly thing to do would be to light a lamp. Oddly, her fingers shook so badly she nearly couldn't accomplish the task. When she finally managed it, she felt so flustered she almost didn't bring the thing to him.

It's only Micah Tate. Ruby lifted the lamp then steadied it with her other hand. *And Micah Tate irritates me on a good day.*

She stepped into the dining room. The wrecker didn't bother to look up. Setting the lamp in the middle of the table seemed silly since

it barely cast enough light to reach to the far edges.

Slowly and with care, Ruby edged nearer Micah. When he looked up, a startled expression on his face, she realized he'd been deep in thought and not merely careless with his attention.

"Oh, I. . ." He rose so quickly the chair fell backward and clattered to the floor. Tossing his notes onto the table, Micah retrieved the chair then checked it for damage. "I'm sorry," he finally said. "I didn't hear you come in." He looked at the lamp then glanced out the window. "It's late," he said. "I should go."

While Micah made to pack his things, Ruby reached for one of the loose pages. "Forgiveness," she read, "is the business of God. Ours is to allow Him to wipe the slate clean."

He snatched the paper from her and set it on the pile in front of him. "Just notes," he said. "Not a real sermon yet."

Ruby settled across from him and reached for another page. "White as snow, He washes us, though our scarlet sins would surely—"

"Really, Miss O'Shea." Again he took the paper from her. "It's not in a form I am ready to share yet."

She nodded but made no attempt to leave. "You're welcome to work on it here," she said. "I'll be putting the girls to bed soon, but that certainly won't affect anything happening in this room."

He nodded and muttered a word of thanks.

"So take your time." She rose. "And let yourself out should you finish before I come back downstairs."

Another nod, and he bowed his head over his work, one hand guarding the pages he'd filled with scribbles. Rising, she left to fetch the girls and see to their bedtime routine. Through it all, she continued to listen for the door to close, signaling the departure of her guest.

Finally, the girls settled into slumber, and Ruby had her chance to do the same. Exhaustion played at the corners of her mind, as it always did this time of night, and her body ached. Any other night, she might have heated water for a bath.

Somehow with Micah Tate under the same roof, it seemed improper. So did lying down to sleep with him sitting in her dining room.

Perhaps it was the long discussion she'd had with the girls about him. While Ruby had been careful not to commit to anything, Tess had decided Micah would make a fine papa for them. Maggie agreed, but Carol kept silent.

"I still have a papa, don't I?" Carol whispered as Ruby had kissed her good night.

What to say? Reflecting on it now, Ruby cringed with the lie she'd told. Someday she'd tell them the truth—someday when they were old enough to understand.

"What a joke," she whispered. "I'm two decades past them in age, and I still don't understand."

And with Micah Tate remaining seated at her dining table, she'd do well not to contemplate more than one male at a time. So she rose from the chair where she'd collapsed only minutes earlier and adjusted the braid that had come loose while wrangling Tess into her nightclothes. While she could do nothing about the smudges of exhaustion under her eyes, she did pinch her cheeks to return some semblance of life to her face.

As she stepped out into the hall and closed the door, Ruby felt a strange fluttering in her stomach. Surely Micah Tate was not the reason, for no more irritating a man walked the earth. Yet when she bypassed the next to last step—the one that always creaked—in order to keep him from hearing her approach, Ruby had to admit it was so she could watch him undetected.

He kept himself well-groomed, this rough-hewn wrecker, though his clothing bore signs he might have patched it himself. With rusty hair trimmed short enough to touch a jaw with no trace of whiskers, the wrecker almost looked like a gentleman. A lawyer, perhaps, or maybe if she forgot about the way he made her feel when he stood too close, a preacher. Only his hands, overlarge and covered with the calluses a working man accumulated, gave him away.

He'd moved the lamp closer, causing most of the dining room to be plunged into darkness. The stern portraits of Judge and Mrs. Campbell took on a sinister look on one wall, while the curtained windows offered nothing but the black night sky and the sound of the waves lapping against the rocks at the base of the hill some distance away.

Another book lay in front of him along with the Bible, but its name she could not discern. As she edged closer, Ruby could read the binding.

Robinson Crusoe.

What in the world?

The wrecker wasn't writing a sermon at all. At least it appeared he hadn't given much thought to the needs of a congregation, unless he would be speaking to them about castaways and uninhabited islands.

Ruby felt her temper flare as Micah picked up the book, slowly turned a page, and allowed his eyes to lazily follow Mr. Defoe's words across the page. *How nice he has time for such frippery.*

While she'd been hard at work taming girls, Micah Tate had turned her dining room into a reading room. *Of all the nerve.*

CHAPTER 20

Emboldened, Ruby stepped into the dining room. "Shouldn't you be working on a sermon, Mr. Tate?"

Micah let the book fall to the table, where it landed with a thud. Again he made to rise; again the chair wobbled against long legs. This time, however, he caught it before it toppled.

"Yes, well, I was—"

"Reading." Ruby retrieved the novel. "I know. I am a fan of Mr. Defoe, though I must admit I've not found the time to read this book in quite some time. Years, in fact."

She paused to decide whether to continue. *Oh, why not?*

"I'm far too busy with the raising of children and the running of a boardinghouse to take on such a novelty." She sounded like a shrew, yet the words were out and there was nothing to be done for it.

Ruby returned the book to its place on the shelf nearest the window then slowly turned to face Micah Tate. "If you were waiting for me to come back downstairs before you departed, you needn't have."

He looked crestfallen, something that surprised her. Even more of a surprise was the guilt she once again felt at speaking with such a sharp tongue.

An apology rushed to her lips, yet she bit it back as she settled across the table from him once more. What was it about this man that brought out her less-than-nice side?

Ah yes, it was the irritation he caused nearly every time he crossed her threshold.

Yet at this moment, he seemed as nice as could be. Not a bit of irritation about him.

Ruby glanced past the lamp to the pages he'd been so unwilling to share earlier. "Have you finished your sermon, Mr. Tate?"

Micah shrugged. "I've done a passable job of putting something together, but I'm not certain I'll do the opportunity justice."

Leaning against the back of the chair, Ruby regarded the wrecker across the table. The words tumbled from her mouth even as she wished not to say them. "Perhaps you'd read me what you've got." She paused. She was tired. So very tired. "Try your sermon out on me," she continued. "If you want," she hastily added. "You're certainly under no obligation."

Gratitude replaced a blank stare. "You'd listen?" He paused. "Surely you've other things more pressing than to hear me ramble."

Here was her chance to plead her cause and remove herself to the soft bed that awaited in her attic room. "No," she said carefully, "nothing that won't wait until you've read your sermon to me."

"I go by notes," he said almost apologetically. "An outline, really. I don't actually read. And I have to stand. Can't sit."

Micah paused, and unless Ruby missed her guess, he seemed a bit flustered. Was it her or the sermon? She'd not ask, though she'd dearly love to know.

"I'm not making a lick of sense, am I?"

"No," she said, "but I've come to understand that's a part of conversing with you on occasion, Mr. Tate. So please begin doing whatever it is you do." Ruby gave him a mock-serious look. "Or should I don my Sunday hat and gloves so as to give you more of the atmosphere of church?"

"I believe I can close my eyes and imagine it, but I do thank you all the same," he said with equal formality and a twinkle in his eye.

"If you're certain, then," she teased. "Though I rarely imagine a church smelling of conch chowder and fresh-baked pie."

"I have it on good authority, Miss O'Shea, that the Lord is fond of those things he's created, namely conch chowder and fresh-baked pie, so why not scent His churches with such things?"

Ruby giggled like a schoolgirl. "Mr. Tate, I'm no authority on these matters, so I will, of course, defer to you, but I cannot recall ever reading in the Bible that the Lord either created or prefers to smell pie and chowder."

Micah reached for his Bible and began to thumb through the pages. When he found what he sought, he met Ruby's gaze and cleared his throat. "I beg to differ," he said. "Right here in Philippians, chapter 4: 'But I have all, and abound: I am full, having received of Epaphroditus the things which were sent from you, an odour of a sweet smell, a sacrifice acceptable, wellpleasing to God.' "

She leaned forward to try to see what he'd read. "I fail to see where there's any talk of chowder and pie."

"Oh, that's right here," he said. "Where Paul mentions the sweet smell and a sacrifice acceptable and pleasing to God."

He turned the Bible around, and Ruby read it. Sure enough, it said what he claimed. "I'm new at this," she said. "So I'm going to trust your interpretation, though I suspect you're teasing me just a bit."

The wrecker's gaze met hers. Again there was amusement in his expression. "I'm not a man given to much speculation about heaven, Miss Ruby, but I suspect what the Lord's got for us to eat up there, if indeed we're fed, will be at least as good as your pie and chowder."

"Oh, now, Micah," she said then regretted her use of his first name. "Mr. Tate, that is."

"I prefer Micah."

Ruby nodded. "Anyway, I don't see how the Maker of the universe cares for human things like smell and taste. It doesn't make sense. After all, He's God."

"Ah, but it does make sense." Micah rested both hands on the table and seemed to be daring her to argue the point.

"Show me in there." She pointed to the Bible. "I want to see where God talks about things like that."

"Like taste, perhaps?"

"Yes," she said. "Start with taste."

Micah seemed to warm to the challenge. His grin broadened then slowly faded until he'd shuffled the pages and found his place. " 'O taste and see that the Lord is good.' " He looked up. "Psalm 34. Want one more?" When she nodded, he set about finding another. " 'As the apple tree among the trees of the wood, so is my beloved among the sons. I sat down under his shadow with great delight, and his fruit was sweet to my taste.' " Again he looked up. "Song of Solomon."

She shook her head. "That makes no sense. Explain what he's talking about there."

Micah looked at the page, and by degrees, his face turned nearly as red as his hair. "Actually, I'd really rather try out my sermon on you if that's agreeable."

Ruby nodded, although she wondered about the man's strange reaction. She'd have to go find that book Song of Solomon and see what in the world had the wrecker so embarrassed.

"All right. Let me find my place." Clearing his throat, Micah Tate set the Bible aside and shuffled through his pile of pages. With a glance in her direction, he stood and began.

"We are," Micah said, "a people who demand much from God but more from ourselves. When God shows Himself to be God and ignores our demands, we are surprised, angry even. When we prove human and fail, we have the same reaction only directed at ourselves."

As he spoke, she listened as much to his voice as to the words he said. His accent, touched at the edges with a slow drawl, was familiar. Texas, perhaps. Or possibly some other state nearby.

No, she decided, he was a Texan. She knew from her days in Galveston what a man from Texas sounded like.

And what he was capable of.

This much she shook off with a roll of her shoulders as she returned her concentration to his words rather than his voice. His oversized feet wearing a rut in the floor, Micah began to speak of God's ability to cast our past behind us and see only our future. Would that she could depend on this.

Somehow Ruby never could quite feel washed clean. Perhaps it was the continuing specter of Papa, of Thomas Hawkins, and of men like Jean Luc Rabelais and nameless others, even the passing thought of Remy Dumont, that kept her past from being past.

Or perhaps the problem lay with her inability to forgive herself.

This much Micah discussed at length, not as it related specifically to her, of course, but as a generality.

Then he said something completely outlandish, and Ruby held up her hand to stop him. "One minute, please. I'm willing to believe God cares about human things like taste and smell, but I fail to see how He can just wipe the slate clean and declare that none of those bad things I've done count anymore."

Micah stopped his pacing but said nothing for what seemed like a full minute, maybe more. "That's a tough one." He set the papers on the table and rested both hands on the back of the chair. "I know what the Bible says, but I have to admit I don't always feel like it applies to me."

"A fine preacher you'll be, then." As soon as the words were out, she clamped her hands over her mouth. "I'm sorry," she said through her fingers. "That was awful."

His shoulders slumped. "No, it's the truth."

Shaking her head, Ruby stumbled from her chair. "Really, no," she said. "Your sermon, it was very good."

Micah seemed doubtful, though he remained silent.

"Truly good," she said. "Why, I was, well, I was. . ."

"Speechless?" he asked.

"Yes, well, no, actually." She pressed her palms on the table and leaned toward him. "Honestly, Micah, I think you're trying too hard. The things you said, they were really good. You speak from your heart. It's just that, well. . ."

"Go on."

She lowered her gaze. "I liked it better when you were explaining things to me."

"Better?"

Ruby braved a look and saw he seemed neither displeased nor particularly happy. "Yes, when you preach, you're different. But when you're answering my questions, oh, Micah, I mean Mr. Tate, you make me understand."

When Ruby attempted a grab for the notes, Micah swiped them away. "Go on," he said as he straightened and crossed his hands over his chest. "You don't need these to tell me how you feel."

"No, I suppose not."

She walked around the table to pick up Mrs. Campbell's copy of *Robinson Crusoe*. "Do you ever feel like this man, Mr. Tate? Like the whole world is going on somewhere beyond your horizon and you've no way to leave the place you find yourself in order to join them?"

Micah's nod was barely discernible in the dim lamplight.

"Well, that's what I feel most Sundays when I listen to people who understand the ways of the Lord much better than I do. I feel like I've landed myself on this island where I'm stuck with my sinful self, and meanwhile there are all these good people who have something I'm missing out on." She sighed. "I'm not making a bit of sense, am I?"

Micah's eyes widened, and he sank into the nearest chair. For a moment she thought she might lose him to apoplexy or some other aptly named condition. He certainly appeared unable to breathe, to speak, or to do anything but stare at her as if she'd grown a second nose.

"I'm sorry," she said, her voice sounding more like the squeak of a mouse than that of a woman with an opinion. "Oh, I've really done it, haven't I? Please don't listen to me."

While the wrecker seemed powerless to stop her, Ruby snapped up the sermon notes and shook them. "This, Mr. Tate, is a good sermon. I'm a silly fool who's only just learning who this God is I promised to serve." She paused. "Seven weeks now," she said. "No, wait, it's eight now, isn't it? Yes, it's eight. Oh, I'm rambling."

Setting the notes back on the table, Ruby turned to take a walk of shame toward the stairs. *Leave it to me to chase a future preacher away from the ministry.*

"I've done enough damage here, Mr. Tate," she said over her shoulder as she reached the stairs. "Please promise me you'll do two things: Forget you were ever here, and let yourself out when you're finished using the dining room."

Ruby got three steps up the stairs when she heard the familiar squeak behind her. She froze. "Mr. Tate, is that you standing on my squeaky step?"

CHAPTER 21

I t is," Micah said.

Ruby gripped the handrail to steady herself. "I distinctly requested that you do two things. Following me up the stairs was neither."

"Turn around, Miss O'Shea. Ruby." His voice was low but firm. "I refuse to talk to your back," he added in an even softer tone.

"No," she said.

"I'd like very much to continue this conversation." Again the stair squeaked, giving her hope he'd stepped backward. "Please," he added, and she knew he'd only moved closer.

Close enough to cause her to look toward the top of the stairs and wonder if she might be better off racing toward her room than remaining in this ridiculous predicament. Yet something kept her rooted in place.

Shame—yes, that's what it was. Her old familiar friend.

"Look," she said slowly. "I've done you a terrible disservice, Mr. Tate, and while there's no way to make up for it, I'd like to—"

"Ruby." His hand touched her shoulder, and she resisted the urge to shrug it off. "Please." Gently he turned her until she faced him. "Stop talking."

What happened next was unclear, for Ruby found her feet no longer touching the ground while the room spun around her. She regained her senses as Micah Tate deposited her in a chair just inside the circle of lamplight.

His hand cupped her jaw while his face wore a strange expression. "You," he said, "are a source of continual amazement."

She opened her mouth to reply, but the wrecker placed his finger across her lips. "My turn to talk," he said. "Though I need a minute to decide what to say."

"All right."

He gave her a look of mock irritation then stood to take up his pacing, stepping in then out of the light until she grew weary of watching. Her eyes grew heavy, and she quickly blinked to keep them from closing altogether.

When Micah snapped his fingers, Ruby's eyes flew open. "I'm sorry," she mumbled, "I'm just—"

"Tired? Yes, I can see that." He disappeared behind her then returned holding the novel that had started all this trouble. "Have you read this book?"

Nodding, Ruby watched him retrieve his Bible. "And this one? Have you read it?"

Ruby shook her head. "I intend to, but all I've seen of it is parts."

"Parts."

She couldn't tell whether he was contemplating her answer or making jest of it. "Yes, you know. Whatever parts Rev. Carter talks about in church, I read. Then when I get a spare minute—which isn't nearly as often as I'd like, I'm afraid—I go back and read it again, starting where I left off and going until something makes me stop. Most times I'll lose all track of time reading. It's a fascinating book."

"Yes," Micah said, "it is, but I am doing the talking, remember?"

She covered her mouth. "Sorry," she whispered.

"Ruby, you're brilliant. That thing you said about *Robinson Crusoe*? It was everything I wanted to say and more." He grabbed a handful of sermon notes and crumpled them. "You're the one who should be preaching on Sunday, not me."

At this, Ruby laughed. She couldn't help it. "Oh my, that's a good one." She leveled a direct stare at the man who now stood strangely still. "Do you have any idea what kind of woman I was?"

Micah waved away her statement. "Don't you see, Ruby? It doesn't matter. That's the old you."

She ignored his look of warning and pressed on. "You don't even know the half of what I've done. How can you say that?"

"I've done things, too, Ruby. Things I'm not proud of." Micah faltered a moment before giving the answer he knew in his mind—if not completely in his heart—to be true. "But they're in the past."

Even as he said the words, Micah wondered what sort of things this hardworking mother of three might have done. Sins of gossip or envy perhaps, though he could barely conjure up those.

"Ruby," he said just as he decided it, "there's nothing I need to know." He shook his head. "That's not completely true. I need to know if you'll allow me to use what you said about *Robinson Crusoe*."

He couldn't tell if she was relieved or confused. "Is that all?"

Micah glanced at the clock and noted the late hour. Too late to rouse the judge. "For tonight, yes."

As Micah reached to gather his things, Ruby stood. "Nothing else?" she asked.

"No," he said. "Nothing else."

Did he detect disappointment? Micah suppressed a smile as he stuck his notes into the Bible and moved toward the door. With Ruby a half step behind him, Micah got all the way to the door before stopping to turn around.

Was that a hopeful look? Likely he only imagined it, yet it emboldened him.

To his delight, she barely missed falling into him. "Actually," he said as he caught Ruby by the arm and righted her, "there is one more thing."

"Oh?" she asked, eyes wide.

Again he checked the clock. If only the time hadn't slid past so quickly. He'd spend yet another night keeping watch and another day glancing toward the white house on the hill far more than he ought.

"Yes." Micah released her then watched Ruby rub her arm where he'd touched her. "Might I borrow the book? I don't own a copy of *Robinson Crusoe*."

Ruby turned to fetch the novel, and Micah followed. "Ruby O'Shea," he called. "I've changed my mind. It's you I want, not the book. Is tonight the night you finally say you'll marry me?"

She hid her face behind the leather volume, but only for a moment. Unfortunately, he learned too soon that what the book hid was not a smile. "There are things about me you need to know, Mr. Tate," she said. "Things I must tell you before you decide to take on the girls and me."

"Ruby," he said as he removed the book from her arms and gathered her to him. "There's time for that. But not tonight."

"No?"

"No," he said, "and once again, you haven't answered my question. I owe you protection, Ruby O'Shea, and I think you'd make a fine wife. Will you marry me?"

"The cad! He'll not get away with this." Remy pounded his fist into the arm of the chair.

Viola jumped. "Really, you don't have to resort to violence," she said as she felt her hands begin to shake. "I'm fine, truly."

She wasn't, though Viola would never let her brother know that Dan Hill's abrupt departure from Fairweather Key with only a note of explanation was a shock from which she'd not soon recover.

The truth—and it pained her—was that she'd suspected a change in the doctor well before this. More often he'd spoken to her of the medical than the personal, and the last time she'd seen him—nearly three days ago—he'd said more than once that she was as capable as he of acting as doctor to the people of the island.

She'd laughed then and felt a measure of flattery. But something in how he said it made her wonder, if only in passing, whether she might someday be thrust into the position.

Now she had been.

Viola's fingers shook as she wrapped them around the key in her palm. She'd found it this morning folded inside the note.

Someone should be told, but Viola couldn't form the words to speak to anyone about it. The judge. Indeed, he should be the one to initiate a search for another doctor. His was, after all, the job of caring for the needs of the townspeople.

She glanced at Remy, who was studying her carefully. To his credit, her brother said nothing. "Will you accompany me to the judge's office? I think he should be informed."

He nodded then left to return with his hat and hers. "I respect that you'll not allow me to read what the doctor wrote, but you must understand that there's not a thing he could say—good or bad—in any letter that would change my opinion of him."

"It's not that I'll not allow it," she said. "But it says nothing of value. He's gone. He wants me to run the clinic in his absence." She shrugged. "Beyond that, there's nothing."

Viola donned her hat and shawl then followed Remy outside into sunshine that failed to warm the chill in her bones. On the walk to the courthouse, she likely passed numerous familiar faces, but she acknowledged none of them. Such was the numbness in her mind that had Remy not guided her, she might have continued to wander the streets of Fairweather Key completely oblivious to the reason for her outing. By the time she found herself seated at Caleb Spencer's desk, she'd all but given up any pretense of feeling anything.

The judge leaned back in his chair, his fingers steepled. "How can I help you today, Miss Dumont?" He looked to Remy. "Mr. Dumont, it is?"

Remy offered a curt nod. "You can right the wrong that has been perpetrated on my sister," he said. "And you can find that doctor of yours and haul him back to answer to me as representative of my family."

Judge Spencer let his hands drop to his lap. "These are serious charges, sir." He looked to Viola. "Perhaps you will fill in the details?"

She offered up Dan's note instead.

"How did you come to have this?" he asked.

"The bell rang early this morning, and I rose thinking I was heading to another birthing. Instead, I found this note on my porch." She paused. "Accompanied by a key."

Remy shot her a reproving look. "You didn't tell me he left a key."

"To the clinic," she said as she set the key on the desk.

For a moment all was silent. The judge seemed to be considering the situation. It was almost more than Viola could stand to try to wrap her mind around the fact that the man she loved was gone.

Not gone but vanished, leaving only a note of apology and the key to the clinic in his wake.

"I repeat my request that you find this man and call him to task for his behavior," Remy said.

Caleb offered the note back to Viola, but she declined to touch it. "Did Dr. Hill make any promises to you, Miss Dumont?"

Remy rose, and the chair toppled backward. "Look here, I fail to see—"

"Of marriage? We discussed it."

"See there," her brother said.

Viola slid him a warning glance, and he reluctantly righted the chair and sat in it. "We discussed it in generalities but never in specifics." She paused. "My purpose in bringing this to your attention is not to cause him to return, but rather to allow you notice so you might search for a new doctor."

"I see." Caleb rested his elbows on the desk. "And what of your expertise, Miss Dumont? Might you have the abilities we need to take the doctor's place?"

"Me?" She shook her head. "No, and even if I were able, I'd not be able to commit to such a responsibility. You see, I'll be leaving soon."

The statement surprised her almost as much as Remy. His smile was brief but sincere.

The judge, however, kept his expression blank. "Will you stay until another doctor can be found?"

"Honestly, I prefer not to face those who will want to console me. Leaving for a place where none knew of my. . ." Viola paused. "Of my attachment to the doctor," she continued, "would give me great comfort. I am willing, however, to sacrifice that comfort for a short while rather than leave these good people without medical care."

She looked to Remy, who offered an almost imperceptible nod. The decision made, she sighed. At least the course of her future would no longer depend on the indecision of one man or the death of another.

"If the search for a new teacher at Fairweather Key School is any indication," the judge said, "I fear this might take some time."

"What is this?" Remy asked. "You're searching for a teacher?"

"A headmaster, actually," he said, "or headmistress. The candidate must be willing to act as both educator and administrator."

"I see." Remy edged forward on his chair. "And what are the requirements for this position?"

Viola gave him a look.

"He or she must be a person of good character. Must offer up proof of some sufficient education." Caleb looked to the ceiling as if thinking. "And of course, a contract would need to be signed. If a woman, the term of employment would end with marriage. Which is why the position is open."

Remy inquired, "Might there be an interim position available? Say for a well-qualified fellow with a diploma?"

Caleb looked askance at Remy. "You've a university degree?"

"From Harvard," Emilie Gayarre said from the door. "I'm ashamed I didn't think to ask you about taking on the job of teaching the children. I suppose I expected you were only here visiting." She looked at Caleb and must have noted his solemn expression. "I'm interrupting. I'll just come back."

"No, don't go," Viola said. "He's gone, Em." Viola ran to meet her halfway and fell into Emilie's arms as the tears she'd held at bay began to fall. "Dan's gone."

CHAPTER 22

"All right, Micah," Ruby said as the last of her resolve melted. "Yes."

Perhaps it was for the best, as she'd spent most nights barely sleeping for worrying whether this would be the night Jean Luc returned. Or worse, Tommy Hawkins.

Then there was the issue of avoiding Remy Dumont. Marriage would certainly cure the habit of lying awake and brooding about what man would press his way into her bed.

From now until she took her last breath—or until he took his—it would be Micah Tate. That was somehow comforting.

His smile almost showed. Almost but not quite. "Yes what, Ruby?"

"Yes," she said as she exhaled a long breath, "I will marry you."

"You're serious."

"I am," she said just as the butterflies in her stomach threatened to take flight.

"All right, then."

When Micah set down his books and lifted her into his arms, then headed for the door, Ruby squealed, "Stop! Where are you going?"

"To wake up the judge," he said. "I told him if you ever said yes to me, I'd haul you over there on the spot before you had a chance to change your mind."

"Put me down." She pushed against his chest until he set her feet on the ground. "I've got sleeping girls upstairs to think of, Mr. Tate."

"Under the circumstances, I think it's safe to call me Micah, don't you?" He gestured to the door. "Now let's go. If we hurry, we will likely not catch the judge in his nightclothes. If it'll make you feel better, we can fetch someone to stay here with the girls while we're gone."

She reached for his arm. "Slow down," she said. "Can't this wait until tomorrow when the girls are awake? And why the judge? Don't most weddings on Fairweather Key happen in the church?"

Ruby could tell the wrecker hadn't thought of these things. Then came something else she hadn't thought of until now.

"Micah," she said gently, "I know ours will be a marriage based on promises that are a bit different than most. Strange as it sounds, it would mean something to me if it didn't look that way."

He paused. "I see your point. I suppose I can sleep with one eye open one more night," he said.

"I know you're teasing." Ruby released her grip on his wrists. "But I have wondered where you've been. Given the fact that you did say you'd be watching out for me—for us—after what you did to Jean Luc."

Her words must have stung, for he shrugged and walked to the door. "I've not slept more than a few hours at a time, Ruby, since the day I defended you. When I do, I find someone willing to take watch. I told you that, but I see you didn't believe me."

For a moment she had no words. "I didn't know," she finally said. "I thought you'd—"

"Given up? Hardly." Micah shook his head. "I've heard there is a certain appreciation that comes along with missing someone. I decided to test the theory."

"I thought. . ." She shook her head. "Never mind. I'll ask that you find your own bed tonight, Micah, and tomorrow we can revisit the topic of marriage."

"Then expect me for breakfast, Ruby." He gestured to the door. "I'll be sleeping on the front porch."

"Oh no, you won't," she said, though her heart was not in the argument.

She watched Micah leave then extinguished the lamp and made her way upstairs. It seemed as though she'd barely climbed into bed when the rooster crowed and her day began.

Trudging through her morning routine, Ruby paused in front of the mirror before heading downstairs to begin breakfast. Dark smudges framed her eyes, and her hair seemed intent on going every direction but the one in which she attempted to tame it.

Using a length of blue cotton cut from an old apron, Ruby tied back her hair; then she pinched her cheeks and made a face. "If this is what Micah Tate is marrying, he's definitely the loser in this bargain."

As the boarders began to file in, drawn no doubt by the smell of fresh coffee, Ruby poured a cup of the steaming brew and slathered butter on a biscuit, then went to look for Micah. She found him curled against the wall on the far end of the back porch, his jacket rolled up as a pillow and his boots set neatly side by side.

Rather than rouse him, she knelt a distance away and watched. Indeed, he made the same snorts and snores as other men, but he also smiled. A man who smiled in his sleep was a novelty she could get used to.

To her it showed a happiness of heart that came from the inside out.

There I go thinking silly thoughts again.

The coffee was warm, as was the morning, and Ruby soon felt beads of perspiration dot her forehead. She should awaken the sleeping guard, or at least hand him his coffee and flee for the safety of the kitchen.

Instead, she rose and tiptoed toward him. When Micah didn't awaken, she knelt once again, this time directly beside him.

He's to be my husband. I'm certainly entitled to. . .

Before she could talk herself out of it, she set the coffee cup on the porch and leaned over to kiss his forehead. A compromise from what she intended, but a kiss after all.

Micah's lack of response was a mixed blessing. How to explain was as difficult a prospect as why she'd done it. Better that she didn't have to speak of either.

She rose, knowing there would be a dining room full of boarders demanding refills for their empty plates and three girls who didn't want to leave their beds. Turning her back to tiptoe away, Ruby thought she heard him rouse.

"Next time try the lips, Ruby. It makes for a much more effective kiss."

"I'll keep that in mind," she tossed over her shoulder as she hurried inside.

"Oh, Ruby," he called.

Leaning out the window, she found him up on one elbow as he ran his hand through spikes of hair that needed a comb. "Yes?"

"Do you remember that day on the beach when I told you I saw a miracle?"

She did, but barely.

"Well, it occurs to me that you never did ask me what that miracle was, and I never took the time to tell you." He sat up and reached for the coffee to take a sip. "Ah, that's good. Now as I was saying, the miracle. Have you figured out what it was?"

Searching her mind, Ruby came up blank. "The sand dollar?" she asked, though that seemed a silly answer.

"No." Another sip as he made her wait for his response. "Come back out here a minute."

"You'll have to wait. They need me in the dining room."

"Ruby," he called.

"What?" This time her response was tinged with irritation.

"The miracle."

"Not now, Micah," she said.

She got halfway across the kitchen when she heard him call her name once again. She determinedly completed her duties as hostess before returning to the kitchen. The wrecker sat on the steps, his boots on and his hair combed. Only his jacket bore signs of having spent the night out on a porch. Micah, to her surprise, looked quite well rested.

"I'm working," she said.

"About that." He pointed to the door. "I've taken the liberty of finding someone to care for the boarders for the rest of the week."

"You found someone. . ." Ruby was at a loss for words. "Who told you to do. . . That is, how could you just. . . ?"

He rose and walked toward her, his long strides slow and easy, his face all smiles. "Ruby," he said softly, "you said you wanted our marriage to look like a real one. Who's going to believe we married for anything but convenience if we leave the church and come back to the boardinghouse in time for you to roast a chicken for dinner?"

"Actually, I'd planned stewp."

"Stew," he corrected.

"No, stewp." She held up her hands to counter any questions he might have. "It's a long story that begins with Tess."

He nodded. "Then perhaps you'll tell it to me later when we're alone."

Alone.

"I see I've taken you by surprise." Micah shrugged, moving close enough to hand her his empty coffee cup. "I'm going to do this your way, Ruby, and I'm doing it because I owe you and your three girls the protection I promised."

Your three girls.

He stood very close, so close that Ruby had to look up to meet his gaze. "About the girls, Micah. There's something I should tell you."

The wrecker cupped her jaw then gently pressed his forefinger to her lips. "Nod if this is something that happened in your past." When she did, he looked away. "Ruby, Ruby, Ruby. We've already talked about this. I don't want to know any of that. If God has washed you clean of it, what business do I have to hold it against you?"

"You're certain?" She paused. "I'm willing to come clean and tell you all of it."

Ruby searched his face, stared into eyes that were the color of strong coffee, and prayed this man told the truth. For if he didn't and he knew even a part of what she'd done, who she was, and how she came to have those three girls, he'd likely forget any promises he made to her.

"Mama," a sleepy voice called. "I'm hungry."

Micah lifted his finger from Ruby's lips, and she answered, "I'll be right there, Maggie."

"Lest you think I'd leave this place and those children with just anyone, you should know the Carters will be running things while we're away."

"Josiah and Isabelle?"

"No, Josiah's parents, Mary and Hezekiah." He smiled. "Last night I had a long talk with the reverend. I figured it best to speak to him ahead of time rather than surprise him with a wedding. He's most pleased for us, by the way."

"Good," she said for lack of anything else to say.

"As your husband, which I will be in a few hours, I'll be insisting the girls not sleep here in our absence. I've arranged for them to stay with Mary and Hezekiah. Should the worst happen and the thug return, at least he won't be able to find them."

"You're very kind," she said. "I thank you for thinking of them."

"Mama," Tess called.

"The only question left," Micah said, "is when to tell them."

Ruby smiled. "After breakfast?"

"Exactly what I was thinking." She'd nearly departed when his fingers encircled her wrist and stopped her. "Ruby, the miracle? Remember I asked if you recalled my saying I'd seen one that day?"

She nodded.

"It was your smile," he said. "Until that day, I'd not seen it." Again he cupped her jaw, and the feel of his calloused hands against her skin gave her an unexpected shiver. "You should know I've grown fond of it and will do my best to find it more often."

"Mama." Carol stepped out onto the porch. "What's *he* doing here, and why's he standing so close to you?"

"I *told* you he was courting her," Maggie said.

"What's courting?" Tess called from somewhere inside.

Micah seemed to be deliberately standing his ground, for he didn't move even when Carol tugged on Ruby's sleeve. "Come inside," she said. "We're hungry."

"Girls," Micah said, "your mother and I aren't finished with our conversation, but we will be in just a minute or two. Why don't you wait inside?"

"But I—"

"Carol," Micah said, "you'll go inside now."

Ruby looked up in surprise but saw no anger on his face. "Listen to Micah," she said. "And after breakfast, we have a surprise for you."

His nod was almost imperceptible; his smile was not. "You're sure that's how you want to tell them?"

"I am," she said, "but I have a question. How'd you know that was Carol? The girls are identical, and Tess and I seem to be the only ones who can tell them apart."

Micah winked. "I guessed. Now let's go in and—"

"No. Not yet." Her smile faded. "Walk with me. Please."

"What of their breakfast?"

Ruby nodded. "Then give me just a minute."

It took her almost five, but Micah waited with all the patience of a man who would take a wife before sunset. When Ruby returned, she offered no explanation, only a gesture toward the front gate.

"After you," he said as he trotted along behind her. "I'm at your command."

She turned to face him, one hand on the gate. "I'm not much of a commander," she said.

He looked down at a face he knew he'd die for and grinned as he touched the tip of her nose. "Well then," he said as he reached beyond her to brush the small of her back as he opened the gate. "I think we're going to get along fine, because I am."

"You're what?" Her tone was part teasing, part taunting.

"I'm a man who is comfortable leading, Ruby. You'll not have to worry for anything."

Was that relief or concern in her eyes? Before he could decide, she turned and headed down the road, leaving him to follow.

He did so at a leisurely pace, for the view was not altogether unpleasant.

"And tonight she'll be my wife," he whispered as his pulse quickened.

She turned the corner at Main and glanced back to see if he still followed. That was when he saw the look on her face. His heart sank.

CHAPTER 23

With that one look, Micah developed a nasty suspicion things were about to go terribly wrong. Ruby certainly hadn't seemed tense when she gave the older girls their instructions for what to do until they returned, nor did she have that look on her face when she teased him at the gate.

Having left the main road to start up the footpath to the beach, however, Ruby's back had gone straight, and her arms were crossed over her chest. She'd not said a word, though he figured it was contemplation and not something else keeping her silent.

Now with the trade wind blowing her hair and dusting their clothes with fine white sand, Ruby O'Shea looked as though she were marching to her death.

Micah judged the distance to the beach and thought to try to lighten her mood with a joke but could come up with nothing suitable to say. Instead, he matched his pace to hers and tried to block the wind as much as possible.

It seemed as though she might walk the entire circumference of the island, for they'd certainly trudged down the half of it before she abruptly stopped and began to remove her shoes. While Micah watched, she rolled down her stockings and set them aside, too.

A brazen thing to do, yet he was to be her husband soon. Then, without sparing him a glance, she lifted her skirts above the lapping waves and walked into the surf.

Now *that* was truly beyond the pale. "Ruby, what in the world are you doing?"

She ignored him.

"Come back here," he called as she showed no signs of slowing, though the water reached nearly to her knees.

Were he not about to meet her at the altar, Micah might have wondered about the propriety of a man who would be standing in the pulpit on Sunday now standing at the water's edge watching a half-deranged woman soak her skirts. Yet something about the way she moved through the surf, the way she stared at the horizon, beckoned him to join her.

He shouldn't, of course, for who knew who might find them?

Yet his fingers moved of their own accord to toss aside his jacket, to remove his boots and roll up his trouser legs. Still, he stood at the water's edge, hoping Ruby would come to her senses and remember she did not dance in the ocean unwatched.

At least it appeared she was dancing. It started with a leap over a wave; then when she landed, she leapt again. By the time Micah reached Ruby, she'd begun to twirl, her blue dress circling her exposed knees and her hair loose and flowing about her shoulders.

Micah caught her and whisked her into his arms, ignoring her protest. "What's gotten into you?" he demanded. "You're acting like—"

"A lunatic?" She met his stare then turned her face to the sun, her eyes falling shut.

"What? No." He struggled to think even as he worked hard to keep both of them upright in the surf and as he took in every curve and line of her face. Of cheeks burnished by the sun and shoulders that bore much more responsibility than they should.

If the fool who left her to raise those girls alone wasn't already dead, Micah knew he could easily dispatch him.

A wave slammed his back, and Micah stumbled then righted himself. Ruby curled toward him and rested her head against his chest. "But I am, Micah. That's what I've tried to tell you. Now you've seen it for yourself."

His mind raced as he reached damp but firm sand. What sins could this innocent possibly have committed?

When he said nothing, Ruby slid from his grasp and ran back into the water. "Enough, Ruby," he said as he shielded his eyes against the sun. "You've made your point; now come out of the water before we both miss the wedding."

She turned but said nothing. Nor did she move or even bother to hold her skirts above the tide. He took a step toward her, and Ruby moved back. With each movement in her direction, she took another away.

Finally, his temper flared. "I find no humor in this," he said.

"Nor I, Micah." Ruby turned her back on him, further fueling his irritation. "Aren't you curious about my life before I came to the key?"

He was. "It doesn't matter." Not completely the truth, but it would become so with time. And with prayer.

"And the girls." She continued to walk away, making her voice reed thin on the wind. "Aren't you curious about their father?"

"I'll admit I am." He paused and prayed for the right words. "But I assume he is no longer a factor in their lives. And so I will endeavor to treat them as if they were my own."

When she didn't answer, he decided to take action. Nothing good could come from this conversation. "Come out of the water this instant," he said, "or I'll—"

"You'll what?" She glanced at him over her shoulder, swiping a curtain of damp red hair from her face to stare in his direction.

"I'll show you what," he said as he stormed across the sand, intent on hauling his bride-to-be back onshore and into the nearest church so he could marry her before he, too, lost his mind.

The response seemed to be the one she sought, for Ruby froze.

Rather than fear, Micah saw. . .what? It certainly wasn't surprise.

He sloshed toward her, heedless of where the waves hit him until he came close enough to speak to her without raising his voice. What he would say did not require much speaking.

"You were trying to provoke me." Not a question, so no answer was required.

Nor was it needed.

Right there in the surf, he knelt before her. A wave slammed him in the chest and washed across his face. He ignored it, spitting salt water until the words would come again.

"What will it take for me to make you understand that I don't want to hear about your past? I don't need to."

She continued to look doubtful even as a wall of water washed over him and sent him spinning facedown onto the ocean floor. Micah sputtered to the surface, but not before he spied something he felt was truly a sign from God.

"Look here, Ruby," he said as he lifted the sand dollar in her direction. "A wedding gift."

Just when he didn't think Ruby would accept it, she did. Still, she remained silent.

"Call yourself what you want, Ruby O'Shea." He had to pause until another wave passed. "Dance in the waves or in the middle of downtown in your wet skirts. I truly don't care. My job is to protect you and those three girls, and that's what I'm going to do. Now let's go back to the boardinghouse. I warrant by the time we return, your assistants in this endeavor will have arrived."

"Assistants?" She reached for his hand, still clutching the sand dollar in the other. "What plans have you made?"

Micah shrugged. "Not many." Another wave, this one sending salt water over his head and into his eyes. He bobbed to the surface, weary of the beating from the waves but reluctant to move from a position that seemed to be working.

"I only spoke to the reverend briefly." He entwined his fingers with hers. "But his wife did mention she would see to outfitting the bride properly."

Outfitting the bride? Ruby felt a wave lift her feet then set them back again. Poor Micah was practically drowning in that ridiculous position.

"Get up, please," she said, "and tell me exactly what that means."

"I know it's. . ." He sputtered as a swell caused him to swallow seawater. "It's customary for the bride to pick out her attire, but in the interest of time, I made the decision for you."

"*You* chose my wedding dress?"

"Not exactly. Viola offered, and I—"

She shook her head. "Slow down. You said you only spoke to Rev. Carter. How does Viola Dumont figure into this?"

"Didn't I mention she was at the Carter home when I arrived? As were Emilie and Isabelle. Seems as though I chose quilting night to make my announcement."

"Wonderful." She turned her back on a wave and let it crash against her. "I suppose they found it odd that you would be making this announcement without me."

"No, actually," he said. "I explained that your duties at the boardinghouse kept you from joining me, which was the truth."

It was. She had to give him credit for that much.

"And I mentioned my concern at your not having a mother to guide you in the process of preparing for a wedding. That's when the ladies offered to step in and help." He paused. "They really like you, Ruby, and I'm not sure you know that."

"Well, of course I do," she said, though she'd have been hard-pressed to say for sure. "I suppose I wouldn't have thought to ask for help." Mainly because she hadn't completely settled in her mind the reality of the situation. That, and the fact that after she was done with him this morning, Micah Tate might very well change his mind.

His expression showed he was ready for a change in topic. Still, she had to ask one more thing. "Did you tell them?"

"Tell them?"

Ruby licked the salt from her lips. "About why you're marrying me?"

"They didn't ask. I suppose they thought the reason was obvious. That we are in love," he added with some measure of haste.

"But we're not," she said, "and a woman knows."

"I guarantee these did not. Why, they were planning and plotting as much as they were whooping and cheering." Micah moved closer but remained a safe distance away. "It's not how many would start a life together, but I'm bound and determined to keep my promise to take care of you and the girls."

"I believe you, but why?" She released his hand and backed away, the desire to run bearing down on her. "Why would a perfectly nice single man just up and decide to take on the care of a woman and three girls he barely knows? It's not normal, Micah." Ruby shook the sand dollar at him. "And don't tell me God said. I just won't believe it."

"At least you admit I'm perfectly nice." He rose but remained rooted in place as she continued to back away. "Ruby, I'm not going to try to explain it. I can't. Not yet. I just know you're my second chance, and I'm not going to let this second chance get away."

"Second chance?" That was something she hadn't considered. Certainly a man couldn't reach Micah's age and not have some sort of past that included a woman or, more likely, women. The men she'd known surely hadn't escaped that.

But a second chance at something? And did she want to know what that something was?

Ruby allowed the waves to propel her toward the shore, and when the water fell behind her, she collapsed onto the sand. This game, and it felt very much like a game, had become all too real.

Chapter 24

Indeed, Micah Tate was responsible for chasing away the one man who'd protected Ruby from Thomas Hawkins, both before and after the shipwreck that led her to Fairweather Key. The arrangement Ruby had made with Jean Luc had been simple if not fraught with troublesome guilt, especially since her meeting with Jesus at the altar of Rev. Carter's church some weeks past.

Since that day, she'd come to understand that many things from her old life would not work in her new one. She'd decided to pray away the specter of the smuggler Rabelais, figuring God wouldn't allow him to return to the key as long as she continued to petition Him. How wrong she'd been.

Now her mistake, and the result of it, lay before her in the form of a marriage to a man she barely knew.

The object of her thoughts hauled his soaking self up beside her and flopped onto the sand. "Ruby, I'm not a man given to thinking about how marriage proposals and weddings are done, but I've got to tell you. . ." He paused to swipe a mixture of sand and seawater from his eyes. "This isn't how I figured to do it." Another swipe. "No offense, of course."

Ruby glanced at him. "None taken."

For a moment they sat in silence. Fishing vessels dotted the waters where the depth dropped off, and gulls swooped and circled each. The sun rode just above the water line. Midday would come soon. The girls would be wondering where she'd gone off to, and the boarders would be wanting their next meal in a few hours.

Still, she sat with the sun baking her skin and drying the fabric of her dress into a wrinkled sandy mess. Ruby leaned forward and brushed back her hair, which she only now realized had come loose.

What a heathen she must look to the pastor-to-be. But then, that had been the point, hadn't it? If Micah Tate wouldn't listen to her past, the least she could do was give him a glimpse at what could be his future.

She exhaled, letting the air out of her lungs and, along with it, the last of her pride. Or was she merely trying to rid herself of the one man who'd treated her well and offered her nothing but his protection and his good name?

Ruby watched the horizon, where an unfamiliar vessel, a brig it seemed, unfurled its sails to skirt around the far reaches of the reef.

She knew this part of the ocean for the dangers it brought. An accidental zig to the left or zag to the right, or even an unexpected wind, and a ship could be blown off course and into rocks so jagged they could slice right through the strongest of hulls.

And the sound—it defied description. Even now, she could hear wood scraping, giving way under the razor-sharp coral. Could hear men shouting, screaming, crying. . .or had that been the sound of a ship giving way unto itself? Ruby could never be sure.

This vessel slid over the horizon unscathed, and Ruby let out another long breath.

"You're quiet for a woman." He winked—or perhaps he had more sand in his eye. "I like that about you."

Ruby elbowed him but said nothing.

"Thank you for proving my point."

"So as long as I don't talk much, you're happy? No wonder you don't mind a wife dancing in the waves and carrying on like a fool."

"Actually, I sort of liked that." His grin broadened. "You're an interesting woman, Ruby."

If you only knew.

Micah rolled onto his side, seemingly heedless of the sand clinging to him. Coffee-colored eyes searched her face as his hand reached out to cover hers. "I know you don't completely understand why I'm doing this. Marrying you, I mean."

The words poured forth. "I don't, Micah. It just doesn't make a lot of sense. Unless you feel guilty for—"

"Guilt? No." He shook his head. "I've an obligation to you, that's for sure, but it's more than that."

"I still don't understand."

He looked away. "No, I don't reckon you do. Maybe someday I'll tell you all of it, but today all you need to know is that sometimes we get second chances, and there's not a doubt in my mind that you and the girls are my second chance."

At what? she longed to ask. Yet Ruby didn't dare lest she give up being curious as to why he married her in favor of spending a lifetime disappointed at the truth.

Another look, another sigh. She could do worse than spending her life with Micah Tate. He was easy on the eye, easy to talk to—or remain silent with. He'd certainly proven himself capable of handling his anger when she purposely provoked him in the water.

She allowed herself to wonder for a moment what her sister, Opal, might have thought of this deliberate deception Ruby was allowing to continue. Likely she'd say that no matter where they hid, Tommy would not be far behind. And when he found them, the girls would once again be in want of a mother.

Better to stand behind a man who'd pledged to fight for her than to stand alone and lose everything. Or to allow herself to fall into the arms of a man like Remy Dumont, who promised nothing other than an afternoon's dalliance and, likely, a broken heart.

Micah patted her hand then stood. His look told her he'd decided their conversation was done. For her part, Ruby had all but forgotten what they had been discussing.

"I'm talking myself into this," she whispered as she watched him walk to the water's edge and make an attempt to rid his soggy trousers of sand. It was a poor attempt, though the wrecker gave it a good try. Finally, he shrugged and came back to flop down beside her.

"I've been thinking about something else," he said as he rolled onto his stomach. "I've got another reason to marry up with you, and

I'm going to admit to you and the Lord right now that it's a selfish one." He leaned in to touch her hair then wrapped a strand around his finger. "Ruby," he said slowly, his attention focused on the coil of hair in his hand, "you write a better sermon than me. So there." His gaze collided with hers. "I'm not proud of it, but that's the truth."

She started to giggle. The thought of her—uneducated and uninformed about most things outside of baking biscuits and making gravy—competing in any way with a man of Micah Tate's intelligence was beyond silly.

Yet she loved the idea of it.

Her giggle became a laugh as Micah pretended outrage. "I'll not have you making light of this serious problem," he said in a grave tone, though the twinkle in his eye dispelled any ideas Ruby might have about whether he was teasing. "Can you imagine how it will look if the news gets around town that Micah Tate cannot write a sermon without his wife? And what if I was forced to attempt it alone?"

"I doubt that will happen, Micah," she said through her grin.

"You'd better believe it won't." He sat up, the sand once again clinging in sheets to his shirt and skin. "That's why I have to marry up with you. It'll keep you where I can find you."

She studied the mess that was his shirt and trousers for a moment, then shook her head. "No, I think you're just looking for someone to wash your clothes."

Micah laughed and shook a bit of grit in her direction, and she squealed as she scooted away. He made a slow grab for her that included a full roll sideways until he reached her and wrapped his sand-caked arm across her waist.

"Stop that," Ruby managed through her laughter as she scrambled to her feet. "You're completely uncontrollable."

Micah looked up, his face a mask of innocence and guilt. "Not completely, Ruby." Ruby noticed that lest he allow her to think he might have gone serious, the wrecker winked. "Were that the case, I'd have hauled you up and dunked you in the surf for frightening me."

"Well, at least that's something we can give thanks for."

She glanced at the sun and cringed. Surely her return was long overdue, a concern she'd have to address with the girls. And then

KATHLEEN Y'BARBO

there was the condition of her clothing. Ruby looked down at the soggy mess that was her blue frock. How would she manage a walk through town without becoming the source of speculation?

She gave Micah an accusing look before doing her best to attack the clumps of sand weighing down her skirt.

"You started it, Ruby," he said, "by dancing in the surf. So you must admit your wet clothing is completely your responsibility."

"True," Ruby responded, "though the worst of this sand is your responsibility."

Micah drew near, suddenly intent on inspecting the damage done to her favorite frock. He shook his head. "Doesn't appear to be anything a good washing won't take out. Here, let me see if I can help."

"Really, it's not—"

"Let me help you."

The horizon tilted as Micah lifted her over his shoulder and bounded toward the surf.

CHAPTER 25

"Put. Me. Down."

"Hold your breath, Ruby. Here comes a big one." Micah held her at arm's length and waited until the wave hit to dunk her. She came up sputtering as he set her on her feet, holding tight to her arms to keep her from bobbing backward. "There," he said as he pointed to her frock. "No more sand."

Ruby tried to be angry. She truly did. As she pulled away the tangled curtain of her matted hair, she even managed to frown. Then she looked up into eyes that searched her face, seemingly wondering if he'd pushed his joke too far.

How simple it would be to allow him to believe he hadn't just endeared himself to her with his humor. She might have, had her grin not gotten the best of her.

It began as a smile that touched the corners of her lips and caused them to quiver. Then came the giggle, bubbling up from a place she'd forgotten existed after all these years.

Micah released her to duck beneath the water then in one fluid motion pop up from the waves like a fish. He caught her laughing and seemed to be taken aback.

"Why are you staring at me?" she managed. "Haven't you ever seen a woman amused at a foolish man?"

He disappeared beneath the next wave, and when he emerged from the water, he'd come near enough to wrap both hands around her waist. "Ruby," he said, "if you'll promise to laugh like that at least once a day, I'll promise to stay foolish the rest of our lives."

She pretended to think about it as Micah inched closer. A wave pushed her forward into Micah, but strong hands kept her above the surface.

"Ruby," he said as he righted her, "either we have to get out of the water, or I'm going to have to kiss you."

Rather than respond, she stood on her toes and, with the next wave, aimed for his lips. Embarrassment at her boldness didn't occur until after she ended the kiss.

"I don't know why I did that," she said softly.

"I suppose now would be the time," Micah said, his lips now touching her cheek, "to remind you that you may have done that because tonight I'm to become your husband."

Ruby sighed. "Perhaps," was all she could manage as Micah laced his fingers with hers and led her out of the water. At the shoreline, he retrieved her shoes and stockings along with his own and folded the jacket he'd shed around them.

"Follow me, and I'll get you back to the boardinghouse without walking through the middle of town," he said as he stepped across the sand on bare feet then turned to head up a hill that led to the bluff above the ocean, his bundle thrown across his shoulder. From there he pointed west, and Ruby followed. "Up there is my home," he said as he pointed to a modest structure a distance away.

She recognized the place. "It must have a lovely view," she said.

"It does," he cast over his shoulder as he cleared the path of a fallen limb. "I'm afraid there's not much inside to recommend it, but I tend to forget once I stand on the edge and look out at the water. It's almost like being aboard ship."

"Sounds wonderful."

"I suppose, though all I've managed to furnish it with is a bed and a few dishes. Until now, that's all I needed."

"About that." Ruby braved a look up at Micah. "We've not discussed where we would live. I assumed the boardinghouse since I am obligated to Mrs. Campbell to run it until her return."

He seemed to consider the statement. "I agree you've got an

obligation, but no wife of mine's going to be working like you do longer than I can help it. Mrs. Campbell will have to hire someone to replace you, though she'd likely do better hiring two for as much work as you do."

Micah stepped ahead to push back a tangle of brush so Ruby could pass. They walked in silence for a few minutes.

"Here's what we'll do," Micah said. "I'll write to the Campbells and let them know they will need to either return or find your replacement soon. Once the babies start coming, it wouldn't be healthy for you to exhaust yourself the way you do."

The babies? Ruby suppressed a sigh. Indeed, the wrecker was getting a bit ahead of himself, though she had to applaud his honesty in stating his expectations. At least she'd likely have no trouble discerning what he wanted.

"And until you're free to leave your work, I'll agree to move into the boardinghouse." He looked at her. "What sort of arrangements do you have?"

"Arrangements?"

Micah nodded. "Sleeping arrangements."

"Oh." She paused. "There are two bedchambers and a sitting room on the third floor at our disposal." Sensing her answer had been too sparse for him, Ruby continued. "Mrs. Campbell was kind enough to allow us to choose our furnishings from her husband's warehouse. It's rather amusing how fancy the items are that the girls chose."

When her companion glanced at her, she clamped her mouth shut. Surely Micah Tate had little care for the small details of the O'Shea women's world.

"Go on," he urged, and she nodded.

"Well, the twins—they share a bed—they're rather partial to fancy bed coverings and beds with tall posts and curtains around them, so that's what they chose." She paused to see if Micah still seemed interested. When she decided he did, she continued. "Tess, now she's not like the other two. Her only request was that her bed be high enough to have a step stool. You should see her climbing into that tall bed like she's the queen of England or something. Half the time she's got somebody's petticoat fastened around her so she's got the train and everything."

Micah laughed with her, and she relaxed. Perhaps her husband-to-be really did care for the mundane things of their lives.

"As I said, the space is quite generous. The sitting room looks out toward the west, so the light's good until late in the day." She paused to step over a low spot then continued. "I'm sure you'll find your bedchamber comfortable."

"Our bedchamber," he corrected.

"Yes, well." She bit her lip and watched a flock of orangequit rise above a stand of mango trees and take wing. "You see, Tess is just a baby, really."

"Ruby." The warning in his tone was unmistakable. "I understand there may be a period of difficulty until the sleeping arrangements are complete, but I would insist on two points. First, Tess is neither a baby nor incapable of sleeping in a room with her sisters and without her mother."

He looked to Ruby as if he expected her to protest. In truth, she welcomed a night without awakening to a tiny foot in the small of her back or, worse, pressed against her cheek.

"Agreed," she said, though how the good idea would become a reality was beyond her understanding.

"Second," he said, "despite my appearance as such, I am not a patient man. I will not spend our wedding night separated from my bride. I've mentioned it before, but I will repeat that I think it's in the best interest of both of us to send the girls off to stay with Mary and Hezekiah for the evening."

She opened her mouth to protest then thought better of it. If Micah was to become her husband, the time for bowing to his reasonable requests was now. Much as she wished for another solution, this was a reasonable request.

"Agreed," she said, though she knew the separation would be much harder on her than it would be on the girls.

"And lest you think me heartless or believe me to be compromising my promise of safety for the four of you," he said, "I've made arrangements for two members of the militia to be at the Carters during our absence. A third will stay at the boardinghouse."

Ruby let out a long breath. It was more than she could have asked for, yet Micah had thought of the plan before she had. "Thank you," she managed to say as she turned to look back over her shoulder at the ocean.

"I'm to warn you that the Gayarre sisters along with Miss Dumont are more than excited about assisting you with whatever it is women do before they marry. At least that's the message Mary Carter asked me to give you." He gave her a hopeless look. "I won't even guess what that means, but I do know it will be happening around two this afternoon. The wedding is at seven."

She smiled. Having women friends was a new experience, one that made the loss of Opal all the more bittersweet.

Micah stopped and gestured to a tree trunk near the juncture where the footpath met the road to town. "We'll continue on this same path, but as the captain of the militia, I'd rather not be caught barefoot by some citizen out for a stroll."

Ruby looked down at the dress that had already begun to dry in the morning sunshine. Micah looked no worse for wear, though his trousers hung at the knees and bore wrinkles and spots of sand all the way to his toes. His linen shirt was ruined, though a good washing might make it serviceable again.

Her eyebrows rose. "I'm not sure our bare feet will be the first thing noticed."

"I'll not disagree. Sit there," he said, and she complied, observing him as she did her best to braid her hair back into submission.

While she watched, the wrecker set his jacket on the ground and opened the knot he'd tied. He retrieved one of her stockings then slipped it over her foot. Gently he slid it above her ankle then paused to look up at her. Without words, he told her his restraint was not easy.

"Perhaps I should don the other on my own."

"Perhaps," he said, though his voice sounded strained.

She slipped the stocking over her foot then adjusted her wet skirts to cover her legs. "There," she said when she'd sufficiently righted herself.

Micah lifted her shoe from the bundle and pointed to her foot. "Right foot," he said then laughed when she complained. "All right. I suppose you'll want to do this, too."

She nodded and quickly stuffed her wet and sandy foot into her shoe, all the while trying to tame her suddenly shaking hands. Somehow she managed the feat then allowed Micah to help her stand.

His hand continued to grasp hers. "Ruby." Micah spoke her name so softly that it almost disappeared on the wind. "There's much you don't know or understand about me, and I know that. By my choice, the same can be said for what I know about you." His gaze shifted past her. "It's enough for me. I've only one thing more I'd like you to know: This time, I won't fail."

CHAPTER 26

*T*his time."

Two words that taunted Micah all the way back to the boat, where he left his boots on the deck then jumped into the water fully dressed. Unlike his swim with Ruby, slipping under the lapping waters of the bay offered a few seconds of peace and quiet.

Holding his breath, Micah opened his eyes and waited for the familiar sting of the salt water to subside. A shaft of sunlight pierced the murky water and illuminated a pair of tussling lobsters on the ocean floor. Any other day, he'd have dived down and brought up dinner.

Tonight, however, he'd not need the feast, though he could certainly offer them to the Carters for the favors they'd be performing. Using a skill that had filled his hungry belly more times than he could count, Micah made short work of tossing both of the combatants onto the deck of his ship, where he'd tend to them once he finished his swim. Without much effort, he found two more and added them to the pair, who now seemed more intent on exploring than escaping.

Dropping back into the water, he kicked off the hull and propelled himself a decent measure away from the vessel. A sail off to the south caught his attention. Though he rarely judged these things from water level, it appeared the ship was sailing dangerously close to the reef.

Watching a moment longer, Micah decided the angle at which he viewed the sail seemed to be the reason. With the weather as fine as it was today, any decent sailor captaining a vessel in these waters would know the dangers and steer clear.

Micah gave the vessel one last look then turned to float on his back. Above him, the Lord had set the slightest wisp of cotton clouds against a sky so blue it hurt to look at it.

Blue as Ruby's eyes.

Not since he mistook his friendship with Emilie for something more had he paid such close attention to a woman. Always he'd been too busy to concern himself with the confusing process of wooing a woman.

His thoughts tumbled back to Caroline. She had required little of him, and sadly, he'd obliged her by spending too many hours planting and plowing only to return with just enough energy to eat and fall into a sleep that seemed to last only minutes. Then he got up and did it all over again. Just as his pa had done, and likely his pa's pa.

Even when Caroline begged him to stay, he chose his allegiance to Texas over allegiance to her. "I promise, Lord," he whispered. "Not this time."

Micah rolled onto his belly and ducked beneath the surface, then rose up to commence floating on his back once again. The move did nothing to change the direction of his thoughts, though it did cause his eyes to sting again.

Or were those tears?

He shook off the foolish notion and tugged at his water-soaked trousers. With the sun full overhead, his belly complained. Only then did he realize he'd eaten little of what Ruby had brought to him for breakfast.

She was a fine woman, that Ruby O'Shea. He smiled to think of the gift that was even now likely being delivered. That the book he'd ordered would arrive the day before his wedding was something only the Lord could have managed. Since the day he first laid eyes on her, he'd thought of the verse in Proverbs that he'd written inside the cover last night while lying on the porch.

"Her price is far above rubies. The heart of her husband doth safely trust in her. . . ."

Indeed, Ruby O'Shea was a woman in whom he could safely trust.

And in a few hours, he'd promise before God to be a husband she, too, could safely trust.

But first he had to try to make himself presentable.

Closing the distance to the boat, Micah shed his gritty shirt. Then, while he treaded water, he did his best to wash away the sand that remained. This accomplished, he tossed the shirt onto the deck and went about the business of trying to clean his trousers without removing them.

"Ahoy, Tate. Where are you?" Josiah Carter called.

Micah lifted himself up over the side and landed on the deck. "Took a bath," he said as he shook the water out of his hair then reached for his shirt to begin wringing it out. "And did my laundry, too."

Josiah shook his head. "Things are about to change, sailor," he said. "Starting with proper baths and cleaner clothes."

A lobster scampered toward his bare foot, and Micah swatted at it with his shirt. "All well worth the home cooking and soft bed." He swung his attention to his best friend. "What brings you here today?"

The wrecker grinned. "Your wedding."

"Is that so?" Micah slung the wet shirt over his shoulder and gestured for Josiah to follow him into the cabin. While Josiah sat, Micah found the last of the jerky and offered a portion of it to his friend.

"There'll be no more of this, either," Micah said. "So I warrant I'll not be disappointed in the things I have to give up. Ruby's cooking is worth the sacrifice."

"So it's her cooking that's got you marrying her so quickly." Josiah stared intently. "I wondered."

Something in his expression seemed wrong. "You've known me too long to keep a concern from me, Carter. Out with it."

Josiah shifted positions and bit off a piece of jerky.

"I'll wait," Micah said as he took his own bite of the nearly vile meal. As he chewed, he tried not to think of what the diners up at the boardinghouse were eating. *Something much better than this, no doubt.*

"All right," Josiah finally said. "I'll not tell you this is a marriage that seems hasty, but I will ask you whether you're sure what you'll be vowing this evening is something you can promise."

"Meaning?" Micah asked as he took another bite.

"Meaning I wonder if you're not. . ." He paused. "I know you fancied Emilie, and what with Caleb now married to her, I've got to wonder if Ruby might be. . ." The wrecker seemed to run out of words.

"Be?" Micah felt his ire rising, but he took a deep breath and tried to ignore it. This was, after all, his best friend, a man who would tell him the truth when no one else would.

Josiah gave up all pretense of eating the jerky and tossed the remainder of it in Micah's direction. "Did you make this? It's awful." His stare must have worked, for Josiah shook his head. "I'm not a man to talk all around a subject."

"I respect you for that," Micah said as he added Josiah's portion of jerky to his own then leaned back and stretched out his legs as he shook more water from his hair. "So go to it. Whatever you've come to say, say it."

"I'm concerned that Ruby is just a substitute for Emilie." He, too, leaned back in his chair. "There, I said it. Now go ahead and hit me if you feel so compelled."

Micah did, though he'd not act on the impulse just yet. "Why?" he managed to ask through clenched jaw.

"It's just that. . .well, how well do you know the woman? I mean, she and those fair-haired girls washed up on the island without any history at all, and far as I know, no one's asked them about it." Josiah paused. "You were there, Micah. You saw the remains of that vessel we pulled them from. It belonged to Hawkins and had so much loot in the hold that the criminal was using gold and silver as ballast."

"Agreed," Micah said. "But that proves nothing save the fact that Ruby and the girls were fortunate to have been rescued. I don't even want to think of what they were made to endure."

"That's the problem, Tate. You don't want to think." Josiah gave him an even stare. "Think now." His voice raised a notch. "You were there. You pulled her off that ship and handed her to me to carry back to my boat. Did she look like she was being held prisoner?"

A black anger rose as his fists clenched beneath the table. Saying nothing felt preferable to the foul words Micah longed to unleash on his friend.

"You don't remember, do you?"

Again Micah said nothing.

Josiah rose and moved toward the cabin door as if to check the weather or feign some interest in the goings-on out on the bay. When he turned, his face was hidden in shadows by the sun shining at his back.

"The explosion that broke your arm and sunk the *Caroline* stole your memory of that night, didn't it?"

Something he'd told no one. It seemed shameful that he'd lost time and could not account for it, an odd thought now that Josiah presented it as such. Slowly Micah nodded.

Josiah came to sit across from him again. "Nothing about that night remains?" he asked as he pointed to Micah's forehead.

"Nothing after the call of wreck ashore," he admitted. "The next memory is of Doc Hill patching me up by wrenching my arm back into place. Told me I'd likely never remember what happened." Micah's laughter held no humor. "Would that I could remember what I've forgotten."

"I'll help you, then. She and those girls were in a nicely appointed stateroom off the starboard bow." He paused. "Best I could tell, it was attached to the captain's quarters." Another pause. "The little one, Tess—she was calling for her papa."

Micah rested his elbows on his knees and cradled his head in his hands. The implications were obvious. "So you think she was Hawkins's woman."

A statement, not a question. It was obvious he did, but Micah wanted him to admit it.

Josiah slammed his palms on the table. "She's a redhead, Micah, and those girls have blond hair. I've seen Hawkins, and so have you."

Micah looked up. "That means nothing. Hair color changes with age. Half the children in the key are fair-haired."

"And the fact that Hawkins protected them?"

Numb, Micah rose and stumbled toward his sea chest and opened it. "I need your help," he said. "You're my second in command. Go and pick three good men. Men who can be trusted to keep their silence. Offer them a fair wage for an afternoon's work and bring them to the back gate of the boardinghouse in half an hour. Can you do that?"

" 'Course I can, but do you mind if I ask why?"

Micah heard the scrape of a chair that indicated Josiah was on his feet. Meanwhile, he reached beneath the ragged quilt he'd slept under as a child to find the only decent set of clothes he had left—his militia uniform.

While he'd intended to marry in it, wearing the uniform for this purpose would have to do. The more he thought on it, it seemed only right. He found his comb and yanked it through his wet hair.

The verse that had only hours ago given him comfort now rose in his mind to taunt him.

"For her price is far above rubies. The heart of her husband doth safely trust in her. . . . She will do him good and not evil all the days of her life."

Phrases that formed part of a whole. *Lord, show me the truth.*

"Micah?"

A piece of leather to tie his hair back, and Micah was ready to take a deep breath then answer the question. "I've a mind to see my bride," he said simply.

"Before the wedding?" Josiah came to stand beside him. "Are you serious? You can't do that."

Micah reached for a length of toweling and dried his chest and shoulders. "I can, and I will."

"With the militia?" Josiah shook his head. "Whatever you've got in mind, I won't be a part of it."

"Then why did you come here?" He pointed at his best friend. "To warn me that I might not be getting what I expected out of this marriage bargain?" When Josiah said nothing, Micah continued, his voice as calm as he could manage. "What did you think I would do?"

"Get angry, maybe, but call out the militia? That I hadn't expected." He touched Micah's arm, and it was all Micah could do not to pull away. "Maybe postponing the wedding is what needs to happen."

"Postpone until when? I intend to get to the bottom of this mystery right now." He looked down at his water-soaked trousers then back at Josiah. "In a half hour, that is. Now find these men, and meet me at the boardinghouse's back gate."

"Why not go alone?"

"Think about it," Micah said. "If you're right and she's in league with the smugglers, they may have been watching since the day I chased off the Frenchman."

The wrecker took a step back and crossed his arms over his chest. "What Frenchman?"

Micah waved away the question. "I'll need a man each for the front and back gates and one for the back porch. Since the front door is close to the gate, that will be under the watch of the man at the front gate."

Josiah nodded. "What about me?"

"You'll be stationed on the stairs. No one goes up or down until I am satisfied of the answers I get from Ruby."

"But my mother's there. What if she wants to pass?"

Micah gave Josiah a less-than-patient look. "Find the men, please. Time's wasting."

Josiah disappeared around the corner only to shout Micah's name.

When he stepped onto the deck, he found the wrecker with a lobster attached to his finger. "What are you doing?"

"Get this thing off me," he said. "I saw it skulking about and thought to throw it into the bucket."

"You're supposed to pick it up by the middle, not by the tail." Micah tried not to laugh but failed miserably as he removed the crustacean and dumped it into the bucket. "Best meet me in an hour instead."

"Why?" Josiah asked as he shook his injured finger.

"I've got three more of these to catch and I should probably inform Caleb of this field exercise of ours."

"Oh, it's a field exercise now?"

"Yes," Micah said, "and unless I've missed my guess, getting past Viola and the Gayarre sisters will be much more difficult than any battle either of us has fought."

CHAPTER 27

*T*his time."

Two words that haunted Ruby all the way up the back stairs at the boardinghouse as she held her skirts just high enough to keep the floor from being dusted with sand. Even with the precaution, Ruby got to the top of the stairs and saw to her dismay she'd left a trail behind her. Worse, while she hoped the girls might not be waiting for her, she walked into the sitting room to find all three sitting happily on the floor with Mary Carter and Viola Dumont, having what looked to be a tea party.

"Oh," Ruby said, "I thought you'd be here this afternoon."

Viola rose while the elderly Mrs. Carter merely smiled and continued to sip what was surely water from one of Tess's tiny teacups. "I hope you don't mind," she said, "but once I heard the news, I decided to come on over this morning. The Gayarre sisters still plan to keep their appointment this afternoon, but I couldn't wait." She grinned. "I thought perhaps you might be in need of. . ." She glanced down at the girls then back up at Ruby. "Why don't I just show you?"

Thankfully, Viola said nothing of the disheveled way Ruby looked. She'd begun to think the damage her morning escapade had done was not nearly as visible as she thought. Then she heard Tess's sweet voice follow them into her bedchamber.

"What happened to my mama? She's a mess."

Ruby glanced over her shoulder, her mind ticking through any number of possible responses that might be understandable to a child. All three girls were staring, which made the thinking even harder.

"It's quite windy this morning," Mrs. Carter said as she winked at Ruby. "Likely her morning errands took her too near the water, the poor dear."

"Yes," Maggie said. "I'm sure that's it exactly. Now have another sip of tea, Tess."

"She was with that *man*." Carol shot Ruby an angry glance. "I don't think I like him."

Viola tugged Ruby into the bedchamber and closed the door. "Best you let Mrs. Carter handle this conversation," she said. "I'm sure she'll be able to speak to them with a bit less passion than you might."

Passion. An interesting word choice. Ruby had wavered between anger and guilt but would have called neither emotion passion.

"I hope you don't mind," Viola said as she walked toward the armoire. "I've taken the liberty of bringing you something for tonight. I'll understand if you don't want to. . ." The midwife shook her head. "Let me just show you."

She opened the door to reveal a lovely gown hung between Ruby's two other dresses: the sum total of her wardrobe. *A pale flower among common onions, for sure,* came the silly thought as Ruby watched Viola retrieve the pale blue garment and spread it across the bed.

Ruby gasped. "This," she managed when her voice returned, "is the most beautiful dress I've ever seen." She took a step back and shook her head. "I can't wear it," she told Viola. "It's too beautiful. Just far too beautiful."

Viola studied the gown a moment then reached over to run her hand over what appeared to be real pearls sewn into the bodice. For a second, her expression changed. Just as quickly, her smile returned.

"No, I insist." She paused. "It would mean very much to me if this dress was finally used for its intended purpose."

"I can't possibly try that beautiful gown on in this state." Ruby looked down at the dress then back at Viola. "I'm sure you're wondering how I managed to get myself into this condition."

"A better woman would say no." Viola grinned and flopped onto the bed beside the dress. "But I'm not a better woman. What in the world did you do? Decide to go swimming in your clothes?"

"Actually. . ." Ruby met Viola's astonished gaze.

"Ruby? You did?" Her laughter was contagious. "What came over you?"

As she considered the question, Ruby tried to decide how to explain the answer. "I think it might have been a test," she finally said.

"For you or for Micah?" She pointed a finger at Ruby. "Don't look so surprised. I saw the two of you walking down the street this morning."

"For both of us."

"I would ask if you passed, but I fear it's none of my business." Viola scooped the dress into her arms. "Go and get yourself cleaned up," she said. "We've got work to do." She reached for the knob then seemed to think better of it. "I'm going to hate myself if I don't ask. Did he pass the test?"

"Yes," Ruby said as she felt a blush slide up her neck. "Yes, he did. Now if I'm going to have the boarders fed on time, I'll need to wash this sand off and do something with the mess I've made of this dress."

"Don't you worry about feeding those boarders," Viola said. "I'll manage it. You get yourself cleaned up and put the dress on. Call me when you're ready to have the dress fitted."

As she heard the doorknob click, Ruby began to shed her wet things. The basin of water was a poor substitute for a true scrubbing, but she managed. Though she still felt as if she wore a layer of sand on her skin, Ruby finally gave up and set the towel aside, then slipped into her chemise.

She gathered up her soiled clothing and felt something land on her foot. Looking down, Ruby spied the sand dollar Micah had given her that morning. Sinking to the bed, she held the cool shell to her cheek as she closed her eyes.

"Opal, I miss you," she whispered. "But I'll not let anything happen. I promise."

"Ruby, are you ready?" Viola called.

"I fear I'll need help," she said as she glanced at the mantel clock then opened the door. "I've never worn anything so beautiful. I don't know where to start."

Viola set a bag on the edge of the bed. "Before you can don the dress, you've got to start with the underpinnings—else it won't lie right."

Five petticoats of different varieties, a dress improver tied at the waist and properly fluffed at the back, and a snugly laced corset later, Viola finally reached for the gown and helped Ruby into it. While the back was being fastened, Ruby sneaked a peek of herself in the mirror.

Beyond the hair that had yet to be tamed, she looked like someone else. From the wide sleeves to the waistline that would soon be tucked to fit her, the dress was the height of elegance.

Ruby sighed. She looked like quality. In all her imaginings of what the Lord had done to her heart, she'd sometimes wondered what she would look like on the outside if that were to show through.

Now she knew.

Viola stepped away and gave her an appraising look. "What do you think?"

"It's. . .it's. . ." Ruby stopped trying to speak and turned to hug her friend.

"It is, isn't it?" Viola adjusted the ribbons at the shoulders then turned Ruby around to face the mirror once again. "I think just a nip and a tuck and this will fit you beautifully. It won't take but a short while to have this dress ready to wear." She looked down at Ruby's feet. "Show me what you usually wear to parties and such."

Heat began to flood Ruby's cheeks as she looked away. "I've not been to a party," she mumbled. "So my boots are all I have."

Viola came to stand behind her once more. "Honey," she said, "don't cry. Isabelle has the most beautiful kid slippers, and I know she will be happy to pass them on to you."

"What? No." She shook her head to emphasize the point. "I couldn't possibly."

"Now that she's in her second confinement, she can no longer wear them, and my feet wouldn't squeeze into them. Emilie's either." Viola began the process of unfastening the back of the dress. "One welcomes babies, but the changes they bring to their mamas are not always expected or pleasant." She paused to help Ruby step out of the dress then swept it away. "But then, you know that."

Ruby's throat caught. Indeed, she'd been the beneficiary of a number of Opal's things after the twins' birth. "Yes," she said based on that alone, "I do know that."

"You're still tiny though. Gives me hope that if I ever have a baby of my own, perhaps I will have some chance of keeping my figure." She paused to look down then back at Ruby. "Such as it is," she added with a shrug.

Viola flipped the dress inside out and finished her measuring and pinning while Ruby stood quietly, unsure of what to do next. To remove all these ridiculous layers would require help that Viola could not give until she finished whatever calculations she was making.

Finally, the midwife looked up from her work. "Oh, mercy, I've left you standing there. You've an hour or so before it's time to start preparing for the ceremony, so why don't you just relax?"

"*Relax?*" A foreign word with a concept she'd yet to decipher. "But I've got work to do," she protested.

"Not today, you don't. Nor tomorrow." She gestured to the rarely used chair. "For two days, you are a lady of leisure courtesy of me, Mrs. Carter, and the Gayarre sisters. Oh, and there's something else in the bag for you." Viola grinned. "A gift from your intended."

"My intended?" Ruby frowned. "I didn't give him anything. Is that something couples do before exchanging vows?"

"Ruby, I warrant you'll be gift enough to that man."

"Gift? Me?" Understanding dawned, and Ruby felt a blush climbing her cheeks. Odd how the thought of her wedding night made her feel so squishy inside. She certainly knew what was expected. And likely nothing new had been invented in the short time since she'd given up her old life.

Still, something about the thought of Micah Tate as her husband had begun to cause a strange sensation to snake down her spine and coil in her belly. At least since this morning.

Her toes curled as she thought of how he'd gently helped her don her soaked stockings. Of how he knelt before her in the surf and pledged to care for her and the girls as long as he lived.

That had certainly been a new promise. None who came before him had ever made that vow. Perhaps that was the source of this emotion she couldn't quite name.

"Ruby." Viola pointed to the bag. "Just look inside. The lad who delivered it said I'm to be sure you read the inscription."

She reached into the bag and pulled out an exquisite leather-bound book. Instantly she recognized the title, though the copy was not the one she'd loaned Micah. This one looked never to have been read.

"Open it and see what he wrote," Viola urged. "And no, I didn't read it, though the temptation was strong."

Ruby held the volume to her chest as she walked toward the window. She found the horizon and scanned it, then opened the book to the first page.

In masculine but neat handwriting were these words:

> *Who can find a virtuous woman? for her price is far above rubies. The heart of her husband doth safely trust in her, so that he shall have no need of spoil. She will do him good and not evil all the days of her life.*
>
> *—Proverbs 31:10–12*

Beneath the verse, Micah had written, *To my Ruby, in whom I safely trust.*

He'd signed and dated the note, and she ran her fingers over the M and then the T. Before nightfall, she, too, would sign her name as Tate. Ruby Tate.

Again she traced the letters. "Safely trust," she whispered as she turned her attention to the horizon once more.

Emilie Gayarre burst into the room, and Ruby tore her attention from the water's edge.

"I'm here to help. Mrs. Carter's taken over the kitchen. Isabelle brought Joey, and the girls are having a wonderful time with—" She looked from Viola to Ruby then back to Viola. "I didn't get to see her in the dress."

"It looks beautiful on her, but it needs a little work," Viola said as she lifted the dress to show Emilie her marks. "Just a few tucks at the waist, and it should work just fine."

The fabric swished as Viola climbed onto the bed where Ruby had never once slept and settled the dress in her lap. She looked at the mantel clock and smiled. "A wedding. How wonderful." Her fingers started to shake, and she dropped the needle.

Emilie retrieved it while Ruby perched on the chair then adjusted her layers of underthings to find something close to a comfortable spot. Strange objects poked her and pulled at her, making Ruby wonder how ladies of quality managed to accomplish anything at all.

A hasty exit seemed the best response.

"I should go and help Mrs. Carter," Ruby said as she rose and tugged at the strings attaching her to the aggravating bustle. "I'm sure the boarders have more than sent her into fits by now. Some of them can be quit difficult to please."

"No," Viola said as she stabbed the needle into the dress then swiped at her eyes. "Please stay. I consider you a friend, Ruby, and there are no secrets between friends."

The statement stung as Ruby returned to the chair, lugging her wedding gift and a bellyful of guilt at the secrets piled up in her heart. She'd never reveal those to anyone, except perhaps to her husband if he were to allow it. Which he'd made plain he wouldn't.

Yet she smiled and nodded as if she agreed.

"I've not asked, Vi, but I'll ask you now." Emilie knelt before Viola, taking both of the midwife's hands in hers. "What happened?"

Viola took a deep breath and let it out slowly. "Quite simply, nothing." She paused to take a shuddering breath. "And I mean that in all seriousness. Remember when we first arrived on the island? I took one look at Dan Hill and knew he was the man for me. Some months later, he told me he'd felt the same."

"Of course," Emilie said as she turned to Ruby. "The three of us arrived together—Isabelle, Vi, and me—and there was some trouble with the ship that left Isabelle injured. Without Dr. Hill and Vi as his nurse, my sister might have died."

"Oh my," Ruby said.

"Dan showed me I had an aptitude for medicine that I didn't know was there," Viola said. "In all honesty, I only took on the challenge because I was smitten. Had he been some old codger with

ear whiskers, I might still be unaware of my calling."

Viola fell silent then picked up the needle and went back to her work.

Emilie rose and walked to the door to close it. "I've an idea what this is about," she said, "and I fear I'm the cause."

"You?" Viola looked up sharply. "How so?"

"I encouraged Papa to make the match between you and Andre. I had no idea of my brother's penchant for angry outbursts. My only explanation is that he must have hid them from me just as Papa did."

"Oh, Em, no."

Emilie held up her hand to silence Viola. "I'm of a mind to clear my heart of this, Vi, so let me do it. I thought helping you escape Andre before the wedding was the answer. I figured finding you on the steps of the cathedral was the Lord's way of showing me He wanted you with us aboard the *Jude*. I never expected Andre to follow." She looked over at Ruby. "He was my brother."

Ruby nodded.

"Vi, do you think the shooting was what kept Dr. Hill from making good on his plans to marry you?" When Vi remained silent, Emilie shrugged. "I know time has passed, but I can't think of any other impediment." Her eyes widened. "Oh, you don't think he had a wife somewhere else or maybe some deep hidden secret that finally caught up with him, do you?"

The needle continued its motion even as Viola shook her head. "I don't know what to think, Em. I suppose I could use the key and see if he left any clues at the clinic." She glanced over at Ruby. "But that's something to be done another day. Today we're celebrating, aren't we, Ruby?"

She tried to nod but found moving impossible. The story she'd heard troubled her. If someone as nice as Dr. Hill had a deep hidden secret that caused him to disappear, leaving the woman he loved, how much more so would the things she hid affect Micah should they come to light?

"Ruby?" This from Emilie, who looked at her with concern. "Something wrong?"

"Perhaps the new-bride jitters?" Viola offered. "She's thinking about tonight, I'll bet."

"Tonight?" Ruby flushed yet again. "I, well, that is. . ."

"Leave her alone, Vi," Emilie said. "You're embarrassing her."

"All right, then." Viola returned her attention to the gown, proceeding to add a few more tucks at the waist.

"Have you any hairpins, Ruby?" Emilie asked.

"Only the ones I use to keep my bonnet on."

"Then we'll improvise." Emilie reached up and let her own dark curls loose, pin by pin, until she had a stack of hairpins. Hastily she fashioned a braid and used three of the pins from the pile to fix it in place atop her head. "Now," she said. "Let's get to work making you the prettiest bride Fairweather Key has seen since my sister walked down the aisle."

Ruby bowed her head to allow Emilie to begin combing out her tangles. As she sat thus bowed, she took advantage of the position to offer up a prayer of thanks for the women the Lord had dropped into her life. And for the man who would officially and forever take away the fictitious name O'Shea as well as remove all vestiges of her former life as an O'Connor.

Her prayers were interrupted by a tap on the door. "I'll handle this," Viola said as she set the silk aside and opened the door just enough to peer out.

"You can't come in here, Micah Tate," Ruby heard the midwife say. "She's not decent, and you're not supposed to see her before she steps inside the church."

Micah. Ruby's heart slammed against her chest. *He knows.* She swallowed hard and lifted her head, oblivious to Emilie's protest.

"Emilie," she said, "I've a clean dress in the wardrobe. Might you hand it to me?"

"Ruby, no," Viola called from the door.

"Listen to her," Emilie said. "Make him wait."

CHAPTER 28

R uby," Viola warned from her spot at the door, "you absolutely cannot walk through this door. It's just. . .wrong." She looked to Emilie, who nodded.

"Ruby," Micah called. "Please."

His voice held a note of pleading that went beyond the words he spoke. Pleading did not indicate anger, did it? Nor did it mean he'd found her out. No, something else had Micah Tate riled up, and she'd rather know about it sooner than later.

"All right, Micah," she said, her decision made. "Just give me a minute." She motioned to Emilie then pointed to the bustle's knotted ties. "Help me get this thing off so the dress will close."

With fingers far more used to the underpinnings of the silly underthings, Emilie made short work of the tangled ribbons. As the cagelike contraption fell to the ground, Ruby squared her shoulders and yanked the dress shut, then started fumbling with the buttons.

"Here, let me," Emilie said.

A glance at the mirror while Emilie worked on the buttons told Ruby she looked half done, what with the topmost portion of her hair piled up in a fancy style and the rest curling in spirals down her back. The effect was that of a woman who couldn't seem to make up her mind whether to go to the ball or mop the ballroom floor.

"It's bad luck," Viola hissed as she closed the door and leaned against it.

"Do we believe in luck, or is that God's department?" This, shockingly, from Emilie, who came to stand by the midwife. "Perhaps we should let Ruby decide."

A look passed between the two, and slowly Viola opened the door just enough to stick her head out. "You've got nerve coming here like this, Micah," she said. "If anyone were to—"

"They won't," came the gruff response. "I've got men stationed on all sides, with Josiah waiting on the stairs. No one's coming in or out until I give the word."

"Does Caleb know about this?" Emilie called. "I'm not sure he'd approve of using the militia to facilitate a romantic interlude."

"Emilie," he said evenly, "seeing as how Caleb's recently become a married man, I'm going to guess he'd do just about anything to 'facilitate a romantic interlude.' Seems to me you've forgotten the lengths he went to just to—"

"All right," Emilie said, "that's enough. Just don't think Vi and I are going far. We'll be right outside this door."

"And for the record, I'll be filing an official report later this afternoon that will term this a field operation for the purpose of gathering information," Micah added. Ruby could hear the chuckle even through the door. "That's the way Caleb said I should handle it."

The pair of women slid outside, and for a moment, Ruby stood alone in her chamber. Then the door opened, and Micah Tate's silhouette filled the door frame. He moved forward, and a slice of sunlight caught his face.

He wore the clothing of a man who commanded a militia. The change from wrecker to captain was startling. And quite appealing. Beneath his officer's coat, he wore a neatly pressed shirt, and his boots shone. The only diversion was his hair, which had been captured with what appeared to be a length of leather. He held his hat in his hand.

How handsome he is, was her only rational thought.

"Ruby, I—"

As he moved out of the sunlight, his smile froze, and her heart lurched. "What is it? Is something wrong?"

Without looking away, he reached for the door and closed it. Still, he wore the peculiar expression.

Ruby endured the silence as long as she could manage. Finally, she turned to walk to the window. As he'd stated, a man in the uniform of the militia lounged on the back porch, a plate of whatever Mary Carter had served for lunch in his hand.

She looked past him to the ocean, where a vessel she didn't recognize glided along the horizon. At that moment, the ship could have belonged to Tommy himself, and she wouldn't have cared.

"I knew it," she said. "It was all too good to be true."

The floor creaked as his footsteps drew near. In the glass's reflection, she could see Micah standing behind her. To turn and fall into his arms might cause him to change his mind and marry her anyway, but her pride wouldn't let her do it.

She watched the strange ship until it disappeared behind the tall silhouettes of the mercantile and the courthouse. *Keep the watch, Claire. Always keep the watch.*

"Ruby? I'll keep the watch. Turn away now." Almost a whisper, yet unmistakably a command.

Her spine straightened as her breath caught. How had he known?

His hand spanned the small of her back, soft, proper in its placement. "Turn away now." A bit louder. Somewhere between a plea and a command.

Ruby swallowed hard as her feet refused to move. The hand, however, traced her spine and tangled in her hair as Micah closed the distance between them. They stood for what seemed like an eternity, not quite touching yet so close Ruby could hear Micah breathe.

"I don't hear anything," Viola called from the other side of the door.

"Hush, Vi," Emilie said.

Had Micah not stood so close, Ruby might have laughed. Instead, she resolved to end the standoff. "Just tell me you're not marrying me," she said, "then go. I'd rather you get it over with than make me stand here and wait."

"I agree."

Shock caused her to turn and face him. "You do?"

"Yes, I do." He seemed to be searching her face until his gaze rested on her eyes. "The color of the sea on a calm day," he said softly. "I never noticed until now. I'd always thought they reminded me of the sky, but no. . .it's the water. But then, that's more changeable, no?"

"What is? I don't understand."

"Your eyes, Ruby. They're so blue it hurts to look at them," he said as his hand pressed against her back and moved her into his embrace.

She craned her neck to look up at the man who by equal measures irritated and interested her. "Why are you here? I'm confounded completely."

"As am I," he said as he leaned down. "You see, I'd planned on a marriage based on one thing, but I've come to think there's more to it."

"Again I don't understand." She focused on the topmost button on his shirt rather than look Micah in the eye and risk forgetting what she intended to say. "What could you possibly want to learn by calling out the militia and barging into my private chambers on our wedding day?"

"It occurred to me," he said slowly, "that our marriage will not be legal if either of us is not free to marry."

"What are you asking?"

"The Frenchman. Who is he to you?"

She thought a minute. "He is no one, Micah. Only someone I once feared and now only want to forget."

Micah seemed to consider the statement for an eternity. Outside the window, a bell clanged and a horse and buggy rolled past. Still, he looked down at her without speaking.

"Why did you fear him? Was it because he hit you?"

How much to say? She decided to speak the truth judiciously. "No," she said slowly. "I feared him because of what he could do to the girls. I would give my life for them, and he knows it."

"Then my vow to keep you safe will stand." Her husband-to-be looked away. "Tell me you don't love him."

Something akin to warmth flooded a heart that had gone icy. "Oh, Micah. No, no, no. I never loved him." She reached up to grasp his face and turn it toward her. "You've made a vow to protect me. I would like to make a vow of my own."

"Oh?"

"I vow," she said softly, "that I will be a wife you can safely trust."

His nod was curt, though she thought his expression appeared to soften. When he scowled, however, her hopes for an end to his questions plummeted.

"Ruby, there's another issue that's pressing, and I must handle it before I can possibly consider taking you as my wife."

"I see." She tried to wriggle from his embrace, but he tightened his grasp.

"Be still," he commanded. "This is a problem in need of immediate remedy."

"All right," she said.

"You must admit that while you did attempt a passable kiss down at the beach this morning, I think it's safe to say that one didn't quite reach the mark. Neither did that kiss you thought I didn't notice back on the porch."

She felt the heat rising and stifled a smile. "You make it sound like I'm some sort of shameless hussy bent on kissing you at every opportunity."

Her words nearly stopped her heart as she realized how close the statement of her character was to the truth—before she met the Lord.

"I'm doing the talking here, Ruby," he said. "So try to keep quiet and follow along. Now as I said, I figure it is important that I rectify the wrong that's been done here, what with those two pathetic attempts at a kiss being all that I've got to go on as far as your expertise in this department."

Ruby's grin took hold, but she reined it in. "Is that so?"

"It is, and while I'd still marry you even with this troublesome situation hanging over our heads, I'm a man of action. I'd rather fix the situation so we can marry up without having to wonder whether we'll ever kiss right."

"Kiss right?" Now her grin refused to be tamed. "Exactly what does that mean?"

"Well, that's the question of the moment, isn't it?" He shrugged. "Far as I can tell, there's only one way to find out, isn't there?"

"Mr. Tate," she said with mock surprise. "I'm about to be a married woman. Are you suggesting I should—"

Micah's hand cupped her cheek, and her ability to speak fled once more. With excruciating slowness, he traced a path down her jawline with his knuckles until he reached her chin. Tilting her chin with the slightest nudge, Micah succeeded in making Ruby look at him.

"The question, Miss O'Shea, still stands."

"Question?" she managed. "Was there a question?" Her gaze collided with his. "I've forgotten."

"Stop teasing and kiss her," she thought she heard Emilie say.

"Hush, Em. He'll do it when he's ready, won't you, Micah?" Viola responded.

Micah's smile was broad, but it lasted only long enough for his lips to reach hers. As the kiss deepened, Ruby felt her feet leave the floor. The mantel clock ceased to tick, and time fell away just as the floor had. Only when Micah set her back on the ground did she come to her senses.

At least in part.

If the kiss she attempted in the waves that morning was her way of learning whether Micah was a suitable husband, this kiss surely was Micah's way of learning whether he had a suitable wife.

"Micah," she whispered when she could. "What happened?"

"I got my answer," he said. "That's what happened."

"No, I mean, my feet left the ground. Didn't you feel it?"

"They did?" Eyes half closed, Micah gathered her to him once more. "No, I didn't. We'd better try that again."

When the same thing happened three times more, Viola barged in with Emilie behind her. Even Josiah had joined them, and he now stood a few paces behind them with a broad smile.

"Enough of that," Viola said as she reached for Micah's arm and hauled him toward the open door. "It's time for Ruby to finish her preparations for the ceremony."

Micah pulled free and walked back to where Ruby stood. "I'll see you at the church."

"Yes, you will," she said with an enthusiasm that was diminished only by her lack of ability to stand without leaning against the chair.

He moved close enough so that he could whisper in her ear. "My promise stands, Ruby. You're safe with me. I'll not fail this time."

CHAPTER 29

*T*his time."

Ruby walked through the rest of the preparations for her wedding day with those two words foremost in her mind. Why hadn't she asked for an explanation?

She squared her shoulders and gave her hair one last look. "Because I don't need one."

Yet Micah's cryptic statement followed her up the aisle of Fairweather Key Church. It wrapped around the promise she made before God to be a helpmeet for Micah Tate and snagged on her heart when she said, her eyes on her three girls instead of the groom, "I will."

"Before I declare this couple man and wife," Rev. Carter said, interrupting Ruby's thoughts, "I would like to read a verse from Scripture that I feel is appropriate for this occasion."

Ruby looked up at her groom, who reached to grasp her hand. Something in that gesture and the gentle, almost shy smile that accompanied it gave her pause. Had she truly found a man who would keep his promises?

Perhaps so.

"From the book of Proverbs," the pastor continued. " 'Who can find a virtuous woman? for her price is far above rubies. The heart of her husband doth safely trust in her, so that he shall have no need of spoil.' " Rev. Carter paused to offer Micah a nod. " 'She will do him good and not evil all the days of her life.' "

"Safely trust in her."

Yes, she vowed, from this moment forward her husband would safely trust in her. She'd see to it. They might have entered the marriage in a more practical way than most, but Micah Tate would have a wife who was everything that verse said and, if she could manage it, more. It was what he deserved.

Surely the Lord would protect this man who'd sworn to protect her. Of course, she would pester God every day on that, just as she pestered Him to keep His hand on Carol, Maggie, and Tess.

"Ruby?" came the whisper.

She glanced up at Micah, who looked at her curiously. "What?" she replied.

His eyes crinkled at the corners as his grin broadened. "Did you hear what the pastor said?"

"Oh," came out like a squeak. "Yes, absolutely, I will," was much louder. Loud enough, in fact, to elicit laughter from those at the altar and even a few behind her.

She didn't care.

"No, sweetheart," he said as he turned her to face those assembled then leaned to speak into her ear. "You already said you would. Now it's time to show them we did."

"We did?" She shook her head. What had she missed while her mind wandered? "Did what?"

"We got married, Ruby Tate," he said. "Rev. Carter just told everyone who was listening. Obviously that wasn't you."

"Ruby Tate." She let out a long breath even as her groom led her down the aisle. How like this God she was only learning to know to bless the name she'd chosen by linking it to such a beautiful verse.

Today Claire O'Connor had officially and forever become Ruby Tate, a virtuous woman whose price was far above rubies. As she walked out of the church on the arm of her husband, she prayed that nothing would ever change that.

"You were a beautiful bride," Mary Carter said as they reached the steps of the church.

"Yes," Viola echoed. "Beautiful."

Ruby excused herself to greet the Gayarre sisters. Emilie, tall and dark with lovely curls, and Isabelle, fair and fine-featured, walked toward them with little Joey Carter holding one hand of each woman. Trailing a distance behind were Josiah and his brother, William, a younger version of his older brother down to the tilt of the head and the intent look in his eyes as their voices rose in congenial conversation.

"I see you brought your escort," Ruby said as she knelt to hug little Joey. "He just gets bigger every day."

"And so do I," Isabelle said as she wrapped her arm across her slightly rounded abdomen. "Though I cannot complain, as Josiah treats me like a queen. He'd have a houseful of little ones if he had his way."

Ruby rose to receive hugs from Isabelle and Emilie. "You're next," Ruby said to Emilie.

"Soon perhaps," Emilie responded as her palm pressed against her abdomen.

"There you are," Micah said as he reached for Ruby's hand. "We should bid these kind people good-bye and be on our way."

Viola raised a dark brow and seemed to be having trouble taming what appeared to be the beginnings of a grin. "Of course," she said then leaned close to Ruby. "It appears your husband's intent on helping to build my business."

"Business?" Ruby shrugged. "What do you mean?"

"Ruby," she said patiently, "I am a midwife. Remember?"

"But I'm not in that way," Ruby said. "That is, it's a bit too soon for that." Only when she turned to see all eyes on her did she realize she might have protested a bit too loudly.

"What's Mommy talking about?" This from Tess, who'd somehow slipped up behind Ruby without being noticed.

"It means a baby's in her tummy," Maggie offered.

Carol released a long sigh and put on an expression of dire exasperation.

"My mommy's got a baby in her tummy?" Tess began to dance and twirl, her celebration drawing the attention of anyone who might not already be staring.

"No, dear," Emilie said softly as she wrangled the girl by lifting her into her arms. "Miss Isabelle, *she's* going to welcome a new baby in a few months, not your mommy."

But the damage was done, and Tess refused to be convinced that a baby would not be joining their newly blended family anytime soon. Perhaps Ruby imagined it, but more than a few sets of eyes suddenly seemed interested at what she might have hidden beneath the large bow at her waist.

Micah took Tess from Emilie and walked over near the fence to carry on what appeared to be an animated and, on Micah's part, frustrating conversation. While Ruby and the ladies watched, Micah's face grew suddenly red, and he stood up. Grasping Tess's hand, he walked toward them.

"I think we should go now," he managed to say without meeting anyone's stare.

"Ask them," Tess said. When Micah ignored her, Tess tugged on his sleeve. "You told me you'd ask my mommy how to get a baby with her." Tess stared right at Emilie. "He doesn't know how, Miss Emilie."

"Th-thank you all for being here today," Micah stammered as he lifted Tess onto his shoulders. "I'm just going to take my new family home before I end up having to leave town."

"We understand, Micah," Isabelle offered. "I cringe when I think of the things Joey has said already."

Josiah joined them, along with William, who instantly took little Joey onto his shoulders. While Tess and Joey giggled, Josiah gave his best friend a concerned look. "What's wrong? Change your mind about the marriage already?" His wink let Ruby know he was joking. "Nah," he continued. "Can't be that. You've certainly ended up with a woman far above your caliber." Again he laughed.

"That much is true," Micah said with a chuckle, "though it's possible I might need to spend a bit of time conversing with my new daughters before we attempt another family outing in public."

"What happened?" Josiah asked, and Micah proceeded to tell him.

"Did he just call us his daughters?" Carol protested. Ruby gave Carol a look that told her she'd allow no talk of that sort, but the sullen girl ignored her.

"Excuse us," Ruby said as she wrapped her arm around Carol's shoulder and stepped away from the crowd.

At nearly nine, Carol lacked but a few years' growth from being as tall as Ruby. "He's not my papa," the girl said before they'd come to a stop. "I know what you're going to say, but he's just not."

"No," Ruby said, "he's not, but he is the man whom I've married, and I expect you to be respectful of that." When the girl looked away without comment, Ruby sighed. "Look, honey, I know you and your sisters have had a rough go of it. Don't you see that by me marrying Mr. Tate, we will no longer have to worry about. . ." She paused to shake her head. "What I mean is we won't have to worry at all," she amended.

Carol turned her attention to Ruby, her eyes narrowed to slits. She tried and failed to shrug away from Ruby's grasp. "I'm not stupid," she said when she quit resisting.

"No, of course you're not." Ruby pushed away fair hair from a face that wore an angry pout. "I know how very much you loved both your mother and your papa."

More than loved. Until the day her mother died, Carol rarely left her side. The irony was that while the girl tried to become like her mother, the resemblance was stronger in Maggie, who found only amusement in what others would call the cares of this world. Carol, however, not only held her sisters close to her heart, but also claimed the responsibility of keeping them safe.

Sadly, upon her mother's death, the girl had shifted her protective instincts to her father. Somehow the girl figured to play guardian angel to a man who made his living smuggling whatever cargo he could hide in his holds to whoever offered up the most money.

Not a man who needed a child's assistance.

Ruby glanced back at Micah, who seemed to be trying not to be obvious in watching her. He gestured a question as to whether she needed him to join her, and she shook her head.

"I saw Papa's friend."

"What?" Ruby swung her gaze back to Carol. "What friend?"

"That man who talks funny." She gave Ruby an accusing look. "I saw him."

Only a moment passed until Ruby had collected her composure

and put on a casual face. "I'm sure you were mistaken," she said.

"You fought with him. In the parlor." Carol dared Ruby to deny it. "Until he made him go." She pointed to Micah. "I tried to follow him, but he was too fast for me."

Ruby's heart sank. "Follow him? Why?"

"Because I knew he would lead me to my papa." Fair brows gathered. "I know you said he was dead, but I don't believe you."

Maggie ran over to join them. "Mr. Tate says it's time to go."

Ruby looked past her to nod at Micah then turned her attention to Carol. "Sweetheart, I know you loved your father very much, but your life is here now with me. Even if your papa were alive, he'd not be able to care for you like I have, now, would he?"

The girl looked as if she were remembering those last months at sea. Slowly she shook her head as she bit her lip.

"Then we must believe God had a purpose in allowing us to end up here on Fairweather Key. Don't you have nice friends?" When Carol nodded, Ruby continued. "And we have a lovely home that neither leaks nor runs aground."

"And we're no longer shot at," Maggie added.

"Yes," Ruby said. "See, we're safe here."

"And wherever Papa is," Carol said, "he's safe now, too, right?"

Ruby gathered Carol to her then reached to include Maggie in the embrace. "I pray he is," Ruby said. "Was," she corrected, though the familiar guilt pierced her heart.

Someday she might have to tell the girls the truth about their father. Today, however, it was still best they believe their lives no longer had any possibility of being included in his.

Mrs. Campbell's Bible told her that the Lord was her protector now, and He had sent her Micah. Between the two of them, there was no reason to give thought to her concern that someday she might awaken to find that Thomas Hawkins had snatched the girls from their beds while she slept unaware.

CHAPTER 30

The fear of Tommy somehow spiriting away Carol, Maggie, and Tess was a worry Ruby had nearly forgotten by the time she returned to the boardinghouse to pack her things for what was to be her first night as Micah's wife. Only when she knelt at the parsonage gate to kiss her girls good-bye did it return.

"They'll be plenty safe," he said as if he'd anticipated her concern. "I've posted several men to keep watch. Good men."

Ruby looked up at the man she'd married, the wrecker she'd staked her girls' safety on. "Thank you," she said. "Mind your manners, girls, and don't be a bother to the Carters."

Maggie ran into her embrace while Carol hung back. Meanwhile, Tess had launched herself into Micah's arms. "See to your sisters," Ruby whispered against Maggie's ear. "And remember, it's just one night away. Think of it as an adventure."

"Why can't you stay at the boardinghouse?" Maggie looked up at Micah. "Don't you like our house?"

"Yes, of course I do," he said, "but your mother and I are going away to get to know one another."

"They're courting," Tess said.

"I think the courting's over," Carol muttered. "Now we'll never get rid of him."

Ruby released the younger twin to offer a smile at the elder of the pair. "Carol, aren't you going to come and say good-bye?"

KATHLEEN Y'BARBO

"It's just one night," she said, not budging an inch. "And he's not my papa."

"No," Micah said, "I reckon I'm not." He set Tess back on the ground then adjusted his hat. "Don't intend to try to be, though I do plan to be here in his stead if you need me." He directed a look at Carol. "I bet you miss him, don't you?"

Her lower lip quivered, but only Ruby would have noticed. "Sometimes," was all Carol would admit.

Micah nodded. "I miss mine, too. It's an awful lonely feeling to wish for a papa and feel like God isn't listening."

Carol turned away.

"Sweetheart," Ruby called, "won't you come and tell me good-bye?"

"It's only one night," she said. "Come on, Tess. I promised to braid your hair, and now's as good a time as any."

Tess trotted away with Carol in the lead, ever the dutiful sister. She'd nearly reached the parsonage door when she turned and came tearing back. "I almost didn't get to kiss you," she said. "I can't forget, not ever."

Ruby grinned and pressed fair curls away from the girl's face. How lovely this child, and how much she made her heart proud. "That's right, not ever."

Tess tangled her fingers in Ruby's hair and lifted the strands to her nose. "Smells sweet, Mama. Like you." She looked over at Micah. "Does this mean I get a baby now?"

"Come on," Carol called, and Tess hurried away, sparing Ruby from giving an answer. Maggie lingered a moment longer, time enough to give Micah a guarded look.

"Is she going to be all right?" he asked. "Your sister, I mean."

Maggie's eyes narrowed. One thing the girls had learned early on was how to spot someone who couldn't tell them apart. "Which sister?"

Micah looked to Ruby for help, but she decided to give him no assistance. He'd need to learn sooner or later.

"Carol," he said, though the name lacked a certain enthusiasm.

Maggie nodded. "Yes," she said after a moment. "She'll be fine."

Mrs. Carter waved from the door then waited until Maggie

198

pressed past her to disappear inside. Though the door had shut, Ruby remained at the gate.

A hand rested lightly on her shoulder, and then, gently, her husband reached for her elbow and helped her to her feet. Though the street remained busy with the normal foot traffic and rolling carts of any workday, Ruby suddenly felt alone.

Even with Micah standing there.

"They'll be fine," he said. "Let's go."

Ruby took a few steps alongside him then turned to look over her shoulder. "I wonder if Tess remembered to bring her dolly. It's her favorite, and she can't sleep without it."

Micah guided her forward. "If she's forgotten it, Mrs. Carter or the reverend can go and fetch it."

"True." Their walk took them along the same stretch of beach where they'd stood that morning. The same stretch where she'd showed Micah who she really was.

She thought of the gift, of the sand dollar he'd almost magically produced from the ocean floor. It certainly hadn't been there a moment before when she'd been stomping about like a woman gone mad.

Out of habit, she glanced at the horizon. No new vessels dotted the waters, nor did there seem to be anything out of the ordinary.

She'd keep watch anyway.

Micah turned her from the beach and pointed to a path carved from the brush and rocks. Above it all stood a house on the bluff. "Just a little farther," he said. "If you're tired, I can carry you."

"Don't be silly, Micah," she said. "We've barely left the main road."

She looked into his eyes and saw disappointment. Evidently the protection he promised extended to climbing hills as well as fighting off smugglers.

"Yes," she said slowly as she warmed to the topic. "It has been an exhausting day. I'd actually be—"

Before she could finish, Micah scooped her into his arms and raced up the hill. At the door, he placed his boot in the center and it flew open. Ruby stifled a scream then slowly began to giggle.

"Something funny?" he asked as he leaned against the door with his shoulder and slammed it shut.

"No," she said, and then, "Yes, actually."

Micah stopped midway across the sparsely furnished room to stare down at her. "If it's me you're laughing at, I'd prefer you not tell me about it."

"No," she said, "I'm not sure at all why I'm laughing, but it's definitely not because of you."

He lifted a dark brow as he continued to stare at her. "You're sure?"

"Micah Tate, I haven't been sure about anything related to you since I met you." She shrugged. "No, that's not true. There was a time I was sure you were completely, certifiably crazy."

Her husband chuckled. "When was that?"

Ruby leaned her ear against his chest and traced her finger across his lapel. "When you asked me to marry you."

"Which time?" he asked as his footsteps echoed in the broad expanse of space.

She braved a look and saw him staring. "Every time."

"And what's crazy about asking you to marry me, Ruby? You're a good cook and fair company." He paused to turn sideways and step into the bedchamber. "A man could do worse, Mrs. Tate."

"*Fair* company, Mr. Tate?"

Micah carried her across the almost empty main room and through a doorway that led to a bedchamber. The first thing Ruby saw was the elegantly carved bed, its four posts draped in beautiful white linens that stood in stark contrast to the rough boards of the walls.

Beyond the bed, long windows had been opened to welcome the sea breeze and offer up a view of the sun as it dipped beneath the horizon.

"Oh my," she whispered. "I didn't expect this."

"Wrecking has its privileges," he whispered against her ear, "as does marriage. Now perhaps we can discuss how you might change my opinion of your company from fair to outstanding."

"Mr. Tate," she said, "ours was to be a marriage of convenience. Your protection for my—oh!" She paused as her protector parted the bed curtains and dropped her in the center of what turned out to be quite a soft mattress.

"Your what, Mrs. Tate?" he asked as he doused the lantern and plunged the room into soft twilight.

"My cooking," she managed to say.

Gradually the room brightened from deep purple shadows to a softer hue that allowed her a full view of her new husband. He seemed unwilling to do anything other than stand there and stare at her.

"So perhaps I should go and make dinner, then." Ruby made to climb off the bed, but Micah blocked her way.

"Are you hungry, Ruby?" he breathed against the skin of her neck.

"No," she said as she watched his shirt land on the floor. "Are you?"

"I will be," he said as he closed the bed curtains. "Tomorrow."

Her laughter matched his as their lips met.

Later, with the stars shining, Ruby lay in Micah's arms, her eyes open wide. "Micah?" she whispered. "Are you awake?"

When he didn't immediately respond, Ruby rose to follow the silver path of the moon to the window. The sea breeze tossed her hair, which hung loose about her shoulders, and sent a chill down her spine as it blew across her skin.

She was a married woman. A woman married to a man who not only commanded a militia but would soon take over the duties of Judge Spencer as well.

Ruby's chuckle held no humor. What would Tommy say to that? She shrugged off the question with a roll of her shoulders, for what did it matter tonight? Why ruin a wonderful evening with thoughts of a man who no longer had a place in her life or the lives of the girls? She leaned as far as she could outside the window. In both directions, the seas were calm, no sails that she could spy.

Nothing but the moon teasing the waves.

"Can't you sleep?" This from Micah, who leaned up on one elbow to watch her.

"Perhaps it is the unfamiliar room." She forced her back to the sea, offering the suggestion even though she knew the real cause lay elsewhere.

Micah rolled over to light the lamp, casting the room in a brilliant golden light. "Perhaps." He stretched and leaned back against the pillows, the sheet tangled around his legs and torso. "Might I entice you to return to bed, Mrs. Tate?"

"Of course." Ruby averted her gaze and felt uncharacteristic heat rise in her cheeks. Where was the woman she'd been? The woman who in years past had felt nothing when faced with a man wearing only a sheet and a smile.

This man was declared before God to be my husband.

And I am declared clean and new through Jesus.

She went to him then as his wife. As a woman already smitten with a man she'd married only for the protection of the children in her care.

" 'Who can find a virtuous woman? for her price is far above rubies,' " Micah whispered against the sensitive skin of her neck as he lifted the sheet to cover her. " 'The heart of her husband doth safely trust in her, so that he shall have no need of spoil. She will do him good and not evil all the days of her life.' "

"That's beautiful," she whispered. "So very beautiful."

"It's the Lord's promise," he said, "for a husband with a wife such as you. The woman I safely trust."

Safely trust. Ruby's heart lurched. Would Micah always feel this way about her?

"Far above rubies," he said as he extinguished the light. "I warrant it is no accident you are so aptly named." Micah embraced her then kissed her forehead. "It's the girls, isn't it? You're worried about them."

She remained silent, unwilling to mar their wedding night with her fears.

He touched the tip of her nose then gathered her closer. "Would you feel better if we went and got them?" A pause. "The truth. Always the truth from now forward."

Always the truth. Ruby sighed. From now forward, she'd never have to worry about telling the truth. *Thank You, Lord, for letting me start over. And for Micah.*

"Yes," she said as she turned in his arms to face him. "I think I would like that very much, though I wonder if the Carters would mind the intrusion on their evening."

As it turned out, they neither minded nor asked why the newlyweds had returned so soon. Rather, the pastor offered to carry a sleeping Tess himself, while Mrs. Carter promised to come and cook breakfast for the boarders just as she'd planned.

Ruby's protest fell on deaf ears; thus she found herself faced with the unexpected luxury of lying abed past the time the sun rose. With the girls safely asleep in their own beds, even Tess, Micah Tate returned with two cups of coffee and a smile.

Luxury indeed.

"I cannot linger but a moment," he said as his lips brushed her cheek. "I've a meeting with Caleb to discuss his departure. Thanks to the Dumont fellow taking on Emilie's duties as teacher, it appears they'll be sailing in a few days."

Ruby accepted the coffee then held it out at arm's length until Micah had settled on the end of the bed. "Thank you," she said after taking a sip of the heavenly brew. "Mrs. Carter makes wonderful coffee. I'll have to ask her what her secret is."

"I made the coffee," he said as his gaze scorched her, "and I'm sure you'll pry the secret out of me somehow."

Ruby blushed to her roots. "Micah, honestly."

Micah took two gulps of coffee then cradled the dainty teacup in his oversized hands. "Ruby, I know you don't love me yet, but I hope in time that you will. Until then, I'm going to be the husband to you that I ought to be." He paused to study the cup then swung his attention back to her. "You're a wife who would make a man proud. Just so you know."

"Thank you, Micah."

She should have told him somewhere between yesterday's swim in the ocean and last night: She'd found feelings for him that might surely bloom into a love that would last. She should have said that she, too, felt proud to be the wife of a man like Micah Tate.

Instead, she set the cup on the bedside table and rose up on her knees to make her way toward her husband, dragging half the bedcovers with her. What Ruby meant as a quick kiss caused Micah to latch the door and miss a meeting.

CHAPTER 31

After a full month of married life, Ruby had almost managed to forget what life was like waking up with Tess's foot in her back. Now she awoke to snores in the night, to be sure, but at least when Micah touched her, it usually was not in his sleep.

Blushing at the thought, she turned away from the stove to swipe at her forehead with the corner of her apron. This morning's letter from Mrs. Campbell had offered encouragement that perhaps a replacement had been found for her in the boardinghouse kitchen. She'd tucked the letter in the Bible Micah studied after supper each night so he'd be sure to find it.

What she would do once her days weren't filled with cooking and cleaning for the ever-changing array of boarders, Ruby couldn't quite imagine. She pressed her hand to the belly that just this morning had rebelled against breakfast. Dared she hope there might be a babe to tend to by then?

A flash of color in the distance caught Ruby's attention, and she went to the window. From her vantage point, she watched Maggie returning from school with Tess following a few paces behind. The older child seemed to be doing her best to keep the younger from catching up.

Ruby frowned. Tess must have done more than her usual best to bother Maggie. They rarely walked any way but hand in hand.

Straining her neck, Ruby looked to see if perhaps Carol was lagging

again. Since Micah had joined their family, Carol seemed bound and determined to leave it.

"Where's your sister?" she asked as the girls arrived on the porch.

Maggie shrugged past Ruby and walked through the kitchen without stopping while Tess made her way to the plate of treats cooling on the windowsill. Stepping onto the porch, Ruby looked both ways in case Carol had chosen another route home from school.

Seeing no sign of Carol, Ruby came back inside to follow Maggie to the stairs and watched her until she reached the topmost landing. "Maggie, I asked you a question. Where is Carol?"

"Dunno," Maggie muttered as she opened the door to their rooms and slipped inside.

"Now that was strange." Preoccupied with the fact that Maggie had ignored the treats altogether, Ruby almost missed Tess's attempt to stuff a spare one into her apron pocket. "Put that back," she said. "What's gotten into you?"

Just yesterday she'd found the child filling a bucket with food from the larder. When caught, all Tess would say was that she'd decided to play house and needed things for her kitchen.

She waited until the child returned the contraband to the plate before lifting her into her arms and swirling her around the kitchen. Tess giggled but held firm to her treat until Ruby set her on the stool and gave her a plate.

"So, Tess," she said as casually as she could manage, "is something wrong with Maggie?"

Her mouth full, Tess said something that sounded like "Carol" and then perhaps "scenic house." Or was it "secret mouse"?

"Carol has a mouse?"

When Tess shook her head, Ruby tried again. "You have a mouse?" Another no with Tess still chewing, and Ruby was about to give up. "Secret house?" she finally said.

Tess froze, and her face took on the look she wore when she'd been caught at something naughty. Or had given away a secret.

As she swallowed with some difficulty, the child's eyes widened. "How did you know?"

Deciding to play along, Ruby shrugged. "Mamas know things,

sweetheart," she said. "But what I wonder is why Maggie seems upset about this secret house."

"That's 'cause Carol says Maggie has Micah for a papa." She took another bite and turned her attention to the window. "What kind of bird is that?"

Still puzzling through Tess's statements, Ruby took a moment to answer the question. "An orangequit," she finally said when Tess asked her once again.

"But it's not orange," she protested.

"You're right about that." Ruby paused. "Tess, can you tell me what a secret house and Micah being Maggie's papa have to do with one another?"

The front gate banged. Carol walked through the front doorway. Ruby looked up as she paused at the dining room door. "Come and have a treat with us."

"It's yummy." Had there been any doubt, the goo on Tess's face would have given away the truth of her statement.

"Here, Tess," Ruby said as she handed the girl a length of toweling. "You've a mess that needs washing off."

Footsteps retreating gave Ruby notice that Carol, too, had chosen an escape upstairs over indulging in the treats that were their favorite. Something was wrong.

"Carol," she called from the base of the stairs. "I'd like to see you in the kitchen, please." When the girl paused but did not turn around, Ruby added, "Now."

Reluctantly Carol made her way back down the stairs to stop at the kitchen door. "At the table." She placed two treats on Tess's tray. "Go on upstairs and take this one to Maggie." Before Tess could ask, Ruby added, "And you might consider sharing the other with her, too."

The prospect of even half another treat seemed to placate Tess's obvious disappointment at being banished from the impending conversation. Ruby placed two more treats on a fresh plate and brought them to the table.

"Here, sweetheart," she said to Carol, who merely sat with her all-too-familiar sullen look. "All right, then."

Ruby crumbled a corner off the treat and popped it in her mouth, all the while praying it would stay down. Just this morning, she'd had an awful experience with scrambled eggs that made her reluctant to attempt lunch. Now that it was halfway to dinnertime, her stomach seemed to be warring with the dual missions of being fed and staying empty.

While Carol studied the ceiling, Ruby studied the situation. With Maggie and Tess, the direct way was best. A question asked was usually a question answered. Only when they had something to hide did she find she must chase the tail of the trouble for a bit before she arrived at the source.

But Carol, she was different. Too much like her mama and too quick to both love and hate. It was a fine balance, this art of conversing with the high-strung oldest child.

With the first bite successfully down, Ruby attempted a second. The instant she bit into it, she realized her mistake.

Yet she had a mystery to solve.

As she chewed slowly, she watched Carol's eyes dart back and forth between the ceiling, the floor, the window, and just about anything else she could look at other than Ruby. Even as Ruby's stomach began to protest, something more troublesome niggled at the corners of her mind.

House.

Micah.

Papa.

A thought occurred, and immediately Ruby prayed she was wrong. Tommy was back, and he'd hidden himself somewhere on the key then found the girls and coerced them into bringing him food. No, she corrected, not Maggie. That would explain why she seemed to be on the outs with the other two.

"Do not move," she said to Carol as she stumbled from the table and out into the afternoon sun to find a place behind the outhouse where she could once again relieve her roiling gut.

When she returned, Ruby found the girl sitting obediently in place. Though Ruby noticed Carol had wolfed down one of the treats in her absence, she said nothing. Rather, she found a knife and cut the other treat in half, then pushed the untouched portion toward Carol.

"Are you sick again?" she asked, her eyes narrowing.

KATHLEEN Y'BARBO

"What do you mean 'again'?"

Carol picked at the edge of her treat much as Ruby had done, though she made no move to eat it. "I saw you this morning," she accused, "and I know what you and that man have been doing."

Instantly Ruby felt her cheeks flood with heat. "What are you talking about?"

"I see him looking at you and saying things in your ear that we aren't supposed to hear," she said. "And I know what that means."

Ruby let out a long breath and sent up a quick prayer for wisdom. When she took on the raising of these precious girls, she never expected there would be times like this.

She swung her gaze up to meet the girl's stare. "Perhaps you should tell me what that means, Carol."

Carol pushed away from the table with such force the chair fell backward. "It means you are going to have a baby and you won't want us anymore." She flung the statement at Ruby then grabbed the plate and stormed from the room.

A baby. Hearing the words she'd just only begun to hope were true spoken in this fashion caused Ruby's breath to freeze in her throat. "Carol O'Shea, come back here this instant," she called when she could manage it.

True to her nature, the girl did as she was told, though her expression plainly showed she wasn't happy about it. For a moment Ruby breathed a sigh of relief that the situation might be easily diffused. "What?" she said with disdain. "And maybe I want to be called Caroline Hawkins like my mama named me."

"Maggie," Ruby called upstairs. "Please watch Tess while Carol and I take a walk before dinner." She waited for Maggie's somewhat sullen response then turned to regard Carol.

Before she could say anything, Carol blurted out, "I don't want to." She took a bite from Ruby's treat and chewed it slowly.

So this is what rebellion looks like with a child who aims to please.

Her gut still protesting, Ruby took a deep breath and let it out with care. Keeping as even a temper as possible, she removed the plate from Carol's hand and placed it less than carefully on the table.

Another calming breath, and she took Carol's free hand. "You're

208

welcome to take the treat with you, but you and I have somewhere to go, and it won't wait."

"Where?" she asked as she swiped at the side of her mouth with the back of her hand.

Again Ruby steadied herself and offered Carol a smile. "I thought perhaps you would tell me."

Carol's face fell, and she looked away. She said nothing, her silence speaking volumes.

Ruby released her grip and caught the treat before it fell to the floor. Carefully she returned it to the plate then snatched up the toweling and dipped it into the basin to clean the girl's sticky hand.

Carol remained silent.

"Look at me, sweetheart," Ruby said as she set the toweling aside. "I know."

Blue eyes swam with instant tears. "Tess told you, didn't she?" Carol stamped her foot. "I knew I couldn't trust her."

Ruby gathered Carol into her arms and rested her chin atop her head. Coming to Fairweather Key seemed God's way of allowing them a fresh start at a decent life. If Tommy had returned and Carol was somehow helping him to stay on the island, how soon until the past was no longer behind them?

"Carol, you know I love you, don't you?" When she nodded, Ruby continued. "And you believe what the Bible says about telling the truth." Another nod. Ruby held her at arm's length. "Then don't you think it's time I heard the story from you?"

"But Tess already—"

"From you," Ruby repeated. "The truth."

"I didn't mean to find him. I know I'm not supposed to go down to the beach alone, but Maggie wouldn't come with me and I knew Tess would tell." Carol paused and blinked back tears that fell anyway. "I saw a ship that looked like Papa's, and I thought he might be coming back for me."

Ruby's pulse jumped. "Carol, I'm disappointed in you."

The comment seemed to light once again the flame of rebellion in her eyes. "You are not my mother."

Five words that could change everything.

CHAPTER 32

"You're right, Carol. I didn't give birth to you, but my sister did, and I'll not let anyone take you from me," Ruby said, her back straight. "That includes Tommy Hawkins."

Carol gasped. "So he *is* alive."

Carol's reaction gave definite proof that whomever Tess referred to, it was not Tommy. For this alone, Ruby could be grateful.

"I said no such thing." Ruby opened the door and ushered Carol out onto the back porch, then latched the door behind her. "You saw the ship go down just as I did. Don't you think if he were alive he'd be back by now?"

Even as she said the words, Ruby's stomach roiled.

They crossed the lawn to the back gate, where one of Micah's militiamen sat whittling in the shade. As he caught sight of them, the fellow scrambled to his feet. "I've a favor to ask," Ruby said. "Jim, isn't it?" When he nodded, she continued. "Carol and I are going for a walk. I wonder if you might keep watch over Maggie and Tess while we're away." He looked about to protest when she shook her head. "We'll be fine, but I do worry about the girls. Micah loves them so, you know."

Jim thought only a moment before nodding. "I'll let Spack know. He's likely up at the front of the place."

"Thank you, Jim," she said as she laced her fingers with Carol's and swept past.

"Why do we need those soldiers watching us all the time?" Carol slid Ruby a glance as she wiped away the last of her tears. "They're watching for my papa, aren't they?"

"Sweetheart," Ruby said slowly, "first tell me where we're going, and then we can discuss other things."

Carol hesitated only a moment. "I'll take you there. It's easier than telling you."

With a nod, Ruby fell in beside the youngster. "So," she said when they'd left the rather public sidewalk for the lane that led toward Emilie's home and, beyond, to the beach. "You asked why we must have the militiamen keeping watch. It's a precaution Micah wishes to take while he is acting as commander and judge."

Carol looked up, and for a moment Ruby felt like she was staring down at Opal again. "But why?"

Ruby sighed. "Micah doesn't want someone who might be upset with him to come and try to hurt us."

They stopped at Emilie's gate, and Carol's eyes went wide. "Would they do that?"

"Likely not," Ruby said as gently as she could. "Our island is quite safe, and there's rarely anything to concern ourselves with. However," she added as casually as she could, "though I want to believe your papa's no longer alive, I wager there is the very slight possibility there are men who might want to find us all the same."

"You want to believe it, but you don't know for sure, do you?"

The sea breeze lifted a strand of hair and tossed it across her cheek as Ruby looked past the girl to Emilie's empty home. "Carol, why are we here?" she asked as she tucked the strand behind her ear. "You know Emilie and Caleb are gone."

Carol looked to the right and then to the left. Slowly she reached for the latch and opened it, then stepped inside the yard.

"I know," she said. "That's why I brought him here."

"Him?" Ruby picked up her pace to catch Carol, who had already turned the corner and headed for the back of the house. On the clothesline, Ruby saw a set of linens from the boardinghouse hanging askance. Upon closer inspection, it appeared they'd been tossed over the line. Beside them was one of Emilie's aprons. At least it appeared to be, though the color was an odd shade of. . .

Ruby touched the still-damp fabric. Only one thing stained linen this color.

Blood.

"Oh, dear Lord, protect my girl." Ruby looked around and found Carol had disappeared. "Carol," she called as she raced for the house and what she now noticed was an open back door. "Carol, where are you?"

She stepped inside and instantly spied a mess that Emilie and Caleb couldn't possibly have left behind. A familiar lunch pail had been upended onto the sideboard, and a variety of foods had tumbled forth. The water basin was missing, and broken pieces of a plate littered the floor.

"Mama?" Carol called from the parlor.

"Coming, honey." Ruby stepped over the mess and raced toward Carol, who stood in the center of an empty but obviously recently occupied room. She gathered the child to her as she surveyed the parlor.

While Emilie kept her home as neat as a pin, the disarray in the kitchen extended to this room as well. A shelf that once held Emilie's collection of novels had been emptied of its contents, and in their places sat a stock of food.

"He's gone." Carol's whisper drew her attention, but only for a moment.

"This room is a mess." Ruby turned to look over her shoulder. "And who is he?"

Carol seemed reluctant to answer.

"Carol," she said slowly. "Why was there blood? Did someone get hurt when the plate broke?"

The girl's lower lip quivered. "Miss Emilie's gonna be mad at me about that."

"Honey," Ruby said carefully, "it's more important that you show me where you were cut." She held out Carol's hands and found no sign of injury. "I don't see anything here." Then it dawned on her. "It wasn't you, was it?"

She shook her head. "No, Mama, I only brought him something to eat. William left it in the kitchen."

"William?" Her heart sank. "Was William hurt badly?"

"No, he's fine."

Ruby paused. Indeed, if the boy were injured seriously, that would have been the topic of Tess's conversation rather than Carol's secret. With no obvious connection to Tommy here, she had to assume Carol had thrown that tidbit in to confuse Tess.

Ruby leaned against the wall and let her shoulders sag. The churning in her belly had returned, and Carol was making less sense the more she spoke. Even so, the picture had become quite clear: The usually well-behaved William Carter and her own Carol had decided to take advantage of Emilie's absence to get into mischief.

All that remained was to determine the extent of it.

"Tess said you had a secret house and something about your papa." She sighed and swallowed back the bile climbing into her throat. "I'm not feeling well, so perhaps that's why I'm so confused. I see a broken plate and evidence of blood that's been cleaned up." She shrugged. "And all I can think is that I'm extremely disappointed in you and William."

"Disappointed?" Carol's surprise almost seemed believable.

"Yes. You've treated Miss Emilie's home like your personal play-house and then lied about the reason, Carol, and I'm very upset about it. Now I want you to go straight home." She paused as a wave of nausea passed. "Later you and I will pay a visit to the Carters to straighten up this situation. Do you understand?"

"Yes, Mama," she said, "but why aren't you coming with me? Are you going to wait and see if he returns?"

"Enough, Carol. There's no one." She looked around and sighed. "And when I'm done, I'll start thinking about your punishment."

"Punishment? But I—"

"No arguments." Ruby stepped over a pile of books and made her way back into the kitchen. "Now run and find William."

"But if he comes back and finds you here, he might—"

"Enough, Carol. Go and do as I said." Ruby held her breath until Carol skittered out the door; then she gradually allowed herself to exhale as she closed her eyes.

When she heard the front gate shut, Ruby opened her eyes and sagged against the doorframe. *Help me to know how to handle this, Lord. What would her mama do?*

"Don't be so hard on her, Miss Ruby," a distinctively male voice said. "She was only trying to help."

Ruby whirled about to see a man standing at the parlor door. His left arm was bundled up in a sling made from what appeared to be a strip cut from one of Mrs. Campbell's lace curtains. Around his injured arm, someone had wrapped a length of toweling now soaked through in spots with blood.

Her stare rose to his face, where she noticed a crescent-shaped scar on his left cheek. "I remember you."

"Drummond, Mrs. O'Shea," he said, his voice now a hoarse whisper. "Clay Drummond."

"Are you sure about this, Dumont?" Micah leaned back in the chair that, until Caleb returned, belonged to him and studied the man sitting across the desk from him. "I fail to understand why Carol would take a pail of food to Emilie's cottage."

"I saw it for myself," was his curt reply.

Remy Dumont was the last man he wanted to trust, though Micah suspected his judgment was colored by the man's obvious affection for his wife. Caleb had surely thought enough of him to name the man headmaster of the school in Emilie's absence, so he figured that was enough to balance his own concerns.

Micah paused to consider his next question. "And just how did you come to follow my Carol, again?"

"I became suspicious of her behavior well before that."

"Suspicious?" Micah reached for Caleb's writing pen and weighed it in his hand. "How so?"

Dumont's expression changed, and he seemed ready to bolt from his chair. "Look, perhaps I've made a mistake in coming here."

He made to rise, but Micah gestured for him to sit. "As Ruby's husband, her daughters are in my care, so I'd appreciate your finishing the story."

"All right, then. One of the girls took bread out of William Carter's lunch pail and put it in her own, though at first I wasn't sure if it was Maggie or Carol. They are nearly impossible to tell apart."

Micah nodded, though he offered no commiseration. He'd learned that the differences were subtle but obvious once you knew what to look for. Perhaps someday he'd tell Dumont, but not today.

Leaning forward, Micah pressed his palms on the desk. "Go on."

"I've never noticed the twins go anywhere but straight home, and they're always together. Once they reach the parsonage, the little one joins them and walks the rest of the way." Another pause. "Often William sees they cross the road safely. He's a good fellow."

Dumont's statement struck a nerve. "It appears you've paid close attention," Micah said carefully. "Do you extend this level of devotion to the other children?"

Viola's brother had the gall to lean back in his chair and grin. "Perhaps it is because I find their mother a delight. The sight of Ruby never fails to make me smile."

Micah rose. "I've heard enough. You will apologize for the familiar way you've spoken about my wife."

Dumont stood. "Or?"

"Or you will live to regret it."

He returned the fool's stare and said nothing further, allowing his expression and fisted hands to speak for him. By degrees, the schoolteacher must have realized his mistake.

"I already do." Dumont shrugged. "I mean no harm. I realize you've come out the better man in all of this. In fact, I've a dual purpose in being here today."

"Oh?"

"Indeed." Remy Dumont removed a document from his coat pocket and thrust it across the desk toward Micah. "My letter of resignation. How Viola remains in this place is beyond me, but I'll not endure it any longer. Two weeks is all you'll get from me."

Micah rose. "Why wait, Dumont? I'm sure we can find someone to replace you." He shrugged. "As judge, I'll call a school holiday until Emilie returns. It's highly improper, but I'd rather have an extended school vacation and a married woman teaching my girls than the likes of you."

CHAPTER 33

Ruby watched the man sway then steady himself against the doorframe. "You're injured," she said even as her eyes darted about in hopes of finding an easy exit.

Mr. Drummond leaned forward then righted himself. "Can't talk now," he said as he pushed past her to stumble through the kitchen and into the hallway. He seemed at a loss as to what to do next.

"You're bleeding," she called after him then cursed herself for a fool. Of course the man had surely noticed this.

She should fetch Micah. He would know what to do.

"You raised a good girl," Drummond said as if mocking her. "She was a help to me. The young fellow, too."

When he made no move toward her, Ruby let her irritation show. "I am Carol's mother," she said. "And may I just say that I'm quite disappointed that you would send children out to steal for you."

"Now hold on a minute, lady." Mr. Drummond seemed sufficiently riled to lean away from the doorframe and hold the pose. "I never asked those kids to do nothing of the kind." He sagged against the wall then shook his head. "I need to sit down, and I'd be obliged if you'd help me."

When Ruby did not move, Mr. Drummond did, turning his back on her to stumble into the parlor. After a moment, she inched toward the door to peer around the corner. She found the man sprawled on the settee.

She glanced at the mantel clock. Likely Carol was home by now.

A thought occurred. Surely someone would come looking for her soon, what with the boarders likely wanting their next meal at the usual time. Perhaps even Micah, should he return to the boardinghouse at a reasonable hour.

She inched forward and nudged Mr. Drummond's boot with her foot, and he did not respond. His even breathing gave her hope he now slept.

"Mr. Drummond?"

Nothing.

Ruby backed up two steps then paused and retraced her steps to the kitchen, where her foot crunched on a shard of what had once been Emilie's dinner plate.

She jerked around to see Mr. Drummond standing a stone's throw away. Other than the toweling still wound around his hand, the man appeared lucid and well able to stand.

"I thought you were—"

"Hurt?" His lips curled into a smile that quickly vanished. "A nasty cut, this here," he said, "but otherwise I can't complain." He moved forward to lean on the edge of the table. "I hope you'll forgive the playacting. I had to be sure you wouldn't run to turn me in to the law before I had a chance to talk you out of it."

"Play—"

"Acting," he said. "I'll get right to the point. Your daughter and her friend have been right helpful, but they don't have any idea who I am."

"Neither do I." Ruby whirled around to see Micah standing in the door, his rifle at his side. "I'm not a man for wasting time, Drummond, and I've got men on every corner of this property. Only a fool would try to run, and you don't look like a fool."

"You remember me." He smiled. "I'm flattered."

Ruby skittered behind Micah then peered around him to watch the injured man raise both hands as Micah raised his weapon and caught Drummond in his sights. "He seems nice, Micah," she said. "Don't shoot him."

"That's enough, Ruby." His tone both stunned and stung. "Go on home now."

"Home, but I don't see how it's safe for you—"

"Home." Micah's shout told her he would listen to no more arguments. "And I'll not tell you again," he added with a tone that told her anything they'd shared in the past month was now forgotten. "Do. You. Understand?"

She did. With little to recommend her save the way she cooked and the fact that she might give him a child, Ruby had ruined the best she'd had. And she hadn't had it but just over a month.

"Yes, Micah," she said. "Would you like me to send Viola to doctor him up?"

"Tell her I'll need her at the jail in an hour."

"You're mighty certain you're going to convince me to leave with you," the stranger said.

Micah kept the weapon trained on the man until the sound of the front gate closing told Micah that Ruby was safely out of harm's way. "More than certain, Drummond." Micah paused. "If that's who you really are."

"It is, but before I trot over to the jailhouse with you, I figure we've got some chatting to do." He paused to level an even stare despite the fact that he was in dire danger of being shot. "You are Micah Tate, captain of the Fairweather Key Militia and until, oh, two or three weeks from now, the acting judge as well. Sorry I missed the wedding, but you got yourself quite the bride, too. Feisty. Bet she's a—"

Micah's trigger finger twitched as his temper flared.

"Hold on there." Drummond waved his hands. "I mean no disrespect." Another pause, his arms still held high. "One lawman to another, that is."

"Lawman?" Micah sneered. "No decent lawman would break into someone's home and use it as a hideout, then convince children to do his stealing for him."

"See, that's where you're wrong." Drummond's hands sank a notch, but they rose again when Micah lifted the gun to adjust the sights. "Look here," he said, "how about you call some of your hired help to keep an eye on me so you don't get too jumpy and shoot me before you realize what I'm saying's the truth?"

Micah ignored the statement. "Where exactly did you find Carol?"

"She found me. I was out at the beach on the east end of the island. You know the spot where the mangroves are thick."

"I do."

"They're quiet, those two, and I was tired," he said. "Otherwise I'd have heard them."

"Not much of a lawman if a couple of schoolgirls can best you, Drummond." Yet he knew the story of the twins going to the beach alone was plausible. Before the Frenchman hit the floor and things changed, it wasn't unusual to see two or three of the O'Shea girls pass within view of his home when he happened to be there.

The stranger shrugged. "I'd have just slipped away quietlike and let those girls go on about their game of missing school, but for something the girl said to me."

"What's that?"

"That one—Carol's her name, I believe." He shook his head. "She called me her pa."

Micah called out for the two nearest men to join him. "Take him down to the jail," he told the first through the door. "I'm going to take a look around."

"Hold up there, Chief," Drummond said. "How about you check my references before you throw me in jail?"

Micah laughed. "What references?"

"I've got a coat somewhere in the back of the house. The girl said she'd hang it up for me."

"What will a coat prove?"

"There's a letter. Inside seam."

Micah waited until the men had Drummond in hand; then he went to the back of the cottage and opened a door. No armoire, only a lone bed and a table covered in books. Likely a spare bedroom.

Opening the door across the hall, he stepped into a room filled with light and flowers. They decorated the bed coverings and pillows, and pictures of them hung at different places around the room.

"If this is how Caleb's going to live, I feel for the man," he muttered as he stepped over a flowered carpet to throw open the door of an armoire that seemed to be the only thing in the room not covered with foolish adornments. Inside, conspicuous among the frilly things, was a man's jacket.

He yanked the jacket from its peg and patted it down for weapons. Satisfied nothing was hidden in it, Micah held it at arm's length as he walked down the hall and into the parlor. There he found Drummond swapping stories of life in Texas with his men.

"Feeling like home, are you, Drummond?" he asked with all the sarcasm he could manage. "I'm glad these fellows were able to entertain you. Stay long enough, and one of 'em just may ask you to waltz."

Both men shrank back to stand in the doorway as Micah stepped into the room and tossed the jacket to the stranger. "What's this going to prove?"

"There's a pocket in the seam." He gestured to a place under the left arm. "Reach in there, and see what you find."

Micah patted it first then slipped his fingers into the seam to retrieve what at first glance appeared to be a slip of paper. As he removed it completely, he could see it was a letter of introduction.

He glanced at the letter then scanned the signature. "Dumont?" Micah shook his head. "Is this—"

"Remy and Viola's elder brother with a second signature below made by their father, along with his seal. You can see by the letter that I am in their employ. If you look at the next page, you'll find a letter written on the stationery of the governor."

Micah turned to the second page. Sure enough, there it was.

"I see that." He shook his head. "What I don't understand is why."

Drummond looked past him to the men standing guard. "As a professional courtesy, I'm here on a private matter and would like it to stay that way."

Micah folded the letter and set it aside, then nodded to the militiaman nearest the door. "Go find Remy Dumont and bring him back here. If he gives you any trouble, tell him it's in regard to his sister." When the fellow had gone, Micah turned back to Drummond. "I doubt you were sent here to hide out in Emilie's house."

Drummond gave the remaining militiaman a glance. "You have

my word I'll not try to escape, Tate, so might we have some privacy?"

Micah gave the matter some thought then gestured to the fellow who waited at the door. "One sound out of the ordinary, and you come in." A pause for effect. "Shoot to kill."

"Yes, sir," he said as he left.

"And let me know the minute you see Dumont coming up the road." Micah waited for the man's response then turned his attention to Drummond. "All right. You've got your privacy," he said, "but I've got my militia."

"Fair enough." He leaned back against the cushions and rested his hands in his lap. "What would you like to know?"

"Start at the beginning," Micah said, "and I'll stop you if I have any questions." He shook his head. "Wait. When you were here last, we checked you out, Caleb and I, and all we could find was that you were an insurance man."

"You could say I've been hiding in plain sight, Tate," Drummond said. "An unfortunate casualty of my line of work is that I must sometimes stretch the truth in order to get to the greater truth." He shook his head. "And in a way, I do indeed work in the insurance field. I insure that the guilty are brought to justice." He shrugged. "So in that way, I'm not all that different from you."

Micah looked down at the stranger. "I doubt that."

"Anyway, the beginning. I came at the behest of both Mr. Dumonts—father and son—and I've been paid to bring the criminal Hill back to stand trial. It appears, however, that he ran off like the coward he is."

"Hill?" Micah shook his head. "Dr. Hill?"

He shrugged. "Doctor or not, he killed a man."

"Emilie's brother," Micah said, "though I understand the case has been closed as the doctor shot in self-defense."

A grin crossed Drummond's face. "I think that's for the courts back in New Orleans to determine."

Micah sighed. "I'll not be any part of vigilante justice, Mr. Drummond, which is exactly what this smells like. If these men want to hang someone, let them consider it might have been Viola who pulled the trigger."

Drummond seemed to give the statement some thought. "Likely

it was, but answer me this, Tate. Where's the good doctor now?"

"Gone," Micah said as he chewed on the words. "And I'll give you this: He didn't exactly leave in broad daylight."

"About a month ago, three weeks at the least?"

His eyes narrowed. "About."

Drummond's expression gave no indication of what he might be thinking. "I suppose that didn't set well with Miss Dumont."

"You can ask her yourself," Micah said. "She'll be the one doctoring you up."

"In the jail."

Micah shrugged. "Depends."

"I believe you're about to find out I'm telling the truth." Drummond gestured to the door. "You won't shoot me if I stand up, will you?"

"Got the schoolteacher, Mr. Tate," he heard the militiaman call as the gate closed.

"Send him in," Micah said, never removing his attention from Clay Drummond, who had begun to chuckle.

"Dumont," Micah said when the teacher walked through the door. "Do you know this man?"

Ignoring the question, Remy Dumont pressed past Micah. "Clay Drummond?" He followed the question by a string of expletives. Then Remy punched him.

To his credit, Drummond barely flinched as Viola's brother continued to deride everything from his parentage to his personal convictions.

"Any question now whether I am who I say I am?" he asked.

Micah nodded to the militiaman, who quickly stepped in to pull the schoolteacher off Drummond. "Guess it's too late to ask if you'd vouch for Drummond's character."

"Oh, I'll vouch for him, all right." Dumont struggled against the militiaman's iron grip. "I'll vouch for the fact my father and brother think the world of him. Funny, since it wasn't that long ago that you were the man they least wanted to see their precious—"

"Enough," Clay Drummond growled.

The stranger held his ground, but Micah couldn't help thinking he'd spring forward to take Dumont by the throat at any minute. Dumont looked ready to return the favor.

"Easy there." Micah moved between the two men. "The jail here's small, but it'll easily hold the both of you."

"I've done nothing wrong," Remy protested, "but this man, well, ask him what he does for my father. No, I'll tell you." He threw a disgusted look at Drummond. "He uses his considerable skills to see that my father and, I assume, my elder brother are kept apprised of anything that might interest them."

"You said you were a lawman." Micah gave the stranger a long look. "You want to change your mind and tell me the truth?"

"Oh, it's true enough," Remy continued. "Clay Drummond's got a long and storied career on both sides of the law. Father found him toiling away in some law office in San Antonio and decided to prey upon his emotions and bring him to New Orleans to work for him. I always suspected it was to keep you where he could watch you, Drummond. Same reason he arranged the situation with my sister."

"Another word," Drummond said through clenched jaw, "and I don't care what your father's orders are."

The teacher froze, his bravado turned to fluster. "What orders?"

Drummond cast a glance at Micah. "I told you the partial truth, Tate, and I'm man enough to ask for forgiveness for it now."

"Go on."

"It's true that I was sent here to get to the bottom of the Gayarre shooting and bring Daniel Hill back to face justice. I'm sure the Dumonts will not be happy that the doctor slipped away before that could be accomplished." He paused to release a long breath. "But the rest of the story is I'm also here to keep an eye on Remy and his sister until both are back home in New Orleans."

Drummond shifted his attention from Micah to Remy. "That's right," he said derisively. "Your father doesn't trust you to be man enough to come back to him alive."

Dumont launched himself at the stranger, surprising the militiaman, who'd eased his grip. In the resulting fray, Clay Drummond made short work of pinning the schoolteacher down despite being handicapped by his bandaged arm.

"Enough of this," Micah shouted as he yanked the stranger back. "You've proved to me who you are, Drummond," he said. "What I haven't decided is what to do about it." He gestured to the militiaman. "Escort Mr. Dumont home; then help him find a ticket back to New Orleans."

He gave Remy a look that dared him to respond, then felt more than a little disappointed when the schoolteacher left without comment. A thought occurred, and he turned to see Clay Drummond inspecting his injured arm.

"You'll be needing medical care." He paused. "But will Viola be willing to help you?"

Drummond surprised Micah with a grin. "I'd like to think she'd be glad to see me."

"I'll take that letter of yours until everything's sorted out." Micah kept his palm on his weapon until Drummond handed over the document.

"Is this where I march off to jail?" he asked with a sarcastic tone.

"I'm tempted," Micah said, "but only to keep tabs on you." He shrugged. "I'll send you over to the clinic with two of my men. After Vi patches you up, I'd like you to meet me back at my office to discuss a few things."

Drummond lifted a dark brow. "Such as?"

Micah shook his head. "You've got to survive your reunion with Viola Dumont first."

"Fair enough." He reached to offer his hand in a firm handshake. "One more thing, Tate. In my line of work, I hear things." A pause. "Recognize the name Thomas Hawkins?"

A blow to the gut, that name, yet he'd not let Drummond know this. "I do," he said as indifferently as he could manage.

Drummond seemed reluctant to continue. "You can take my advice or leave it," he finally said as he turned to leave, "but if I were you, I'd keep close tabs on that family of yours."

Micah caught the man by the shoulder and spun him around. "What do you know?"

"Talk is you've made him mad."

The Frenchman.

"We'll continue this conversation later, Drummond." He stepped back. "Understand if you're with Hawkins, you'll go down with him."

Drummond gave him a curt nod. "If you don't mind, Tate, I'd prefer to stand with you and yours."

CHAPTER 34

Ruby raced toward the beach, tears stinging her eyes. Long as they'd been married, Micah had never raised his voice to her. Now she'd really done it.

She turned off the lane, looking past the stares of those whose greetings she ignored. What if Mr. Drummond had been sent by Tommy to fetch her?

And she'd just chased off the only husband she'd had. The only man who'd been willing to stand by her and not ask for anything but her future. The man whose baby she might be carrying.

At the water's edge, she paused and tossed away her shoes and stockings, then moved forward, her skirts lifted above the tide. Rather than look to the horizon, she lifted her gaze upward. The words stuck in her throat, so she let the tears fall as the water lapped against her bare ankles.

Salt water flowing to salt water. Something appropriate in that.

And then the prayers rose up and burst forth, words spoken to a loving God who would neither forget her nor forsake her. By degrees, she backed up and sank to her knees in the sand, caring not for the mess she made of her frock.

Praise stung her lips until she let the thoughts find voice. Two lines from a song she'd learned only last Sunday bubbled forth. " 'Lo, here I fall, my Saviour! 'Tis I deserve Thy place,' " she sang into the surf. " 'Look on me with Thy favour, Vouchsafe to me Thy grace.' "

She tried to remember more of the song. Failing that, Ruby repeated the lines twice more; then spent, she rose. To her surprise, though she knelt on what felt like wet ground, her dress was only slightly marred by sand that easily dusted off.

This Ruby did quickly as she reached for her shoes and stockings. Beneath them she spied the sand dollar, and the tears began again. "Even if Micah no longer wants me, Lord, I know You do."

Slipping the treasure into her pocket, Ruby carried her bundle down the beach then donned her stockings and shoes to hurry toward home. Likely he'd be even more upset that she'd ignored his demand for her to go straight home.

"Ruby, wait."

She picked up her pace, unwilling to speak to whatever woman called her name.

"Ruby!"

Viola. This time Ruby stopped to allow the midwife-turned-doctor time to catch up. As she leaned into the cool shade of the mercantile, her gut began to protest again. Before Viola could reach her, Ruby had gone behind the store to relieve her stomach of what little contents it still held.

"Ruby?" Viola came to stand behind her. "Oh, Ruby, are you?"

Turning to face the midwife, Ruby held up her hand. "Don't say it. I cannot even consider that I might be. . ." She looked around. "You know."

Viola's grin was broad, her laughter immediate. "Honey, what's wrong with being, well, *you know*? You are a happily married woman, after all."

"I thought I was," she said as she swiped at the corner of her mouth with the back of her sleeve. "Now I'm not so sure."

"What do you mean?" Viola shook her head. "Of course you are."

"No, Micah's mad at me and deservedly so," she said, fully aware of how silly it sounded once the words were out.

The midwife shrugged then greeted one of the townsfolk. "And?" she asked when the matron had passed.

Ruby started walking toward the boardinghouse, anger renewing her purpose. "I thought you of all people would understand. Considering, I mean. He's *mad*."

Her expression changed. "Ruby, does he. . .that is, has Micah been. . . ?"

"What?" Ruby jerked her attention to Viola as the realization of her unasked question found its mark. "Oh no, not at all. Micah's gentle as a lamb. It's just that now, well, I thought he loved me, but now, what with the. . ." She paused to suck in a breath. "I'm rambling."

"No," Viola said slowly, "you're panicking. Take a deep breath. Now let it out slowly. Feel better?" she asked when Ruby had complied.

"Not really." She glanced up at the boardinghouse. "But I have to get back. Dinner won't wait." Ruby set off walking then stopped short. "Viola?" she called to the midwife's retreating back.

Viola returned to her side. "Yes?"

"Micah's got a prisoner at the jail who needs doctoring." She paused to decide how much of the odd saga of Mr. Drummond she should reveal. "He'd like you to come and see to him in an hour." She paused. "Less than that now, actually."

"Any idea of the extent of his injuries?"

Ruby shook her head. "His left arm. Cuts, maybe."

"I see. I'll do what I can, then, but I'll have to go and fetch some things at the clinic first." Viola's dark brows gathered as she gestured to Ruby. "About that. . .well, *you know*?"

Ruby felt heat rise in her cheeks. "What of it?"

"You've been through this twice already, so I don't have to tell you that you'll know soon enough if there's to be a babe come spring." Viola winked. "Let's hope this is just one baby and not two. Though I do love twins, they aren't always the easiest to birth, and they're often smaller than. . ." She shook her head. "Well, *you know*."

"Viola, please," Ruby said as she glanced around at the heavily populated sidewalk. "Do you mind?" she asked in a forced whisper. "If I am, I'd prefer Micah hear it from me and not any old somebody who happened to pass by."

"Of course."

Ruby made to walk away then stalled when Viola caught her by the arm. "About the other thing. Micah being mad?"

Ruby fidgeted with the edge of her sleeve. "What of it?"

"Honey," she said softly, "didn't anyone ever tell you that sometimes people who care about one another—friends or family, let's say—have differences of opinion? Say a sister you might have squabbled with or a mama or papa you didn't get along with."

"Well, sure, I guess," Ruby said as too many images tumbled forth. She chose one, a memory of Opal accusing her of not watching for Papa, and hung tightly to it, her fingers itching for the sand dollars that recalled that time in her life.

"And you still love that person, correct? I mean, one doesn't just up and leave a sister or a mama or a papa because of something like that."

"No," she said slowly, "not for something like that, I suppose." Again her gut roiled. Ruby swallowed hard and sniffed, her back straight. "A sister's always a sister, no matter what," she admitted.

Viola nodded. "That's right. Then you need to understand that you and Micah will sometimes squabble. That does not mean he's ready to stop being your husband." She paused to search Ruby's face. "You don't believe me, do you?"

Ruby took a deep breath and let it out slowly. "I want to."

She looked past the midwife to see her husband making his way up Main Street. "Ruby, wait," he called.

An uncharacteristic feeling curled in her gut, replacing the unsettled nausea. Was that a smile he wore? Then she saw it was for the fellow who ran the funeral home, a man he now had stopped to shake hands with.

Ruby watched her husband nod then tip his hat to a pair of matrons. How tall and proud he stood.

"So now that you've got a minute to spare, tell me about this prisoner. Should I bring Remy with me, or is he harmless?" Viola paused. "What are you looking at?"

Ruby blushed as Micah met her gaze.

"Honey, if you don't stop wearing that expression, the talk of the town is going to be how Ruby Tate is smitten with her own husband." Viola giggled. "What would that do to the other women who are married to mere mortals of less than Micah's caliber? Or worse, to single women like me who have no hope of snagging a—" She pressed her index finger to her lips as Micah neared. "I'll just be going now."

"Vi, wait. Did Ruby tell you about the fellow who needs attention?" Micah called.

She added another wink at Ruby before putting on a serious face and turning toward Micah. "Yes, she did. Anything I should know about him?"

Micah's gaze collided with Ruby's, and she felt the impact down to her toes. "No," he said to Viola. "Except that the plan's changed. I sent him to the clinic." His gaze never moved from Ruby as he went on to describe the attention Mr. Drummond might need. "Ruby, it's time to go home."

His voice held firm, though his eyes strayed downward from her face to slowly scorch a trail that she felt more than saw. Without warning, he pressed past her and headed for the boardinghouse.

"Yes, Micah," she said before reaching to grasp Viola's hand. "Thank you," she whispered as she kissed her friend's cheek then set out to follow her husband's broad back up Main Street.

Viola's nod bade her to walk fast enough to catch up with Micah's long strides. Until he reached to grasp her hand, a gesture both bold in its forwardness and welcome in its familiarity, she still wasn't sure what she was to face.

"We must have a serious discussion with Carol," he said.

"Yes," she said, though she would offer nothing more.

"Lies are lies." He opened the gate for her. "Carol must learn that there are consequences to keeping secrets, even if she felt she did it for a good reason."

"Consequences to keeping secrets. Even if she felt she did it for a good reason."

Again the words to the beloved hymn came to mind. *"Look on me with Thy favour, Vouchsafe to me Thy grace."*

Yes, Lord, please.

CHAPTER 35

Ruby trailed Micah up the stairs until they reached the door to their third-floor apartment. On the other side, the three girls chattered and giggled. As the door opened, however, silence reigned, and three innocent-looking girls sat cross-legged on the floor, a picture book between them.

At the sight of Ruby and Micah, Tess bounded up and threw herself into Ruby's arms. Maggie, however, turned to stare at Carol, who rose. "I'm in big trouble, aren't I?"

Ruby shifted Tess to her hip and looked to Micah. His nod was almost imperceptible.

"Your mother and I will talk to you about this after dinner." He gestured to the door. "For now, you may go downstairs and take down the laundry. Once you've folded everything and put it away, you may sit in the kitchen and wait for your mother."

It was all Ruby could do not to stare at the man who'd so easily slipped into the role of father to the girls. A smile began, but she tamed it lest she be misunderstood.

Carol opened her mouth, seemingly to protest, and then clamped it shut again. Without a word, she turned and left the room to head downstairs.

He turned his attention to Maggie. "Would you please take your sister outside to play? Inside the fence only and making sure you always see at least one of the militiamen."

Maggie climbed to her feet. "Want to get your dolly, Tess?" she called as she reached for a book. "I'll read to both of you."

Tess skittered from Ruby's arms and raced into the room where she now slept every night without exception. A moment later, she returned with her ragged baby doll and yanked at Maggie's free hand. "Hurry before we have to help Carol."

Ruby covered her smile with the back of her hand until the girls were safely out of the room. Micah stepped into her line of vision, his expression stern. "I fail to see the humor in any of this, Ruby. Perhaps you will enlighten me."

"I just, well. . ." She let out a long breath and dropped her hands to her sides as Micah closed the door. "It's just that Tess makes me smile."

"Ruby." The warning in his voice was impossible to miss. "Come here."

She did, though each step toward Micah felt as if she were walking to the gallows. "I'm sorry," she said. "I shouldn't have said anything, and I know I was in the way when—"

He stopped her babbling with a kiss.

"Never," he said, his voice rough and his breath warm against her neck as he held her against him, "never frighten me like that again."

"Frighten you?" She leaned up to look into his eyes. "I frightened you?"

Micah's hands met at the small of her back; then slowly he traced the length of her spine with his palm until he reached the back of her neck. "Men are assigned to see to your safety when I am not here. Until the issue of Hawkins and his crew is settled, you will not leave this place without someone with you. Do you understand?"

"Micah, really," she said, "I don't think it's necessary."

"Don't you?" He held her at arm's length, his grip firm but gentle. "How did you know you weren't walking into a trap at the cottage? That man could've been one of them."

She shook her head. "I was thinking of Carol."

Micah lifted her chin so she would meet his gaze. "I promised I would keep you safe, Ruby, but you're going to have to let me do it."

"I will," she whispered.

Beloved
Counterfeit

"You sure?"

"Yes, I'm sure." She paused. "Micah, about the man at Emilie's home. I—"

"Don't worry about him," Micah said. "I'm satisfied he is who he says he is."

"But that makes no sense." Ruby walked to the window and looked out. From nowhere the horizon seemed to tilt, and she grasped the frame for support.

"You understand I cannot tell you anything more than that he's provided sufficient proof."

Ruby formed a protest then thought better of it. "Yes, of course," she said softly.

He gestured to the back garden where Carol had joined the other two girls. "I've a sermon idea I'd like to run past you," he said, "on honesty."

Ruby gulped back the nausea. "Oh?" was all she could manage to say.

" 'Only fear the Lord, and serve him in truth with all your heart: for consider how great things he hath done for you,' " he quoted. "Wise words from 1 Samuel that I hope you might help me reason through."

She looked up and smiled as her fingers brushed the sand dollar in her pocket. "I would like that very much."

He touched the tip of her nose. "Have you any idea how much I appreciate that you act as a helpmeet in this?"

Tess scrambled into sight, and Ruby watched the girl tumble beneath the laundry drying on the line. True to her word, Maggie followed a close distance behind with the book tucked under her arm.

"Ruby?"

"What?" She found his gaze once more. "I'm sorry. I was watching—"

"The horizon?" he asked with an unreadable expression.

"The girls, actually." A wave of nausea hit her, and she fought to remain upright.

"Shall we go and have a discussion with our daughter, then?" Micah asked.

"Our daughter?" She smiled despite the churning in her gut. "I like the sound of that, Micah Tate." Her smile went south. "Perhaps you should go ahead, though. I'll be right there."

Micah cupped her cheek with his palm. "Are you ill?"

"I'll be fine," she said, though she barely managed to wait until Micah's boots hit the stairs before she found the chamber pot.

When she looked up, she found Micah staring. "You are unwell." A statement and not a question. He crossed the room to give her an odd look. "I figure this to be overwork," he decided, "and thus you will rest today." He lifted her easily and set her on the bed. "Hot tea will ease what ails you."

Though she wished to scramble away, Ruby stayed put. "I'm fine, truly."

A steady look, and then Micah shrugged. "Nonetheless, Carol will bring tea and toast. On my way back to the courthouse, I'll stop in at the Carters' and see if perhaps the reverend or his wife can offer some advice on hiring a cook to take over that part of your duties."

"Truly, Micah, I enjoy the cooking. I've done it all my life, and I'd be lost if I didn't have someone to cook for." The truth.

One of few she'd spoken to him about her past.

"Fine," he said after a moment. "Then someone to take on the other duties." He paused. "What is it you do?" When she told him, he shook his head. "I'll not try to figure how you manage it all, but I'll see to it that you'll not continue to do so."

"Thank you," was all she could manage as she watched her husband walk away.

A moment with her eyes closed, and the ill feeling passed.

"Are you sleeping?"

Carol. Ruby opened her eyes and saw Opal's precious child standing in the doorway with a tray. "Come in, honey," she said.

"Micah told me to bring you tea." She remained in place only a moment before carefully crossing the room to set the tray on the table beside the bed.

The question of how the girl had managed to climb two flights of stairs holding the tray disappeared when she heard heavy footfalls heading back downstairs. Micah. Ruby smiled. "Thank you, Carol.

Won't you sit with me?"

Indecision crossed Carol's face, though she quickly settled onto the settee. Ruby took a sip then set the cup aside.

"He's disappointed in me." Carol looked to Ruby as if asking her to disagree.

"As am I."

She rose. "That's because you're married to him. You've always got to do what he says now. Just like my mama used to do."

"Carol." Ruby kept her voice low and even. "Sit down." When the girl had complied, she continued. "Yes, Micah is my husband, and a wife has a duty to do as he asks. I don't expect you to understand this at your age."

"But. . ." She looked away.

Ruby scooted to the edge of the bed then eased over to sit beside Carol. "This time I agree with Micah, not only because he's my husband, but because I am disappointed, too."

"I thought you would understand," Carol said. "You of all people should know why I had to lie."

"You of all people."

A stab in the gut, and this time not from nausea. "What do you mean?"

Wide eyes shimmered with tears. "You know," she said in a low voice.

She did. She also knew it was the only way they'd survived thus far. But to explain this to a child?

Lately Ruby had trouble explaining it to herself, especially when each night she fell asleep beside a man who trusted her completely. A man who refused to let her tell him about her past.

She sighed. If only she could have the kind of faith Micah professed. *Fix that in me, Lord.*

"That man could have meant you harm," she said, intent on deflecting the topic.

"But he knows Miss Viola and Mr. Remy." She shook her head. "And he had a letter inside his jacket. And he only cut himself because I accidentally tripped him when he was carrying the plate I'd brought him."

Ruby shook her head. "Carol," she said slowly, "the fact remains that you and William have done something terribly wrong. There are always consequences to lying. Micah and I will decide what those consequences are for you."

Carol swiped at her tears, her demeanor now defiant. "If there are always consequences to lying, then you better start worrying, *Mother*."

CHAPTER 36

Viola took cautious steps up the back stairs to the clinic, all the while thinking of the times she'd boldly arrived via the front staircase. Now, however, she could barely force herself to step onto the property, much less face anyone who might see her there.

Had she not agreed to patch up some criminal, she would have happily gone on taking as little interest in the medical issues of the citizens as possible. Thankfully, there had been no wrecks on the reef since Daniel left—bad for the wreckers but good for the shipping commerce and for forgetting about the missing doctor.

"Wait until I get my hands on you, Daniel Hill," she muttered as she slid the key into the lock and turned the knob. "Of all the times you promised you would marry me, we end up like this?"

"The man was a fool."

She jumped, and the key clattered to the ground. Before she could pick it up, a distinctly male hand reached around her to grab it first. Viola turned to follow the length of arm and the breadth of shoulder, finally stalling at eyes the color of a stormy sea.

"Clay?"

Viola caught herself on the porch rail, though her knees still threatened to give way. She looked beyond the familiar face to find two men. Micah's men. Despite her better judgment, she waved them away then watched as they settled themselves on the steps.

She opened the door, stepped aside, and let Clay press past. "Why are you here?" she managed to ask as she closed the door. "You're not the prisoner Micah wanted me to see to, are you?"

"I reckon I am, though it took a good bit of talking to convince Tate I'm on his side of the law." He held up his injured arm. "So, yes, he said you'd patch it up for me. Nice guy, that Tate, though he is a bit protective of his kin." He paused. "Second reason might come as a surprise to you."

"Oh?"

His nod was quick and barely noticeable. "I came to save your skin, Vivi."

"Save my—" She glanced at his poorly wrapped hand. "What happened to you?"

He shrugged. "That's what happens when you let a girl do a job a woman was meant to do." At her outraged look, he held up his good hand. "I'm just teasing you," he said. "I'm ashamed to admit this, but I ran into a little trouble while waiting out the right opportunity to make myself known to you. If it weren't for the gal who found me, you might have been one more almost-husband short."

"Clay, honestly," she said. "That's a joke I don't find funny."

"Last time I hid in plain sight over at the boardinghouse. Even told 'em my real name." He held up his injured hand. "Probably should've done that again, but Tate nearly ruined my cover by asking too many questions. Had to tell him I was a fellow looking to find lost treasure. That, Vivi, wasn't a complete lie."

He moved toward her, so Viola slipped aside to put Dan's examination table between them. Again she took note of his injury. His gaze met hers, and she saw the scar.

"You going to fix me up?" he asked, seemingly oblivious to her discomfort.

"Yes," she said even as the memory of a brash soldier injured dueling for her hand plagued her thoughts.

His grin crinkled the corners of his eyes. "You're thinking about it, aren't you?"

She cleared her throat and reached to move the stool near to the table as if this unexpected reunion hadn't rattled her to the core. "Let's see what you've done to yourself this time, Clay Drummond."

Clay threw a long leg over the stool as he continued to watch her. Finally, he set his arm on the table then stretched out his fingers. "So where's the doc?"

A pause while she touched his fingers to draw his hand within reach. "He's away."

"Temporarily, or is he gone for good?"

She looked up sharply from her work of unwinding the makeshift bandage. "He didn't say. Why?"

Clay shrugged. "Worried about you."

"Everything's fine with me."

Yet as she stood in the spot where Dan Hill should have been, things were anything but fine. Behind her was the door where Andre Gayarre had burst through, the floor where he'd fallen. And gone was the one man she thought she could live the rest of her life with, even after he'd watched her kill a man.

"Is that so?" His chuckle was slow, deep. "Then I guess no one's told you about the suspicion of murder."

"Murder?" Her heart thumped against her chest as she went back to work. "You've got the wrong woman." She paused in her work to let her hands still their trembling. "This is about Andre Gayarre, isn't it?"

"It is."

"You're late on that one," she said as casually as she could. "The shooting was ruled self-defense. Case closed."

"Maybe in Florida, but you know things don't operate the same way in Louisiana," he said as he flexed his now-free fingers. "I did some damage to that, didn't I?"

"At least it's not your trigger hand." Viola forced a calm breath. "Now tell me why a lawman from Texas would come all the way to Florida to drag out an already-closed case."

"Ex-lawman, Vivi," he said. "I hire out now."

She refused to look up from the work of picking glass out of his hand. Memories of the brash fellow who'd tried to court her, only to find opposition from every male member of the Dumont family, were limited by her choice to remember. What Viola did recall was a man who was too smart, too handsome, and too good with a gun for his own good health.

239

She turned his hand over to see that his knuckles had suffered from the same treatment. "This looks like pieces of a whiskey bottle I'm picking out of here, so I'll guess you've bought yourself a saloon."

He didn't smile. "Hardly," he said. "That's part of a dinner plate, by the way. Turns out I'm still as light on my feet as I used to be."

This time his joke did hit the mark, though Viola gave him only the briefest of smiles before her hand slipped and she dropped the instrument. Thankfully, it clattered to the tabletop and not the floor. Easily retrieving it, she went back to work as if everything about the man she'd once entertained the thought of marrying hadn't changed in a heartbeat.

"Did you hear me, Vivi? I'm working for people who need justice now. Can you feature it?"

"I heard you." She set the instrument aside and looked up at him. "Believing you, now that's another thing entirely."

This time his smile was quick to unfold. "I'm sure that's the truth. You'll likely not believe me when I tell you that losing you put me on a course I never expected. See, I didn't leave the Rangers; the Rangers left me." He shrugged. "Actually, after one too many nights associating with the same fellows I was supposed to be rounding up, the captain told me they'd prefer I keep to that company instead of theirs."

She set the instrument aside. Despite her refusal to comment, the thought of Clay Drummond playing any part but the brash soldier was hard to fathom. "So how did you end up changing careers? I figured once a soldier, always a soldier."

"Did time," he said as he once again flexed his fingers. "But it was good for me."

"As in jail?" Another blow to the memory of Clay Drummond. Surely the questions she had would find expression, but for the present, it was all Viola could do not to edge Clay off the stool and seat herself. Only the Lord kept her knocking knees from giving way.

He reached over to rest his free hand atop hers. "I left jail a man who knew two things: the Lord and the law." He noted her look of discomfort and removed his hand. "When I was released, the fellow who prosecuted me in San Antone was more than happy to teach me what he knew about lawyering. I ended up working for him until I got a better offer some months ago."

"Is that so?" The dashing image returned, and with it her resolve not to think of it. "This might sting a bit." She set the basin under his hand and washed his wounds. "Sorry," she said when she was done.

Again he placed his hand atop hers. Her mind tumbled back to the soldier who'd brashly introduced himself, who'd gone to her papa for permission to court her then swiftly ignored the man's refusal and come calling. How tempted she'd been to allow it.

"I'll need to bind that," she said as she slipped her fingers from beneath his.

Clay allowed her to finish her work before he reached for her hand. "Look, I know you're surprised I'm here and likely not too happy to see me."

Viola shook her head. "I haven't decided that, Clay," she said, "but I'm confused. I'll admit that." Their gazes met. "I didn't murder anyone, and neither did Dan."

"Then why'd he leave?"

Viola's hand trembled, so she paused to wait it out then turned her back to begin putting away the instruments. "Maybe he didn't want to marry me," she tossed over her shoulder.

"I'll find Dan Hill and bring him to justice." His boots hit the floor heading away from her. "You're thinking you'll confess to shooting Gayarre and save your man, aren't you? Well, forget it."

"The truth is the truth, Clay, no matter who you work for." She turned to find him at the door, his bandaged hand slipping into his jacket, the other holding his hat. "I'm not sure I believe any of this."

He removed a paper from his pocket and stormed toward her, tossing it onto the table. "It's a letter for you. Read it."

She didn't have to, for the handwriting told the tale. "Papa," she said as her heart sank.

"Indeed."

"But why? Who would be pressing these charges? Andre's father is dead, and Emilie's the only relative still living."

"Isabelle's the heir, Vivi, not Emilie," he corrected. "You know that."

She did, but it stunned her to realize he knew as well. "How did you—"

"Know about Emilie being born to a slave woman?" He paused. "It's my business to know these things." Clay shook his head then slipped on his hat. "The truth is, old Monsieur Gayarre's funeral stirred up quite a fuss. With a daughter off somewhere in Florida and a son killed under mysterious circumstances, an enterprising reporter decided to do some digging. That's when the details of Andre Gayarre's death came out." Another pause. "And with them, his engagement to you."

Viola sighed. Of course her father and brother would be horrified that the family name had been associated with such an affair.

A tip of his hat, and then Clay snapped his finger as if he'd forgotten something important. "You should know, Vivi," he said, "when I was last here, I contacted the good doctor."

"You what?"

"I stayed at the boardinghouse." He shrugged. "Figured I'd get the lay of the land before I decided what to do about you and Dr. Hill."

Something akin to anger boiled to the surface. "What did you say to him?"

Clay's grin spread as he reached for the latch. "That it might be healthier for him if he did his doctoring elsewhere. Guess he agreed with me."

With that, Clay Drummond turned his back to her and walked out the door.

Viola caught up with him before his boots hit the sidewalk. "Come back here, Clay Drummond. I'm not done talking to you."

He stopped short, and she almost slammed into his broad back. "You sure you want to make a scene right here in the middle of town?" he asked as he glanced over his shoulder.

"I've got nothing to hide," she said even as she lowered her voice. Then she spied Micah Tate coming up the road toward them.

Clay looked past her. "Best smile, Vivi. I'd hate to end up in jail again because Micah Tate decided I was a threat."

"He'd be right," she said as she turned to wave at Ruby's husband. "I got your prisoner patched up, Micah. You can go ahead and lock him up now."

"Let's take a walk, Drummond." Micah waved off his men and waited for Clay to fall into step beside him.

"I thought I'd be meeting you at your office."

He gestured to the clinic. "You'll understand if my allegiance is to Vi. I needed to see for myself that she was all right."

"She's a strong woman, if that's what you're worried about. Viola might be missing a fiancé, but she'll be fine."

"The Gayarre case is closed," he said. "And all vigilante justice will do is get you a stay in my jail."

When Drummond had no response, Micah pressed on. "Leave Viola be, Drummond. She's been through enough. If you want to go off chasing Doc Hill, I can't stop you, but I'll not have you bothering an innocent woman. So don't try my patience. In addition to my concerns about Vi, you've gotten my daughter in a heap of trouble."

"Look," he said. "I never intended for that to happen, but I also never intended for them to catch me while I was working. I had to say something."

Micah stared at the fool. "The truth would have been a handy thing to start with, seeing as you're a lawman and all."

Drummond ducked his head and gestured to his bound hand. "You're right, and I'll admit it. I figure that's why the Lord let me fall over my own big feet and land in a mess of broken plate. I likely had it coming."

"Likely." Micah shouldered past a pile of barrels that narrowed the sidewalk, then waited for Drummond to catch up. "Tell what you know about Hawkins."

"He's put the word out that he's looking for a woman he calls Ruby Red. Said she stole something from him and he wants it back."

Micah digested the information. "Why the warning about keeping an eye on my family?"

"You tell me, Tate," Drummond said. "And before you start thinking I'm one of them, realize the Dumonts aren't paying me enough to rot in jail, but they are paying me enough to stay on the right side of the law. I'll stand with you to keep Hawkins off this key if you'll let me."

He glanced at the man. "What do you get out of it?"

"I'm not stupid enough to think I'll get Vivi off this island anytime soon." Drummond paused. "What you don't know is she once meant very much to me. Still does, actually."

The statement surprised Micah. "Go on."

"I know what a man like Hawkins is capable of, and I don't think there's a woman on this island who is safe until he finds whatever he's looking for. Or should I say, *whom* he's looking for." He gestured up the hill. "Looks like we're going to the boardinghouse."

"That's where I'm going." Micah stopped short to allow a pair of ladies to cross the sidewalk ahead of him. "You'll have to find another place, and it won't be Emilie's cottage. I've got men staked out there to be sure of it."

A flash on the horizon caught Micah's attention, and he turned toward the ocean. He saw it again and knew immediately what it was. Pressing past Drummond, he started toward the docks. Before he reached his destination, the cry of "Wreck ashore!" had sounded.

"What's going on?"

He glanced back to see that Drummond had followed. "Ship on the reef. Looks familiar, but I can't place it."

Picking up his pace, Micah weaved through the passing wagons on Main Street to emerge on the other side. There he found lighter foot traffic and a downhill slope that let him break into a full-out run.

When he reached the docks, he made short work of reaching his vessel though the chaos of wreckers. As he yanked on the rope, inexplicably stuck, Drummond vaulted past and landed on the deck.

"Get out of here," he said as he went back to his work.

"I'm one-armed, but I know my way around a deck. Back in '31, I had the misfortune of being aboard the *Sabine* when Brown decided not to pay the Mexicans their export duty." He reached behind Micah to give the rope a yank with his free hand. "Long as I don't have to help you sail this thing from behind a cotton bale with cannons firing at us, I think I can handle it."

Together they had the vessel free in a few seconds. "Thank you," Micah said, "but I'll not tell you again to leave my ship before I have to throw you off."

"You don't have that kind of time." Drummond pointed to the now-flaming wreck. "And I guarantee I'd put up a fight, even without both hands. Now what say we head toward that wreck? You'll do

Beloved Counterfeit

better to get this vessel under sail with me as your crew than with none at all."

He was right, though Micah hated to admit it. "Stay out of the way and do as I say."

With a mock salute, Drummond sprang into action. In short order, they'd joined the cluster of wreckers sailing against the tide toward the reef. It didn't take Micah long to recognize the vessel now partially engulfed as the *Weatherly*, owned by a merchantman who regularly sailed the waters.

Micah eased the vessel alongside the others then called out to ask who the first on scene had been. "Neely's the master on this one," the wrecker nearest Micah responded.

"Duly noted," he said. "What instructions has he given?" After listening and nodding, Micah turned to Drummond. "Lay anchor and stay put."

He only looked back once to be sure the stranger had done as he'd been told. Jumping into the fray meant finding a way to salvage people and goods from a vessel listing to port and burning. As the wreck's master called out that the ship was now emptied of its occupants, Micah surged forward with the other wreckers to search for any cargo that might be salvaged.

Staying low kept the smoke above him for the most part, but Micah still coughed even though he'd tied a length of cloth over his nose and mouth. One closed hold offered up a wealth of goods for the wreckers to offload and bring back into town, but two more were filled with smoke and flames.

"It's no use," he heard the man nearest him call. "The rest'll burn before we can salvage it."

But Micah thought otherwise. "I'm going to give it a go." He gestured toward the end of the passageway. "Just some smoke right now. I think I can make it."

"Suit yourself," he heard from behind him. "But I doubt Neely's going to want to risk you getting hurt again, Tate."

Getting hurt again. Until now, he'd not thought of the last time he'd acted as wrecker with his own vessel. Losing the *Caroline* to the explosion had paled in comparison to the injuries Doc Hill had predicted would sideline him from wrecking altogether.

The doctor was wrong.

Micah shook his head as he turned away. "Neely's got more important things to worry about than me."

The only way to reach the fourth compartment was on his hands and knees, so Micah crawled down the passageway even as the smoke thickened and stung his eyes. As he reached the hold, flames teased the latch, and he knew his mission was over.

Micah felt a tap on his shoulder and turned to see Clay Drummond squatting behind him. "Neely's called us off."

Irritation rose like the flames overhead. "I told you to stay put."

An all-too-familiar groaning noise drowned out Drummond's response. Then came the darkness. No air, just water and stale smoke.

Coughing was as close to breathing as Micah could manage. Something wrenched at his arm, and then, mercifully, came the air.

He scrambled to his feet and found smoke again. This time when he fell, it was to land on knees that took him toward the light streaming through a break in the hull.

Emerging into fresh air and sunshine, he dove into the water and swam toward his vessel. He beat Drummond to the side and hoisted himself over as the stranger caught the anchor's rope.

The lawman took Micah's outstretched hand and tumbled over the rail to fall onto the deck. Micah slid backward on the wet deck and landed on his face.

He could've stood, but lying there inhaling fresh air felt like the better choice. And inhale he did—deeply—ignoring the strangers who stomped around the deck, flailing water and hooting with what sounded like either joy or pain.

Closing his eyes, Micah let the sunshine dry his face. Still, the breaths came deep and clean. Then a shadow fell across his face.

"Still wish I'd stayed put?"

Micah leaned up on his elbows. "Drummond," he said slowly, "didn't your mama tell you when she was raising you that you should listen to your elders?"

"I'm sure she did," he said slowly, "but I probably wasn't listening." He sank down beside Micah and leaned his back against the rail. "Oh,

and for the record, I'm older than you by seven months and a day."

"How do you know that?"

Clay Drummond glanced at him then offered a crooked smile. "It's my job to know things, Tate. Haven't you figured that out yet?"

"What I haven't figured out," he said as he rose, "is how you know them."

"Like I said." Drummond scrambled to his feet then flexed his injured hand. "It's my job. Just like it's your job to guard this pitiful island until Caleb Spencer comes back to claim it."

Micah nodded, deciding the fewer words used in Drummond's presence, the better. Then a thought occurred. "If you know so much, why don't you know where Doc Hill is?"

Drummond reached for his hat and set it atop his wet hair. Taking his time as if considering his response, the stranger finally looked Micah's way. " 'Cause I told him I didn't want to know."

"So you—"

"Suggested he take an extended vacation until people stopped asking what happened to Andre Gayarre?" He nodded. "Yeah. Seemed the best choice for everyone."

Understanding dawned. With Dan Hill's mysterious disappearance, blame for Gayarre's death would shift to the doctor. And away from the midwife.

"Especially Viola Dumont," Micah said.

"Exactly," was Drummond's quick reply.

"So I guess you'll be staying for a while, then?"

Another grin. "Exactly," Drummond said. "Thought I might rent a room at the boardinghouse."

Micah shook his head. "Might as well stay at the doc's place until he returns, seeing as how you two are acquainted and all."

Clay Drummond answered with a solid handshake. "I'll take good care of her," he said.

"And I'm going to pretend I don't know what you're talking about."

CHAPTER 37

Three weeks had passed since the wreck of the *Weatherly*, and soon Caleb would return to take the mantle of responsibility from Micah. The letter now sitting atop his Bible was proof his tenure as judge would end as soon as Caleb could extract his wife from his mother's clutches.

Even as Micah laughed at the image, he looked forward to the pair's arrival with mixed emotions. Less responsibility gave him more time with Ruby and the girls. This much he appreciated, though lately he'd sensed something not quite right with his wife.

While she never failed to respond to him in the dark, her gaze often did not quite meet his in the daylight. Maybe he'd ask Josiah about that. He had far more experience as a husband than Micah did.

Josiah had also sent word that he and Isabelle would be returning early—possibly today. Soon they would be ushering another child into the world, and Isabelle insisted Viola be in attendance for the birth. Micah tapped his pen against the edge of the inkwell then set it aside.

He'd figured to be making those sorts of plans with Ruby by now.

At the sound of footsteps on the front steps, Micah looked up from his corner of the dining table. The boarders, a pair of missionaries awaiting transport to points south, stepped inside, interrupting their animated conversation to greet him, then disappearing upstairs.

Micah returned to his sermon notes but found that his thoughts

refused to follow. He chafed at the reminder that nearly three months after the wedding, he was no closer to moving his family to a home of their own, despite the fact Mrs. Campbell had written to say she would be working on a replacement for Ruby.

Though Micah hated to see Ruby working, even now that he'd hired others to do everything but the cooking, he did welcome the security the big house on the hill provided, especially when his militia duties kept him away.

Thankfully, the Seminole threat seemed to have passed, at least in Fairweather Key. Despite their position far south of any attacks, the militia remained vigilant with at least two men on guard at any time. Later tonight, Micah would take his turn despite the fact that the late shifts had begun to be a point of contention in his marriage.

While he didn't blame Ruby for her concern, it bothered Micah a bit that she didn't appreciate his willingness as a leader to take on the same duties as those he commanded. At least he assumed that was the issue behind her behavior.

The object of his thoughts passed through the room, and he reached out to snag her around the waist. "Micah Tate, you do carry on," she said, though she willingly set aside her basket of laundry and landed in his lap.

"Yes," he said as he kissed her soundly then set her upright again and allowed her to go on her way, "I do, but with good reason."

Indeed, he had plenty of good reasons for carrying on. Ruby O'Shea—Ruby Tate, he corrected—and her three daughters had brought him a happiness he'd never thought he'd have again.

Which brought him to the choice to revisit the idea of second chances.

His sermon idea—or rather, Ruby's idea—using the novel *Robinson Crusoe* was so well received back when he'd given it that Micah had decided to use the idea again. This time, however, he planned to add an exercise. So sure was he that this exercise would be beneficial to the parishioners that he told Rev. Carter that he would first try it at home with Ruby.

The prospect of telling her the whole truth about Caroline and the baby so soon into their marriage troubled him, though Micah knew the Lord would go before him to smooth the way for his news. He wouldn't require anything from Ruby, as he would be telling the congregation the exercise was voluntary though recommended.

Besides, what would she have to confess that he hadn't already guessed? Somehow she'd fallen in with a man who traveled in a rough crowd. Youthful foolishness was his guess. Love brought three daughters, though the man obviously raised his fists to Ruby more than once.

The idea of anyone inflicting harm on her made him shake with rage. *It's a good thing he's dead, or I'd have to kill him.*

Micah looked down at his fists then sat back stunned. *Where did that come from?* He obviously had some business to do with God before he could broach the topic with Ruby of her life before she married him.

Better to keep tonight's conversation centered on him without letting it stray to her. This decided, Micah reached once again for his notes from the earlier sermon. He'd preached this sermon as a man whose wife of only a few days sat in the front row. Staying focused on the topic had been difficult, for somehow he'd become hopelessly besotted with the woman he'd never expected to love.

And it happened in the first hours of their life together.

The door opened again, but Micah ignored it. "Might an old man interrupt?"

He looked up to see Rev. Carter standing in the doorway. Rising to offer the pastor a chair, Micah smiled. "I'd not call your visit an interruption. Do sit." He waited until the old man had settled in his chair before returning to his place. "I hope you've not come to tell me you've changed your mind about Sunday's sermon. I had an idea to do something that I think will be quite effective."

"Oh no, son," he said as he placed a stack of mail on the table. "Rather, I've come for something else."

"The mail?" Micah spied a letter sitting atop the stack that caused his breath to catch in his throat. As he gathered his wits and slid the documents aside, he knew there was only one reason Caleb would be receiving a letter from the authorities in Texas.

Micah's heart sank as Rev. Carter continued to stare.

"Well," Micah said as he cleared his throat and sat up a bit

Beloved
Counterfeit

straighter. "I do appreciate the favor of delivering these, though I hate that you went to all the trouble." Again he slipped a peek at the letter.

"No trouble at all. I happened to be strolling past the mail boat and offered to deliver these as I was already headed this way." Josiah's father leaned his cane against the table, and the silver lion's head caught the light. "Though perhaps you'll wish I'd chosen to discuss one Sunday rather than a multitude of them."

"A multitude, sir?"

"It cannot come as a surprise that I would extend the offer of handing over my pastorate to you, Micah," he said.

"Why now?" was all Micah could manage.

Hezekiah Carter's brows rose. "In a word, William." He shook his head. "The boy's bright. He was headed for school in London when he and Josiah arrived here."

"I didn't know that," Micah said, "though I have noticed the boy's of above-average intelligence."

"Indeed, he is," the pastor said, "and I wish to reward his studious nature by showing him the Continent."

Unannounced, Josiah Carter stepped into the room and embraced his father. "And to think when I was William's age you only wanted to show me the door." Before the reverend could protest, Josiah waved his objections away. "I deserved far worse, Father," he said, "and I can admit that now."

Micah rose to shake his friend's hand. "Welcome back. You've been missed."

"And it appears I almost missed something important here." He claimed the chair next to his father. "Am I wrong, or are you ceding your spot in the pulpit to my friend Tate here?"

"I am," Hezekiah said. "And with no hesitation."

Micah froze, unable to speak. For a moment, he considered tossing the letter from Texas into the fire.

Josiah smiled. "It appears a celebration is in order."

"Not yet, Son," Rev. Carter said. "The lad's not yet agreed."

"What?" Josiah swung his gaze to Micah. "Well, put the man out of his misery and tell him you'll do it."

"I don't know." Micah returned to his seat and laid his palm over the stack of letters. "It's a big job. I wonder if I'm up to it."

Rev. Carter reached for his cane then pointed it toward Micah. "Promise me you will never lose that feeling of inadequacy, and I'll hand over the keys to the parsonage this very minute."

The parsonage.

A home of their own.

Micah swallowed hard and tried to think of what to do next. Of what to say.

"Surely you've been praying about the day this would happen," Josiah said.

"I have," Micah managed to say. "I just didn't think it would happen so soon."

"Have you told him the rest of it, Father?" Josiah asked.

"Not yet." Hezekiah leaned forward. "I've a further piece of information for you, Micah." He paused as a look passed between him and his son. "Our Isabelle has made a purchase with the inheritance she received from her late father." Another pause, this time to tame a grin. "Mrs. Campbell drove a hard bargain, but our Isabelle is now the owner of the boardinghouse. Or rather," he said with a chuckle, "she and Mary, as the two ladies have been plotting this for quite some time."

"Isabelle and Mrs. Carter?" Micah struggled to take in all the news. "Why? What possessed her to. . ."

Josiah shrugged. "I advise not to try to logic it out, Micah. Between Isabelle and my mother, the place will be in good hands, though I'm sure they will be looking to Ruby for the occasional recipe and possibly help with the menus."

"I'm sure she'd be willing to do whatever is asked of her," he said. "Though she will be the one to tell you that for certain."

Hezekiah rose, ignoring his son's offer of help. "We shall consider it settled. You're already preparing a sermon for Sunday."

"I am," Micah said as he stood on shaking legs.

"Then with your permission, I shall make the announcement of your pending pastorate at that time."

Micah nodded. "I'll speak to Ruby first, of course." *And the authorities in Texas.*

"Of course," he said. "And you'll let her know she'll be handing her pots and pans over to my wife as soon as the switch can be managed?"

"I will." He rounded the table to shake Rev. Carter's hand as Josiah clapped him on the back. "But I must ask, are you certain of all this?"

"I am."

And with the reverend's firm assertion, Micah knew his life had taken an interesting turn. Or it might have had his past not caught up with him. Even as he stepped out onto the porch to bid the Carter men good-bye, he was plotting how he might best tell the news to Ruby.

He walked back into the dining room like a man heading for the gallows. Again the fireplace beckoned.

Lifting the letter, Micah held it to the light. It was certainly within his authority to open any correspondence sent to the person in charge. He'd been doing just that ever since Caleb left.

Micah broke the seal and opened the letter, then held it against his chest while he petitioned the Lord to care for his wife and the children he would surely soon leave behind.

His eyes scanned the page.

"No offense found," he read. "No offense found." Micah's heart soared as he read sentences offering him up as a man with whom the state of Texas could find no fault.

"I'm free." He stood then fell back into the chair as the welcome relief of laughter overtook him.

"What's so funny in there, Micah Tate?"

Ruby. He smiled as his laughter faded to a chuckle. He should tell her all of it, but where to start?

In one brief conversation, all his prayers had been answered. Well, he decided, almost all of them. *But there will be a babe soon enough.*

Micah returned to his sermon notes then gave up his studies and leaned back against the chair, closing his eyes. *Lord, I am a man truly blessed.*

"Sleeping on the job, are you?" Ruby ruffled his hair as she passed by again, well aware of his habit of praying during the sermon preparations, which were coming at regular intervals of late.

"Research for Sunday's sermon. Also, I'm pondering answered prayers." Micah paused. "Might I count on some time with you after dinner? I could use your listening ear on both topics."

"Yes, of course," she said as she swiped at her forehead with the corner of her apron. "Something wrong?"

"No, of course not," he said. "I'm merely in need of a bit of sermon help." He swiveled to face her. "If you're agreeable, that is."

Ruby nodded and went back to her work. "I'll see the girls are in bed early."

True to her word, Ruby had the twins settled and Tess sleeping soundly well before their usual bedtime. "How did you do that?" he asked when she returned to their bedchamber and closed the door.

"Prayer," she said. "And a promise to begin reading *Robinson Crusoe* to them as soon as their papa was finished with it. Which I told them I would ask you about tonight when we had our special conversation."

Papa.

His mind hung up on that word and took in very little of the rest, though he did manage a nod and a murmur of agreement.

Papa.

Micah grinned as he thought of moving his family of five—soon to be more, he hoped—into the parsonage. It had taken Maggie and Tess very little time to warm up to him. Carol, however, still maintained a distance that only the rarest of smiles could sometimes breach.

Likely she'd not be thrilled to know her mother associated her with the other two traitors, as he'd overheard Carol call them when they referred to Micah in fatherly terms. She alone of the three maintained that her father would someday return for her, though both Maggie and Tess had assured him their father had drowned when his boat was sunk.

Micah found it troublesome that Ruby did not correct Carol, though he'd thus far kept his peace on the matter. Once Carol decided he was not a stranger to be ignored—or worse, an interloper who meant to take her mother away—then perhaps they would broach the topic of what to call him. After that, they would tackle the subject of her father's death.

"Micah?"

He turned to find Ruby already at her dressing table, unpinning her hair. "Yes, sorry," he said as he moved to push her fingers away and do the work of allowing her hair to fall about her shoulders.

She looked up, eyes narrowed, then captured his hands with hers. "Micah Tate. You didn't want to work on a sermon at all, did you?"

The question brought him to a dilemma. No, he didn't; not anymore. Nor did he want to even discuss the good news with her at this moment. Indeed, the thought on his mind was singular and bordering on desperate.

Yet there was no putting this off.

Micah slipped from her grasp then knelt before her. "Ruby, I've been working on another sermon about how God forgives us even though we tend to hold things against ourselves." He looked up at her. "Perhaps you remember the previous one."

Her grin was sufficient response.

"This time I'm feeling as though I need to challenge those in attendance to look within and do some contemplating over what God might be asking them to forgive."

She nodded. "A worthy exercise."

"That's it, indeed." Micah kissed his wife then forged ahead, knowing how easy it would be to leave this conversation while they were both smiling. "I've known for several days that before I could expect the parishioners to search their hearts, I had to search my own."

Ruby nodded then reached for her hairbrush. "I think that makes good sense."

Micah leaned back to rest his palms on Ruby's knees. "The Lord's been clear in telling me I need to speak to you about some things." He cupped her chin and directed her gaze to meet his. "Things that are difficult."

"Difficult?" Her eyes widened. "You're frightening me."

He rose to lift her to her feet then wrapped his arms around her. "No, don't be frightened. The truth is all it is, Ruby, and once it's out, we'll both be the better for it."

CHAPTER 38

So he knows.

Ruby searched the face of the man she'd come to know as husband and found no trace of the emotions she expected. Had God really given her someone who could know of her many, many sins and still hold such love for her that it showed on his features?

It appeared so.

"Perhaps it is time for such a discussion," she said. "Though I am a bit confused as to how you—"

"Come and sit with me," he said, and she followed him to the settee. "Now to begin."

He took a deep breath and appeared to be waiting for her to start. Again she studied his expression and found nothing to cause her to believe he was angry.

"Yes, well, it all started with a particularly hot afternoon when I was barely out of the nursery. Not that we had a nursery, Opal and I." Her hand shook, and she hid it in the pocket of her skirt. "Mother wouldn't have hired anyone decent to staff it, anyway. We ran wild mostly, unless Papa was on the island."

Micah stared at her as if she'd said something foreign. "What?" she asked.

"Go on," was all he said, though she distinctly felt he had more on his mind.

"The day came when we couldn't hide from Papa anymore. And

when he found us. . ."

"You and Opal?" Micah supplied.

"Yes. When he found us, well, let's just say he likely thought he'd killed us, and we let him believe it. If it wasn't for Opal's friend, we'd have been left on that beach the same way he left our mother."

"Your mother?" His tone held an unmistakable chill.

The memory of the woman lying in the surf rose only to disappear. She'd not allow herself to spend a moment thinking on it.

Her husband shook his head. "Am I to understand your father murdered your mother and left you and someone named Opal—"

"My sister."

"Your sister, Opal," he continued, "for dead?"

Ruby could only nod. In all the years since she had left O'Connor Plantation, she'd never told the whole sordid tale to anyone, not even Mrs. Campbell. As far as she was concerned, it died with Opal.

"But you were rescued." He reached for her, and Ruby allowed herself to be drawn against his shoulder. "That's quite a testimony, Ruby, that God was able to deliver you from that horrible situation."

"Yes," she said as she slid a look up to see if perhaps Micah Tate was toying with her. Surely if he knew the rest of her story, he wouldn't have been so grateful that God allowed her to go from one tragedy to the next without doing much, if any, delivering.

Micah shifted her around to face him then slid her across his lap. "What happened to Opal?"

Ruby refused to allow her mind to recall the image. Somehow she forced herself to say the words: "Thomas Hawkins killed her."

"Hawkins." Micah swallowed hard then set his jaw. A vein in his neck twitched, and he seemed unable to speak. "You were his prisoner."

Indeed, she did not desire to be aboard the smuggler's vessel, but had she taken the opportunity Tommy offered to depart in Havana, the girls would have had no one to protect them. He would certainly never let them remain behind. Thus, though she traveled with Hawkins and his men, she *was* truly a prisoner, bound by the ties of family obligations. With only the slightest twinge of guilt, she nodded.

"And this Frenchman?" Now his temper had obviously flared,

even though his voice softened. "What was his role?"

"He protected me," she said without meeting his stare, "and the girls, too."

Once the statement hung between them, Ruby looked into eyes filled with the closest thing she'd seen to unconditional love. In that moment, also, she knew he had no idea about any of this.

"Ruby?" he said slowly. "Is there something else?"

"No," she said. Never would she hurt her husband by telling him what Jean Luc Rabelais demanded in return for that protection.

But as she settled against his chest, she felt another twinge of something akin to guilt. Was it really Micah she was protecting, or had she ignored a chance to tell Micah the whole truth?

"Ruby?" His voice rumbled against her ear. "I appreciate your honesty. Might I tell you my story now?"

She almost blurted out a loud no accompanied by the full truth of her life before landing on Fairweather Key. Almost told him about Claire and the piano lessons in Galveston. And the fathers of those girls, the men who made scheduled nighttime assignations with her while, during the day, their daughters learned their scales and plinked out silly tunes.

If what Micah had said in church was the truth, then God had forgiven her for all of it the moment she confessed her actions and promised never to repeat them. Micah had promised everyone present that Sunday that the Lord would cast the ugliness into the depths of the sea where He would think of it no more.

But could she?

More important, could Micah?

Ruby knew the answer to the first question, but she refused to take a chance on the second. Thankfully, she was a wrecker's wife and not someone who might be expected to be held to a higher standard.

Leave that for women like Mary Carter. I've got miles to go before I can manage that sort of spotless reputation.

"Your story?" she said. "Yes, of course."

"I had a wife," Micah began, and Ruby closed her eyes. She kept them closed as her husband told the story of a battle he wished he hadn't gone off to fight and a wife and child he'd expected to be

Beloved Counterfeit

waiting when he returned.

He tightened his grip and spoke of coming home to find graves rather than family, and Ruby felt tears welling. "It wasn't your fault, Micah," she whispered. "You couldn't have known."

"I'm coming to believe that," he said, "though I'm still not completely convinced."

Micah cupped her cheek with his hand and softly kissed her forehead. "I failed my fellow soldiers and my family," he said, his voice thick with emotion and his eyes full of unshed tears. "You have my word I won't fail you. Not this time."

"This time."

The words carried a much different meaning now that she understood. So, too, did she understand his devotion to his duties as head of Fairweather Key's militia. More important, she understood his need to protect her and the girls.

She also understood what it must have taken for a man with his principles to admit something like this. Certainly Micah Tate believed what he preached, that God took sins and cast them to the depths.

His faith shamed her, as did the guilt that refused to let up.

"Micah," she said as she pushed away far enough for him to see her face. "There's more to my story, though I've already told the Lord the details and asked for His forgiveness." She paused to wait until Micah nodded. "You've given me reason to believe that perhaps I should tell you all of it."

"Shh, Ruby," he said. "There's no need of it. You're forgiven by God and thus by me. Now let me tell you of the news the Carters brought this afternoon."

"Micah," she pleaded. "The Lord's not going to let me rest until the whole truth is out." A pause. "And neither are the girls."

"The girls?" He shook his head. "I don't understand."

"You will," Ruby managed as she steeled herself to tell the rest of the story.

CHAPTER 39

"I was born the daughter of a man whose anger was offered as quickly as my mother's charms," Ruby said. "And both were considerable. Opal was the image of my mother, while I, well, suffice it to say none would wonder whether I belonged to Clement O'Connor. A man proud to tell all who would listen how he had been a prizefighter in his youth," Ruby said. "He killed more than one with his fists, in and out of the ring." She had to look away. "Including my mama and her beau."

Micah's sharp intake of breath was almost her undoing. "I'm sorry," he said.

"As am I. Opal and I might have been next. You see, there was this place under the porch steps where we thought he wouldn't find us, but he did."

She had to stand. To go to the window where a view of the ocean lapping against the horizon sent her back to that day.

"With Papa chasing us, we ran. He caught Opal when she stopped to fetch Mama's baubles, but I wouldn't let him hurt her." Ruby winced. Even now she could feel the blows and see the glint of Jamaican sunshine against the jeweled necklace hanging from Opal's fingers.

A mainsail pierced the horizon, and she watched it until her voice returned. "Opal had a friend. I never approved of him, but he was kind to her. His papa hid us away on his ship and told Clement O'Connor he'd shoot him if he tried to fetch us home."

Micah came to stand behind her, and with care he kissed her neck and wrapped his arms around her. "So he cared for you?"

"In a matter of fashion. He was a trader of slaves and other contraband, so his was not a vessel fit for children. Tommy never seemed to mind, but I don't recall a single night's sleep aboard that ship. The sounds. . ." She shook her head. "I still hear them upon occasion."

"Would that I had known you then," he said against her ear. "No harm would have come to you."

"Yes, well, he put us out in Galveston where he offered us up to someone he called a relative, though I have my doubts. They were nice enough and elderly, and they certainly had need of two extra sets of hands to cook and clean."

Micah came to stand beside her. "So I've this woman to thank for the quality of your cooking, then?"

"Yes," she said as she studied the ship, now fully over the horizon and headed for port. "I certainly learned much in her kitchen, though Opal was hopeless at all of it."

"You did her work and yours, didn't you?"

Ruby glanced up sharply. "How did you know?"

He cupped her cheek with his palm and kissed her soundly. "Continue your story," he urged.

"All right." She rested her palms on the windowsill. "As I said, they were elderly. The fever came through and claimed them both, leaving us to make do as best we could."

Micah's hand moved from her cheek to her shoulder. "Oh, Ruby. This is a tale I'd not wish on anyone."

"Yet the story is incomplete," Ruby said, even while everything in her begged for a change of topic. "I was not unskilled. I'd learned to play the piano. I offered lessons for a price, but the money soon proved to be insufficient. I had to seek a second means of employment."

"And Opal?"

"She did things," Ruby said, "but it was difficult for her to find something that suited her. Opal was delicate."

"I see."

He didn't; Ruby could tell from his expression. Before Micah asked just what that second career might be, she hurried on. "This is difficult. I've not been that person for so long now that I can barely remember what it was to be her. To be Claire."

"About that," Micah said. "Why the change of name?"

"When Tommy came for Opal, I left with them. I knew Opal couldn't care for herself. She'd married him and was no longer an O'Connor."

His hand fell from her shoulder to wrap around her waist. Ruby leaned back against her husband, a man of strength, faith, and so much more than she ever expected to be blessed with.

"So you chose to rid yourself of the name as well?" he asked.

"In a manner of speaking, though it didn't happen quite so easily as that." She paused.

Offered for a price. The phrase taunted her. Only the look of trust in Micah's eyes allowed her to go on. "Seeing the city disappear over the horizon made me feel like I had a new beginning. And for a time, it was. Tommy appreciated how I cared for his wife and made sure I was treated well."

Micah cringed at the mention of the man's name. That she referred to the fiend as Tommy made it all the worse. "So you lived aboard his vessel? Plying the seas for plunder?"

"No." She muted the edge in her voice as best she could. "There are many small islands in the southernmost parts of Louisiana. We had a lovely home and lived as normal people do, though the location might be considered a bit remote. Tommy's vessel carried items of use that were unavailable. He would talk of the many important people who would come or send their agents when his goods were sold upriver."

"So he was a smuggler?"

She nodded. "Still is, I assume, though if pirating were to pay as well, he'd be likely to have taken it up."

Micah sighed. Judge Caleb Spencer, grandson of seafaring people of Benning ancestry, had bested Tommy twice. "We've become all too well acquainted with Thomas Hawkins here in Fairweather Key. He is no friend to us."

"No, and with good reason."

"Ruby," Micah said gently. "What of your husband?"

She turned to put her back to the window and the ocean beyond. The eyes she saw looking down at her were filled with what she hoped was love, though her husband had not yet declared it verbally. "Perhaps you've heard enough. It's as you say. I am a new person thanks to Jesus, and maybe that's where we should leave it."

Micah kissed her, and for what seemed like an eternity, he held her. "Your story pains me, Ruby, and makes me love you all the more for the woman you are now."

Love. He said it. Her heart soared even as she realized the silliness of wanting a man who had married her out of an obligation to protect her to actually find feelings for her.

Then he shook his head. "I've shared my story about Caroline. I would hear of Mr. O'Shea."

Mr. O'Shea.

Ruby felt trapped in the arms that gently held her. She slipped from his grasp to rest her shaking knees by sinking onto the settee. "Ruby?" he said as he came to sit beside her. "How did Claire O'Connor become Ruby O'Shea?" When she did not respond, he cleared his throat. "I would have an answer."

Ruby weighed her options. Either she responded and accepted whatever her husband might think, or she kept her silence and risked worse. "You've met Jean Luc."

Micah recoiled, anger flashing in his eyes as he jumped up. "The Frenchman? He is your husband?"

"No." She grasped his hand and urged him to return to her side. "But he *is* Mr. O'Shea."

"Ruby. Explain yourself."

The edge in his voice gave her pause, yet she managed to speak. "I went along with the ruse to survive. There were Opal and the twins to think of, and it seemed harmless to pretend to be the wife of an Irish businessman."

He shook his head. "I don't follow, Ruby."

"Tommy needed someone who appeared trustworthy to negotiate for him in certain situations. He and Jean Luc decided an Irishman with a wife would be the solution. Jean Luc has quite the ability to mimic, and all I had to do was remain silent and pretend to be his wife."

"I see."

Again she could tell he didn't. "It kept me alive, Micah," she said, "and it kept the girls safe, even after Opal died."

"So he was not your actual husband."

"No."

His face wore a pained expression. "And is he the father of Tess and the twins?"

"No! Of course not." She took a deep breath and let it out slowly. This much was the truth. More she'd rather not tell, though Ruby knew if Micah questioned her, she would have to be honest.

"And is their father alive?"

Here was her chance for the honesty she'd only just now feared. "Alive?" She weighed the question even as she weighed the cost of the answer. Should Micah Tate find he had taken on the raising of Thomas Hawkins's children, might he change his mind?

Though she prayed she knew him well enough to believe he would not, she could not take the risk.

Micah's hand rested on her shoulder gently and moved lightly toward the nape of her neck. His eyes seemed to hold no anger. "Ruby?" he said softly. "I would have an answer."

"Alive? No," she said. "He is dead." *To us.*

The ringing of the too-familiar warning bell prevented her from continuing. Micah rose, as did she. For a moment, he seemed not to know what to say. For her part, Ruby knew what to say but could not force herself to go back and tell him the truth.

"Ruby," he finally said, "we're not done with this, and I've much else to tell you, but you know I have to go."

"Yes," she whispered. "But before you go, there's one more thing you should know."

Again the bell rang, and this time Micah leaned past her to look out the window toward the sea. "What?"

She reached for her husband's shirtsleeve and gave it a tug, then waited until he met her stare. "I said vows before God two times since I came here to this island. The first time was when I told Him I'd let

him have whatever He wanted of me and my life. The other time was when I married you." She swallowed hard to keep the tears at bay. "I'm not proud of who I was before I came here, and I'm offering no excuse, but both times I meant those vows."

Ruby paused. Now, she knew, was the time to tell him the truth about Tommy. To explain that she told him Tommy was dead because she feared what he might do.

The bell rang again, and Micah was gone, racing out the door and down the stairs with only a quick kiss and a smile. Ruby fell onto the settee, first listening for the door downstairs and then watching the road until she saw him hurry past. Some minutes later she found his sail among the others heading toward the reef.

Likely Clay Drummond was with him. Lately the man had taken to stopping by to visit with Micah and, she surmised, had become her husband's friend. She knew from Viola that Clay often sailed with Micah when the need arose.

Ruby turned her thoughts back to their conversation of moments ago. Guilt gnawed at her, but she pushed it away to concentrate on the emotion she normally felt when Micah answered the alarm bell: first fear and then, by degrees, a measure of peace.

So many times she watched this same process, yet Ruby had never quite lost the butterflies that teased her stomach when the bell rang and the wreckers responded. Micah had been hurt badly salvaging the very wreck that brought Ruby and the girls ashore, and she knew the ache in his healed bones still plagued him on occasion. Knowing it could happen again set her on edge, though she worked hard not to let it show.

Ruby watched until she could no longer remain upstairs. Until a replacement arrived, she'd not have the luxury of rest. The fact that Mrs. Campbell hadn't yet responded to her last letter irked Ruby a bit.

If her prayers were answered—and Ruby had no reason to believe they would not be—then soon she would find herself carrying Micah's child. Her husband had already declared she would no longer work as she did now once the Lord blessed them in that way.

As she closed the door behind her, Ruby touched her abdomen.

That she did not yet carry Micah's son or daughter was of some concern. The nausea of those few days last month had passed, and then came the unmistakable evidence of the absence of any possible pregnancy.

Ruby sighed. At times such as this, she ached for the lack of a mother. If only she had someone she could ask what she—or rather they—might be doing wrong.

Banishing the thought, she donned her nightgown and climbed beneath the covers to await her husband. Heavy footsteps roused her from sleep, yet when the mattress sagged indicating that Micah had joined her, Ruby chose to feign sleep. A few moments later, Micah's snores told her that his sleep was, indeed, genuine.

When she awoke the next morning, however, his side of the bed was empty. Dressing without lighting the lamp, she hurried downstairs to find that Micah was gone. She fumbled through breakfast preparations, certain that the truth, partial as it was, was the cause.

Once the boarders were fed, Ruby took breakfast upstairs to the girls. While the twins dressed, Tess bounced about with more than her usual amount of chatter. Ruby tried to be patient, but only removing herself to her bedchamber kept her from snapping at the child.

There she saw the pillow where her husband had barely rested his head. Tears threatened. Somewhere between the need to protect Opal's girls and last night, she'd managed to realize that she wanted a real marriage with Micah.

Moving to his side of the bed, she sank to the mattress and placed her palm in the center of the pillow. Her eyes closed as she pictured her husband in sleep. The impossibly long lashes dusting high cheekbones tanned from hours in the sun. The hair, so like her own, that fell across his face as he lay on his side. The slow, even breaths that invariably led to soft snores.

I'm an idiot.

Yet as she opened her eyes, Ruby couldn't say whether her idiocy came from sentimental thoughts or too much of the truth—or from not enough of it.

In any case, the result was the same. Micah Tate couldn't live with a woman whose past hadn't stayed where it belonged.

"Mama?"

Ruby turned to see Tess standing in the doorway. She had dressed herself and wore an interesting combination of her sisters' adornments in her hair. As had become her habit, Tess had chosen a book from the shelf and held it to her chest in preparation for her walk down the street to the parsonage.

Ruby had worried that Tess might be imposing until the morning when she took Mary Carter up on her offer to peer through the window unobserved and see what a delight and a helper Tess had become to the Carter women. Indeed, the moment Isabelle arrived to spend the morning with her mother-in-law, Tess sprang into action and kept little Joey occupied.

Before the family left on their trip to Santa Lucida with Emilie and Caleb, Tess had even begun to read to the child, though Ruby doubted how much of her talent was actual and how much was made-up words. It mattered not, for little Joey would sit and listen, even taking his turn at naming items in the pictures.

At yesterday's news of Joey's return, Tess had begun planning her visit. How to tell her that she must now stay put because Micah, her faithful companion on the daily walk, was nowhere to be found?

"I'm ready to go."

"Honey," Ruby said gently, "don't you think Joey's grandmother might like a morning to herself? After all, they've been away for several weeks."

Tess's expression told her she didn't understand.

"We'll walk with her to the parsonage," Maggie called. "But only if she's ready to go now."

"Just a couple of adjustments to her hairstyle, and she'll be ready," Ruby said as she reached for the brush. When Tess made to protest, Ruby shrugged. "All right, then. I suppose you'll stay here and help with the laundry."

Her eyes narrowed. "Micah told you to hire someone to do that. I heard him."

"Yes, well, first off it's quite impolite to listen in on adult conversations, Tess," Ruby said as she began to remove the first of several knotted ribbons.

"She does it all the time," Carol said from the door. "We told her to stop, but she won't. I think she needs to know there are consequences."

Carol's choice of words stopped the breath in Ruby's throat. "Yes," she said, "I agree a discussion is in order."

When she looked up, Carol was gone. Still, Ruby's unease at the jab remained. Her fingers shook, and Tess cried out.

"Sorry, darling," she said as she removed the last of the ribbons and employed the brush to create a more appropriate braid for the girl's silky locks. "It appears you're ready now."

Yet before she could release the girl to send her off to the parsonage, Ruby gathered her into her lap and held her tight. If only Micah could see into her heart and know how very much these girls and their safety had tangled up the line between truth and lies.

Then again, this line had starting knotting well before their births. Best she could figure, things had begun to muddy well before Opal married Tommy Hawkins.

"Isn't this a pretty picture?"

"Micah!" Tess screeched against Ruby's ear.

While the child scrambled to the floor and vaulted herself into Micah's arms, Ruby could only remain very still and watch. Her heart hurt for the innocence Tess would lose with Micah's departure.

"Tess, c'mon," Maggie called. "We're leaving without you."

Micah set the girl on her feet and patted her head. "I'll come to fetch you later or send someone if your mama or I can't go."

With that, Tess raced out the door, calling back a quick good-bye. Three sets of footsteps clattered on the stairs; then, as Ruby rose, the door slammed downstairs. Though the boardinghouse was filled to the rafters with guests, suddenly Ruby felt very alone.

"Ruby?"

Soft. Almost gentle. Still, dread wrapped tentacles around her heart that surely burned like stinging sea creatures.

His expression, she decided when she braved a glance, gave away none of what he might be thinking. Again he said her name, this time with a touch more firmness.

"You must be tired." Ruby tried to slide past, but Micah caught her wrist. "I thought I'd make fresh coffee," she said without looking up.

"You were a criminal."

Four words, yet they carried the weight of a hundred. His grip tightened, and she studied his hand. Noted the scar that traced a path across his knuckle to disappear into his sleeve.

"Ruby. Look at me."

She couldn't.

"Ruby," he said softly as his free hand cradled her jaw then gently lifted her chin. "You were a criminal."

Searching his face, she hoped for some sign of what he might say next but found none. "Yes," Ruby managed. "I was a criminal because that's what kept those girls safe. It plagued me something awful, but Rev. Carter says Jesus wiped away that sin along with all the others I've committed." Emboldened, she continued. "But I remember enough about my criminal days to know how to disappear." The briefest of pauses. "If that's what you want."

CHAPTER 40

Micah couldn't deny parts of Ruby's story would be hard to get over. Other things likely he'd never quite learn to live with. He'd never tell her that, of course, but it pained him to admit the truth.

Thinking of his wife in any way other than as a mama of those girls was too much for him. Imagining her taking part in a smuggler's ruse went beyond what he thought he could stand.

Knowing she'd done those things to survive blunted the blow to his pride at marrying a woman whose past was not what he'd expected. And believing the Lord had washed her clean kept him from walking away.

"I wasn't sure you'd come back."

His wife's direct look broached no nonsense, yet he had a suspicion that beneath the surface she was not nearly so calm. He'd seen her wild eyes, watched her stare at the horizon as if some specter might pierce it and come after her. He was no stranger to her occasional walks to the beach to gather the sand dollars that were now piled several rows high in a bucket beside the back door.

So her story, now that he'd had time to think on it, filled in the gaps and told him the why of her actions.

"Micah? I hate it when you stare at me like that."

He blinked hard. "I'm sorry. Leave? Why?" He shrugged. "I'll admit it hurt my pride to know I'd married a woman with a past that I didn't expect."

"I tried to tell you, but you—"

"Hold on, woman," he said. "It isn't entirely true that I didn't expect something awful had happened to you. Remember, I was there when they pulled you and the girls off that animal's ship. I saw."

Her nod urged him to continue, but he wouldn't until she looked into his eyes. He cupped her cheek once again, his favorite thing, and gently guided her gaze toward his. "Ruby," he said as softly as he could, "I'm no saint, either. I just didn't think. . .well, I expected the four of you had been kidnapped."

Ruby's chuckle held no humor. "Ironically, on that trip, we had. Tess was complaining of a sore ear, and the twins were both getting over bouts with some sort of stomach bug. I told Tommy I'd not go anywhere with them in ill health. I awoke to find them gone. Tommy had them. Said he'd let me board the ship and go with them, but only if I did as he said."

Micah let out a long breath while his temper cooled down a notch. Would that he'd come across the pirate in a fair fight. He'd have demanded payment for all of these wrongs and more.

"But the vessel was not headed toward New Orleans, Ruby," he said, the easiness in his tone hopefully masking the concern he felt at this new piece of information. "And in the ship's belly was a fortune in what we figure to be stolen cargo." He paused to take another long breath. "Did you know about what you were walking over?"

"No," she said quickly, and he could tell she didn't. "Tommy only said he had to leave due to what he called 'business trouble.' I always figured the law was about to catch him—else he wouldn't have gone without Jean Luc."

"Or the rightful owner of the treasure he was using as ballast." Micah shrugged. "Maybe they are one and the same, this Frenchman and the treasure's owner."

"I don't know. Those men, they never told me anything, and all I did was try to keep the girls and myself out of the way." Her eyes blinked, but her gaze never wavered. "I swear to you I was only on that ship because I couldn't leave those babies with him alone."

"Just like you couldn't leave Opal with him."

Her nod was slow in coming, as if she hadn't put the two memories together until now, and it took all he had in him not to gather her onto his lap and hold her until her smile returned.

"Ruby, here's how I figure it," he said. "The Lord's given us both a second chance. You know my story, and I know yours." Micah paused. "Which means there's nothing left hidden between us."

Was it his imagination, or did his bride hesitate?

"Nothing's hidden," she echoed as she reached across the distance between them to take his hand.

"You're sure."

This time he knew she paused, though he preferred to think it was so she might better search her heart to determine whether she could answer truthfully.

"Good—then you should know you're about to become the pastor's wife." He smiled as her eyes widened. "And we'll be moving into the parsonage while the Carters will be settling in here."

"But what about. . .that is, how will—"

"Later, Ruby. Right now I'd like breakfast."

"Breakfast," she mumbled as she scurried from the room. "Yes, of course. Breakfast."

Micah headed to the courthouse, and Ruby left for the beach. She collected an apron full of sand dollars before dumping them back into the surf. Try as she might, she knew she couldn't be the pastor's wife.

Not until the pastor heard the rest of her story. The part where she admitted that the girls were not hers.

The horizon tempted her, and it seemed an easy solution to stand and stare at it as she'd done as a child. But she was no child, and she had three girls to protect. Surely the new pastor wouldn't turn her out for this one last missing fact.

Two, she decided, for he would also have to know about the other men.

Her knees shook, and she nearly turned around several times before she actually stepped onto the courthouse grounds. When she opened the door, she found Caleb Spencer sitting where she'd expected Micah to be.

"Oh, I'm sorry," she said. "I was looking for my husband."

"You'll find him down at the docks, I believe."

She smiled. "Thank you, and welcome home."

He matched her grin. "I'm very happy to be here," he said. "As is Emilie. Do go by and see her when you can."

"Yes, of course," she said, though she doubted Emilie would want to speak to her once the woman heard of the scandal attached to her name.

Ruby found Micah supervising some sort of work being done on his boat. "Perfect timing," he said as he waved to her. "Come and see this."

She looked past Micah to the man now painting the last flourish on the bow. "*Ruby*," she read.

"My wife in whom I trust," he whispered as he gathered her to him. "I love you, Ruby."

"Might we discuss something?" She slipped from his grasp. "It's important."

"Of course." He gestured to the vessel and led her aboard. "I'm all yours."

"I saw that Caleb's back," she said. "I suppose that means you'll not be the acting judge anymore." A stupid statement, yet it bought time.

"I happily turned over the desk and chair." He sat and urged her to do the same. "I've told Rev. Carter he can have the boardinghouse as soon as he's ready. I'm a bit concerned about the stairs, however, as is Josiah. I think he and Mary will be taking that back bedroom downstairs and leaving the third-floor apartment for Josiah and Isabelle. It means one less room available for guests, but I don't suppose that's a problem."

Micah paused, and her heart stalled. It would be her turn. She wasn't ready.

"Close the door," he said, and she complied. He leaned back and patted the place next to him on the bunk. What came next, she could guess, though he would likely change his mind once she told him her tale.

"I've spoken to Drummond. He's a good man. Didn't think so

273

when I met him, but he's won me over." He shifted to look at her. "I'm turning over my duties as head of the militia to him. Or at least I will once he decides whether he'll accept them. With the Seminole proven not to be a threat, there's really no need to keep the militia on full-time watch, so if Drummond agrees to it, he'll have minimal duties. That much was decided yesterday."

"Is that so?" Ruby perched on the end of the bunk and drummed her fingers on the mattress. "Micah, might I tell you one more thing?"

"One more thing?" He gathered her to him. "Ruby, you can tell me anything. No secrets between us, right?"

"Well. . ." She leaned away then moved back to the edge of the bunk. "Just let me say this, all right?" After a deep breath, she said, "The girls' father. He's alive."

"Oh?"

Ruby dared not look at him lest she be unable to continue. "And they are not mine. The girls belong to Opal, Micah. She died birthing Tess."

"So the girls belong to. . ."

"Tommy," she offered. "Thomas Hawkins," she amended as she risked a glance in his direction.

He leaned forward to rest his elbows on his knees, seemingly heedless of the fact that Ruby had to scramble to get out of the way. "And what more do you have to tell me?"

"You're not mad that I didn't tell you who the girls belonged to?" She let out a long breath. "Well, then there's just one more thing to tell you. You see," she said slowly, "the work I did in Galveston, well, it wasn't. . .that is, it was. . ."

"Out with it, Ruby," he said sharply. "How bad can it be compared to the fact you've lied about the parentage of the girls? I mean, it's not like you were a prostitute or anything. So tell me, what sort of demeaning work did you take?"

Sarcasm, she knew, yet a measure of pain seemed to come through. Or perhaps she only thought so.

"Ruby?"

Somehow she met his gaze. "I was Claire," she said. "When the Lord wiped away my sins, I figured to take another name. The girls

knew me as Ruby because that's what Tommy. . ." She shook her head. "Anyway, now you know."

"Now I know what?" He shook his head. "Ruby, I asked you if you were a—" His expression changed, and he looked away. "Why?"

"Opal was—"

"Delicate. Yes, you mentioned that. And you. . ." Micah shook his head. "No, not you. *Claire*," he said with what sounded like disdain. "Claire spent her free time entertaining anyone with enough coin or promises of protection."

Shock rendered her speechless.

Micah rose. "Why didn't you offer to pay me off that way? Was there something wrong with me?"

His words hit her every bit as hard as any blow she'd taken. Somehow Ruby ended up on her feet, even though she still swayed as she fought to remain standing.

"Please," she managed through the roaring in her ears. "Micah, listen to me. I was a different person then. Nobody had told me about Jesus. Once I learned there was a better way, I changed."

His stare sent her tumbling backward. She crumpled to the floor, helpless to move.

Micah closed the distance between them to scoop her into his arms. For one brief moment she thought perhaps he might be offering his forgiveness.

Instead, he dropped her in the middle of the bunk then took a step backward. "I didn't want to know."

"But—"

"No, *Claire*," he said. "I did not want to know this. This exercise was for me. I never expected you to offer up the sordid details of your life." His laughter held an icy tone. "But then, I never expected there were sordid details."

"Micah, please," she pleaded. "Listen to me, please. I was different then."

"Were you?" He came to her then, pinning her beneath him as he pressed lips that held no love against her neck. "Were you different, Claire?"

Tears stung Ruby's eyes, but she refused to cry. Her husband was a good man, a man who regularly preached the gospel on Sunday mornings. A man who vowed to protect her and who preached that both he and the Lord would forgive her.

A man who'd governed the island, led the militia in protecting its citizens, and preached in its pulpit.

Never had he touched her with anything but tenderness. As he moved away to stand once more, Ruby wondered whether this might be the time when he became like the others.

He must have recognized the fear in her eyes, for abruptly Micah turned and moved toward the door. "Micah?" she called. "Where are you going?"

But he was gone.

CHAPTER 41

Had she the strength, Ruby might have gone after her husband. Instead, she could only trace his path as far as the boardinghouse. As the door slammed behind her, Ruby made her way into the kitchen to prepare lunch as expected. Later she made dinner as well, all the while wondering where her husband was.

The last of the day's work done, she trudged upstairs into the girls' room, where she climbed into bed with Tess and forced back her tears. *He'll be back by morning.*

But he wasn't, nor did he come for his lunch. The warning bell rang at half past two, calling all wreckers to an unfortunate merchant vessel stuck on the reef. This much she determined from the boardinghouse porch, for she'd decided not to go into town to fetch him back.

Her determination wavered a bit when Tess found her. "Is Papa out there?" Tess asked.

Papa. A stab of pain pierced her heart. Lies built on top of lies, all now falling shattered around her.

"Yes, I think I see Micah's boat." She pointed out the most likely vessel. "Do you see it?"

"I see it," she shouted. "Papa's a hero, isn't he?"

"Yes, darling," she managed to say. "Papa is a hero."

Tess laughed then clapped her hands as the vessel in question pulled away, its decks visibly full of what appeared to be persons and cargo. "When he comes home tonight, I'm going to tell him I saw him saving people with his boat."

But her papa didn't come home that night or the next. On the third night, Ruby stopped making excuses and admitted to the girls that she was uncertain as to when Micah would be back.

Maggie and Tess took the news in stride, but Carol's response was sullen silence.

Long after the girls were slumbering, Ruby lay on Micah's side of the bed, her eyes refusing to close. By the light of the moon, she could see the shimmer of the ocean and the cluster of vessels moored at the docks.

Likely Micah was on one of them, unless he bunked elsewhere. "Enough of this foolishness," she said as she threw off her wrapper and donned the dress it seemed she'd only just put away. "You'll come home, Micah Tate, or the girls and I will find another place to live."

She found Micah curled in the tiny cabin, his jacket taking the place of a pillow. Until that moment, Ruby hadn't realized her husband had left with only the clothes on his back.

"Micah, please listen," she said before she knew whether he was awake to hear it.

"Not now, Ruby," he said, shifting position to offer her his back. "It's been a long day, and I'm in no mood to talk to you."

The old fear of a man's fists returned, spurred by the way Micah's voice echoed in the small cabin. To continue could very well provoke him. To leave, likely the best choice.

Yet Ruby couldn't leave, wouldn't let this man go.

Ruby squared her shoulders and faced down her fear. "That's unfortunate," she said. "You're going to listen. What you do with what I say is up to you, but I'd suggest you think carefully before you respond."

Micah sat up and swiped at his hair, then scratched his chin. "All right," he said. "You've got my attention."

"Good." Ruby sent a prayer skyward. Somehow she had to find the words to bring him home. To bring forgiveness.

"I am *not* Claire. Not anymore. Not for a long time, actually."

She paused to see if Micah might respond. When he didn't, she pressed on.

"I'm Ruby," she said. "Ruby Tate. That's who I am, Micah. Not a perfect person, not even a person who is proud of her past."

Ruby ignored his inelegant snort.

"What I am is forgiven, Micah. I listened closely when you spoke about it," she said, "and I read up on the parts I didn't understand by finding all the citations you gave in the Bible."

He seemed about to say something but then looked away.

"What I found was what you said. The Lord, He casts our sins as far as from east to west. We have to ask, and we have to mean it, but if we do, He does it, and then it's done."

Another pause, this time with the hope that Micah would respond. He did not.

"Micah Tate, do you know what you are?"

While his eyes blinked, Ruby couldn't tell whether Micah was listening at all. "You're a hypocrite, Micah Tate. A hypocrite. Oh, you talk like a preacher. You tell people things that the Bible says, but then you turn around and hold them to a different standard." She paused to blink back the tears. "An impossible standard," she continued. "And that's just not fair."

Silence.

Then the gravity of the situation hit her. Not only had she lost her husband to lies, but she'd compounded that loss by her shrewish behavior.

"I'm sorry." She backed up and rammed her elbow into the doorframe. "Come home, Micah."

When he ignored her, she decided to take desperate measures. "Micah," she said softly. "Please." As she said the word, Ruby knelt then molded herself to her husband's back. Snaking her arm around his waist, she began to pray. After a moment, she said softly, "I wanted to be carrying your child by now."

Three months of marriage had not been enough to teach her the ways of her husband's mind, but she'd learned a bit about how to reach his heart. Unfortunately, he slipped from her grasp and stormed outside to stand on the deck.

Dignity did not allow her to follow quickly, but she did follow. "The girls have asked about you," she said when she spied his profile at the far end of the dock. "And Tess? She says you're a hero."

His shoulders slumped, and she could tell her words had hit their target. "Please reconsider what you're doing, Micah," Ruby said.

"Go home," was his only response.

"My home is with my husband."

Micah turned to stare. "I'm not altogether certain you still have a husband, Ruby." He paused. "Or perhaps I should call you Claire."

"Please," fell from her lips in a last-ditch plea, but her husband ignored her.

"All right," she said, "I'm going home, but you said vows before God that makes the bed where I sleep your bed, too. You can do this all you want, but nothing will change the vow you made."

"I am not unaware of this."

"Yes, well." She took a deep breath and let it out in a quick gasp. "And while I'm on the topic, Micah—or should I call you *Reverend Tate*—I would have you think about exactly what you would tell one of your parishioners should he come to you having been told something like this. Would you tell him to leave the wife and children he promised God to care for and go hide out on a boat somewhere? Would you tell him to judge his wife then cast her aside?"

His eyes flashed with what appeared to be anger. "That is unfair."

"As is this situation you've forced me into, Husband. I took you to the beach the day before we wed and tried to tell you everything. I showed you who I was, and you danced in the waves with me." She swiped at the traitorous tears now coursing down her face. "I tried to tell you, Micah. I'm not stupid. I know the story is a difficult one. And yes, I am at fault for leaving out details I should have told you. Details I was ashamed of."

Nothing.

"Micah?"

He showed her his back.

"So that's how it will be? How dare you cause me to fall in love with you, then reject me for my honesty?"

Again nothing but the splash of her tears.

"Very well, then." Ruby turned away, resisting the urge to look back over her shoulder to see if any of her words had penetrated Micah's hard head. With each step she took away from her husband, she prayed he would come after her.

He didn't.

Her footsteps echoed in the silent and deserted streets, and her heart hurt. This was not the return she'd expected, but then, her husband had not given the response she'd expected, either.

What happened to forgiveness?

She wanted to cry out, to shout the question, but awakening the citizens of Fairweather Key to let them know the man chosen as their next pastor did not practice what he preached seemed wrong. Satisfying, yes. But still wrong.

A second set of footsteps joined her, and Ruby stopped to glance over her shoulder. "Just an echo," she whispered as she resumed walking.

Ruby passed the door to Viola's home and slowed, hoping to see lamplight in the upper windows. They were dark, so she picked up her pace.

Ahead she saw the church and its parsonage, also bathed in darkness. The moon, hidden behind clouds that portended rain before morning, offered little light to lead the now-familiar way.

Something moved behind her, and she whirled around to find she still stood alone. She turned toward home, comforted by the fact that one scream would likely bring a dozen people running. The downside to this knowledge was that she would then have to explain why she was skulking about at that hour.

And why her husband was neither with her nor at home.

"Lord, I thought You honored the truth," she whispered. "The Bible says the truth will set me free."

Feeling foolish for speaking aloud, she once again glanced over her shoulder to be sure she hadn't an audience. "The Lord is good, a strong hold in the day of trouble; and he knoweth them that trust in him."

Ruby relaxed at the memory of the verse she and Micah had read together what seemed like just this morning. In truth, it had been the morning of the day he left. Surely God had known she would need to be reminded.

The city fell behind her as Ruby began her walk up the hill to the boardinghouse. "I trust You, Lord," she whispered, though she felt an urgent need to hurry home.

"Don't be silly," she admonished herself as she left the main road for the footpath through the mango grove that was her favorite shortcut. "There's nothing out here that can hurt me."

"Don't be so sure, sweet Claire."

Jean Luc.

She opened her mouth to scream and bit into something that tasted as foul as it smelled. Her hands went behind her, captured into something that bit into her wrists and pained her shoulders.

Her mind began to reel, searching through the choices she had for convincing the man she knew too well to release her. First he would have to see her eyes. Indeed, he'd rarely been able to resist her once she set her mind to it, so a look at her face would do the trick.

Ruby began to relax. In a moment this would be over and Jean Luc would be on his way.

Without warning, her feet left the ground as the horizon tilted. "Be still," the smuggler hissed against her ear. "I did not travel alone tonight."

The statement gave her pause, though Ruby continued to tick through the ways she might be released. Whichever underling Jean Luc had brought would likely pose no less threat than the Frenchman.

Ruby froze. Men were assigned to the boardinghouse when Micah was not in residence. This had become his habit since their marriage. One member of the militia on guard in the front, and another of Micah's men in the back.

Rescue was within reach. The knowledge gave her reason to fight. First she attempted a kick, which only landed in midair. Then Ruby yanked against the bonds on her wrists, and Jean Luc slapped her. A cry of outrage was impossible, and she felt tears roll over her stinging skin. Ruby arched her back, determined to cause her captor to let her go.

Instead, he bundled her like so much baggage through the mango trees and down a path he seemed to be creating himself. Likely with a militia member trailing a safe distance behind.

"Be still," he said in a tone that was almost soothing. "If you are harmed, it will not be at my hands."

She relaxed a notch. Surely her rescuer would arrive soon.

The thought carried her all the way to the beach, where Jean

Luc dropped her into a small skiff then inexplicably stepped back to push her out alone into the surf. As the tiny vessel took float, she searched the narrow expanse of beach for the militia who surely must be standing at the ready by now.

Nary a torch pierced the darkness, nor did she see any sign of those who had sworn to protect the key. *That doesn't mean they're not there. Hiding. Waiting. Looking for the best opportunity to free me.*

Above all, she wondered, *Where is Micah?*

Yet she knew. Her husband, the man who had vowed to keep her safe, vowed never to fail her, was likely asleep on a pillow made from a wrinkled jacket and a healthy dose of self-pity.

The skiff bumped against something, jarring her from her thoughts. A chuckle. Low. Deep.

Familiar.

"Hello, Ruby Red."

CHAPTER 42

How dare you cause me to fall in love with you, then reject me for my honesty?

Ruby's question soaked through Micah's skin and settled into his bones as he tried once again to sleep. He could blame the sleeplessness on poor planning and a lack of decent bunk space, but the truth of it was the lumpy mattress on which he lay was stuffed with pure, stubborn pride.

Micah rolled to his back, then forced his eyes to shut. Dawn would come eventually, and with it another day. A vessel passed in the dark, the waves lapping against the hull and rocking him in a way that once was so familiar. How had he, an avowed sailor, become so hopelessly landlocked?

Yet now his life had moved from the ocean to a house on the hill. He looked in that direction now, his view obscured by poor light and a few ill-placed palm trees. When he stood, however, and looked beyond the palms, he could see a light still burned in the room where he'd last laid his head and slept comfortably.

All the ugly secrets his wife had hidden came tumbling out like stones in a wall forever wedged between them. *"How dare you cause me to fall in love with you, then reject me for my honesty?"*

Again Ruby's question haunted him. Or was she Claire? He'd lost the ability to know.

"Nobody told me about Jesus."

Micah sank back onto the deck and leaned against the rail. Her statement was like a punch in the gut. What excuse did he offer for judging her unfit to be his wife? He exhaled slowly.

"Nobody told me about Jesus."

He pounded his fist against the wood.

"But I can't trust her, Lord," he said, fully aware of how foolish he'd look should anyone catch him speaking aloud to God. "She's lied to me. Left out important things. Done who knows what? She's—"

"Your wife, and no less imperfect than you."

Micah scrubbed his face with his palms. God's truth hurt more than Ruby's truth. Indeed, he'd failed. Not in the same way as Ruby, yet did the Lord use some sliding scale to weigh one's sins? Had one of his parishioners come to him with the question, he would have said no.

Why then, now, did he wish desperately the answer was yes?

Stepping into his boots, Micah made short work of returning home to the boardinghouse. There he found his wife gone and the girls sleeping soundly.

Thomas Hawkins's girls, he corrected. Yet the thought did not hold the sting it had before. He went back into their bedchamber and slipped into bed to await his wife's return.

Of all the nights to be without a militia guard, he thought as he rolled over onto his back. Had he a man stationed around, he might have some idea of where his wife had gone.

"I remember enough about my criminal days to know how to disappear."

Micah shrugged away the thought. *That was then; this is now.* His wife was indeed a new creature in Christ, and he'd been an idiot to forget that.

At least he could be reasonably sure she was safe, given the fact that neither smugglers nor Indians had dared show themselves at Fairweather Key. Still, he found that sleep evaded him, so Micah finally made his way downstairs to wait for Ruby on the porch.

Ruby gagged as Jean Luc stuffed the putrid cloth into her mouth. While her eyes pleaded with her former protector, her heart knew

285

she'd lost all hope the moment Micah slammed his fist into the Frenchman's face.

The cabin was small, tiny by Tommy's standards, yet the lamp overhead illuminated only a small circle of weak light. A glint of silver caught her attention, and Ruby saw the knife in Tommy's hand.

"You'll likely not believe me, but I am sorry it's come to this." A moment of silence. "Leave us," Tommy said as he moved into the lamplight.

A slam of the door. The creaking of wood. Footsteps as Tommy moved toward her.

Ruby stared at his eyes and tried to think of how they were blue like Tess's. She saw fair hair that belonged to all three girls and a tall stature that both Carol and Maggie would likely inherit.

Seeing these things kept her from thinking of what might happen next.

"My girls," he said. "I want them back."

She froze. Had the gag not been in place, she might have told him to kill her now, for he'd never find them. He sheathed the knife and removed her gag. His expression told her he'd release her in a heartbeat if she'd only give him what he wanted: his daughters.

Indeed, before her stood Tommy, the man who'd saved her more than once.

"I know you have them," he said, "though Rabelais was unsure as to where you've hid them."

Ruby let out the breath she'd been holding. At least Jean Luc had been faithful to protect her in that.

For that she gave thanks.

"They're all I have left of her, Ruby Red," he said, though she didn't believe for a minute that he wanted them as some memento of time spent with Opal.

"You're a fool to bring me here," she said. "My husband and his men will have your hides."

Tommy laughed as he rested his palm on the knife's handle. "Not before I have yours." He leaned close, placing his knuckle against her jaw. "One more chance," he said. "Tell me where my girls are."

Ruby looked him in the eyes and said nothing.

"All right, pigeon," he said. "I always did think you were the more interesting O'Connor sister." His knuckle traced a path down her jaw and around to grasp the back of her neck. As Tommy drew her forward, she remained still. "Last chance." Closer still. "I want them back."

Again she met his stare. "Never," she said.

"I'm almost disappointed." He wrenched her toward him and stuffed the gag back into her mouth.

Tommy's hands spanned her waist to lift her up, and for a moment she thought he might release her. "Don't worry, Ruby Red," he said as he tossed her like a rag doll onto the bunk then removed the knife and set it aside. "I'll not use this on you tonight." Tommy moved closer, and by degrees, she realized his intentions. "Because I want this night to be our little secret. Just something you think of when you think you might want to lie to me about where my girls are."

"No," came out like a muffled groan.

"Yes," he said. "And know I'll be watching you. I'll come for them," he said, "but first I want to leave my mark on you."

She lay still, eyes closed, and tried to remember how to pray. Tried to think. Then tried not to think.

"Fight me, pigeon," he said against her neck as he untied her wrists. "Give me a reason to hurt you."

She didn't.

But he hurt her anyway.

Afterward, he forced her to stand and then to walk out of the cabin and across the deck. At the rail, he handed Ruby her wrinkled dress then gave her a shove.

She landed in the water, where Jean Luc was waiting for her in a rowboat. He said nothing of her unfinished state of dress, which she quickly remedied with the soaked dress. Rather, he guided the boat into a cove and turned away as she scrambled onto the beach.

Run.

That was all she could do.

But where?

Ruby followed her feet as the sound of waves lapping against the shore drowned out the sobs she finally allowed. To go home might be best, but how could she know whether Tommy was watching?

Still, she ran, scrambling across the sand toward the path that led into town. She spied a light in the distance at Emilie's cottage and raced toward it. *May the Lord forgive me for leading the wretched smuggler here.*

As the gate banged shut behind her, Caleb appeared at the door. He brought Ruby inside, never asking about her appearance. Rather, he called to Emilie, who gathered Ruby into an embrace while Caleb slipped away.

"Micah?" Emilie asked, and when Ruby shook her head, she added, "Where are the girls?"

"Home," she managed through chattering teeth. "Need to get them."

"I'll send Caleb. Are you worried about their safety?"

Ruby nodded then reached for Emilie when she backed away. "Don't tell Micah," she said. "Promise me. He would never believe me."

"Of course he would," Emilie said. "He's your—"

"No." Ruby made to stand but swayed instead.

"All right, I won't tell him, and neither will Caleb. You need a doctor, though. And something warm to drink. You're shivering."

"All right, but see to the girls first." It seemed as though Ruby lay alone for hours, though surely it was only a few moments. When Emilie returned, she brought a basin and towel and a nightgown.

"Caleb's going to the boardinghouse, and then he'll get Vi." She dipped the towel in the basin and offered it to Ruby. "Can you do this yourself?"

Ruby managed it, but only after Emilie left the room to heat water for tea. By the time Emilie returned, she'd scrubbed herself nearly raw, finally giving up on ever feeling clean again, and donned the gown. She huddled under a blanket and only lifted her head to sip at the tea Emilie offered.

When Viola arrived, Ruby closed her eyes and allowed the midwife to see to her. "No permanent damage," she finally said, "though the man who did this to you should be shot."

"It wasn't Micah," Ruby managed to say, though her teeth still chattered.

Viola looked up, her gaze steady. "I know that."

She took a long breath and let it out slowly as she shifted positions. "And the girls? Are they with you?"

"No, they're with Micah," Emilie supplied. "Caleb found him sitting on the porch at the boardinghouse. He said he figured you'd gone for a walk, and he was waiting for you."

"What did Caleb tell him?"

"That you were with me," Emilie said.

Ruby closed her eyes and felt exhaustion wash over her in waves. She could have remained beneath the blankets in the care of these women.

But her husband was waiting.

She threw off the blanket and reached for her dress. "I've got to go home."

"Ruby, no," Viola said. "You need a night's rest, at least."

"Micah will know. I need to go home," she repeated as she threw off the gown, caring not for the fact that she was not alone in the room. She managed soon enough to set herself aright and even braided her hair with Emilie's help.

"Just like on my wedding day," Ruby said then bit back a sob.

"Oh, honey." Viola came to her and held her while she cried. "This animal should be locked up. Just give Caleb the name, and he'll see to it."

Ruby squared her shoulders and swiped at her face. "No," she said. "But I'll accept his help in keeping my girls safe. I fear they're in danger of being taken."

She repeated the statement to Caleb a moment later, adding that the one who might steal them away was Thomas Hawkins. This she said without allowing any connection between what had happened to her and what might happen to them.

A look passed between Emilie and Caleb. "I do miss your mother," Emilie said. "I wonder if she might welcome me back with three visitors."

So it was decided that Emilie, her trunk still not unpacked from her voyage home, would sail on the morrow with the girls to Santa Lucida. "But I can't be without them," Ruby said, her mind reeling from the decisions she felt helpless to make.

"Hawkins will follow you," was Caleb's unwavering answer. "Do you want that?"

"No, but they've never been without me." A sob jerked through her, sending Caleb from the room. "What if something happens and I'm not there? I'd never forgive myself."

"You've not met Caleb's mother," Emilie said gently, "but I warrant no more tenacious woman has been put on this earth. Have the girls known either of their grandmothers?" When Ruby shook her head, Emilie continued. "Then they are in for a treat." A pause. "Or would you rather they stay with you and fear for their lives?"

"No." Yet her heart hurt at the thought of going home to pack the girls' things and send them away. "What will I tell Micah?"

"The truth?" Emilie supplied.

CHAPTER 43

Micah awakened to the moon high in the sky and Ruby's hand on his shoulder. "Come to bed," she said lightly as she led the way inside. When he made to light the lamp, she quickly stepped out of its glow.

She slipped behind the armoire door to emerge a moment later in her nightgown. "Might you dim the lamp?"

He took her question and her quick move to climb beneath the blankets as an invitation to join her. She was shivering, likely from the damp dress now lying in a heap on the floor.

As he gathered her to him, Micah considered chastising her for the swim he figured she'd taken before paying Emilie a visit. Or perhaps after.

He knew too well Ruby's penchant for tromping about in the waves when riled, and he also knew he'd given her plenty of reason to be riled tonight. Not that he didn't have more than his own share of reasons, too.

Yet this was the wife the Lord had given him. The wife he'd sworn to keep safe.

Micah fitted her against him and breathed in the salty scent of seawater from her hair. Indeed, they would have a talk tomorrow about her habits. But tonight was not the night for words.

His lips found her forehead, and he kissed her. "Ruby," he whispered. "I want to be the husband God made me to be, but I've got a long way to go. Will you forgive me?"

Silence.

"Ruby?"

He almost believed she'd slipped into slumber. Until he heard the sniffle.

Something deep in his gut wrenched, and his palm reached to cup her damp cheek. "Ruby, sweetheart. I'm sorry. So very, very sorry."

"The girls," Ruby said. "I've decided to send them to Santa Lucida."

"Santa Lucida?" He rolled back to rest on his elbow. "Why?"

"I think it's better for. . ." Her shuddering gasp told him her tears had intensified.

"For us?" He gathered her to him. "Sweetheart, you don't have to do that. We'll get past this."

"I know," she said, "but I think some time alone would be good for us, don't you think?" She sniffled again, but her tears seemed to have slowed. "Emilie will be with them, so their schooling won't suffer. She's excited about the prospect of showing the girls Santa Lucida."

Something didn't make sense in all of this, but Micah was loath to figure out what it was. Rather, he took hope in the fact that he hadn't caused his wife to want to leave with them.

"Ruby," he said, "I don't care what happened before now. Nothing else matters except that you're here with me." His lips found her ear and the spot that always made her sigh. Instead, Micah felt her stiffen in his arms. "I love you, Ruby," he said against the curve of her neck. He tugged at her gown, but she pulled away. "Don't do this to me, Ruby," he whispered as she turned her back to him. "Tonight I need to be your husband. Please let me show you that I love you."

Afterward Ruby cried as much for the pain Hawkins had knowingly inflicted as for the pain Micah had no idea he'd caused. She closed her eyes, knowing she would take both facts to her deathbed.

Her next thought was that she hoped that moment would come sooner rather than later.

Ruby rolled onto her side to stare out the window at the horizon. What the moon did not illuminate, her fears did. When the first rays of orange teased the horizon, she rose and donned her wrapper without feeling the slightest need for sleep.

Moving quietly, she went to the attic and cast about for a suitable trunk. Finding one beneath a stack of quilts, she hauled it down the stairs to their sitting room despite her body's protest.

Then she went about the process of gathering up what the girls would need during their time away. Time away. "I will not cry," she said even as she swiped at her damp eyes with the back of her hand.

By the time Carol stirred, Ruby had nearly accomplished the deed.

"What are you doing?"

Ruby forced a smile. "I have a surprise," she whispered. "You're going on a trip."

"Did you say we're going on a trip?" Maggie asked as she wandered in. "Where are we going?"

"Now that's where it gets really fun." Ruby closed the trunk. "The three of you are going with Miss Emilie to Santa Lucida. Do you know where that is?"

"He wants us gone, doesn't he?" Carol gestured to the closed door. "I knew he didn't really want to be our papa."

"No, that's not true at all," Ruby said. "It's just that Miss Emilie asked if you three might want to go with her for a visit, and I told her—"

"She just came back," Carol said.

"I know that." Ruby saw Tess climb from her bed and snatched her up into her lap. "Did you hear about the trip you're taking today?"

"Are you going, too?" Tess asked.

"No, sweetheart, I'm not, but Micah and I hope to come and fetch you back soon." Ruby pulled the precious child to her chest and buried her face in her hair. "You know I can't be without you long." She gestured to the twins. "Come here and give me a hug, dears. You know it must last a week or two."

Likely more, though she'd not tell them that.

"Is Joey going?" Tess asked.

"No, I don't think so. Girls only this time."

Micah opened the door and offered a lazy smile as he stretched then swept hair from his face. As he walked toward her, Ruby's heart flip-flopped.

He knelt down to kiss Ruby on the cheek and then took Tess from her arms. "Am I the only one who thinks girls only is a bad rule?" he asked as Tess giggled.

Carol tugged on Ruby's sleeve. "Do you promise to come and get us?"

Ruby entwined her fingers with Carol's. "I promise with all my heart," she said. "And the sooner the better."

"Don't come too soon," Maggie said. "I think a vacation from school sounds fun."

Micah shook his head. "I think perhaps Emilie remembers a thing or two about being your teacher."

The twins groaned, but Tess smiled. "Do you think she'd teach me now? I'm much older than before."

"Yes, you are," Ruby said with a smile. It was all she could do to keep her smile in place until Emilie and Caleb arrived to fetch the girls.

Caleb did not meet Ruby's gaze as Emilie linked arms with her and moved her into the kitchen. No words passed between them, though Ruby tightened her grip when Micah walked through with the trunk.

"Did you tell him about Hawkins?" Emilie whispered when the men were safely outside the gate.

"I couldn't," Ruby breathed as she turned her attention out the window to the rooster crowing like a fool on the other side of the yard. "I didn't even try."

Emilie sighed. "I know this man Hawkins. Were it not for Caleb Spencer, I might have a similar story to tell."

Ruby jerked her attention from the window. "What?"

She looked away. "He is evil, Ruby, and not a man from whom a woman might easily free herself. Please do not question yourself."

"How can I not?" The gate opened then banged shut as Ruby stifled a sob.

Heavy footsteps climbed the back porch steps and stopped at the door. Micah. "This is difficult for her," she heard Emilie say.

Then her husband's arms were around her. Ruby allowed her

head to rest on Micah's chest, her ear snuggled against the sound of his beating heart. And she let him comfort her even though he did not know the depth of her sorrow or its true source.

"Don't cry, Mama," Maggie said as she wedged herself into the space between Ruby and Micah. "Else I'll have to cry, too, and then so will Tess."

"Traitor," came a voice that could only belong to Carol.

"Mama, is it time to. . ." Tess launched herself past Carol. "It's a family good-bye, Carol. Come on."

Ruby recognized that stubborn look as one she'd worn herself. "Honey," she said to the reluctant twin. "Please. You're a part of us, too."

With as little enthusiasm as she could muster, Carol edged forward.

Micah stepped aside to offer his attention fully to her. "Come on, sweetheart," he said gently as he dropped to one knee. "I'm gonna miss you something awful."

Carol ran, stumbling toward Micah's open arms.

"It's time." This from Caleb, who stood at the kitchen door. "We'll need to get you safely aboard, ladies."

Safely aboard. Thankfully, Micah seemed oblivious to the importance of those words as he rose.

Caleb had brought a wagon, a treat for the girls, and they now scrambled past to vie for a coveted spot up front. "Slow down," Micah called, "and come tell your mother good-bye before you go running off."

Maggie was first, her smile firmly in place as she wrapped her arms around Ruby's waist. Then came Tess, who attached herself to Ruby's apron with two fistfuls of calico. "I want to take you with me."

Reaching behind her, Ruby untied the apron. "Want to keep this safe for me until I can come for it?" Tess grinned and allowed her to tie the embroidered cotton around her waist. "There," Ruby said. "You'll find something special in the pocket. Don't lose it, you hear?"

Tess reached into the pocket to find the sand dollar Ruby had retrieved only yesterday on her early morning walk. How long ago that seemed.

Carol edged her sister out of the way. "I love you." A look crossed the child's face that gave Ruby pause. "Mama," she added loudly enough for

Micah to hear. And then came the smile. Pure and genuine. "Mama," Carol repeated, this time soft enough for only Ruby to hear.

"Yes, baby." Ruby gathered the girl to her. "Mama," she echoed. While her heart tore in half, Ruby fixed on a smile. "Take care of your sisters," she said, though the statement was unnecessary.

Of course she will.

CHAPTER 44

Ruby was standing at the kitchen window when the gate closed. Had she the luxury to show her emotions, her knees might have given way. Instead, she reached for the spoon and channeled her feelings into lunch preparations.

When Micah came up behind her, Ruby held her breath. "We need to go see them off."

A statement that did not appear to offer an option, yet the prospect of being seen with the girls terrified her. "I'm not feeling well," she said. The truth.

So Micah went with them, and Ruby left the kitchen to climb the stairs and slip into bed. Sometime later, she became aware of sounds. And smells. Someone had made lunch.

Or perhaps it was dinner.

It didn't matter. Didn't matter who cooked. Who cleaned. Or even who lay beside Micah Tate. None of it mattered.

She might have looked outside, but the effort of opening the curtains seemed too much. Micah came in and lay beside her, but she refused to acknowledge his presence. Sometime later he left, and even then she did not allow herself the luxury of tears.

Only when Caleb Spencer threw open the curtains and forced the sunshine into the room did she respond. And not well.

"Go ahead and be angry with me," Caleb said. "I prefer that to seeing you give up. And yes, I know it's quite improper to walk into a woman's bedchamber like this, but I promised Emilie I would do this for her."

Ruby rolled away from the blinding light and covered her head with the pillow. When Caleb snatched it up, she couldn't manage a protest.

"Leave me be," she said.

"I won't." When Ruby didn't respond, Caleb walked to the armoire and opened the door. Selecting her blue frock, he returned to the bedside. "I'm going to walk out that door, and I want you to put this on."

"Really, Caleb. Go away."

"Ruby Tate," he said as he threw the dress at her, "if you want to lie there for the rest of your days, that's between you and the Lord. Keep in mind that what you're doing right now, however, is letting Thomas Hawkins win."

With that, he turned on his heels and stormed toward the door.

"Wait," she called as Caleb placed his hand on the knob. "Why do you say that?"

"He wants you like this. Don't you see?" He glanced back over his shoulder. "Micah can protect you from Hawkins. You just have to let him."

"No." Ruby reached for the dress, allowing her fingers to brush across the soft material. "The girls are safe, and that's what matters."

Caleb leaned against the doorframe and studied the floor for a moment before turning his attention to Ruby. "Hawkins came after Emilie once," he said. "Twice, actually."

This news caught her attention and held it. "She mentioned something. . . . I didn't know that."

"I'm not asking you what happened the other night." He looked away. "I don't want to know."

Ruby felt her lower lip begin to quiver.

"What I do know is the Lord gave me Emilie to love and protect. Had she not been truthful with me about Hawkins. . ." He shrugged. "Suffice it to say God allowed me to keep her safe." A pause. "I thought I'd killed him," Caleb said. "You'll never know how very much I hate the fact I didn't."

"I wish you had," she whispered as she shifted positions and tried not to wince.

"Tell Micah what happened," Caleb said. "Let him take care of you, Ruby."

"I can't," she whispered as she gathered the dress to her.

"Then I'll tell him for you."

"No!" She lowered her voice. "You can't. Promise me you won't."

He looked reluctant.

Ruby's heart pounded as her fingers clutched the fabric. "Promise me. You have to."

"First, you must understand I will not lie. Not for you or for anyone."

She nodded. "I'm living proof nothing good comes of lies."

"Will you get out of bed and get back to the business of living, Ruby?" His expression changed. "I cannot be held to a promise if I know it to be against your best interests."

"What's going on here?" Micah pushed past Caleb to glare at Ruby. "Why is he here?"

Caleb opened his mouth to speak, but Micah whirled around to punch him, sending the judge reeling backward into the hallway. "Micah, no!" she shouted. "Don't! He's only here because he's worried about me."

"I'm sorry, Micah," Caleb said as he massaged his jaw. "I promised Emilie I would see how Ruby is faring without the girls. She was quite insistent."

Micah looked unconvinced.

"Yes, well, I'll just be going, then." He looked past Micah to meet Ruby's stare. "I'm sure you two have plenty to talk about anyway."

When the squeaky step sounded, Ruby knew Caleb was likely out of earshot. "That man is your friend, Micah Tate," she said with more bravado than she felt, "and you owe him an apology."

"Do I?" He seemed to be studying her. "Am I to understand it's appropriate now for you to entertain men in our bedchamber?"

"Micah, no," she said. "What a thing to say."

"Is it?" He crossed his arms over his chest. "Where were you the night before the girls left, Ruby? Caleb said you were with Emilie, but I wonder. And why did you leave without taking a guard with you?"

"Yes, I was with Emilie, and she'll tell you that's the truth."

"So you spent all that time with Emilie. You didn't go anywhere else? Like down to the beach?" A choice between the truth and a convenient lie was impossible, so she said nothing.

"I see."

"Ruby?" Viola called. "Are you up there?"

Micah looked away.

"Give me a minute," Ruby called.

"Ruby," Micah said. "You're my wife, and I'll have an answer to where you were all night."

She held the dress against her chest in the hopes it might cover the evidence of her breaking heart. "Micah, please. You alone are my husband." Ruby met his gaze. "And I think of none other in that way, nor do I desire to."

The truth.

He came to her then, standing between her and the dreams she knew would be shattered if she spoke. Reaching to grasp her wrist, Micah gently pulled her to her feet.

She swayed, and he caught her. An embrace that once brought comfort now took her breath away. When his hand moved down her spine to rest at the small of her back, she froze.

What to do? A glance at what lay beneath the nightgown, and he would see. Would know. His hand pressed her against him, leaving no doubt of his intentions. "Ruby?"

She looked past him to the door. "Viola's downstairs waiting for me."

"Tell her to go away."

When Ruby did not respond, Micah held her for a moment then released her. Without a word, he turned and walked out the door.

Numb, Ruby shed her nightgown and quickly donned the blue dress lest Micah return and see her bruises. She'd find a way to keep him from knowing.

She had no choice.

Micah stormed from the room, determined to get to the bottom of the mystery. Obviously Caleb knew more than he was saying, so he'd head there first. Viola greeted him at the bottom of the stairs, but he had no stomach for pleasantries.

"Go on up," he said to the midwife. "Likely she'll be happier to see you than me."

Words he regretted as he slammed the door and stormed down the porch steps. The last thing he needed was yet another citizen of Fairweather Key to know of his marital troubles.

He reached the gate before a thought occurred and he stormed back inside. Catching Viola midway up the stairs, Micah called to her.

"Your brother, has he left yet?"

Viola gave him an odd look. "This morning, actually," she said.

"I see." He swallowed hard and worked to keep any trace of irritation from his voice. "So where was your brother two nights ago?"

"Two nights ago?" The midwife astonished him by blushing. "I'm not exactly certain."

"And might I inquire as to why that is?"

She smiled. "I suppose it's all right to tell you. I was with Mr. Drummond until an hour that might be considered a bit late for a younger woman. You see, it was a lovely night, and the stars were out. I hope you don't think less of me. I assure you he's quite the gentleman."

"Drummond?" He shook his head. "No, of course. Thank you."

Micah's imagination took over, and by the time he reached Caleb's office, he'd determined that his wife had indeed succumbed to Dumont's questionable charms. The judge, however, quickly dismissed Micah's concern.

"I guarantee you're wrong," Caleb said.

"Wrong about what?" The door closed behind Josiah, and he smiled. "What did I miss?"

"Not much," Micah said. "I'm only trying to find out where my wife was two nights ago. I don't suppose you would know."

The statement obviously stunned the normally talkative Josiah into silence.

"You were right," Micah said, warming to the topic. "You warned me about her, and I didn't listen."

Josiah held up his hands. "Wait a minute. What are you talking about?"

"He's out of his mind," Caleb said. "Ruby's a good wife, Micah. Trust her. That's all I'm going to say about it."

Caleb's words chased him down the steps and out into the afternoon sun. He wanted to believe them. But with every step he took, Micah found reason to disagree.

The silence. The way she stiffened when he touched her. The fact that she would neither look him in the eye nor account for her whereabouts. The odd way she sent off the very children she'd married him to protect.

The memory of their last time together as husband and wife intruded, and Micah shrugged it off. Better to concentrate on the *now* rather than the *then*.

Josiah fell into step beside him. "You can't just walk out and leave like that."

Micah stalled. "I won't talk about this."

Josiah studied him a minute. "All right," was all he said before shaking Micah's hand and heading off in the opposite direction. "Oh, Micah," he called. "I almost forgot why I was looking for you. Isabelle's heard from the Campbells. It appears the boardinghouse is officially hers. She wanted me to let you know."

"Well then," Micah said. "That's great news." It wasn't, but he'd not let Josiah know this.

"There's no hurry in moving out," Josiah added. "I'm sure Ruby will need time to prepare."

"Time?" Micah shook his head. "No," he said, "with the girls gone, I think preparing for a move is exactly what she needs now." He paused. "And what I need as well."

What he didn't tell Josiah was that while Ruby would be preparing to move into the parsonage, he would move back to the boat. There he could consider what to do next.

The folly of that plan became apparent when he stepped aboard and settled onto the bunk. The citizens of Fairweather Key would never stand for a pastor who didn't live under the same roof as his wife.

Try as he might, there was no way around it. He had to go home.

But not tonight, and maybe not tomorrow night. No, it might take a few days before he was ready to climb under the covers with that woman.

Saturday night Ruby sat at the table and picked at the food Mrs. Carter had left for her. Micah had been in and out of the boardinghouse many times, but each night when she went upstairs to bed, she went alone.

Tonight, with the girls gone, the house seemed impossibly quiet. Even the fact that the second floor was full to the brim with boarders and the front and back porches held a militiaman, each ready to guard her with his life, did not keep Ruby from feeling completely alone. With Mr. Defoe's *Crusoe* as her companion, Ruby pushed away the untouched plate and drew the lamp closer.

When the door opened and closed again, she ignored it. Now that the Carters were taking on the kitchen duties, she was merely another boarder.

"Ruby."

Micah. She did not look up.

"I'll be staying here tonight," he said.

Again she did not respond. Rather, she turned the page, even though she'd not read a word on it. The creaking step sounded, and he was gone.

Only then did she allow a single tear to fall before going back to join Crusoe on his island. After a while, she gave up and closed the book, unable to recall a word she'd read.

Trudging up the stairs gave her time to decide what to say to Micah. The truth of her absence would set her free. But could he touch her knowing Tommy had defiled her?

She stopped in the parlor then turned to open the door to the room where the girls slept. Or rather where they used to sleep.

The girls.

Yes, that was the solution. No one in Fairweather Key would fault her for going to be with her girls. And likely Emilie would be wishing to return to her husband. Indeed, it was the perfect solution.

Closing the door, she walked across the small living area and into her bedchamber with renewed purpose. She'd expected to find Micah asleep, thus giving her time to consider the words she would use to convince him.

Instead, he was waiting for her.

"I've come to a conclusion," he said. "Our arrangement is not working."

"Our arrangement or our marriage?" Ruby skirted the lamplight to move toward the armoire.

"We will be moving into the parsonage next week," he said, ignoring the question. "I'll expect you to conduct yourself as a proper pastor's wife."

Ruby froze as her dress sagged to the floor. "That won't be a problem, Micah." She slipped on her nightgown and turned toward him, her shaking fingers still working to close the buttons. "For I came to tell you I'll be joining the girls in Santa Lucida."

Had he begged her to stay, she would have. Instead, Micah nodded then extinguished the lamp.

She climbed into bed beside him and waited for the words she hoped would come. When his breathing slowed, she knew she'd not hear them. "Micah," she said in a voice loud enough to wake him. "Why did you come here tonight?"

He shifted toward her. "Tomorrow's Sunday, and I'm the pastor. Where else would I be?"

"Of course," she said as the last of her pride evaporated. So he'd only come back to her for appearance's sake. "And tomorrow night? Where will you sleep then?"

"Stop, Ruby." He slid his hand around her and hauled her against him. "What do you want from me?"

Pressing her hands to his chest, Ruby slipped from his grasp. *I want you to love me.*

But the words went unsaid.

On Monday morning, she climbed aboard a vessel that would take her to Santa Lucida. What Micah didn't know when he left her on the docks was that she had no immediate plans to return.

By the time she stumbled numbly off the ship and into the sympathetic embrace of Caleb's beautiful mother, she'd determined to stay until Micah came for her. Or, she amended, until the Lord sent her home.

Wherever that was.

CHAPTER 45

I don't ever want to leave," Tess said as she stretched out in the canopied bed. "It's lovely here."

"Indeed, it is." Ruby kissed the girl's forehead then settled the blankets around her. "But remember, we're only visiting."

"When will our papa come for us?" Carol asked from the bed she shared with Maggie on the opposite side of the expansive bedchamber.

Ruby sighed. Evidently she'd been mistaken when she assumed Carol had given up on seeing Tommy again. Perhaps now was the time for the truth.

"Don't you miss Micah?" Carol asked.

Ruby took a second to gather her wits. "Of course," she said, "but isn't it nice of him to allow us this vacation?"

"I don't want a vacation," Maggie said. "I want to go home."

"Me, too," Tess whined as she placed the ever-present sand dollar on the table beside the bed. "I want to sleep in my own bed."

Ruby extinguished the lamp and moved by the light of the moon toward the open door and the balcony beyond. From the corner of her eye, she spied Caleb's mother on the opposite end of the balcony.

"Am I intruding?" Mary Fletcher asked as she moved toward Ruby.

"I welcome your company," she said, "though I wonder if we might talk where we'd be less likely to bother the girls."

As Emilie had predicted, in the months since Ruby had arrived on

Santa Lucida, Mary Fletcher had become the mother Ruby never had. She'd also proven herself to be a grandmother worthy of celebration to the three girls under her roof.

But it was her ability to listen that endeared the woman to Ruby. Mary's exploits failed to match her placid exterior, and more than once they'd discussed what it meant to be a woman with a past.

A woman who sought the Lord now, though she'd not always stayed on so narrow a path.

Watching the reed-thin woman making her way across the balcony, the wind whipping hair that only slightly glistened with threads of silver, put Ruby in mind of a woman more suited to walk the floors of a castle in some far-off land.

"I would like that very much." Mary's gaze settled on Ruby's eyes then dropped as she reached for her arm. "I have it on good authority that Fletcher has anticipated our need for just such a conversation and put water on to boil."

Fletcher treated Mary like the newlywed she was. The pair put Ruby to shame with their endearments, and more than once she had caught them kissing as if they were many decades younger than their actual ages.

It was quite sweet, and often it made her want to cry.

But then, lately everything made her want to cry.

They walked together downstairs to the large gathering room that served as a parlor in this tropical paradise. "Tea?" Mary asked as Ruby settled on the settee. So much about this room, this island, reminded her of the home of her childhood.

"Thank you, but no."

"Of course. It wouldn't settle well, would it?" She gave Ruby a look. "What with a baby coming."

"How did you know?" It was something Ruby hadn't even admitted to herself. Yet the signs were obvious.

"He's coming for you," she said. "I know it."

"It's been four months, almost five. Wouldn't he have come for me before now?"

Mary shrugged and settled back with her tea. "I just know he will. It is not for a woman to determine a man's timing."

Thus, when the vessel docked at Santa Lucida nine days later, Ruby was not completely surprised to see Micah Tate at the helm. "I've come for my wife," he called to Caleb's mother and Fletcher. Mary's response was a knowing smile and a gesture to the balcony where Ruby stood.

With the girls dancing around Micah like fools, Ruby held back to see what he would do. He came to her, walking down the wide expanse of balcony as if he owned the place.

Her heart jolted at the sight, so Ruby tried to look away.

She failed.

"Get your things, Ruby. We're going home."

He was impossibly handsome standing there, though she again tried not to stare. A bit gaunt about the jaws and somewhat worse for wear, but handsome all the same.

"And if I don't wish to go with you?" she asked.

He moved toward her but did not touch her.

The distance between them might have been a mile, yet he was close enough for Ruby to hear him breathing.

"You misunderstand." His fingers found her wrist, and he gently led her to him. "I didn't ask."

He smelled of soap and fresh sea air, and she inhaled even as she tried to ignore the way he made her feel. She could have easily slipped from his grasp, but heaven help her, she didn't want to.

"Look at me."

She did and nearly toppled into him. He caught her and, in the moment before their lips met, offered a smile.

Ruby allowed the kiss, though her heart still complained of his absence. "I was an idiot," he said as if he'd heard her thoughts. "Come home with me?"

"Are you asking now?"

His hand cupped her jaw then slid down the curve of her neck. "No," he whispered against her flushed skin. "I'm begging."

Any other time, Micah might have lingered on Santa Lucida. Today, however, he had a mission: to get his womenfolk home safely. But as he slid the ship past the protection of the reef and into open waters, he could only pray that mission might be accomplished.

To be sure, he'd not come alone or unarmed. Yet when it became evident he was being followed, Micah knew he had a decision to make. To turn and take on the shadowing vessel would put Ruby and the girls at risk, likely from the pirate Hawkins. But to race the ship to Fairweather Key meant inviting trouble right at his doorstep.

The memory of his palm resting on the swell of his wife's belly less than an hour ago hit him hard, and he called to unfurl the sails. He would live to fight another day, but tonight Ruby Tate would sleep under his roof once more.

Thus the vessel split the waves and made for home while the offending ship fell behind and eventually disappeared from the horizon. Micah did not allow relief to come until his hand touched the gate of the parsonage, where just last week he'd allowed himself to move in.

"You'll likely want to move things around to suit yourself," Micah said as he opened the door to the home and watched Ruby walk through. The girls ran about until he directed them to the nursery that would have to be added onto soon.

He'd taken the liberty of purchasing a few things for them, with the help of Isabelle and Emilie, and from the squeals, it sounded as if the girls approved.

"You'll be safe here," he said as he held his wife a moment longer then released her. "I've an errand to run that might take a while."

Ruby seemed to understand, for she merely smiled.

"Have the girls in bed when I return," he said with a wink.

When he shut the door behind him, the last of Micah's good humor evaporated. Already, two dozen men surrounded the parsonage. "Keep out of sight," he said to Neely, who'd come to take charge. "I'll be back as soon as I can."

"You bring back my men in one piece, you hear?" Neely said with a good-natured grin.

"You know I will," Micah tossed over his shoulder.

"Yes, I do, sir," Neely said. "You're the best there is. Now go with God and rest assured the men and I'll be right here watching and praying."

Micah turned to focus on the militiaman. "As I'll likely be in great need of both, I do appreciate it."

He got all the way to the courthouse before doubts about involving the navy sent him doubling back to the boardinghouse to try to raise Josiah from his bed. When he realized he'd only draw unwanted attention to a mission neither Josiah nor Caleb would approve of, Micah turned on his heels and headed toward the one man who not only owed him but would likely come along for the pure adventure of it all.

With only the briefest of stops to pull Clay Drummond from his bed, Micah and a skeleton crew sailed out into the night to capture Hawkins. "I'd not do this for just anyone," Drummond complained even as he smiled. "Last thing I need is to propose to Vivi with my backside full of buckshot."

"I guarantee it won't be buckshot that hits you," Micah said, "though what better wife could a man like you take on than one who does her own doctoring?"

"Good point."

"There is something," he said. "I wonder what'll happen if Doc decides to come back."

"He won't." Drummond nodded toward the horizon. "See anything yet?"

Micah shook his head. "You're pretty confident of it. Dare I ask how you know?"

Clay shrugged. "It was part of the deal."

"I see." He did, though whether he approved was another matter. Micah had never known Doc Hill to be anything other than a good man, though one never knew everything about a person. This he realized all too well.

Again Drummond gestured toward the horizon. "Nothing out there?"

"No, but I know what I'm looking for." *And likely whom.* He gave the order to extinguish the lanterns then watched with satisfaction as his crew jumped to their duties in silence.

He'd chosen well.

Micah's pulse raced as he turned his face into the east wind. How easily he could be distracted by his thoughts. Revenge, his ever-present

Beloved
Counterfeit

temptation, bore hard tonight.

Yet he could not give in to its pull.

While Micah kept watch, the hull chased the silver path of the moon across the waves. Then he spied it, this vessel that had dogged his wake. It lay at anchor some distance from the flats, and he could hear what sounded like rousing merriment.

"What now?" Drummond asked.

"We'll not fire on it unless fired upon," Micah said. "Though be at the ready."

He turned to gesture to the nearest sailor, and immediately the sails were trimmed. He reached for the spyglass and held it to his eye. Quite a celebration was taking place on the aft deck.

Scanning the deck, he searched for Hawkins until he found the sorry excuse for a man lifting a bottle and laughing. Anger, white hot and unexpected, simmered just beneath the surface as he watched the fair-haired man upend the liquor then raise it high again.

How a man could live with half of what Hawkins had done was beyond understanding. Were it incumbent on him to choose between praying for the man's soul and killing him, Micah knew which he'd prefer.

He also knew which the Lord preferred.

Lowering the glass, he thrust it into the hands of the sailor who stood at his elbow. A long, slow exhale, and the rage, while not gone, was under control.

As Micah turned the wheel to head toward the vessel, Clay placed his hand atop his arm. "What are you going to do?"

"Take back what's mine."

"What's that?" Clay asked.

"Peace of mind," Micah said as he tamped down his anger all over again. "This man will no longer haunt my wife's nightmares or be a threat to the girls." He paused to correct the trajectory of their path. "Nor will I continue to wonder whether I'll be forced to kill him."

"Is that why we're here, Tate? To kill Hawkins?"

Micah had to think on the question longer than he liked before he could answer. "Would that I could," he said, "but vengeance is not mine to have." He paused. "Yet were I called on to defend myself to the death, there would be neither hesitation nor a question of which of us would fall."

His look dared Drummond to comment. When he only nodded, Micah went back to the work of slipping up on the vessel undetected. Steering the vessel away from the moon's path was easily done. Keeping it moving at a speed slow enough to maneuver was not.

Upon his silent command, the men of the *Ruby* took up their arms and waited.

Coming alongside the smuggler's vessel, he realized what a foolhardy move he'd made coming out with none but Drummond and a handful of true but not tried sailors. Still, he kept to his plan. Capturing Thomas Hawkins had become a personal matter and nothing he'd want delegated to Caleb and the navy.

Three dozen men, maybe more, were visible on Hawkins's vessel, but most were in the latter stages of becoming falling-down drunk. Those who remained upright blended voices with those who found themselves unable to find their sea legs to serenade a captain who leaned dangerously over the quarterdeck with not one but two bottles in his fists.

By the time the lashing hooks were thrown, the *Ruby* had been spied. What would be done about this invading menace, however, seemed to be a matter of confusion for Hawkins's crew.

For Hawkins, however, it appeared a personal affront. "See here," he called as he grabbed for the rail, causing one of his bottles to crash to the deck below. "How dare you attempt to come aboard without proper invitation."

"We've a mutual friend," Micah called as he rested his palm on the weapon lashed to his belt. "This precludes any need for invitation." Micah turned to order the crew to stand their places. Drummond looked away and did not respond. "I'll do this myself," he told Clay. "Though I'd be obliged if you were to keep watch and see that my hide's safe."

"I'd be delighted," he said, "but I'll be going with you, so let's get on with it."

Arguing would take more time than ignoring the man, so Micah chose to turn his attention to Hawkins without comment. As his ropes

landed on the enemy vessel, Micah noted that Hawkins's men had neither ceased their merriment nor paid them much attention. Their only concession to the goings-on seemed to be their lack of singing. Rather, they stood—or lay—mute.

"Who might I say is my guest?" Their gazes met, and Thomas Hawkins had the audacity to grin as he looked away and took a long drink from the bottle.

"I've something you want, Hawkins," Micah called as he felt for the knife lashed beneath his coat. "Four somethings. And you'll never lay a hand on them."

Again, he almost said, though there was no proof. At least none that Micah wanted to explore.

Hawkins's laugh floated over to Micah, along with the invitation, "Come down below and let's discuss things," as Micah reached for the rope coiled beside him.

"Don't do it," Drummond cautioned, but Micah ignored him and tossed the line over to where Hawkins now strolled the deck. A moment later he found himself face-to-face with the smuggler.

"Join me in my quarters for the evening meal," the smuggler said as he gestured to a passageway that led into the ship. "I've a succulent dish awaiting me."

Something in the way he said the words made Micah think the man referred to something other than food. The image that followed roiled in his belly, and he spat on the deck to shove it away.

"Thank you, no." Micah's palm found the pistol, and his fingers closed over it. He could kill the man now and likely scramble back to his ship untouched.

"I wonder if Ruby asks about me," Hawkins said, oblivious to the danger he was about to face.

So Hawkins knew with whom he dealt. Good.

Micah looked about and found the deck populated with drunk men, who simply jeered and lifted their cups as if watching their captain's defeat was quite the show. "Why would she?" Micah asked as he glanced back to see Drummond watching.

"You tell me." Hawkins paused to wipe a grin from his face. "Oh, of course. She didn't tell you about our night together." He chuckled, an action that under other circumstances might have landed him sprawling across the deck. "No, I don't suppose that's something a woman tells her husband."

White-hot anger engulfed him, but Micah held it in check. Barely. "I'll not allow lies to be told about my wife," he said through clenched jaw.

"Lies?" Hawkins laughed. "Tell me, Tate. Did your wife fail to come home one night, oh, might be some four months ago? Or maybe it was five." He shrugged. "Doesn't matter. You'll know when the baby comes."

Micah hit him. Hard. When Hawkins scrambled to his feet again, Micah landed another blow. And then another. Such was his blind rage that none aboard the vessel would come near him. Rather, the drunken sailors had begun to jeer at their captain, seemingly placing lots on who might take his place.

With Drummond nearby and a shipload of men covering him with their weapons, Micah turned his attention back to Hawkins. It was all he could do not to spit in the now-bleeding face.

Hawkins smiled. "She was a tasty tart."

Micah might have killed Hawkins if someone hadn't held him back. "Vengeance isn't yours to be had," Drummond reminded him as he threw Micah aside and scraped what was left of Hawkins off the deck. "Now help me get this sorry excuse of a man to Cuba so the authorities can hang him for the pirate he is."

Micah shoved Drummond away, and Hawkins stumbled then landed in a heap. As Micah watched the smuggler try and fail to gain his footing, the rage and hate boiled away, leaving only a mind-numbing exhaustion. His breath came in short gasps as he checked to see if Hawkins could still manage.

When Hawkins groaned, Micah rolled him onto his back. Drummond reached to help, but Micah shouldered him away. With one last look at the deck, which his men had cleared of anyone associated with Thomas Hawkins, he hefted the smuggler onto his shoulders and heaved him over onto the deck of his own vessel.

There the militiamen swarmed and then by degrees fell back to allow Micah into their midst. "I'll do it myself." Though everything

in him wanted to kill the man, Micah stumbled into the hold with Thomas Hawkins and threw him behind a door that he bolted more to keep himself out than to keep Hawkins in.

"What now?" Drummond asked. "Home or Havana?"

Micah thought of Ruby, his baby in her belly, lying in the bed she'd not yet shared with him, and the temptation to go home hit him hard. Yet it wouldn't do to leave the dispatch of this man to anyone else.

The job was his alone, and he'd not leave his post.

"Havana, but by the fastest means possible."

His mission accomplished, Micah fell into a fitful sleep that night and awoke in Havana Bay to the sound of Clay Drummond singing. "Enough," Micah said as he forced his eyes open. "Let's get Hawkins off this tub before I change my mind."

"Will we be staying to watch the hanging?" Clay asked as they left the courthouse some hours later.

Micah clamped his hand on Drummond's shoulder. "I think I'd rather go home to my wife. What about you?"

Clay nodded. "There's a certain appeal to that," he said. "Though I'm not certain Viola's ready to call herself my wife yet."

Micah chuckled, though exhaustion tugged at the corners of his mind. "Maybe you should ask her."

"Maybe so," Drummond said. "But for now, what say I take the wheel? Like as not, you'll want to be at your best when you explain to your wife where you've been since this time yesterday."

Though he wasn't at his best, Micah did appreciate the time he had to prepare for the moment when Ruby opened the parsonage door and let him in. To her credit, she didn't ask why he'd not come home, nor did she seem to want to know.

Rather, she fussed over him and served him two helpings of conch chowder before setting an oversized slice of pie on his plate. "You're spoiling me." He caught her wrist as she tried to slip past. "Now go and put the girls to bed."

She did as he asked then joined him in the parlor, where he'd been playing at planning Sunday's sermon. No notes were necessary for this one. He already knew what God had put on his heart.

"Come now, and let us reason together, saith the Lord: though your sins be as scarlet, they shall be as white as snow; though they be red like crimson, they shall be as wool."

He rose to meet Ruby, struck by her beauty, and he prayed for the right words to come. "You should know Hawkins will no longer bother you or the girls."

Ruby stopped short. "How can you know this?" She paused, her hand on her belly. "You killed him."

"No. I delivered him to the authorities but elected not to stay for the hanging." He took a deep breath. "I wonder if I might ask something of you," he said. "Something important."

"You've spoken to Hawkins." She lifted her gaze to meet his, her expression tentative. "I want no further secrets between us. You see, I never knew how to tell you that the night I didn't come home, I was—"

He silenced her with a kiss. "I know," he whispered, "and there's no need to say more."

"You know?" she said as her eyes fell shut.

Micah refused to allow her tears. This was not an occasion for sorrow. "Do you love me, Ruby?"

"Love you," she whispered. "Yes, I do love you."

"Then nothing else matters," he said as he swept her off her feet. Her squeal was quickly ended by yet another kiss. "I love you, too, Ruby, with all that I am."

"Our baby," she said as he cradled her against his chest. "It might be—"

"Hush, Ruby," he said, unwilling to give thought to what he knew she was trying to say. "The child God gives us will be mine, and I'll have no further discussion about it."

Then he showed her how much he loved being her husband, and she responded as a wife who'd missed her man.

Very much.

EPILOGUE

"You can't quit now, Ruby," Viola said. "Just one more push."

"I can't," was all Ruby could manage to say before falling back onto the pillows. How long she'd been at this, she couldn't say, though she knew she'd long since stopped caring about anything except whether the child she labored to bear would be healthy.

The silly fear that she might be giving birth to a baby who did not belong to the man she loved with all her heart was too cruel to consider for more than a moment. Another pain shot through her, and the thought evaporated.

"I truly cannot," she cried in response to Viola's urging.

"You can, and you will," the midwife demanded, though the rest of her words disappeared when the pain returned.

"All right, now rest," Viola finally said.

Ruby's head fell back on the pillow. Silence. Then Micah's voice. Soft. Gentle. Pleading with God to bring this baby into the world. She rested. Eyes closed. Safe in her husband's embrace.

He said something about sand dollars. "Have I ever told you the story of the sand dollar, Ruby?" he asked as he pressed his palm against her damp cheek.

She managed to mouth a silent no.

From his pocket, Micah retrieved a perfect sand dollar. "For you," he said, "though I warrant you'll need me to hold it for you."

When she did not respond, he frowned. "The story," he said,

KATHLEEN Y'BARBO

"starts with the five points here around the edges. They represent the Easter story. You see. . .four nail holes from the crucifixion and a fifth one here. That's the one made by the spear of the Roman soldier."

She concentrated until the sand dollar came into focus. Indeed, as Micah said, there were the five holes.

"See, here's the star that led the wise men." He flipped the shell over. "And there's the Christmas flower. Now watch this." Micah grasped the sand dollar and cracked it in half.

"You broke it," she said as little pieces littered the blanket.

"Five doves," he said as he gathered the bird-shaped pieces into his palm. "Representing peace and goodwill."

"Beautiful," she managed as waves of exhaustion hit her.

"Yes," he said. "You are."

She looked up into eyes that held no guile. "Even now?"

His lips touched her forehead then her nose. "Especially now," he said as his lips met hers.

Pain. Again it came without warning. Shuddering, screaming pain like nothing she'd ever known. Micah spoke again, but the words were blurred by the pain.

Viola's voice joined Micah's.

Something about breathing. Something else about biting the length of rawhide she'd brought.

None of it mattered.

There was only pain.

Horrendous pain.

Then—a baby's cry. The pain ceased.

"You've a son," Ruby heard someone say, and then came other voices. A man. She fought to open her eyes and found Micah crying.

Her lips formed a weak question: "What's wrong?"

"Nothing's wrong," he said. "We have a son, and he's perfect. All his toes and fingers, and, well, he's perfect." The image of her husband faded then appeared again.

"Unless you've a better idea," he said, "I'd like to call him Micah after his pa. 'Course we'd call him something to differentiate between the two of us. Mike, maybe. Or Mikey, though he's going to grow out of that soon enough."

Relief flooded her, along with the realization that she'd indeed given birth to Micah's child. "Oh, Micah," she managed, "a son. Our son."

He moved close, touching her as if she were something rare and fragile. The pride on his face was unmistakable. "Yes, *our* son, and there'll never be a doubt of it. Not now; not ever. Now rest. I'll be here if you need me."

She did until the baby's lusty cry woke her. "I believe someone's hungry," Micah said as he helped Ruby sit up then lifted the baby from his cradle.

As Ruby watched her husband hold their crying son, she began to shed tears of her own. That God would bless her not only with a second chance but also with Micah Tate was more than she could fathom.

"Are you in pain?" he asked. "I sent Vi home with Clay, but I can fetch her if need be."

"No, I'm fine." She smiled as Micah settled the baby in her lap. "More than fine. Now let me get a look at my son." She slipped the blanket from around her son.

Her fair-haired son.

Ruby froze.

"He's hungry," Micah urged. "There'll be time enough later to examine him to see if all his fingers and toes are intact, though as I said, I have it on good authority they are."

"But, Micah," she said, her heart thudding to a stop. "He's—"

"Ours," her husband said with a look that told her he'd brook no further argument. "And no one will ever dispute it, least of all, me."

ABOUT THE AUTHOR

KATHLEEN Y'BARBO

Kathleen first discovered her love of books when, at the age of four, she stumbled upon her grandmother's encyclopedias. Letters became words, and words became stories of faraway places and interesting people. By the time she entered kindergarten, Kathleen had learned to read and found that her love of stories could carry her off to places far beyond her small East Texas town. Eventually she hit the road for real—earning a degree in marketing from Texas A&M before setting off on a path that would take her to such far-flung locales as Jakarta, Tokyo, Bali, Sydney, Hong Kong, and Singapore. Finally, though, the road led back to Texas and to writing and publicizing books.

Kathleen is a bestselling author of more than thirty novels, novellas, and young adult books. In all, more than half a million copies of her books are currently in print in the U.S. and abroad. She has been named as a finalist in the American Christian Fiction Writers Book of the Year contest every year since its inception in 2003, often for more than one book.

In addition to her skills as an author, Kathleen is also a publicist at Books & Such Literary Agency. She is a member of American Christian Fiction Writers, Romance Writers of America, the Public Relations Society of America, Words for the Journey Christian Writers Guild, and the Authors Guild. She is also a former treasurer of the American Christian Fiction Writers. Kathleen has three grown sons and a teenage daughter.

You can read more about Kathleen at www.kathleenybarbo.com.